Merry Christmas 2003
Love Wendy and Ray

WRITING THE RAILS

WRITING THE RAILS

Train Adventures by the World's Best-Loved Writers

Edited by Edward C. Goodman

BLACK DOG
& LEVENTHAL
PUBLISHERS
NEW YORK

Published by
Black Dog & Leventhal Publishers, Inc.
151 West 19th Street
New York, NY 10011

Distributed by
Workman Publishing Company
708 Broadway
New York, NY 10003

Manufactured in the United States

Design by 27.12 Design Ltd, NYC

ISBN: 1-57912-205-1

h g f e d c b a

Pages 363-365 constitute a continuation of this copyright page

Library of Congress Cataloging-in-Publication Data

Writing the rails: train adventures by the world's best-loved writers / edited by Edward
C. Goodman.
p. cm.
Includes index.
ISBN 1-57912-205-1
1. Railroads—Literary collections. 2. Railroad travel—Literary collections. I.
Goodman, Edward C., 1952-

PN6071.R3 W75 2001
808.8'0356—dc21   2001046090

TABLE OF CONTENTS

INTRODUCTION

The stories, essays, poetry and other pieces that make up this anthology have been carefully selected to reflect the multifarious glories of travel by rail, from the Orient Express to the New York City subway.

Train travel is a world apart, and its lure has beckoned since the first steam locomotives were invented in the nineteenth century. Taking a train on vacation to Canada, the Rockies, the Riviera and the Alps at one time was an exciting adventure, and the mystique of the Pullman cars in the United States and the wagon-lits in Europe has inspired writers to set short stories and entire novels on the railway.

The authors in this anthology have all discarded the safe cocoon of home and embarked on their own journeys, either fictional or nonfictional, into the world of train travel. I hope you will enjoy reading the selections within and perhaps be inspired to travel by train soon, to try to recapture some of the glamour and mystery of the rails.

I am indebted to everyone at Black Dog & Leventhal. Their dedication to this project was much appreciated and their guiding comments and criticisms shaped the book. I would also like to thank J. P. Leventhal, publisher, for his enthusiasm and encouragement through every stage.

I want to thank my parents, Harry K. and Shirley E. Goodman and my sister Helen J. Goodman for their continued support in my writing. This book is dedicated to my maternal grandparents Chester M. and Helen S. Eisaman, who used to take me to the train tracks to wave at the caboose and who set my heart dreaming of train travel.

Ted Goodman

New York, May 2001

A TRIP ON STEPHENSON'S ROCKET, AUGUST 1830

Fanny Kemble (1809–1893)

A famous British actress from a theatrical family, Fanny Kemble toured America from 1832 to 1834 performing for wildly enthusiastic audiences. Upon returning to England, she recorded the experience in Journal of a Residence in America *(1835), which American critics attacked. In 1834, Kemble married a wealthy Georgia plantation owner, but soon returned to England after witnessing the harsh reality of slavery. She published* Journal of a Residence on a Georgia Plantation *in 1863 in an effort to influence public opinion against slavery.*

My father knew several of the gentlemen most deeply interested in the undertaking (the Liverpool-Manchester railway), and Stephenson having proposed a trial trip as far as the fifteen-mile viaduct, they, with infinite kindness, invited him and permitted me to accompany them; allowing me, moreover, the place which I felt to be one of supreme honour, by the side of Stephenson. . . . He was a rather stern-featured man, with a dark and deeply-marked countenance; his speech was strongly inflected with his native Northumbrian accent. . . .

We were introduced to the little engine which was to drag us along the rails. . . . This snorting little animal, which I felt rather inclined to pat, was then harnessed to our carriage, and, Mr. Stephenson having taken me on the bench of the engine with him, we started at about ten miles an hour. The steam-horse being ill-adapted for going up and down hill, the road was dept at a certain level, and appeared sometimes to sink below the surface of the earth, and sometimes to rise above it. Almost at starting it was cut through the solid rock, which formed a wall on either side of it, about sixty feet high. You can't imagine how strange it seemed to be journeying on thus, without any visible cause of progress other than the magical machine, with its flying white breath and rhythmical, unvarying pace. . . . We were to go only fifteen miles, that distance being sufficient to show the speed of the engine. . . . After proceeding through this rocky defile, we presently found ourselves raised upon embankments ten or twelve feet high; we then came to a moss, or swamp, of considerable extent, on which no human foot could tread without sinking, and yet it bore the road which bore us. This had been the great stumbling-block in the minds of the committee of the House of Commons; but Mr. Stephenson has succeeded in overcoming it. . . .

We had now come fifteen miles, and stopped where the road traversed a wide and deep valley. Stephenson made me alight and led me down to the bottom of this ravine, over which, in order to keep his road level, he has thrown a magnificent viaduct of nine arches, the middle one of which is seventy feet high, through which we saw the whole of this beautiful little valley. . . . We then rejoined the rest of the party, and the engine having received its supply of water, the carriage was placed behind it, for it cannot turn, and was set off at its utmost speed, thirty-five miles an hour, swifter than a bird flies (for they tried the experiment with a snipe). You cannot conceive what that sensation of cutting the air was; the motion is as smooth as possible, too. I could either have read or written.

THE CELESTIAL RAILROAD

Nathaniel Hawthorne (1804–1864)

American author Nathaniel Hawthorne was first recognized for his short stories, which were collected in Twice Told Tales *(1837). His later works, particularly his novels, brought him great fame during his lifetime. Hawthorne is best known for* The Scarlet Letter *(1850), often considered the first American psychological novel, and* The House of the Seven Gables *(1851), which studies the narrowness of Puritanism and its effects on the individual.*

The passengers being all comfortably seated, we now rattled away merrily, accomplishing a greater distance in ten minutes than Christian probably trudged over in a day. It was laughable, while we glanced along, as it were, at the tail of a thunderbolt, to observe two dusty foot travellers in the old pilgrim guise, with cockle shell and staff, their mystic rolls of parchment in their hands and their intolerable burdens on their backs. . . .

We greeted the two pilgrims with many pleasant gibes and a roar of laughter; whereupon they gazed at us with such woeful and absurdly compassionate visages that our merriment grew tenfold more obstreperous. Apollyon also entered heartily into the fun, and contrived to flirt the smoke and flame of the engine, or of his own breath, into their faces, and envelop them in an atmosphere of scalding steam.

FROM *DOMBEY AND SON*

Charles Dickens (1812–1870)

Perhaps the most popular novelist of all time, Charles Dickens is known for shady characters and settings as well as his sharp sense of humor. His talents won him early fame, and he wrote steadily for a large audience, with many of his works first appearing in installments that were later made into books. Among his most popular books are A Christmas Carol *(1843),* David Copperfield *(1849–50),* A Tale of Two Cities *(1859) and* Great Expectations *(1860–61).*

The first shock of a great earthquake had, just at the period, rent the whole neighbourhood (of the Camden Hill cutting) to its centre. Traces of its course were visible on every side. Houses were knocked down; streets broken through and stopped; deep pits and trenches dug in the ground; enormous heaps of earth and clay thrown up; buildings that were undermined and shaking, propped by great beams of wood. Here, a chaos of carts, overthrown and jumbled together, lay topsy-turvy at the bottom of a steep, unnatural hill; there, confused treasures of iron soaked and rusted in something that had accidentally become a pond. Everywhere were bridges that led nowhere; thoroughfares that were wholly impassable; Babel towers of chimneys, wanting half their height; temporary wooden houses and enclosures, in the most unlikely situations; carcasses of ragged tenements, and fragments of unfinished walls and arches, and piles of scaffolding and wildernesses of bricks, and giant forms of cranes, and tripods straddling above nothing. There were a hundred thousand shapes and substances of incompleteness, wildly mingled out of their places, upside down, burrowing in the earth, aspiring in the air, mouldering in the water, and unintelligible as any dream. Hot springs and fiery eruptions, the usual attendants upon earthquakes, lent their contributions of confusion to the scene. Boiling water hissed and heaved within dilapidated walls, whence also, the glare and roar of flames came issuing forth; and mounds of ashes blocked up rights of way, and wholly changed the law and custom of the neighbourhood.

In short, the yet unfinished and unopened railroad was in progress; and, from the very core of all this dire disorder, tailed smoothly away upon its mighty course of civilization and improvement.

But, as yet, the neighbourhood was shy to own the railroad. One or two bold speculators had projected streets; and one had built a little, but had stopped among the mud and ashes to consider further of it. A brand-new tavern, redolent of fresh mortar and size, and fronting nothing at all, had taken for its sign The Railway Arms; but that might be rash enterprise—and then in hopes to sell drink to the workmen. So, the Excavators' House of Call had sprung up from a beershop: and the old-established ham and beef shop had become the Railway Eating House, with a roast leg of pork daily, through interested motives of a similar immediate and popular description. Lodging-house keepers were favourable in like manner, and for the like reasons were not to be trusted. The general belief was very slow. There were frowzy fields, and cow-houses, and dunghills, and dustheaps, and ditches, and gardens, and summer-houses, and carpet-beating grounds, at the very door of the railway. Little tumuli of oyster shells in the oyster season, and of lobster shells in the lobster season, and of broken crockery and faded cabbage leaves in all seasons, encroached upon its high places. Posts, and rails and old cautions to trespassers, and backs of mean houses, and patches of wretched vegetation, stared it out of countenance. Nothing was the better for it, or thought of being so. If the miserable waste ground lying near it could have laughed, it would have laughed it to scorn, like many of the miserable neighbours . . . .

As to the neighbourhood which had hesitated to acknowledge the railroad in its straggling days, that had grown wise and penitent, as any Christian might in such a case, and now boasted of its powerful and prosperous relation. There were railway patterns in its drapers' shops, and railway journals in the windows of its newsmen. There were railway hotels, office-houses, lodging-houses, boarding-houses; railway plans, maps, views, wrappers, bottles, sandwich-boxes, and time-tables; railway hackney-coach and cabstands; railway omnibuses, railway streets and buildings, railway hangers-on and parasites, and flatterers out of all calculation. There was even railway time observed in clocks, as if the sun itself had given in. Among the vanquished was the master chimney-sweeper. . .who now lived in a stuccoed house three stories high, and gave himself out, with golden flourishes upon a varnished board, as contractor for the cleansing of railway chimneys by machinery.

To and from the heart of this great change, all day and night, throbbing currents rushed and returned incessantly like its life's blood. Crowds of people and mountains of goods, departing and arriving scores upon scores of times in every four-and-twenty hours, produced a fermentation in the place that was always in action. The very houses seemed disposed to pack up and take trips. Wonderful Members of Parliament, who, little more than twenty years before, had made themselves merry with the wild railroad theories of engineers, and given them the liveliest rubs in cross-examination, went down into the north with their watches in their hands, and sent on messages before by the electric telegraph, to say that they were coming. Night and day the conquering engines rumbled at their distant work, or, advancing smoothly to their journey's end, and gliding like tame dragons into the allotted corners grooved out to the inch for their reception, stood bubbling and trembling there, making the walls quake, as if they were dilating with the secret knowledge of great powers yet unsuspected in them, and strong purposes not yet achieved.

FROM *THE SEVEN LAMPS OF ARCHITECTURE*

John Ruskin (1819–1900)

John Ruskin was one of the most influential art critics of his time; he virtually determined artistic opinion in nineteenth-century England. Ruskin established his reputation with the five-volume set Modern Painters *(1843–60), but is better known for* The Seven Lamps of Architecture *(1849) and the famous* Stones of Venice *(1851–53). Much of Ruskin's work deals with social reform, and many of his suggested programs, such as organized labor and old-age pensions, are now accepted doctrine. In 1878, Ruskin suffered his first period of insanity, and his later years were marked by many spells of mental instability.*

Another of the strange and evil tendencies of the present day is to the decoration of the railroad station. Now, if there be any place in the world in which people are deprived of that portion of temper and discretion which is necessary to the contemplation of beauty, it is there. It is the very temple of discomfort, and the only charity that the builder can extend to us is to show us, plainly as may be, how soonest to escape from it.

The whole system of railroad travelling is addressed to people who, being in a hurry, are therefore, for the time being, miserable. No one would travel in that manner who could help it—who had time to go leisurely over hills and between hedges, instead of through tunnels and between banks: at least, those who would have no sense of beauty so acute as that we need consult it at the station.

The railroad is in all its relations a matter of earnest business, to be got through as soon as possible. It transmits a man from a traveller into a living parcel. For the time he has parted with the nobler characteristics of his humanity for the sake of a planetary power of locomotion. Do not ask him to admire anything. You might as well ask the wind.

WHAT'S THE RAILROAD TO ME?

from *Walden, or Life in the Woods*

Henry David Thoreau (1817–1862)

Well-known American author and naturalist Henry David Thoreau published only two books in his lifetime: A Week on the Concord and Merrimack Rivers *(1849) and the famous* Walden, or Life in the Woods *(1854), his account of near solitary sustenance living on Walden Pond near Concord, Massachusetts. Thoreau's writings, including his journals, essays and fragments, were published in twenty volumes in 1960.*

What's the railroad to me?
I never go to see
Where it ends.
It fills a few hollows,
And makes banks for the swallows,
It sets the sand a-blowing,
And the blackberries a-growing. . .

I LIKE TO SEE IT LAP THE MILES

Emily Dickinson (1830–1886)

An intense and sensitive individual who preferred solitude to the company of others, Emily Dickinson lived her entire life quietly in Amherst, Massachusetts. Though perhaps one of the greatest poets of nineteenth-century American literature, Dickinson published only seven poems in her lifetime. The rest of her poetry was published posthumously, and she never knew the fame her talent would bring her.

I like to see it lap the Miles—
And lick the Valleys up—
And stop to feed itself at Tanks—
And then-prodigious step

Around a Pile of Mountains—
And supercilious peer
In Shanties-by the sides of Roads—
And then a Quarry pare

To fit its Ribs
And crawl between
Complaining all the while
In horrid-hooting stanza—
Then chase itself down Hill—

And neigh like Boanerges—
Then-punctual as a Star
Stop-docile and omnipotent
At its own stable door.

TO A LOCOMOTIVE IN WINTER

from *Complete Poems and Selected Prose*

Walt Whitman (1819–1892)

One of the greatest American poets, Walt Whitman is best-known for Leaves of Grass *(1855), which revolutionized American literature, though it was unfavorably received by American critics at publication. Nine revised and enlarged editions of the volume were issued from 1856 to 1892. His other works include* Drum-Taps *(1865),* Democratic Vistas *(1871) and* Specimen Days *(1882). Whitman also edited the* Long Islander *and several papers, and wrote prose and verse for New York and Brooklyn journals.*

Thee for my recitative,
Thee in the driving storm even as now, the snow, the winter-day declining,
Thee in thy panoply, thy measur'd dual throbbing and thy beat convulsive,
Thy black cylindric body, golden brass and silvery steel,
Thy ponderous side-bars, parallel and connecting rods, gyrating, shuttling at thy sides,
Thy metrical, now swelling pant and roar, now tapering in the distance,
Thy great protruding head-light fix'd in front,
Thy long, pale, floating vapor-pennants, tinged with delicate purple,
Thy dense and murky clouds out-belching from thy smoke-stack,
Thy knitted frame, thy springs and valves, the tremulous twinkle of thy wheels,
Thy train of cars behind, obedient, merrily following,
Through gale or calm, now swift, now slack, yet steadily careering;
Type of the modern—emblem of motion and power—pulse of the continent,
For once come serve the Muse and merge in verse, even as here I see thee,
With storm and buffeting gusts of wind and falling snow,
By day thy warning ringing bell to sound its notes,
By night thy silent signal lamps to swing.

Fierce-throated beauty! Roll through my chant with all thy lawless music, thy swinging lamps at night,
Thy madly-whistled laughter, echoing, rumbling like an earthquake, rousing all,
Law of thyself complete, thine own track firmly holding,
(No sweetness debonair of tearful harp or glib piano thine,)
Thy trills of shrieks by rocks and hills return'd,
Launch'd o'er the prairies wide, across the lakes,
To the free skies unpent and glad and strong.

DICKENS IN DANGER

from *Letters of Charles Dickens*

Charles Dickens (1812–1870)

Gad's Hill Place, Higham by Rochester, Kent.
Tuesday, Thirteenth June, 1865.

My Dear Mitton,

I should have written to you yesterday or the day before, if I had been quite up to writing.

I was in the only carriage that did not go over into the stream. It was caught upon the turn by some of the ruin of the bridge, and hung suspended and balanced in an apparently impossible manner. Two ladies were my fellow-passengers, an old one and a young one. This is exactly what passed. You may judge from it the precise length of the suspense. Suddenly we were off the rail, and beating the ground as the car of a half-emptied balloon might. The old lady cried out "My God!" and the young one screamed. I caught hold of them both (the old lady sat opposite and the young one on my left) and said: "We can't help ourselves, but we can be quiet and composed. Pray don't cry out." The old lady immediately answered: "Thank you. Rely upon me. Upon my soul I will be quiet." We were then all tilted down together in a corner of the carriage, and

stopped. I said to them thereupon, "You may be sure nothing worse can happen. Our danger *must* be over. Will you remain here without stirring, while I get out of the window?" They both answered quite collectedly "Yes" and I got out without the least notion what had happened.

Fortunately I got out with great caution and stood upon the step. Looking down I saw the bridge gone, and nothing below me but the line of rail. Some people in the two other compartments were madly trying to plunge out of the window, and had no idea that there was an open swampy field fifteen feet down below them, and nothing else! The two guards (one with his face cut) were running up and down on the down side of the bridge (which was not torn up) quite wildly. I called out to them: "Look at me. Do stop an instant and look at me, and tell me whether you don't know me." One of them answered, "We know you very well, Mr Dickens." "Then," I said, "my good fellow, for God's sake give me your key, and send one of those labourers here, and I'll empty this carriage." We did it quite safely, by means of a plank or two, and when it was done I saw all the rest of the train, except the two baggage vans, down in the stream. I got into the carriage again for my brandy flask, took off my travelling hat for a basin, climbed down the brickwork, and filled my hat with water.

Suddenly I came upon a staggering man covered with blood (I think he must have been flung clean out of his carriage), with such a frightful cut across the skull that I couldn't bear to look at him. I poured some water over his face and gave him some drink, then gave him some brandy, and laid him down on the grass, and he said: "I am gone," and died afterwards. Then I stumbled over a lady lying on her back against a little pollard-tree, with the blood streaming over her face (which was lead colour) in a number of distinct little streams from the head. I asked her if she could swallow a little brandy and she just nodded, and I gave her some and left her for somebody else. The next time I passed her she was dead. Then a man, examined at the inquest yesterday (who evidently had not the least remembrance of what really passed), came running up to me and implored me to help him find his wife, who was afterwards found dead. No imagination can conceive the ruin of the carriages, or the extraordinary weights under which the people were lying, or the complications into which they were twisted up among iron and wood, and mud and water.

I don't want to be examined at the inquest and I don't want to write about it. I could do no good either way, and I could only seem to speak about myself, which of course I would rather not do. I am keeping very quiet here. I have a—I don't know what to call it—constitutional (I suppose) presence of mind, and was not in the least fluttered at the time. I instantly remembered that I had the MS. of a number with me and clambered back into the carriage for it. But in writing these scanty words of recollection I feel the shake and am obliged to stop.

Ever faithfully,

Charles Dickens

FROM *NOTHING LIKE IN THE WORLD*

Stephen Ambrose (1936–)

One of America's most prolific contemporary historians, Stephen Ambrose has written over 20 books, including multi-volume biographies of Eisenhower and Nixon, an examination of the D-Day landing, and a retelling of the journey of Lewis and Clark, among many other topics. He has produced works on famous generals such as Custer, military battles like D-Day and famous explorers such as Lewis & Clark. A retired professor of the University of New Orleans, he is the founder of the Eisenhower Center in New Orleans and President of the National D-Day Museum in New Orleans.

Ogden would be the terminus for the Central Pacific coming from Sacramento and the Union Pacific coming from Omaha, but the initial meeting point for the two lines would be the basin at Promontory summit. The companies pulled back their men, their tents, their cooking facilities, their equipment, their wagons, horses and mules, everything.

Still, the rivalry between the two railroad lines continued. The competition had become a habit. At the end of April 1869, even though the race had been over for nearly three weeks, that competition captured the attention of the people of the United States.

In 1868 Jack Casement, the UP construction boss, had seen his men lay down four and a half miles of track in single day. "They bragged of it," Charles Crocker, who was in charge of CP construction, later said, "and it was heralded all over the country as being the biggest day's track-laying that was ever known." Crocker told James Strobridge, his burly, profane, supremely capable overseer, that the CP must beat the UP. They got together the material, talked to the men, and did it, spiking down six miles and a few feet in a single day in 1868.

Casement had come back at them later that year, starting at 3:00 a.m. and keeping at the task until midnight. At the end of the day, the UP had advanced the end of track eight and a half miles.

"Now," Crocker said to Strobridge, "we must take off our coats, but we must not beat them until we get so close together that there is not enough room for them to turn around and outdo us." Ten miles ought to do it, he figured.

"Mr. Crocker," Strobridge said, "we cannot get men enough onto the track to lay ten miles."

Organize, Crocker replied. "I've been thinking over this for two weeks, and I have got it all planned out."

Crocker's plan was to have the men and the horses ready at first light. He wanted iron cars with rails, spikes, and fishplates, all ready to go. The night before, he wanted five supply trains lined up, the first at the railhead. Each of the five locomotives would pull 16 cars, which contained enough supplies for two miles of track. When the sun rose, his Chinese workers, the men who had punched the line through the Sierra, would leap into the cars of the first train, up at the end of track, and begin throwing down kegs of bolts and spikes, bundles of fishplates, and the rails. That train would then back up to a siding, and while the first two miles were laid, another would come forward. As the first train moved back, six-man gangs of Chinese would lift the small, open flatcars onto the track and begin loading each one with 16 rails plus kegs of bolts, spikes, and fishplates.

As this operation was being mounted, three men with shovels, called "pioneers," would move out along the grade—that is, the right-of-way prepared to receive the track—aligning the ties that had been placed there the night before. When the loaded cart got to the end of the track, right after the pioneers, a team of Irish workers, one on each side, would grab the rails with their tongs, two men in front, two at the rear, race them forward to their proper position and drop them in their proper place when the foreman called out, "Down!"

The spikes, placed by the Chinese workers atop the rails, would dribble onto the grade as the rails were removed. The bolts and fishplates, which joined the rails together at their ends, were carried in hand buckets to where they were needed. When the cart was empty, it would be tipped off the grade, and the next one brought on. Then the first would be turned around, and the horses would be rehitched, to race back for another load.

Next would come the men placing and pounding in spikes. Crocker admonished Strobridge to have enough spikes on hand so that "no man stops and no man passes another." The crew placing the telegraph poles and stringing the wire would keep pace.

Strobridge heard everything Crocker had to say, considered it, and finally said, "We can beat them, but it will cost something." For example, he insisted on having a fresh team of horses for each car hauling rail, the fresh horses to take over after every two and a half miles.

"Go ahead and do it," said Crocker.

They waited until April 27, when the CP had only 14 miles to go, the UP 9. Crocker had offered a bet of $10,000 to Thomas Durant, vice president of the UP, saying that the CP would lay 10 miles of track in one day. Reportedly, Durant was sure they couldn't and accepted the wager.

What the CP crews did that day should be remembered as long as this Republic lasts. White men born in America were there, along with former slaves whose ancestors came from Africa, plus immigrants from all across Europe, and more than 3,000 Chinese. There were some Mexicans with a touch of Native American blood in them, as well as French Indians and at least a few Native Americans. Everyone was excited, ready to get to work, eager to show what he could do. Even the Chinese, usually methodical and a bit scornful of the American way of doing things, were stirred to a fever pitch. They and all the others. They had come together at this desolate place in the middle of western North America to do what had never been done before.

The sun rose at 7:15 a.m. First the Chinese went to work. According to the San Francisco *Bulletin's* correspondent, "In eight minutes, the sixteen cars were cleared, with a noise like the bombardment of an army."

The Irishmen laying track came on behind the pioneers. Their names were Michael Shay, Patrick Joyce, Michael Kennedy, Thomas Daley, George Elliott, Michael Sullivan, Edward Killeen, and Fred McNamara. Their foreman was George Coley. The two in front on each 30-foot rail would pick it up with their tongs and run forward. The two in the rear picked it up and carried it forward until all four heard "Down." The rail weighed 560 pounds each.

Next came the men starting the spikes by placing them in position, then the spike drivers, then the bolt threaders, then the straighteners, finally the tampers.

"The scene is a most animated one," wrote one newspaper reporter. "From the first pioneer to the last tamper, perhaps two miles, there is a thin line of 1,000 men advancing a mile an hour; the iron cars running up and down; mounted men galloping backward and forward. Alongside of the moving force are teams hauling tools, and water-wagons, and Chinamen, with pails strung over their shoulders, moving among the men with water and tea."

One of the Army officers, the senior man, grabbed Charlie Crocker and said, "I never saw such organization as this; it is just like an army marching across over the ground and leaving a track built behind them."

When the whistle blew for the noon meal, at 1:30 p.m., the CP workers had laid 6 miles of track. Strobridge had a second team of tracklayers in reserve, but the proud men who had put down the first 6 miles insisted on keeping at it throughout the rest of the day. By 7:00 p.m., the CP was 10 miles and 56 feet farther east than it had been at dawn. Never before done, never matched.

To demonstrate how well the track had been laid, the engineer Jim Campbell ran a locomotive over the new track at 40 miles an hour. Jack Casement turned to Strobridge. "He owned up beaten," Strobridge later commented. But so far as can be told, Durant never paid Crocker the $10,000 he lost in the bet.

Grenville Dodge, the UP's chief engineer, sneered at the record. "They took a week preparing for it," he declared. "I never saw so much needless waste in building railroads." But Dodge ended with a comment that summed up the triumphs and troubles he had seen, one that put his, the UP's, and the CP's achievement in reaching Promontory into perspective. He noted that "everything connected with the construction department is being closed up" and concluded, "Closing the accounts is like the close of the Rebellion."

When the Golden Spike went into the last tie to connect the last rail, it brought together the lines from east and west. Lee's surrender four years earlier had signified the bonding of the Union, North and South. The Golden Spike meant the Union Was held together, East and West.

In the twenty-first century, everything seems to be in flux, and change is so constant as to be taken for granted. This leads to a popular question: What generation lived through the greatest change? The one that lived through the coming of the automobile and the airplane and the beginning of modern medicine? Or the one that was around for the invention and first use of the atomic bomb and the jet airplane? Or the computer? Or the Internet and e-mail? For me, it is the Americans who lived through the second half of the nineteenth century. They saw slavery abolished and electricity put to use, the development of the telephone and the completion of the telegraph, and most of all the railroad. The locomotive was the first great triumph over time and space. After it came, and after it crossed the continent of North America, nothing could ever again be the same. It brought about the greatest change in the shortest period of time.

Only in America was there enough space to utilize the locomotive fully, and only here did the government own enough unused land or possess enough credit to induce capitalists to build a transcontinental railroad. Only in America was there enough energy and imagination. "We are the youngest of the peoples," proclaimed the *New York Herald*, "but we are teaching the world how to march forward."

One year before the rails were joined at Promontory, Walt Whitman began to celebrate this new force when he wrote in his "Passage to India":

I see over my own continent the Pacific

railroad surmounting every barrier,

I see continual trains of cars winding along

the Platte carrying freight and passengers,

I hear the locomotives rushing and roaring

the shrill steam-whistle,

I hear the echoes reverberate through the

grandest scenery in the world,

I cross the Laramie plains, I note the rocks

in grotesque shapes, the buttes,

I see the plentiful larkspur and wild onions,

the barren, colorless sage-deserts…

Tying the Eastern to the Western sea,

The road between Europe and Asia…

Parts of the Union Pacific and the Central Pacific ran through some of the grandest scenery in the world, but the spot where the two were joined together was improbable and undistinguished. No one had ever lived there, and shortly after the ceremony no one would ever again, as it is today a National Park. The summit was just over 5,000 feet above sea level, a flat, circular valley, bare except for sagebrush and a few scrub cedars perhaps three miles in diameter. The only "buildings" were a half-dozen wall tents and a few rough-board shacks, set up by merchants selling whiskey.

The ceremony was scheduled for May 8. The Central Pacific's regular passenger train left Sacramento at 6:00 a.m. on May 6, with a number of excursionists. A special train followed, carrying Leland Stanford, the former governor of California and president and director of the CP; the chief justice of California; the governor of Arizona; and other guests. Also on board were: the last spike, made of gold; the last tie, made of laurel; and a silver-headed hammer.

The Stanford special moved along briskly with its excited and expectant passengers. But up ahead, just over the summit, some Chinese were cutting timber above the entrance to Tunnel No.14. After seeing the regular train pass, with no way to know that another, unscheduled train was coming right behind, they skidded a 50-foot log down on the track. The engine struck the log and was damaged. A telegraph was sent ahead to Wadsworth to hold the passenger train until Stanford's coach could be attached.

This was done. The locomotive pulling the passengers train was named *Jupiter*. It was the CP's Engine No. 60, built in Schenectady, now headed toward a permanent place in railroad history.

On Friday afternoon, May 7, the train arrived at Promontory Point, but there was no one from the UP. Stanford sent a message to the UP's Ogden office, demanding to know where the hell the delegation was. Casement replied that because of very heavy rains, the UP wouldn't get its trains to the summit before Monday, May 10.

Stanford and party were stuck in one of the least scenic spots, with the fewest residents, on a train that had food but made no provisions for entertaining its passengers on a two-day layover. Stanford had the train pull back to a more pleasant location at the Monument Point siding, 30 miles west of the summit, where at least there was a view of a lake. There he and his party spent a quiet Sunday. For most of the day, it rained. The *Alta California* correspondent spent the day poking around the summit, looking for a story. He got it. As he was watching, the Wells Fargo Overland Stage No. 2 came into Promontory summit with its last load of mail from the West Coast. "The four old nags were worn and jaded," he wrote "and the coach showed evidence of long service. The mail matter was delivered to the Central Pacific Co., and with that dusty, dilapidated coach and team, the old order of things passed away forever!"

The dawn on May 10 was cold, near freezing, but the rising sun heralded a bright, clear day, with temperatures riding into the seventies. Spring in Utah, as glorious as it can be. A group of UP and CP workers began to gather, but there were not many of them left, and the best estimate put the crowd at 500 or 600 people, far fewer than the predictions (some had gone as high as 30,000). During the morning, two trains from the CP and two from the UP arrived at the site, bearing officials and their guests, as well as spectators.

Among those representing the CP were Stanford, Strobridge, and some minor officials, plus George Booth, engineer of the *Jupiter*; R. A. Murphy, the fireman; and Eli Dennison, the conductor. The UP contingent included Dodge, Durant, and Casement. Sam Bradford was the engineer on No. 119, the opposite number to the *Jupiter*, with Benjamin Mallory as conductor. Cyrus Sweet was the fireman (twenty years old, he would live through World War II and die on May 30, 1948).

A battalion of soldiers from the 21st Regiment, under Maj. Milton Cogswell, was there. The soldiers had come by train and were headed to the Presidio of San Francisco, which surely must make the 21st the first Army unit to cross the continent by rail. The military band from Fort Douglas, Wyoming, was also there, along with the Tenth Ward Band from Salt Lake City.

In the twenty-first century, public-relations officials from the two companies would have long since taken over the ceremony, but as things were, almost nothing had been planned. Still, it had been decided to have a telegraph wire attached to the Golden Spike, with another to the sledgehammer. When the Golden Spike was tapped in, the telegraph lines would send the message all around the country. (The spike would be placed in a hole already drilled, so that it only had to be tapped down and then could easily be extracted; the spike today is at Stanford University.)

If it worked, this would be a wholly new event in the world. People in New York, Philadelphia, Boston, Chicago, St. Louis, Milwaukee, San Francisco, Sacramento, Seattle, and Los Angeles, even people in Montreal, Halifax, Nova Scotia, and London, England, would participate, by listening, in the same event.

Many other decisions had to be improvised. Before the scheduled time to begin, which was at noon, Dodge, Durant, and Stanford are said to have argued for nearly an hour over who should have the honor of putting in the Golden Spike. "At one time the Union Pacific positively refused connection," the San Francisco *News Leader* reported, "and told the Central people they might do as they liked, and there should be no joint celebration." Just a few minutes before noon, Stanford and Durant settled the controversy.

Strobridge and Samuel Reed the UP's superintendent of construction, came forward bearing the laurel tie. Alongside them was a squad of Chinese, wearing clean blue frocks and carrying one rail, and an Irish squad with the other rail. The *Jupiter* and the No. 119 were facing each other, a couple of rail lengths apart. The engineers, Booth and Bradford, pulled on their whistle cords to send up a shriek. Cheers broke out. One veteran said, "We all yelled like to bust."

The crowd pressed forward. On the telegraph, W. N. Shilling, a telegrapher from Western Union's Ogden office, beat a tattoo of messages to impatient inquiries from various offices: "TO EVERYBODY. KEEP QUIET. WHEN THE LAST SPIKE IS DRIVEN AT PROMONTORY POINT, WE WILL SAY 'DONE!' DON'T BREAK THE CIRCUIT, BUT WATCH FOR THE SIGNALS OF THE BLOWS OF THE HAMMER."

The preacher was introduced. Shilling clicked again: "ALMOST READY. HATS OFF; PRAYER IS BEING OFFERED."

The spikes were brought forward. Shilling clicked, "WE HAVE GOT DONE PRAYING." Stanford gave a brief, uninspired speech. Dodge spoke up for the UP. He mentioned Senator Thomas Hart Benton and Christopher Columbus. Shilling again: "ALL READY NOW; THE SPIKE WILL SOON BE DRIVEN. THE SIGNAL WILL BE THREE DOTS FOR THE COMMENCEMENT OF THE BLOWS."

Strobridge and Reed put the last tie, the laurel tie, in place. Durant drove in his spike—or, rather, tapped it in, for it was partially seated in the predrilled hole already. Then came Stanford. When he tapped in the Golden Spike, he would signal the waiting country. Reporters compared what was coming to the first shot fired at Lexington.

Stanford swung and missed, striking only the rail. It made no difference. The telegraph operator closed the circuit and the wire went out, "DONE!"

Across the nation, bells pealed—even the venerable Liberty Bell in Philadelphia. Then came the boom of cannon, 220 of them in San Francisco at Fort Point, 100 in Washington D.C., and countless others. Everywhere there was the shriek of fire whistles, firecrackers and fireworks, singing and prayers in churches. In New Orleans, Richmond, Atlanta, and throughout the old Confederacy, there were celebrations. Chicago had its biggest parade of the century, seven miles long.

A correspondent there caught exactly the spirit that had brought the whole country together. The festivity, he wrote in the Chicago *Tribune*, "was free from the atmosphere of warlike energy and the suggestion of suffering, danger, and death which threw their oppressive shadow over the celebrations of our victories during the war for the Union."

At Promontory, the *Jupiter* and the UP's No.119, uncoupled from their trains, moved forward ever so slowly, until their pilots touched. The photographer A. J. Russell urged the crews to form a wedge radiating out from the point of contact. When he told

his subjects they were free to move, two more whistles joined the others across the nation and a roar exploded from the crowd. Champagne bottles were smashed against each engine.

The engines backed up and hooked onto their cars. No.119 then came forward until it had crossed the junction of the tracks, halted for an instant, then reversed. *Jupiter* came forward, crossed the junction, and also backed away. The transcontinental railroad was a reality.

Stanford invited the UP officials to his car for a celebratory lunch, with plenty of California fruit and wine to mark the occasion. Telegrams went out and came in. To President Grant: "Sir: We have the honor to report that the last rail is laid, the last spike is driven, the Pacific Railroad is finished." Signed by Stanford and Durant. Another from Dodge to Grant. One to Vice-President Schuyler Colfax. One from Dodge to Secretary of War Rawlins, with a nice touch: "The great work, commenced during the Administration of Lincoln, in the middle of a great rebellion, is completed under that of Grant, who conquered the peace."

Of all things done by the first transcontinental railroad, nothing exceeded the cuts in time and cost it made for people traveling across the continent. Before, it took months and might cost more than $1,000 to go from New York to San Francisco. But after Promontory, a man or woman could go from New York to San Francisco in a week, and the cost, as listed in the summer of 1869, was $150 for first class, $70 for emigrant.

Freight rates by train also fell incredibly. Mail that once cost dollars per ounce and took forever now cost pennies and got from Chicago to California in a few days. The telegraph, meanwhile, could move ideas, thoughts, statistics—any words or numbers that could be put on paper—from one place to another from Europe or England or New York to San Francisco or anywhere else that had a telegraph station, all but instantly.

Together, the transcontinental railroad and the telegraph made modern America possible. Things that could not be imagined before the Civil War now became common. A nationwide stock market, for example. A continentwide economy in which people, food, coal, and minerals moved wherever someone wanted to send them and did so cheaply and quickly.

Mistakes had been made all along the line, caused by both errors of judgment and a certain cynicism, encouraged by Congress and cheered on by the populace at large. There was an emphasis on speed rather than quality, on laying as much track as possible, without regard for safe grading. On September 4, 1872, the New York *Sun* had a bold headline:

THE KING OF FRAUDS.

How the Credit Mobilier Bought

its Way Through Congress.

COLOSSAL BRIBERY.

Congressmen who Have Robbed the

People, and who now Support

the National Robber.

HOW SOME MEN GET FORTUNES.

Princely gifts to the Chairmen of Committees in

Congress.

The newspaper had launched what became the biggest scandal of the nineteenth century. The House of Representatives had a series of hearings to inquire into the working of the Crédit Mobilier—the limited-liability stock company incorporated in 1864 to finance construction of the UP—and into the workings of the UP itself, as well as of the CP. Every official from the companies was required to testify, and in virtually every case the testimony was twisted and given the worst possible interpretation. The hearings went on for a full six months, featuring for the most part acrimony and sensationalism, although most charges were true and would be proved.

The UP and the CP were the biggest corporations of their time and the first to have extensive dealings with the federal, state, county, and township governments. They could not have been built without government aid in the form of gifts—especially land grants, plus state and county purchases of their stock and loans in the form of national government bonds. The CP's directors became extraordinarily rich thanks to the railroad and the way it was financed. The men who held stock in the Crédit Mobilier also got rich from it. In large part this was done by defrauding the government and the public, by paying the lowest possible wages to the men who built the lines, and by delaying or actually ignoring payments of bills to the subcontractors and workmen. In many ways they used their power to guarantee profit for themselves. Most Americans found it difficult, even impossible, to believe that they had actually earned those profits. The general public sentiment was: We have been bilked.

The case was a smash hit. People couldn't get enough of it. As in so much else since the road began, the Union Pacific was once again leading the way as the central character in the action. As well it should have been, since what was being argued about was nothing less than the relationship between government and business. Practical matters were involved, such as when government intervention or regulation is justified.

The Central Pacific, or more particularly the line's Contract and Finance Company, which underwrote it, was also investigated, but all its books had been burned—whether deliberately or by accident was and is in dispute—so nothing was pinned on its directors, even though they were as vulnerable as the UP's.

Congress felt it had the right, the responsibility, and the power to go after the UP and the CP, because the companies would not have existed had Congress not loaned them government bonds and given them land grants. This has caused enormous controversy ever since. Both companies have been accused of stretching out their rail lines in order to get more land grants, a notion that is completely wrong. Despite 130 years of working to reduce the length of the lines, only a few miles have been shaved off, and that mainly caused by the fall of the level of the Great Salt Lake, which allowed the railroad to make a shortcut below Promontory Summit by erecting a causeway through the water.

The land grants are much misunderstood, especially by professors teaching American-history survey courses. The grants are denounced, lambasted, derided. In one of the most influential textbooks ever published, *The Growth of the American Republic*, Samuel Eliot Morison and Henry Steele Commager, who were two of the most distinguished historians of their day, if not of the whole twentieth century, wrote: "The lands granted to both the Union Pacific and the Central Pacific yielded enough to have covered all legitimate costs of building these roads." A colleague of theirs, also distinguished, Fred A. Shannon, wrote, "The half billion dollars in land

alone to the land grant railroads was worth more than the railroads were when they were built.

It was the land grants and the bonds the government passed out that caused the greatest outrage, at the time and later. Still, although the concern of the investigators was justified—it was, after all, the people's money that had been taken—there is another side.

The land grants never brought in enough to pay the bills of building either railroad, or even to come close. In California, from Sacramento to the Sierra Nevada range, and in Nebraska, the railroads were able to sell their strips of land at a good price, $2.50 per acre or more. But in most of Wyoming, Utah, and Nevada, the companies could never sell the land. Unless it had minerals on it, it was virtually worthless, even to cattlemen, who needed far more acres for a workable ranch. So too the vast amount of land the government still owns in the West.

The total value of lands distributed to the railroads was estimated by the Interior Department's auditor as of November 1, 1880 at $391,804,610. The total investment in railroads in the United States in that year was $4,653,609,000. In addition, the government got to sell the alternate sections it held on to in California and Nebraska for big sums. Those lands would have been worth nearly nothing, if it had not been for the building of the railroads. As the historian Robert Henry points out, the land grants did "what had never been done before—provided transportation ahead of settlement."

With regard to the government bonds, generations of American students have also been offered a black-and-white view: The government was handing out a gift. Now for those of us who were in college in the 1950s, our classes were taught by professors who were likely to have taken their own graduate training in the 1930s and had thus been brought up to blame big business for everything that went wrong, especially the Great Depression. Those professors who were not New Deal Democrats were socialists, and they all knew that it helps the anti-big-business case if you can call those bonds a gift.

But they were not a gift. They were loans, to be paid back in 30 years or less. The requirement was met. In the final settlement with the railroads, in 1898 and 1899, the government collected $63,023,512 of principal plus $104,722,978 in interest, making a total repayment of $167,746,490 on an initial loan of $64,623,512. Professor Hugo Meyer of Harvard looked at those figures and quite rightly said, "For the government the whole outcome had been financially not less than brilliant."

An automatic reaction that big business is always on the wrong side, corrupt and untrustworthy, is too easy, and the error is compounded if we fail to distinguish between incentives and fraud.

It is well, perhaps, to remember what Charles Francis Adams, Jr., a man of iron rectitude and the scourge of the Union Pacific's financing, later wrote of the road's original directors, after he became president of the line: "It is very easy to speak of these men as thieves and speculators. But there was no human being, when the Union Pacific railroad was proposed, who regarded it as other than a wild-cat venture. The government did not dare to take hold of it. Those men went into the enterprise because the country wanted a transcontinental railroad, and was willing to give almost any sum to those who would build it. The general public refused to put a dollar into the enterprise. Those men took their financial lives in their hands, and went forward with splendid energy and built the road the country called for. They played a great game, and they played for either a complete failure or a brilliant prize."

Both railroads have gone through major changes in the century and a third since they were built. The UP went into receivership in 1893, but as the country turned into the twenty-first century, it remained one of the oldest and richest corporations in the world, and its holdings included what had once been the CP.

In a way, the personnel have changed less. The men who built the CP were mainly Chinese. For the most part, as individuals they are lost to history, but many of them stayed with railroad work. The Irishmen working for the UP also found jobs on other railroads. They too were discriminated against—"no dogs or Irishmen allowed"—but not so thoroughly as the Chinese. They and their sons and daughters and their grandchildren and great-grandchildren went on to participate actively and successfully in American life.

Firemen, brakemen, engineers, conductors, mechanics, welders, carpenters, repair-shop men, the clerical force, the foremen, directors, supervisors, and people in every job for either the UP or the CP stayed with the railroads for their careers, and so did their children, followed by the third generation and beyond. These are the people who run the modern railroad. They repair it, improve it, take care of it, make sure the damn things go. More than in almost any other profession, railroading is something a family is proud of and wants to remain a part of.

Railroad people are special. Like all the rest, they lose jobs, have to move, are underpaid, and otherwise have a lot to gripe about. But on the job, they love being responsible for all that fabulous machinery. Their spirit is a living tie to a momentous achievement.

The dreamers, the politicians, and the financiers; the surveyors, the soldiers, the engineers; the contraction bosses, the railroad men, the foremen; the Chinese, the Irish, and all the others who picked up a shovel or a sledgehammer or a rail; and the

American people who insisted that it had to be done and who paid for it: They built the transcontinental railroad.

Things happened as they happened. It is possible to imagine all kinds of different routes across the continent, or a better way for the government to help private industry, or maybe to have the government build a railroad and own it. But those things didn't happen, and what did take place is grand. So we admire those who did it—even if they were far from perfect—for what they were and what they accomplished and how much each one of us owes them.

BURYING GROUND BY THE TIES

from *Collected Poems 1917–1982*

Archibald MacLeish (1892–1982)

An American poet known for addressing concerns with social issues, Archibald MacLeish won two Pulitzer Prizes in Poetry for Conquistador *(1932) and* Collected Poems *(1952), as well as a Pulitzer Prize in Drama for* J. B.: A Play in Verse *(1959). He was the Librarian of Congress from 1939 to 1944 and taught at Harvard from 1949 to 1962. His* Collected Poems 1917–1982 *(1985) was published posthumously.*

Ayee! Ai! This is heavy earth on our shoulders:
There were none of us born to be buried in this earth:
Niggers we were, Portuguese, Magyars, Polacks:

We were born to another look of the sky certainly.
Now we lie here in the river pastures:
We lie in the mowings under the thick turf:

We hear the earth and the all-day rasp of the grasshoppers.
It was we laid the steel to this land from ocean to ocean:
It was we (if you know) put the U. P. through the passes

Bringing her down into Laramie full load,
Eighteen mile on the granite anticlinal,
Forty-three foot to the mile and the grade holding:

It was we did it: hunkies of our kind.
It was we dug the caved-in holes for the cold water:
It was we built the gully spurs and the freight sidings:
Who would do it but we and the Irishmen bossing us?
It was all foreign-born men there were in this country:
It was Scotsmen, Englishmen, Chinese, Squareheads, Austrians . . .

Ayee! but there's weight to the earth under it.
Not for this did we come out—to be lying here
Nameless under the ties in the clay cuts:

There's nothing good in the world but the rich will buy it:
Everything sticks to the grease of a gold note—
Even a continent—even a new sky!

Do not pity us much for the strange grass over us:
We laid the steel to the stone stock of these mountains:
The place of our graves is marked by the telegraph poles!

It was not to lie in the bottoms we came out
And the trains going over us here in the dry hollows . . .

FROM *THE INNOCENTS ABROAD*

Mark Twain (1835-1910)

Narrator and social observer Mark Twain (pseudonym of Samuel Clemens) first won recognition as a humorist with the short story "The Celebrated Jumping Frog of Calaveras County" in 1865. His first book, The Innocents Abroad *(1869), described his trip to Europe and the Holy Land and made him famous. Hannibal, Missouri, Twain's boyhood home, provided the literary background for* The Adventures of Tom Sawyer *(1876) and* The Adventures of Huckleberry Finn *(1885), Twain's masterpiece, which has been called the first modern American novel.*

We have come five hundred miles by rail through the heart of France. What a bewitching land it is!—What a garden! Surely the leagues of bright green lawns are swept and brushed and watered every day and their grasses trimmed by the barber. Surely the hedges are shaped and measured and their symmetry preserved by the most architectural of gardeners. Surely the long straight rows of stately poplars that divide the beautiful landscape like the squares of a checker-board are set with line and plummet, and their uniform height determined with a spirit level. Surely the straight, smooth, pure white turnpikes are jack-planed and sandpapered every day. How else are these marvels of symmetry, cleanliness and order attained? It is wonderful. There are no unsightly stone walls, and never a fence of any kind. There is no dirt, no decay, no rubbish any where—nothing that even hints at untidiness—nothing that ever suggests neglect. All is orderly and beautiful—every thing is charming to the eye.

We had such glimpses of the Rhone gliding along between its grassy banks; of cosy cottages buried in flowers and shrubbery; of quaint old red-tiled villages with mossy mediaeval cathedrals looming out of their midst; of wooded hills with ivy-grown towers and turrets of feudal castles projecting above the foliage; such glimpses of Paradise, it seemed to us, such visions of fabled fairy-land!

We knew, then, what the poet meant, when he sang of—

> "—thy cornfields green, and sunny vines,
> O pleasant land of France!"

And it is a pleasant land. No word describes it so felicitously as that one. They say there is no word for "home" in the French language. Well, considering that they have the article itself in such an attractive aspect, they ought to manage to get along without the word. Let us not waste too much pity on "homeless" France. I have observed that Frenchmen abroad seldom wholly give up the idea of going back to France some time or other. I am not surprised at it now.

We are not infatuated with these French railway cars, though. We took first class passage, not because we wished to attract attention by doing a thing which is uncommon in Europe, but because we could make our journey quicker by so doing. It is hard to make railroading pleasant, in any country. It is too tedious. Stage-coaching is infinitely more delightful. Once I crossed the plains and deserts and mountains of the West, in a stage-coach, from the Missouri line to California, and since then all my pleasure trips must be measured to that rare holiday frolic. Two thousand miles of ceaseless rush and rattle and clatter, by night and by day, and never a weary moment, never a lapse of interest! The first seven hundred miles a level continent, its grassy carpet greener and softer and smoother than any sea, and figured with designs fitted to its magnitude—the shadows of the clouds. Here were no scenes but summer scenes, and no disposition inspired by them but to lie at full length on the mail sacks, in the grateful breeze, and dreamily smoke the pipe of peace—what other, where all was repose and contentment? In cool mornings, before the sun was fairly up, it was worth a lifetime of city toiling and moiling, to perch in the foretop with the driver and see the six mustangs scamper under the sharp snapping of a whip that never touched them; to scan the blue distances of a world that knew no lords but us; to cleave the wind with uncovered head and feel the sluggish pulses rousing to the spirit of a speed that pretended to the resistless rush of a typhoon! Then thirteen hundred miles of desert solitudes; of limitless panoramas of bewildering perspective; of mimic cities, of pinna-cled cathedrals, of massive fortresses, counterfeited in the eternal rocks and splendid with the crimson and gold of the setting sun; of dizzy altitudes among fog-wreathed peaks and never-melting snows, where thunders and lightnings and tempests warred mag-nificently at our feet and the storm-clouds above swung their shredded banners in our very faces!

But I forgot. I am in elegant France, now, and not skurrying through the great South Pass and the Wind River Mountains, among antelopes and buf-faloes, and painted Indians on the war path. It is not meet that I should make too disparaging compar-isons between hum-drum travel on a railway and that royal summer flight across a continent in a stage-coach. I meant in the beginning, to say that railway journeying is tedious and tiresome, and so it is—though at the time, I was thinking particularly of a dismal fifty-hour pilgrimage between New York and St. Louis. Of course our trip through France was not really tedious, because all its scenes and experi-ences were new and strange; but as Dan says, it had its "discrepancies."

The cars are built in compartments that hold eight persons each. Each compartment is partially subdi-vided, and so there are two tolerably distinct parties of four in it. Four face the other four. The seats and backs are thickly padded and cushioned and are very comfortable; you can smoke, if you wish; there are no bothersome peddlers; you are saved the infliction of a multitude of disagreeable fellow-passengers. So far, so well. But then the conductor locks you in when the train starts; there is no water to drink, in the car; there is no heating apparatus for night travel; if a drunken rowdy should get in, you could not remove a matter of twenty seats from him, or enter another car; but above all, if you are worn out and must sleep, you must sit up and do it in naps,

with cramped legs and in a torturing misery that leaves you withered and lifeless the next day—for behold they have not that culmination of all charity and human kindness, a sleeping car, in all France. I prefer the American system. It has not so many grievous "discrepancies."

In France, all is clockwork, all is order. They make no mistakes. Every third man wears a uniform, and whether he be a Marshal of the Empire or a brake-man, he is ready and perfectly willing to answer all your questions with tireless politeness, ready to tell you which car to take, yea, and ready to go and put you into it to make sure that you shall not go astray. You can not pass into the waiting-room of the depot till you have secured your ticket, and you can not pass from its only exit till the train is at its threshold to receive you. Once on board, the train will not start till your ticket has been examined—till every passenger's ticket has been inspected. This is chiefly for your own good. If by any possibility you have managed to take the wrong train, you will be handed over to a polite official who will take you whither you belong, and bestow you with many an affable bow. Your ticket will be inspected every now and then along the route, and when it is time to change cars you will know it. You are in the hands of officials who zealously study your welfare and your interest, instead of turning their talents to the inven-tion of new methods of discommoding and snub-bing you, as is very often the main employment of that exceedingly self-satisfied monarch, the railroad conductor of America.

But the happiest regulation in French railway government, is—thirty minutes to dinner! No five-minute boltings of flabby rolls, muddy coffee, questionable eggs, gutta-percha beef, and pies whose conception and execution are a dark and bloody mystery to all save the cook that created them! No;

we sat calmly down—it was in old Dijon, which is so easy to spell and so impossible to pronounce, except when you civilize it and call it Demijohn—and poured out rich Burgundian wines and munched calmly through a long table d'hote bill of fares, snail-patties, delicious fruits and all, then paid the trifle it cost and stepped happily aboard the train again, without once cursing the railroad company. A rare experience, and one to be treasured forever.

They say they do not have accidents on these French roads, and I think it must be true. If I remember rightly, we passed high above wagon roads, or through tunnels under them, but never crossed them on their own level. About every quarter of a mile, it seemed to me, a man came out and held up a club till the train went by, to signify that every thing was safe ahead. Switches were changed a mile in advance, by pulling a wire rope that passed along the ground by the rail, from station to station. Signals for the day and signals for the night gave constant and timely notice of the position of switches.

No, they have no railroad accidents to speak of in France. But why? Because when one occurs, *somebody* has to hang for it! Not hang, maybe, but be punished at least with such vigor of emphasis as to make negligence a thing to be shuddered at by railroad officials for many a day thereafter. "No blame attached to the officers"—that lying and disaster-breeding verdict so common to our soft-hearted juries, is seldom rendered in France. If the trouble occurred in the conductor's department, that officer must suffer if his subordinate can not be proven guilty; if in the engineer's department, and the case be similar, the engineer must answer.

The Old Travelers—those delightful parrots who have "been here before," and know more about the country than Louis Napoleon knows now or ever will know—tell us these things, and we believe them because they are pleasant things to believe, and because they are plausible and savor of the rigid subjection to law and order which we behold about us every where.

But we love the Old Travelers. We love to hear them prate, and drivel and lie. We can tell them the moment we see them. They always throw out a few feelers; they never cast themselves adrift till they have sounded every individual and know that he has not traveled. Then they open their throttle-valves, and how they do brag, and sneer, and swell, and soar, and blaspheme the sacred name of Truth! Their central idea, their grand aim, is to subjugate you, keep you down, make you feel insignificant and humble in the blaze of their cosmopolitan glory! They will not let you know any thing. They sneer at your most inoffensive suggestions; they laugh unfeelingly at your treasured dreams of foreign lands; they brand the statements of your traveled aunts and uncles as the stupidest absurdities; they deride your most trusted authors and demolish the fair images they have set up for your willing worship with the pitiless ferocity of the fanatic iconoclast! But still I love the Old Travelers. I love them for their witless platitudes; for their supernatural ability to bore; for their delightful asinine vanity; for their luxuriant fertility of imagination; for their startling, their brilliant, their overwhelming mendacity!

By Lyons and the Saone (where we saw the lady of Lyons and thought little of her comeliness;) by Villa Franca, Tonnere, venerable Sens, Melun, Fontainebleau, and scores of other beautiful cities, we swept, always noting the absence of hogwallows, broken fences, cowlots, unpainted houses and mud, and always noting, as well, the presence of cleanliness, grace, taste in adorning and beautifying, even to the disposition of a tree or the turning of a hedge, the marvel of roads in perfect repair, void of ruts and guiltless of even an inequality of surface—we bowled along, hour after hour, that brilliant summer day, and as nightfall approached we entered a wilderness of odorous flowers and shrubbery, sped through it, and then, excited, delighted, and half persuaded that we were only the sport of a beautiful dream, lo, we stood in magnificent Paris!

What excellent order they kept about that vast depot! There was no frantic crowding and jostling, no shouting and swearing, and no swaggering intrusion of services by rowdy hackmen. These latter gentry stood outside—stood quietly by their long line of vehicles and said never a word. A kind of hackman-general seemed to have the whole matter of transportation in his hands. He politely received the passengers and ushered them to the kind of conveyance they wanted, and told the driver where to deliver them. There was no "talking back," no dissatisfaction about overcharging, no grumbling about any thing. In a little while we were speeding through the streets of Paris, and delightfully recognizing certain names and places with which books had long ago made us familiar.

FORS CLAVIGERA

from *Letters to the Workmen and Labourers of Great Britain*

John Ruskin (1819–1900)

There was a rocky valley between Buxton and Bakewell, once upon a time, divine as the Vale of Tempe; you might have seen the Gods there morning and evening—Apollo and all the sweet Muses of the Light—walking in fair procession on the lawns of it, and to and fro among the pinnacles of its crags. You cared neither for Gods nor grass, but for cash (which you did not know the way to get); you thought you could get it by what the Times calls 'Railroad Enterprise.' You Enterprised a Railroad through the valley—you blasted its rocks away, heaped thousands of tons of shale into its lovely stream. The valley is gone, and the gods with it; and now, every fool in Buxton can be at Bakewell in half an hour, and every fool in Bakewell at Buxton; which you think a lucrative process of exchange—you Fools Everywhere.

FROM *THROUGH THE LOOKING-GLASS AND WHAT ALICE FOUND THERE*

Lewis Carroll (1832–1898)

Probably the most renowned children's book author in the world, Lewis Carroll (a pseudonym for Charles Lutwidge Dodgson) achieved widespread fame with Alice's Adventures in Wonderland *(1865). The book was originally written to amuse his young friend, Alice Liddell, whose father was dean of Christ Church, which Carroll attended.* Through the Looking Glass *followed in 1872 and also became a favorite. Additional children's books by Carroll include* The Hunting of the Snark *(1876) and* Sylvie and Bruno *(1899).*

Tickets, please!" said the Guard, putting his head in at the window. In a moment everybody was holding out a ticket: they were about the same size as the people, and quite seemed to fill the carriage.

"Now then! Show your ticket, child!" the Guard went on, looking angrily at Alice. And a great many voices all said together ("like the chorus of a song", thought Alice), "Don't keep him waiting, child! Why, his time is worth a thousand pounds a minute!"

"I'm afraid I haven't got one," Alice said in a frightened tone: "there wasn't a ticket-office where I came from." And again the chorus of voices went on. "There wasn't room for one where she came from. The land there is worth a thousand pounds an inch!"

"Don't make excuses," said the Guard: "you should have bought one from the engine-driver," and once more the chorus of voices went on with "The man that drives the engine. Why, the smoke alone is worth a thousand pounds a puff!"

Alice thought to herself, "Then there's no use in speaking." The voices didn't join in this time, as she hadn't spoken, but, to her great surprise, they all thought in chorus (I hope you understand what thinking in chorus means—for I must confess that I don't), "Better say nothing at all. Language is worth a thousand pounds a word!"

"I shall dream about a thousand pounds tonight, I know I shall!" thought Alice.

All this time the Guard was looking at her, first through a telescope, then through a microscope, and then through an opera-glass. At last he said, "You're traveling the wrong way," and shut up the window and went away.

"So young a child," said the gentleman sitting opposite to her (he was dressed in white paper), "ought to know which way she's going, even if she doesn't know her own name!"

A Goat, that was sitting next to the gentleman in white, shut his eyes and said in a loud voice, "She ought to know her way to the ticket-office even if she doesn't know her alphabet!"

There was a Beetle sitting next the Goat (it was a very queer set of passengers altogether), and, as the rule seemed to be that they should all speak in turn, he went on with "She'll have to go back from here as luggage!"

Alice couldn't see who was sitting beyond the Beetle, but a hoarse voice spoke next. "Changes engines," it said, and there it choked and was obliged to leave off.

"It sounds like a horse," Alice thought to herself. And an extremely small voice, close to her ear, said, "You might make a joke on that—something about 'horse' and 'hoarse', you know."

Then a very gentle voice in the distance said, "She must be labeled 'Lass, with care', you know."

And after that other voices went on ("What a number of people there are in the carriage" thought Alice), saying, "She must go by post, as she's got ahead on her—" "She must be sent as a message by the telegraph—" "She must draw the train herself the rest of the way—" and so on.

But the gentleman dressed in white paper leaned forwards and whispered in her ear, "Never mind what they all say, my dear, but take a return-ticket every time the train stops."

"Indeed I shan't" Alice said rather impatiently. "I don't belong to this railway journey at all—I was in a wood just now—and I wish I could get back there!"

"You might make a joke on that," said the little voice close to her ear: "something about 'you would, if you could', you know."

"Don't tease so," said Alice, looking about in vain to see where the voice came from; "if you're so anxious to have a joke made, why don't you make one yourself?"

The little voice sighed deeply: it was very unhappy, evidently, and Alice would have said something pitying to comfort it, "if it would only sigh like other people!" she thought. But this was such a wonderfully small sigh, that she wouldn't have heard it at all, if it hadn't come quite close to her ear. The consequence of this was that it tickled her ear very much, and quite took off her thoughts from the unhappiness of the poor little creature.

"I know you are a friend," the little voice went on; "a dear friend, and an old friend. And you won't hurt me, though I *am* an insect."

"What kind of insect?" Alice inquired a little anxiously. What she really wanted to know was, whether it could sting or not, but she thought this wouldn't be quite a civil question to ask.

"What, then you don't—" the little voice began, when it was drowned by a shrill scream from the engine, and everybody jumped up in alarm, Alice among the rest.

The Horse, who had put his head out of the window, quietly drew it in and said, "It's only a brook we have to jump over." Everybody seemed satisfied with this, though Alice felt a little nervous at the idea of trains jumping at all. "However, it'll take us into the Fourth Square, that's some comfort" she said to herself. In another moment she felt the carriage rise straight up into the air, and in her fright she caught at the thing nearest to her hand, which happened to be the Goat's beard.

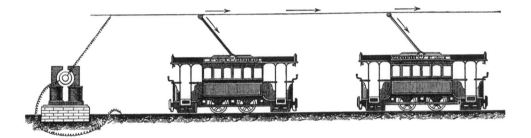

FROM *THE DAILY MAIL*

Thomas Cook (1808–1892)

Britain's most famous travel agent, Thomas Cook was the first to organize and advertise excursions on a regular basis. His tours to the Great Exhibition of 1851 in the Crystal Palace, London, sparked a series of expeditions to famous shows and sites throughout Europe. The Paris Exhibition of 1855 and the Grand Tour of Europe in 1856 helped develop his business into a full-fledged tourist agency. This report to The Daily Mail *comes from his first world tourist trip in 1872.*

The open cars of the American lines afford facilities of contact, and meet the necessities of long journeys far better than the sectional and boxed-up system of English carriages. Conductors have thorough command of trains and can meet any emergencies of travellers without difficulty. Passengers, too, are provided with many conveniences which cannot be afforded under the English system. . . .

The speed of trains is not equal to that of the English lines. The Pacific express of the Union and Central Pacific lines, in connexion with the fastest trains east of Chicago, only attains an average of about 19 miles per hour between New York and San Francisco, including short stoppages of 20 or 25 minutes three times a day for refreshments, and longer delays at the junction of lines. It takes about 170 hours to go 3,300 miles, and that includes seven nights in succession in the sleeping car. . . .

On the Erie line we travelled from New York to Buffalo in a really pleasant drawing-room car, beautifully carpeted and furnished with elbow chairs, mounted on columns, and capable of being turned about in any direction. This was our pleasantest ride in the 3,300 miles, for which we paid extra $2.50 each passenger.

FROM A RAILWAY CARRIAGE

from *A Child's Garden of Verses and Underwoods*

Robert Louis Stevenson (1850–1894)

One of England's best-loved authors, Robert Louis Stevenson was stricken with tuberculosis early in life and traveled extensively in search of healthful climates. An Invalid Voyage (1878), chronicling his canoe trip in Belgium and France, was his first published book. The adventure novel Treasure Island (1883), an instant success, was followed by the collection of children's poems A Child's Garden of Verses (1885), the science-fiction thriller The Strange Case of Dr. Jekyll and Mr. Hyde (1886) and Kidnapped (1886). In 1889 he bought an estate in Samoa where he continued to write.

Faster than fairies, faster than witches,
Bridges and houses, hedges and ditches;
And charging along like troops in a battle,
All through the meadows the horses and cattle:
All of the sights of the hill and the plain
Fly as thick as driving rain;
And ever again, in the wink of an eye,
Painted stations whistle by.

Here is a child who clambers and scrambles,
All by himself and gathering brambles:
Here is a tramp who stands and gazes,
And there is the green for stringing the daisies!
Here is a cart run away in the road
Lumping along with man and load;
And here is a mill, and there is a river:
Each a glimpse and gone for ever!

FROM A MANUAL OF DIET IN HEALTH AND DISEASE

Thomas King Chambers (1818–1889)

Medical writer Thomas King Chambers strove to change the eating habits of the nineteenth-century upper class. His numerous books on the topic include Corpulence, or Excess of Fat in the Human Body *(1850),* Digestion and its Derangements *(1856) and* The Indigestions, or Diseases of the Digestive Organs Functionally Treated *(1869).*

When actually on a carriage or railway journey it is unwise to make large meals. They are sure to be swallowed in a hurried manner, and in a state of heat and excitement very unfavourable to digestion. The best way is to make no meal at all until the journey is over, but to carry a supply of cold provisions, bread, eggs, chickens, game, sandwiches, Cornish pasties, almonds, oranges, captain's biscuits, water, and sound red wine or cold tea, sufficient to stay the appetites of the party and let a small quantity to be taken every two hours.

If this plan be adopted, not only is activity of mind and body preserved, but that heat and swelling of the legs which so often concludes a long day's journey is avoided. Attention to the matter is particularly necessary when the journey continues all night, and for several days in succession, since varicose veins and permanent thickening of the ankles have sometimes resulted from this exertion being combined with too long fasts and hurried repletion at protracted intervals.

HOBO'S TRAIN

from *The Autobiography of a Super-Tramp*

W. H. Davies (1871–1940)

Born in Wales, William Henry Davies left home in 1883 to find fame in the United States. After losing a leg while hopping a train, he returned to Great Britain discouraged. His self-published first book, The Soul's Destroyer and Other Poems *(1905), caught the eye of George Bernard Shaw, and Davies soon found himself in the whirlwind of London literary life.* The Autobiography of a Super-Tramp *(1908) describes his years as a vagabond.*

Brum informed me of a freight train that was to leave the yards at midnight, on which we could beat our way to a small town on the borders of the hop country. Not knowing what to do with ourselves until that time arrived, we continued to drink until we were not in a fit condition for this hazardous undertaking—except we were fortunate to get an empty car, so as to lie down and sleep upon the journey. At last we made our way towards the yards, where we saw the men making up the train. We kept out of sight until that was done and then in the darkness Brum inspected one side of the train and I the other, in quest of an empty car. In vain we sought for that comfort. There was nothing to do but to ride the bumpers or the top of the car, exposed to the cold night air. We jumped the bumpers, the engine whistled twice, toot! toot! and we felt ourselves slowly moving out of the yards. Brum was on one car and I was on the next facing him. Never shall I forget the horrors of that ride. He had taken fast hold on the handle bar of his car, and I had done likewise with mine. We had been riding some fifteen minutes, and the train was going at its full speed when, to my horror, I saw Brum lurch forward, and then quickly pull himself straight and erect. Several times he did this, and I shouted to him. It was no use, for the man was drunk and fighting against the over-powering effects, and it was a mystery to me how he kept his hold. At last he became motionless for so long that I knew the next time he lurched forward his weight of body must break his hold, and he would fall under the wheels and be cut to pieces. I worked myself carefully towards him and woke him. Although I had great difficulty in waking him, he swore that he was not asleep. I had scarcely done this when a lantern was shown from the top of the car, and a brakesman's voice hailed us. "Hallo, where are you two going?" "To the hop fields," I answered. "Well," he sneered, "I guess you won't get to them on this train, so jump off, at once. Jump! d'ye hear?" he cried, using a great oath, as he saw we were little inclined to obey. Brum was now wide awake. "If you don't jump at once," shouted this irate brakesman, "you will be thrown off." "To jump," said Brum quietly, "will be sure death, and to be thrown off will mean no more." "Wait until I come back," cried the brakesman, "and we will see whether you ride this train or not," on which he left us, making his way towards the caboose. "Now," said Brum, "when he returns we must be on the top of the car, for he will probably bring with him a coupling pin to strike us off the bumpers, making us fall under the wheels." We quickly clambered on top and in a few minutes could see a light approaching us, moving along the top of the cars. We were now lying flat, so that he might not see us until he stood on the same car. He was very near to us, when we sprang to our feet, and unexpectedly gripped him, one on each side, and before he could recover from his first astonishment. In all my life I have never seen so much fear on a human face. He must have seen our half drunken condition and at once gave up all hopes of mercy from such men, for he stood helpless, not knowing what to do. If he struggled it would mean the fall and death of the three, and did he remain helpless in our hands, it might mean being thrown from that height from a car going at the rate of thirty miles an hour. "Now," said Brum to him, "what is it to be? Shall we ride this train without interference, or shall we have a wrestling bout up here, when the first fall must be our last? Speak!" "Boys," said he, affecting a short laugh, "you have the drop on me; you can ride." We watched him making his way back to the caboose, which he entered, but every moment I expected to see him reappear assisted by others. It might have been that there was some friction among them, and that they would not ask assistance from one another. For instance, an engineer has to take orders from the conductor, but the former is as well paid, if not better, than the latter, and the most responsibility is on his shoulders, and this often makes ill blood between them. At any rate, American tramps know well that neither the engineer nor the fireman, his faithful attendant, will inform the conductor or brakesman of their presence on a train. Perhaps the man was ashamed of his ill-success, and did not care to own his defeat to the conductor and his fellow brakesmen; but whatever was the matter, we rode that train to its destination and without any more interference.

THE GLOOM AND GRANDEUR OF CENTRAL ASIA

from *A Train on the Trans-Caspian Railway, 1888*

George Curzon (1859–1925)

From 1891 to 1892, George Curzon served as undersecretary of state for India, and then, from 1895 to 1898, as undersecretary for foreign affairs. Russia in Central Asia *(1889)*, Persia and the Persian Question *(1892), and* Problems of the Far East *(1894) were inspired by his travels in Asia. As viceroy (1898–1905) of India, Curzon traveled extensively in the Near and Far East and set up the North-West Frontier Province. Following World War I, he was named foreign secretary and held the post until 1924.*

In these solitudes, the traveller may realise in all its sweep the mingled gloom and grandeur of Central Asian scenery. Throughout the still night the fire-horse, as the natives have sometimes christened it, races onward, panting audibly, gutturally, and shaking a mane of sparks and smoke. Itself and its riders are all alone. No token or sound of life greets eye or year; no outline redeems the level sameness of the dim horizon; no shadows fall upon the staring plain. The moon shines with dreary coldness from the hollow dome, and a profound and tearful solitude seems to brood over the desert. The returning sunlight scarcely dissipates the impression of sadness, of desolate and hopeless decay, of a continent and life sunk in a mortal swoon. The traveller feels like a wanderer at night in some desecrated graveyard, amid crumbling tombstones and half-obliterated mounds. A cemetery, not of hundreds of years but of thousands, not of families or tribes but of nations and empires, lies outspread around him: and ever and anon, in falling tower or shattered arch, he stumbles upon some poor unearthed skeleton of the past.

"TO UNITE THE GREAT SIBERIAN PROVINCES ..."

Czar Alexander III (1845–1894)

Czar Alexander III wrote this letter to his son and successor, Nicholas II, on May 14, 1891, establishing the Great Siberian Railroad across Russia. Czarevitch Nicholas, the last Czar, broke ground for the railroad at the Eastern terminus in Vladivostok on May 31, 1891.

Your Imperial Highness!

Having given the order to build a continuous line of railway across Siberia, which is to unite the rich Siberian provinces with the railway system of the Interior, I entrust you to declare My will, upon your entering the Russian dominions after your inspection of the foreign countries of the East. At the same time, I desire you to lay the first stone at Vladivostók for the construction of the Ussúri line, forming part of the Siberian Railway, which is to be carried out at the cost of the State and under direction of the Government. Your participation in the achievement of this work will be a testimony to My ardent desire to facilitate the communications between Siberia and the other countries of the Empire, and to manifest my extreme anxiety to secure the peaceful prosperity of this Country.

I remain your sincerely loving

ALEXANDER

FAINTHEART IN A RAILWAY TRAIN

Thomas Hardy (1840–1928)

Thomas Hardy's notion of the impending tragedy of human life surfaces in his novels The Return of the Native *(1878),* The Mayor of Casterbridge *(1886),* Tess of the d'Urbervilles *(1891) and* Jude the Obscure *(1895). After the generally poor public reception of* Jude, *Hardy wrote only verse.* Wessex Poems *was published in 1898, followed by* Poems of the Past and Present *(1901) and several additional poetry volumes.*

At nine in the morning there passed a church,
At ten there passed me the sea,
At twelve a town of smoke and smirch,
At two a forest of oak and birch,
And then, on a platform, she:

A radiant stranger, who saw not me.
I said, "Get out to her do I dare?"
But I kept my seat in my search for a plea,
And the wheels moved on. O could it but be
That I had alighted there!

FROM 722 MILES: THE BUILDING OF THE SUBWAYS AND HOW THEY TRANSFORMED NEW YORK

Clifton Hood

Clifton Hood is assistant professor of history at Hobart and William Smith Colleges in Geneva, New York. He was formerly a curator of the LaGuardia Archives at LaGuardia College, City University of New York.

The Geology of Manhattan

Manhattan's geology is forbidding. Although the island has a total of only twenty-three square miles, it harbors an unrivaled range of geological features that posed a severe challenge to the IRT's builders.

Manhattan is shaped like an irregular rectangle. Seven miles long from the Battery to the Harlem River, the island has a width of roughly two miles up to 125th Street, and then it tapers into an elongated neck that ends at Inwood. It has three main topographical zones. The first zone encompasses Manhattan's southern end, the tongue of land below 23rd Street. The terrain there is flat and featureless, rising almost imperceptibly from sea level at the Battery into low, undulating hills that have long since been covered by a grid of streets and buildings. The topography of the second zone, from 23rd to 103rd Street, is much rougher, with steep hills and rocky outcroppings that gave a rough, corrugated appearance. The natural landscape of this zone, like that of the first, has been all but erased.

The third zone, above 103rd Street, is the most varied. Northern Manhattan is dominated by a line of ridges along its western shore. The Manhattan Ridge goes from 103rd Street to about 160th Street, where it divides into two spurs: Fort Washington Ridge, which parallels the Hudson River to the head of the island, and Fort George Ridge, which borders the Harlem River as far north as Dyckman Street. These ridges increase in elevation from south to north, peaking near 185th Street and Fort Washington Avenue, where a rocky point rises 268 feet above sea level, the highest point on the island. Upper Manhattan also has two plains: the broad Harlem lowlands, which stretch east from Morningside Avenue and St. Nicholas Avenue to the Harlem River, and the smaller Inwood lowlands, above Dyckman Street on the Harlem River. In addition, two major faults bisect the island diagonally from northwest to southeast. One fault crosses from 125th Street on the Hudson River to Ninety-sixth Street on the East River, and the other follows Dyckman Street from the Hudson River to the Harlem River. The consequence of water seeping into areas of intensively shattered rock since the Paleozoic era 600 million years ago, these faults cut through the bedrock hundreds of feet below the sea. Although partially filled with glacial deposits of sand, silt, and gravel that raised the level of the ground, the two faults remained important barriers to transportation at the turn of the century.

The island's rock formations are formidable, too. Although a relatively soft rock, called dolomitic marble, overlays the Harlem and Inwood lowlands, the rest of the island is covered by a much more difficult type of rock, Manhattan schist. A well-foliated rock that has alternating black and light gray bands, schist weathers to a dark brown or black color after being exposed to the air and is speckled with coarse mica flakes that shimmer in the sunlight. Manhattan schist can thwart subterranean construction. A metamorphic rock forged deep within the earth's crust under intense pressure and great heat, Manhattan schist is a very hard rock that is murder to cut through. More serious than its hardness, however, is the fact that it is not uniformly hard. Most formations are strong and durable, but this rock is susceptible to decay and can fracture or collapse without warning. This combination of overall hardness plus occasional decay makes schist highly unpredictable and dangerous.

William Barclay Parsons

The man who had to tackle this geological nightmare was William Barclay Parsons, the chief engineer of the Rapid Transit Commission. Parsons was the scion of a proud, old New York family that had belonged to the city's Anglo-American elite during the colonial era. His mother was a descendant of one of North America's most powerful families, the Livingstons of upstate Columbia County; his father was the grandson of the Reverend Henry Barclay, the second rector of prestigious Trinity Church, and a distant relative of Colonel Thomas Barclay, a Tory who fought with the British army during the American Revolution. Parsons' forebears lost most of their political clout when independence severed their ties with the mother country, but they continued to identify closely with Great Britain throughout the nineteenth century as a way of underscoring their elite social standing.

Born on April 15, 1859, William Barclay Parsons inherited a strong dose of Anglophilia from his family. At twelve his parents sent him to an English private school in Torquay, Devonshire, and for the next four years he studied under private tutors while traveling through Britain, France, Germany, and Italy. On this grand tour Parsons formed a lasting admiration for the British upper class as an aristocracy of lofty birth and solid achievement. A dyed-in-the-wool imperialist who credited the British aristocracy with raising the level of civilization around the world, Parsons always tried to emulate its high standards. He went as far as taking his English-sounding middle name, Barclay, as his personal sobriquet, retaining his more ordinary first name, William, for official purposes.

In 1875, Parsons returned to New York and enrolled at Columbia College. A big, strapping youth who was good at games and was popular with his classmates despite a humorless streak that earned him the unattractive nickname "Reverend Parsons," he stroked the heavyweight eight-oared crew to a string of victories on the Harlem River, captained the tug-of-war team, won election as class president, and cofounded the student newspaper, the Spectator. He graduated from Columbia College in 1879 and three years later William Barclay received a degree in civil engineering from the university's School of Mines.

After a brief stint on the staff of the Erie Railroad, Parsons started his own private practice as a consulting engineer in January 1885, with offices at 22 William Street in lower Manhattan. Although he designed a number of water supply systems and railways, Parsons became particularly excited about a scheme that a group of New York City businessmen hatched to build a subway from the Battery to the Harlem River. These entrepreneurs organized the Arcade Railway Company (which, despite its name, was not related to Alfred E. Beach's pneumatic railway) and hired Parsons as a staff engineer. The Arcade was riddled with internal strife, and Parsons and several other dissident employees soon split away to create a rival enterprise, the New York District Railway. The Arcade and the District spent more time fighting each other than planning subways, however, and both companies quickly went bankrupt.

Instead of being disheartened by this failure, Parsons grew fascinated by rapid transit engineering. He pored over topographical maps of Manhattan and hiked through city neighborhoods trying to figure out the best route, motive power, and construction methods for an underground railway. At the same time he exploited his aristocratic connections by cultivating Abram S. Hewitt, William Steinway, Seth Low, and other blue-blooded subway promoters.

Parsons' lobbying paid off. In 1891 the Steinway Commission chose him as its deputy chief engineer. As the principal drafter of the Steinway Commission's subway plan, Parsons earned the respect of other engineers and drew even closer to Hewitt, Low, and Steinway. When the new Rapid Transit Commission replaced the Steinway Commission in 1894, Parsons became its chief engineer.

William Barclay Parsons, thirty-five, now took direct control of subway building. Tall and rangy, with a prominent jaw and piercing eyes that made him appear good-looking in a rough sort of way, Parsons radiated strength and dignity. He stayed calm under pressure and was known for his rigid self-control. Parsons was hardly an amiable or engaging man, and he had little personal warmth. But this stern, demanding patrician nonetheless drew first-rate engineers to his side, inspired their best work, and earned their lifelong loyalty. A journalist later observed that Parsons was a "born general and diplomat" who was "as thorough as a machine" and possessed an extraordinary gift for leadership.

True to his upper-class background, Parsons had a keen sense of social responsibility and believed that engineering entailed much more than narrow technical considerations. He thought of engineering as an instrument for expanding America's wealth and power so that it would eventually surpass Great Britain as the dominant world power. Parsons was an entrepreneurial engineer who worked with capitalists such as J. P. Morgan and August Belmont. At first on his own and later as the founder of a top engineering firm that became known as Parsons Brinckerhoff, William Barclay Parsons built important public works aimed at enlarging the country's commercial domain. In addition to consulting on the Panama Canal, Parsons built docks in Cuba, the Cape Cod Canal in Massachusetts, and hydroelectric plants across the United States.

Parsons found his life's work with the subway. Fervently embracing Abram S. Hewitt's imperial vision of rapid transit as an instrument for guaranteeing New York City's future, Parsons thought of the subway as a mission rather than a mere job.

The Age of Electricity

The first decision confronting William Barclay Parsons and the Rapid Transit Commission was the selection of a motive power for the subway. Their choice was influenced by a technological revolution that had swept surface transit: the adoption of electricity as a new propulsion system.

Engineers had grasped the fundamental principles of electric traction as early as the 1830s. Electricity provided a means of transferring power from the point where it was produced to the point where it was consumed. A coal-burning stationary steam engine, located at a central place, produced mechanical energy, which was converted into electrical current by a machine called a dynamo and then transmitted instantaneously via a conductor to a railway car, where a second machine, the motor, turned it back into mechanical power that drove the wheels. Electricity seemed to have limitless potential as a source of clean, fast, inexpensive, and lightweight energy that could replace the increasingly inadequate animal and steam power. For decades, however, vexing technical problems blocked the development of a satisfactory electric railway, and nobody came close to designing a commercially successful electric railway until the 1880s.

The pioneer of the electric railway was Frank J. Sprague. A graduate of the U. S. Naval Academy and a former assistant to Thomas A. Edison, Sprague founded his company in 1884 to develop electrical motors for factories as well as for railways. In May 1887, Sprague signed a contract with the Union Passenger Railway Company of Richmond, Virginia, to electrify its twelve-mile route. This was a daunting task. The path of the railway wound through a hilly section of the Virginia capital that would test Sprague's new and untried system to the limit, and he also had to improvise much of his equipment on the spot. For instance, he experimented with fifty different trolley poles before finally coming up with one that maintained contact between the overhead wire and the motor.

Sprague beat the odds. Within three months of its February 1888 opening, the Union Passenger Railway was running thirty trolleys at once without experiencing any serious mechanical problems. More important, early electric railways such as Sprague's Union Passenger Railway performed better than competing transportation modes. Their capital costs were 80 percent lower than those of cable railways; their operating costs were 40 percent lower than those of horse railways; and their average speed of twelve miles per hour was about three times faster than that of horse railways.

Frank J. Sprague proved that electrification could be commercially successful on a large scale and under adverse conditions. Consequently, electric street railway construction surged. When Sprague received his Richmond contract in 1887, there were only eight street railways using electric power in the United States (with a mere 35 miles of track). Fifteen years later, in 1902, the total length of electric surface track had multiplied to 21,920 miles. By then the trolley had completely replaced the horse railway as the chief form of surface transport.

But Sprague's Richmond triumph did not ensure that the New York subway could be electrified. When William Barclay Parsons became chief engineer of the Rapid Transit Commission in 1894, electrical traction was still in its infancy in the United States. Only a few rapid transit lines had been electrified so far, such as Chicago's Intramural Railway, a temporary demonstration line built for the World's Columbian Exposition of 1893. Thus, Parsons could not be confident that a technology devised for a twelve-mile-long street railway in a sleepy southern town could be adapted to a high-capacity, high-speed subway for North America's largest metropolis. He remained skeptical about electric traction's possibilities and prudently refused to rule out steam or cable.

Late in the summer of 1894, Parsons sailed for Europe to make a survey of its railways. Because Europe, not North America, was in the forefront of rapid transit operations, it was the best place for Parsons to pick up the technical knowledge he needed to make the right decision. He traveled to Glasgow, where a cable-powered underground railway was being dug that in two or three years would make the Scottish municipality the second city in the world to have a subway; to Paris, where a steam-driven railway circled the urban perimeter; and to Liverpool, where an electric elevated had recently opened along the Mersey.

Parsons went to London, too. London was the birthplace of underground mass transportation, and in the 1890s it remained the center of rapid transit technology. On November 4, 1890, the City and South London Railway had inaugurated the world's first electrically powered subway. Originally intended for cable power, the City and South London converted to electricity at the last moment, and its design resembled a toy train set more than a major urban railway. The new underground was only three miles long, going from the Monument in the city, to Stockwell on the south bank of the Thames River, and its two tunnels had a diameter of just ten feet two inches. Its four-car trains were tiny, seating no more than ninety-six riders, and they averaged just thirteen miles per hour. The passenger accommodations were not ideal, either. Angry riders complained that the small, virtually windowless carriages were stuffy and uncomfortable and that the movement of the trains through the iron-ribbed tunnels created an irritating ringing sound.

Despite these drawbacks, Parsons understood that the City and South London represented a gigantic step forward from London's two steam undergrounds, the Metropolitan Railway and the Metropolitan District Railway. He noted that its stations and carriages were clean and well ventilated, and that its patrons did not ruin their clothes or inhale noxious fumes. But Parsons was more concerned about economics than about the environment. Consequently, he was impressed that the City and South London tallied lower fuel, repair, and labor costs than the two steam undergrounds, suffered relatively few mechanical breakdowns, and made a modest profit. To Parsons this was convincing proof that electricity was the solution.

After returning to New York, Parsons wrote a report for the Rapid Transit Commission advocating the electrification of the subway. Parsons brief, entitled "Report on Rapid Transit in Foreign Cities," removed the commissioners' last doubts about this new energy source and brought the lengthy search for a motive power to an end.

How Deep Should the Subway Go?

As much as he had learned from the City and South London, Parsons knew that the New York subway could not be designed from another underground railway's blueprint. Manhattan's tough physical and urban geography demanded a unique engineering solution, not a carbon copy of another's.

Manhattan' s geological uniqueness had a particularly strong bearing on the question of the subway's depth. The world's first underground, London's celebrated Metropolitan Railway, had been constructed near the surface in order to vent the ashes, cinders, and smoke that its coke-burning locomotives spat out. But the use of electricity eliminated these pollutants from the tunnels, allowing the City and South London to be buried an average of fifty feet below the ground. The City and South London passed mostly through a type of soil called London clay, which was highly stable and uniform. Dense, cohesive, impervious to water yet relatively soft, London clay was perfect for tunneling. Consequently, most of London's subsequent tubes were also built as deep tubes.

New York City was another case. Geologists and engineers recognized that Manhattan schist was a hard, heterogeneous substance that would impede tunneling. What they had not appreciated, however, was that the schist did not lie at an even depth below the surface. In the nineteenth-century the amount of knowledge about New York City's geology was minimal. Before the construction of skyscrapers required digging deep foundations, and only a few public works such as the Croton Aqueduct and the Brooklyn Bridge entailed much underground construction, engineers lacked basic information about the subsurface. William Barclay Parsons himself was among the first to discover that the distance from the ground to bedrock varied from place to place. In 1891, while drilling test holes for the Steinway Commission along the route of its projected Broadway subway, Parsons uncovered a striking phenomenon: The schist came within 20 feet of the surface at Whitehall Street on the Battery; dropped to a depth of 163 feet at Duane Street, three blocks north of city hall; remained at a low level under Greenwich Village; and then climbed back to 16 feet at Thirtieth Street. This U-shaped rock contour had important consequences for Manhattan's growth. For instance, one reason for the emergence of lower and midtown Manhattan as the main business districts was that the schist rose so close to the surface there, it provided an excellent building foundation for skyscrapers.

Parsons' discovery affected the decision of the Rapid Transit Commission about whether to construct the New York subway near the surface, like the Metropolitan, or far below ground, like the City and South London. If the RTC followed the City and South London's lead, its tunnel would cross a mixed face of partly soft earth and partly hard rock. Transiting a mixed face was a poor engineering practice because it would generate high construction costs and produce an unsound structure. One way to avoid a mixed face was to sink the tunnel so deep—as much as two hundred feet below Broadway, the equivalent of two-thirds of a football field—that it would pass only through solid bedrock. But even though this alternative would bring about a structurally sound subway, Parsons warned that it would require the installation of expensive elevators, escalators, and ventilators that would raise capital and operating costs to uneconomical heights.

The answer, Parsons argued, was to build the subway within fifteen or twenty feet of the surface. He claimed that a shallow subway could be constructed by excavating a trench in the street, a relatively simple expedient that would cost less than a deep tube and yet would yield a stable structure. There was one drawback to a shallow subway, however: The space below most city streets was already filled with a maze of electric cables, telephone lines, telegraph wires, water pipes, steam mains, and sewers that would have to be removed and rebuilt elsewhere. Parsons nonetheless concluded that a shallow subway would cost one-eighth as much as a tube, and he strongly recommended that the Rapid Transit Commission opt for a shallow subway.

In early 1895 the Rapid Transit Commission adopted an engineering plan that incorporated most of Parsons' ideas: a shallow railway with four tracks on a single level as far as the Ninety-sixth Street junction, and with two tracks (later enlarged to three in some places) on the Broadway and Lenox Avenue branches. Once the RTC approved its basic engineering design, Parsons had to wait until the commissioners awarded a franchise and then construction could begin. For the chief engineer, the five-year wait for the RTC's plan to emerge from the labyrinth of mayoral, aldermanic, and judicial oversight was torture. Parsons grew particularly concerned when other European and North American cities began passing New York City in the race for rapid transit. Between 1895 and 1900, as New York's courts dickered over the RTC's budget and route, Glasgow, Budapest, and Boston unveiled new underground railways and Paris started to build its first metro. Parsons feared his dream of building the New York subway would not be realized.

Construction of the IRT

Late in 1899 a cable announcing that the RTC's subway plan had finally been approved reached Parsons in Canton, China, where he was surveying a thousand-mile railroad from Hankow to the sea on behalf of a syndicate headed by J. P. Morgan. Overjoyed with the happy news, Parsons immediately quit the Chinese survey and sailed for home. By the time subway construction began on March 26, 1900, two days after a ground-breaking ceremony was held on the steps of city hall, Parsons was already hard at work.

Contemporary building technology was so primitive that the IRT had to be constructed almost entirely by hand. Because there were few steam shovels or bulldozers available in 1900, the burden fell almost entirely on the seventy-seven hundred laborers who made up the workforce at its peak. These workers were predominantly Irish and Italian, although there were also Germans, African-Americans, Greeks, and members of other ethnic groups. Unskilled workers earned from $2.00 to $2.25 per/day, skilled workers about $2.50. Wielding picks, shovels, hammers, percussion drills, and other hand tools, these workmen literally gouged the subway out of the raw earth.

These laborers led hard lives. For instance, one worker who sustained a serious injury building the IRT was an Italian immigrant named Salvatore Mazzella. Born on May 6, 1883, on the small island of Ponza off Naples, Mazzella emigrated to New York City at age seven with his father and grew to be a handsome, blue-eyed six footer. Trained as a tile worker, Mazzella landed a job cementing white tiles to the walls of the IRT stations. He apparently labored on the subway for five or six years, first on the original IRT and then on its extensions; typically, he worked on the IRT during the summer and then returned with his savings to Ponza for the winter. At some point in 1908 or 1909, Mazzella spilled some lead-based tile adhesive in his eye. Mainly because he spoke English poorly, Mazzella did not tell his Irish foreman about the accident until after his eye became badly inflamed. His boss eventually found out and urged him to see a doctor, but it was too late: The doctor had to remove his eye and provide him with a glass replacement. Salvatore Mazzella remained proud of his contributions to New York City for the rest of his life, but he paid a high price for that sense of accomplishment.

Thousands of workers like Mazzella built the IRT subway piece by piece. The standard form of construction was known as cut and cover. The laborers began by cutting a hole the width of the street. Excavating this trench was fairly easy below Tenth Street, where the subway ran through soft soils. It was much more difficult above Tenth Street where much of the route passed through solid rock that had to be drilled and dynamited. In both sections, work gangs had to shore up the old buildings that lined the path of the IRT, maneuver around the underground storage vaults that extended into the streets, and relocate sewers and utilities. Traffic was a concern, too. On busy downtown thoroughfares such as Park Row that had to stay open during construction, workers' covered the trench with a temporary wooden bridge that supported trolleys, carriages, and wagons; on less important arteries the street was closed during construction and the hole remained open.

After completing the trench, the workers erected the structural framework that would house the tracks, signals, third rail, and other equipment. This framework was made of steel and concrete and resembled an elongated rectangular box. Laborers poured a four-inch-thick concrete foundation across the bottom of the trench to form the box's base. They fabricated its sides and roof by planting steel I-beams every five feet and pouring concrete into the gaps between the beams. This technique of embedding steel columns in concrete produced an exceptionally strong structure that could easily bear the weight of the street.

Cut and cover was the most common type of construction, but it could be employed on no more than 52 percent of the subway's total length. Due to the island's hilly topography, abrupt changes in the ground level occurred so frequently that the use of cut and cover would not have kept the rails at grade. To prevent the IRT from resembling a Coney Island roller coaster, the RTC had to build a wide variety of structures, including a 2,174-foot steel arch viaduct across Manhattan Valley between 122nd and 135th streets and rock tunnels in Murray Hill and upper Manhattan.

Of all the techniques used on the subway, rock tunneling was the most demanding. The workers started by sinking a vertical shaft at both ends of the tunnel. Then they isolated a small section at the bottom of each shaft and began driving a narrow heading there. This heading was advanced by drilling holes seven feet into the face of the schist and putting dynamite charges in the cavities. After detonating the explosives, the laborers returned to the face, cleared the rubble, and braced the new section of the tunnel. Then they started drilling again. This cycle of drilling, blasting, clearing, and timbering continued until the two headings met in the middle and the tunnel was completed. The workmen then enlarged the tube to its full size, lined it with concrete, and installed tracks, third rails, and signals.

Boring through Manhattan schist was difficult because the rock was hard; it was dangerous because

the schist lacked uniformity. Drillers often encountered unexpected geological hazards that delayed the project and cost lives—rock slides, pockets of broken rock or loose gravel, and underground ponds. The Murray Hill tunnel, which went up Park Avenue from Thirty-fourth Street to Forty-first Street, illustrated these dangers. A rocky promontory that rose thirty or forty feet above the surrounding landscape, Murray Hill covered the area from Twenty-seventh Street to Forty-Second Street, and from Third Avenue to Sixth Avenue. Although it was not as prominent geologically as the ridges of upper Manhattan, Murray Hill consisted of a highly unstable formation of schist that posed great obstacles to subway building. The rock lay at a forty-five-degree angle that could precipitate rock slides, and it harbored many belts of shattered rock that could lead to cave-ins. The construction of the IRT's Murray Hill tunnel was further complicated because an old trolley tunnel of the Metropolitan Street Railway Company ran below Park Avenue, right in the path of the subway. Consequently, the subway had to be divided into two separate tunnels and shoehorned into the remaining space.

The subcontractor for this section of the subway, thirty-eight-year-old Major Ira A. Shaler, experienced misfortune after misfortune. His first calamity occurred on January 28, 1902, when a wooden powder house, located at Forty-first Street and Park Avenue and containing over two hundred pounds of dynamite, caught fire and exploded, giving off a blinding white flash, a column of dirty yellow smoke, and a powerful shock wave. One New Yorker who witnessed this devastation recalled his fright: "I thought the end of all of us had come." The blast wrecked the Murray Hill Hotel, defaced Grand Central Terminal, and shattered glass for several blocks around. Five people died and another 125 were injured. A grand jury blamed the accident on Shaler's carelessness in storing the explosives and indicted him for manslaughter.

Disaster struck again two months later, on the night of March 21, when a narrow thirty-five-foot crack appeared in the roof of the east tunnel, below Thirty-seventh Street. In trying to shore up the tunnel, Shaler's employees made the alarming discovery that the roof was not covered by a solid mass of schist, as it should have been. Instead, the roof consisted of only a thin shell of hard rock. Above this shell was a loose heap of decomposed rocks, pressing down with the full force of gravity. At 8:30 the next morning an avalanche of boulders, stones, and dirt crashed through the roof with a deafening roar. Although the workers had been evacuated and nobody was hurt, debris partially filled the tunnel, delaying subway construction for weeks. In addition, the break extended to the surface of Murray Hill and undermined the foundations of four homes, causing over $100,000 in property damage.

By now Shaler had been dubbed the "voodoo contractor." His luck ran out completely three months later, on June 17, 1902, when he took Chief Engineer Parsons and Assistant Engineer George S. Rice on an inspection tour of his section. As they reached the upper end of the western tunnel, Parsons stopped, pointed his cane at a rock protruding overhead, and warned that it looked rotten. Major Shaler, insisting that Parsons was wrong and that the rock was perfectly safe, stepped out from the timber bracing for a closer look at the ledge. Suddenly, a one-thousand-pound boulder collapsed. Parsons and Rice had remained under the timber and were not even scratched, but the rock broke Shaler's neck and paralyzed him below the shoulders. He died in Presbyterian Hospital eleven days later.

The subway's most daunting structure was a tunnel that ran over two miles from 158th Street in Washington Heights to Hillside Avenue in Fort George. It ranked as the second longest two-track rock tunnel ever built in the United States, surpassed only by the famous Hoosac Tunnel in western Massachusetts. It was so deep that elevators had to be installed so that passengers could reach the 168th Street, 181st Street, and 191st Street stations; the 191st Street stop is 180 feet below ground and remains the subway system's deepest station today.

The construction of this imposing tunnel attracted miners from all over: eastern Pennsylvania's anthracite coal hills, Colorado's silver lode, the Klondike gold strike, South Africa's gold and diamond fields, Wales, Ireland, Scandinavia, and Canada. These were miners who spent their lives wandering from place to place. They earned up to $3.75 a day, almost twice as much as unskilled workers, and pointedly referred to the tunnel as the "mine" in order to distance themselves from ordinary laborers. During the IRT's construction they lived in boardinghouses in Washington Heights and turned this neighborhood into a tough mining camp that reverberated with the rhythms of work, drinking, and whoring.

The single worst accident that took place during the construction of the subway occurred here in October 1903, near the tunnel's Fort George portal. At the time the tunnel crews were working several hundred feet north of 193rd Street and St. Nicholas Avenue, on the rear slope of Fort George, where the schist lay at a steep angle that was conducive to slides, and in a strata of broken rock that was riddled with fissures and seams. Although these treacherous geological conditions probably should have dictated a cautious approach, only a few hundred feet remained to be excavated before the tunnel was holed through, and the contractor, L. B. McCabe &

Sons, was in a hurry. Consequently, McCabe ordered three dynamite blasts be set off every day instead of the normal two.

This decision proved fatal. Shortly after 10:00 P. M. on October 24 a gang of twenty-two men triggered a series of explosions in the tunnel. Ten or fifteen minutes later foreman Timothy Sullivan returned to the rock face by himself in order to sound the tunnel's walls. He was responsible for making sure that the blast did not loosen any rocks in the roof and walls that might fall on his crew. Thinking the schist looked stable, Sullivan shouted, "Come on, boys, let's get to work." Sullivan was unaware that an underground spring was hidden behind the face, weakening the rock. Shortly after the laborers reached the blast site, a huge three-hundred-ton boulder, measuring forty-four feet long and four or five feet wide, dropped from the roof, killing six men instantly and seriously injuring eight others. The tunnel's walls were splattered with a gory mixture of human blood and spring water, and the air was filled with the moans of badly hurt workers who were buried under mounds of timber, rock, and dirt. Although rescuers freed several of the trapped men, three Italian laborers were crushed so badly that they were beyond saving. The doctors could do no more than ease their horrible suffering with morphine injections. Meanwhile, Father Thomas F. Lynch of St. Elizabeth's Church administered the last rites. Bravely ignoring the possibility that another cave-in might happen at any moment, Lynch stayed with the

three Italians until they died. The doctors did manage to liberate another man who was pinned under the boulder by amputating his leg, but he died not long after being rushed to Lebanon Hospital. Ten people died that grisly October night: Timothy Sullivan, the Irish foreman; William Schuette, a German electrician; and eight unknown Italian laborers.

Two days later William Barclay Parsons arrived at the portal and inspected the accident site. Dismissing the possibility that the contractor's speedup might have contributed to the disaster, Parsons concluded that the mishap was an unavoidable result of Fort George's unforgiving geology. "All possible [safety] precautions had been taken," he assured the Rapid Transit Commission in his annual report.

Parsons lost no sleep over the deaths of these lowly workers of foreign stock. Indeed, although his official report described this loss of life as regrettable, in his private diary Parsons concentrated on the geology of Fort George and did not bother to mention that anyone had died there at all.

As a veteran civil engineer who knew the dangers of heavy construction, William Barclay Parsons unblinkingly accepted the ten Fort George deaths—along with those of the other forty-four workers and civilians who perished during the subway's construction—as the price that had to be paid for progress. To Parsons' cold way of thinking, all that really mattered was keeping the subway on schedule and ensuring that it was a success on opening day.

He got the job done, but at a terrible price.

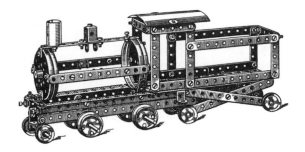

EMIGRANT TRAIN

from *Across the Plains*

Robert Louis Stevenson (1850–1894)

It was about two in the afternoon of Friday that I found myself in front of the Emigrant House, with more than a hundred others, to be sorted and boxed for the journey. A white-haired official, with a stick under one arm, and a list in the other hand, stood apart in front of us, and called name after name in the tone of a command. At each name you would see a family gather up its brats and bundles and run for the hindmost of the three cars that stood awaiting us, and I soon concluded that his was to be set apart for the women and children. The second or central car, it turned out, was devoted to men travelling alone, and the third to the Chinese. The official was easily moved to anger at the least delay; but the emigrants were both quick at answering their names, and speedy in getting themselves and their effects on board.

The families once housed, we men carried the second car without ceremony by simultaneous assault. I suppose the reader has some notion of an American railroad-car, that long, narrow wooden box, like a flat-roofed Noah's ark, with a stove and a convenience, one at either end, a passage down the middle, and transverse benches upon either hand.

Those destined for emigrants on the Union Pacific are only remarkable for their extreme plainness, nothing but wood entering in any part into their constitution, and for the usual inefficacy of the lamps, which often went out and shed but a dying glimmer even while they burned. The benches are too short for anything but a young child. Where there is scarce elbow-room for two to sit, there will not be space enough for one to lie. Hence the company, or rather, as it appears from certain bills about the Transfer Station, the company's servants, have conceived a plan for the better accommodation of travellers. They prevail on every two to chum together. To each of the chums they sell a board and three square cushions stuffed with straw, and covered with thin cotton. The benches can be made to face each other in pairs, for the backs are reversible. On the approach of night the boards are laid from bench to bench, making a couch wide enough for two, and long enough for a man of the middle height; and the chums lie down side by side upon the cushions with the head to the conductor's van and the feet to the engine. When the train is full, of course this plan is impossible, for there must not be more than one to every bench, neither can it be carried out unless the chums agree. It was to bring about this last condition that our white-haired official now bestirred himself. He made a most active master of ceremonies, introducing likely couples, and even guaranteeing the amiability and honesty of each. The greater the number of happy couples the better for his pocket, for it was he who sold the raw material of the beds. His price for one board and three straw cushions began with two dollars and a half; but before the train left, and, I am sorry to say, long after I had purchased mine, it had fallen to one dollar and a half.

The match-maker had a difficulty with me; perhaps, like some ladies, I showed myself too eager for union at any price; but certainly the first who was picked out to be my bedfellow, declined the honour without thanks. He was an old, heavy, slow-spoken man, I think from Yankeeland, looked me all over with great timidity, and then began to excuse himself in broken phrases. He didn't know the young man, he said. The young man might be very honest, but how was he to know that? There was another young man whom he had met already in the train; he guessed he was honest, and would prefer to chum with *him* upon the whole. All this without any sort of excuse, as though I had been inanimate or absent. I began to tremble lest everyone should refuse my company, and I be left rejected. But the next in turn was a tall, strapping, long-limbed, small-headed, curly-haired Pennsylvania Dutchman, with a soldierly smartness in his manner. To be exact, he had acquired it in the navy. But that was all one; he had at least been trained to desperate resolves, so he accepted the match, and the white-haired swindler pronounced the connubial benediction, and pocketed his fees.

The rest of the afternoon was spent in making up the train. I am afraid to say how many baggage-waggons followed the engine, certainly a score; then came the Chinese, then we, then the families, and the rear was brought up by the conductor in what, if I have it rightly, is called his caboose. The class to which I belonged was of course far the largest, and we ran over, so to speak, to both sides; so that there were some Caucasians among the Chinamen, and some bachelors among the families. But our own car was pure from admixture, save for one little boy of eight or nine who had the whooping-cough. At last, about six, the long train crawled out of the Transfer Station and across the wide Missouri river to Omaha, westward bound.

It was a troubled uncomfortable evening in the cars. There was thunder in the air, which helped to keep us restless. A man played many airs upon the cornet, and none of them were much attended to, until he came to *Home, sweet home*. It was truly strange to note how the talk ceased at that, and the faces began to lengthen. I have no idea whether musically this air is to be considered good or bad; but it belongs to that class of art which may be best described as a brutal assault upon the feelings. Pathos must be relieved by dignity of treatment. If you wallow naked in the pathetic, like the author of *Home, sweet home*, you make your hearers weep in an unmanly fashion; and even while yet they are moved, they despise themselves and hate the occasion of their weakness. It did not come to tears that night, for the experiment was interrupted. An elderly, hard-looking man, with a goatee beard and about as much appearance of sentiment as you would expect from a retired slaver, turned with a start and bade the performer stop that "damned thing". "I've heard about enough of that," he added, "give us something about the good country we're going to." A murmur of adhesion ran round the car; the performer took the instrument from his lips, laughed and nodded, and then struck into a dancing measure; and, like a new Timotheus, stilled immediately the emotion he had raised.

The day faded; the lamps were lit; a party of wild young men, who got off next evening at North Platte, stood together on the stern platform, singing *The Sweet By-and-bye* with very tuneful voices; the chums began to put up their beds; and it seemed as if the business of the day were at an end. But it was not so; for, the train stopping at some station, the cars were instantly thronged with the natives, wives and fathers, young men and maidens, some of them in little more than nightgear, some with stable lanterns, and all offering beds for sale. Their charge began with twenty-five cents a cushion, but fell, before the train went on again, to fifteen, with the bed-board gratis, or less than one-fifth of what I had paid for mine at the Transfer. This is my contribution to the economy of future emigrants.

A great personage on an American train is the newsboy. He sells books (such books!), papers, fruit, lollipops, and cigars; and on emigrant journeys, soap, towels, tin washing dishes, tin coffee pitchers, coffee, tea, sugar, and tinned eatables, mostly hash or beans and bacon. Early next morning the newsboy went around the cars, and chumming on a more extended principle became the order of the hour. It requires but a copartnery of two to manage beds; but washing and eating can be carried on most economically by a syndicate of three. I myself entered a little after sunrise into articles of agreement, and became one of the firm of Pennsylvania, Shakespeare, and Dubuque. Shakespeare was my own nickname on the cars; Pennsylvania that of my bedfellow; and Dubuque, the name of a place in the State of Iowa, that of an amiable young fellow going west to cure an asthma, and retarding his recovery by incessantly chewing or smoking, and sometimes chewing and smoking together. I have never seen tobacco so sillily abused. Shakespeare bought a tin washing-dish, Dubuque a towel, and Pennsylvania a brick of soap. The partners used these instruments, one after another, according to the order of their first awaking; and when the firm had finished there was no want of borrowers. Each filled the tin dish at the water filter opposite the stove, and retired with the whole stock in trade to the platform of the car. There he knelt down, supporting himself by a shoulder against the woodwork or one elbow crooked about the railing, and made a shift to wash his face and neck and hands; a cold, an insufficient, and, if the train is moving rapidly, a somewhat dangerous toilet.

On a similar division of expense, the firm of Pennsylvania, Shakespeare, and Dubuque supplied themselves with coffee, sugar, and necessary vessels; and their operations are a type of what went on through all the cars. Before the sun was up the stove would be brightly burning; at the first station the natives would come on board with milk and eggs and coffee cakes; and soon from end to end the car would be filled with little parties breakfasting upon the bed-boards. It was the pleasantest hour of the day.

There were meals to be had, however, by the wayside: a breakfast in the morning, a dinner somewhere between eleven and two, and supper from five to eight or nine at night. We had rarely less than twenty minutes for each; and if we had not spent many another twenty minutes waiting for some express upon a side track among miles of desert, we might have taken an hour to each repast and arrived at San Francisco up to time. For haste is not the foible of an emigrant train. It gets through on sufferance, running the gauntlet among its more considerable brethren; should there be a block, it is unhesitatingly sacrificed; and they cannot, in consequence, predict the length of the passage within a day or so. Civility is the main comfort that you miss. Equality, though conceived very largely in America, does not extend so low down as to an emigrant. Thus in all other trains, a warning cry of "All aboard!" recalls the passengers to take their seats; but as soon as I was alone with emigrants, and from the Transfer all the way to San Francisco, I found this ceremony was pretermitted; the train stole from the station without note of warning, and you had to keep an eye upon it even while you ate. The annoyance is considerable, and the disrespect both wanton and petty.

Many conductors, again, will hold no communication with an emigrant. I asked a conductor one day at what time the train would stop for dinner; as he made no answer I repeated the question, with a like result; a third time I returned to the charge, and then Jack-in-office looked me coolly in the face for several seconds and turned ostentatiously away. I believe he was half ashamed of his brutality; for when another person made the same inquiry, although he still refused the information, he condescended to answer, and even to justify his reticence in a voice loud enough for me to hear. It was, he said, his principle not to tell people where they were to dine; for one answer led to many other questions, as what o'clock it was? or, how soon should we be there? and he could not afford to be eternally worried.

As you are thus cut off from the superior authorities, a great deal of your comfort depends on the character of the newsboy. He has it in his power indefinitely to better and brighten the emigrant's lot. The newsboy with whom we started from the Transfer was a dark bullying, contemptuous, insolent scoundrel, who treated us like dogs. Indeed, in his case, matters came nearly to a fight. It happened thus: he was going his rounds through the cars with some commodities for sale, and coming to a party who were at *Seven-up* or *Cascino* (our two games), upon a bed-board, slung down a cigar-box in the middle of the cards, knocking one man's hand to the floor. It was the last straw. In a moment the whole party were upon their feet, the cigars were upset, and he was ordered to "get out of that directly, or he would get more than he reckoned for." The fellow grumbled and muttered, but ended by making off, and was less openly insulting in the future. On the other hand, the lad who rode with us in this capacity from Ogden to Sacramento made himself the friend of all, and helped us with information, attention, assistance, and a kind countenance. He told us where and when we should have our meals, and how long the train would stop; kept seats at table for those who were delayed, and watched that we should neither be left behind nor yet unnecessarily hurried. You, who live at home at ease, can hardly realize the greatness of this service, even had it stood alone. When I think of that lad coming and going, train after train, with his bright face and civil words, I see how easily a good man may become the benefactor of his kind. Perhaps he is discontented with himself, perhaps troubled with ambitions; why, if he but knew it, he is a hero of the old Greek stamp; and while he thinks he is only earning a profit of a few cents, and that perhaps exorbitant, he is doing a man's work, and bettering the world. . . .

It had thundered on the Friday night, but the sun rose on Saturday without a cloud. We were at sea—there is no other adequate expression—on the plains of Nebraska. I made my observatory on the top of a fruit-waggon, and sat by the hour upon that perch to spy about me, and to spy in vain for something new. It was a world almost without a feature; an empty sky, an empty earth; front and back, the line of railway stretched from horizon to horizon, like a cue across a billiard-board; on either hand, the green plain ran till it touched the skirts of heaven. Along the track innumerable wild sunflowers, no bigger than a crownpiece, bloomed in a continuous flower-bed; grazing beasts were seen upon the prairie at all degrees of distance and diminution; and now and again we might perceive a few dots beside the rail-road which grew more and more distinct as we drew nearer till they turned into wooden cabins, and then dwindled and dwindled in our wake until they melt-ed into their surroundings, and we were once more alone upon the billiard-board. The train toiled over this infinity like a snail; and being the one thing moving, it was wonderful what huge proportions it began to assume in our regard. It seemed miles in length, and either end of it within but a step of the horizon. Even my own body or my own head seemed a great thing in that emptiness. I note the feeling the more readily as it is the contrary of what I have read of in the experience of others. Day and night, above the roar of the train, our ears were kept busy with the incessant chirp of grasshoppers—a noise like the winding up of countless clocks and watches, which began after a while to seem proper to that land.

To one hurrying through by steam there was a certain exhilaration in this spacious vacancy, this greatness of the air, this discovery of the whole arch of heaven, this straight, unbroken, prison-line of the horizon. Yet one could not but reflect upon the weariness of those who passed by there in old days, at the foot's pace of oxen, painfully urging their teams, and with no landmark but that unattainable evening sun for which they steered, and which daily fled them by an equal stride. . . .

To cross such a plain is to grow homesick for the mountains. I longed for the Black Hills of Wyoming, which I knew we were soon to enter, like an ice-bound whaler for the spring. Alas! and it was a worse country than the other. All Sunday and Monday we travelled through these sad mountains, or over the main ridge of the Rockies, which is a fair match to them for misery of aspect. Hour after hour it was the same unhomely and unkindly world about our onward path; tumbled boulders, cliffs that drea-rily imitate the shape of monuments and fortifica-tions—how drearily, how tamely, none can tell who has not seen them; not a tree, not a patch of sward, not one shapely or commanding mountain form; sage-brush, eternal sage-brush, over all, the same weariful and gloomy colouring, grays warming into brown, grays darkening towards black; and for sole sign of life, here and there a few fleeing antelopes; here and there, but at incredible intervals, a creek running in a cañon. The plains have a grandeur of their own; but here there is nothing but a contorted smallness. Except for the air, which was light and stimulating, there was not one good circumstance in that God-forsaken land.

I had been suffering in my health a good deal all the way; and at last, whether I was exhausted by my complaint or poisoned in some wayside eating-house, the evening we left Laramie, I fell sick out-right. That was a night which I shall not readily for-get. The lamps did not go out; each made a faint shining in its own neighbourhood, and the shadows were confounded together in the long, hollow box of the car. The sleepers lay in uneasy attitudes; here two chums alongside, flat upon their backs like dead folk; there a man sprawling on the floor, with his face upon his arm; there another half seated with his head and shoulders on the bench. The most passive were continually and roughly shaken by the move-ment of the train; others stirred, turned, or stretched out their arms like children; it was surprising how many groaned and murmured in their sleep; and as I passed to and fro, stepping across the prostrate, and caught now a snore, now a gasp, now a half-formed word, it gave me a measure of the worthlessness of rest in that unresting vehicle. Although it was chill, I was obliged to open my window, for the degradation of the air soon became intolerable to one who was awake and using the full supply of life. Outside, in a glimmering night, I saw the black, amorphous hills shoot by unweariedly into our wake. They that long for morning have never longed for it more earnestly than I.

And yet when day came, it was to shine upon the same broken and unsightly quarter of the world. Mile upon mile, and not a tree, a bird, or a river. Only down the long, sterile canons, the train shot hooting and awoke the resting echo. That train was the one piece of life in all the deadly land; it was the one actor, the one spectacle fit to be observed in this paralysis of man and nature. And when I think how the railroad has been pushed through this unwatered wilderness and haunt of savage tribes, and now will bear an emigrant for some 12 pounds from the Atlantic to the Golden Gates; how at each stage of the construction, roaring, impromptu cities, full of gold and lust and death, sprang up and then died away again, and are now but wayside stations in the desert; how in these uncouth places pigtailed Chinese pirates worked side by side with border ruffians and broken men from Europe, talking together in a mixed dialect, mostly oaths, gambling, drinking, quarrelling and murdering like wolves; how the plumed hereditary lord of all America heard, in this last fastness, the scream of the "bad medicine waggon" charioting his foes; and then when I go on to remember that all this epical turmoil was conducted by gentlemen in frock coats, and with a view to nothing more extraordinary than a fortune and a subsequent visit to Paris, it seems to me, I own, as if

this railway were the one typical achievement of the age in which we live, as if it brought together into one plot all the ends of the world and all the degrees of social rank, and offered to some great writer the busiest, the most extended, and the most varied subject for an enduring literary work. If it be romance, if it be contrast, if it be heroism that we require, what was Troy town to this?. . .

At Ogden we changed cars from the Union Pacific to the Central Pacific line of railroad. The change was doubly welcome; for, firsts, we had better cars on the new line; and, second, those in which we had been cooped for more than ninety hours had begun to stink abominably. Several yards away, as we returned, let us say from dinner, our nostrils were assailed by rancid air. I have stood on a platform while the whole train was shunting; and as the dwelling-cars drew near, there would come a whiff of pure menagerie, only a little sourer, as from men instead of monkeys. I think we are human only in virtue of open windows. Without fresh air, you only require a bad heart, and a remarkable command of the Queen's English, to become such another as Dean Swift; a kind of leering, human goat, leaping and wagging your scut on mountains of offence. I do my best to keep my head the other way, and look for the human rather than the bestial in this Yahoo-like business of the emigrant train. But one thing I must say, the car of the Chinese was notably the least offensive.

The cars on the Central Pacific were nearly twice as high, and so proportionately airier; they were freshly varnished, which gave us all a sense of cleanliness as though we had bathed; the seats drew out and joined in the centre, so that there was no more need for bed boards; and there was an upper tier of berths which could be closed by day and opened at night. . . .

A little corner of Utah is soon traversed, and leaves no particular impressions on the mind. By an early hour on Wednesday morning we stopped to breakfast at Toano, a little station on a bleak, high-lying plateau in Nevada. . . .

From Toano we travelled all day through deserts of alkali and sand, horrible to man, and bare sage-brush country that seemed little kindlier, and came by supper-time to Elko. As we were standing, after our manner, outside the station, I saw two men ship suddenly from underneath the cars, and take to their heels across country. They were tramps, it appeared, who had been riding on the beams since eleven of the night before; and several of my fellow-passengers had already seen and conversed with them while we broke our fast at Toano. These land stowaways play a great part over here in America, and I should have liked dearly to become acquainted with them.

At Elko an odd circumstance befell me. I was coming out from supper, when I was stopped by a small, stout, ruddy man, followed by two others taller and ruddier than himself.

"Excuse me, sir," he said, "but do you happen to be going on?"

I said I was, whereupon he said he hoped to persuade me to desist from that intention. He had a situation to offer me, and if we could come to terms, why, good and well. "You see," he continued, "I'm running a theatre here, and we're a little short in the orchestra. You're a musician, I guess?"

I assured him that, beyond a rudimentary acquaintance with "Auld Lang Syne" and "The Wearing of the Green", I had no pretension whatever to that style. He seemed much put out of countenance; and one of his taller companions asked him, on the nail, for five dollars.

"You see, sir," added the latter to me, "he bet you were a musician; I bet you weren't. No offence,

I hope?"

"None whatever," I said, and the two withdrew to the bar, where I presume the debt was liquidated.

This little adventure woke bright hopes in my fellow-travellers, who thought they had now come to a country where situations went a-begging. But I am not so sure that the offer was in good faith. Indeed, I am more than half persuaded it was but a feeler to decide the bet.

Of all the next day I will tell you nothing, for the best of all reasons, that I remember no more than that we continued through desolate and desert scenes, fiery hot and deadly weary. But some time after I had fallen asleep that night, I was awakened by one of my companions. It was in vain that I resisted. A fire of enthusiasm and whisky burned in his eyes; and he declared we were in a new country, and I must come forth upon the platform and see with my own eyes. The train was then, in its patient way, standing halted in a by-track. It was a clear moonlit night; but the valley was too narrow to admit the moonshine direct, and only a diffused glimmer whitened the tall rocks and relieved the blackness of the pines. A hoarse clamour filled the air; it was the continuous plunge of a cascade somewhere near at hand among the mountains. The air struck chill, but tasted good and vigorous in the nostrils—a fine, dry, old mountain atmosphere. I was dead sleepy, but I returned to roost with a grateful mountain feeling at my heart.

When I awoke next morning, I was puzzled for a while to know if it were day or night, for the illumination was unusual. I sat up at last, and found we were grading slowly downward through a long snowshed; and suddenly we shot into an open; and before we were swallowed into the next length of wooden tunnel, I had one glimpse of a huge pine-forested ravine upon my left, a foaming river, and a sky already coloured with the fires of dawn. I am usually very calm over the displays of nature; but you will scarce believe how my heart leaped at this. It was like meeting one's wife. I had come home again—home from unsightly deserts to the green and habitable corners of the earth. Every spire of pine along the hill-top, every trouty pool along that mountain river, was more dear to me than a blood relation. Few people have praised God more happily than I did. And thenceforward, down by Blue Canon, Alta, Dutch Flat, and all the old mining camps, through a sea of mountain forests, dropping thousands of feet toward the far sea-level as we went, not I only, but all the passengers on board, threw off their sense of dirt and heat and weariness, and bawled like schoolboys, and thronged with shining eyes upon the platform and became new creatures within and without. The sun no longer oppressed us with heat, it only shone laughingly along the mountain-side, until we were fain to laugh ourselves for glee. At every turn we could see farther into the land and our own happy futures. At every town the cocks were tossing their clear notes into the golden air, and crowing for the new day and the new country. For this was indeed our destination; this was "the good country" we had been going to so long.

By afternoon we were at Sacramento, the city of gardens in a plain of corn; and the next day before the dawn we were lying to upon the Oakland side of San Francisco Bay. The day was breaking as we crossed the ferry; the fog was rising over the citied hills of San Francisco; the bay was perfect—not a ripple, scarce a stain, upon its blue expanse; everything was waiting, breathless, for the sun. A spot of cloudy gold lit first upon the head of Tamalpais, and then widened downward on its shapely shoulder; the air seemed to awaken, and began to sparkle; and suddenly

"The tall hills Titan discovered,"

and the city of San Francisco, and the bay of gold and corn, were lit from end to end with summer daylight.

WRECK OF THE OLD 97

David Graves George

American songwriter and poet David Graves George wrote this poem about the Southern Express train crash of September 27, 1903, which occurred near his Virginia home. The poem was first published in a Chatham, Virginia, newspaper and later set to music. The song would eventually sell over five million copies. Today there is a marker on U.S. Rt. 58 at the crash site.

On a cold frosty morning in the month of
    September
When the clouds were hanging low,
Ninety-seven pulled out of the Washington station
    like an arrow shot from a bow.

Old Ninety-seven was the fastest mail train
That was ever on the Southern line,
But when she got to Monroe, Virginia
She was forty-seven minutes behind.

Oh, they handed him his orders at Monroe,
Virginia, Saying: "Steve, you're away behind time.
This is not 38, but it's old 97
You must put 'er in Spencer on time."

Steve Broady said to his black greasy fireman,
"Just shovel in a little more coal,
And when we cross the White Oak Mountain
You can watch Old 97 roll."
It's a mighty rough road from Lynchburg to Danville
And the line's on a three mile grade.
It was on that grade that he lost his air brakes
And you see what a jump he made.

He was going down hill at ninety miles an hour
When the whistle broke into a scream
He was found in the wreck with his hand on the
    throttle
And scalded to death by the steam.

Now ladies you must all take fair warning
From this time ever more
Never speak harsh words to your true loving
    husbands
They may leave you and never return.

ROMANCE

from The King

Rudyard Kipling (1865–1936)

The author of The Jungle Book *(1894),* Captains Courageous *(1897),* Kim *(1901), and* Just So Stories for Little Children *(1902), Kipling was awarded the Nobel Prize for Literature in 1907. Although modern critics point to the social and racial oppression presented in his works, he was the most popular British author of his day.*

"Romance!" the season-tickets mourn,
"He never ran to catch his train,
"But passed with coach and guard and horn—
"And left the local-late again!"
Confound Romance! . . . And all unseen
Romance brought up the nine-fifteen.

His hand was on the lever laid,
His oil-can soothed the worrying cranks,
His whistle waked the snowbound grade,
His fog-horn cut the reeking Banks;
By dock and deep and mine and mill
The Boy-god reckless laboured still!

Robed, crowned and throned, He wove his spell,
Where heart-blood beat or hearth-smoke curled,
With unconsidered miracle,
Hedged in a backward-gazing world:
Then taught His chosen bard to say:
"Our King was with us—yesterday!"

THE RAILROADS CREATE DEEP ELLUM

from *Deep Ellum and Central Track*

Alan B. Govenar (1952–) and Jay F. Brakefield (1945–)

Alan B. Govenar, an anthropologist and Texas professor of sociology and literary studies, and Dallas Morning News *reporter Jay F. Brakefield culled from oral histories to tell the story of Deep Ellum, a section of Dallas that was once a predominantly African-American community. Govenar's books include* Ohio Folk Traditions: A New Generation *(1981),* Stoney Knows How: Life as a Tatoo Artist *(1981),* The Early Years of Rhythm & Blues: Focus on Houston *(1990) and* Portraits of Community: African-American Photography in Texas *(1996).*

Dallas was founded in 1841 by a Tennessee lawyer, John Neely Bryan, who settled on a bluff about where the former Texas School Book Depository now stands. At that time, long before the Trinity River was rechanneled for flood control, Bryan's bluff sloped down to a natural ford where travelers—first Indian, then white—often crossed. He knew that the Republic of Texas had selected the spot for the junction of two major thoroughfares, one of which survives as Preston Road. Bryan's earliest plan apparently was to found a trading post and to do business with the Indians.

Thus the Trinity River played a vital role in the establishment of Dallas. Despite attempts that continued into the twentieth century, however, it stubbornly resisted navigation. It became obvious that if Dallas was to become a business center, another means must be found. During the Civil War, Dallas served as a regional food distribution center, and the county's black population swelled from around 900 to 2,500, as slaves were imported to harvest crops. The city, relatively untouched by the conflict, had a population of about 2,000 at war's end. Its strong business leadership included men such as William Henry Gaston, a former Confederate army officer who became a banker and major landowner in Dallas. Sarah Cockrell, the widow of one of the city's early leaders, Alexander Cockrell, also wielded considerable power, but because of the male domination of the time, she worked quietly behind the scenes.

These leaders concluded that railroads were Dallas's route to commercial success. In this, of course, they had considerable competition; railroad fever was sweeping the nation. But they had an uncommon determination and were not above a bit of trickery—some would say ruthlessness.

After the war, the Houston & Texas, Central Railroad resumed its northward progress. Its line was to have been built eight miles east of Dallas's courthouse, too far away to do the city much good. Here, Gaston's land holdings saved the day. His home was more than a mile east of the courthouse square—then considered so far from the city's life that he once attempted to recruit neighbors by offering free land to anyone who would build on it. Gaston offered the railroad right of way, and he and the other businessmen sweetened the pot with $5,000 in cash. The railroad accepted the offer. In anticipation of the laying of the track and construction of a station, the city cleared the wooded area and extended the major east-west streets: Elm, Main and Commerce. News of the railroad's coming triggered a boom. "Dallas is improving rapidly," lawyer John Milton McCoy, later Dallas's first city attorney, wrote to his brother in Indiana in December 1871. "The prospects are very flattering indeed. Everything points to the crossing of two great roads here. Property is at exorbitant prices. The people are crazy, talking about Dallas being the Indianapolis of Texas for a railroad center. Emigration pouring in and everybody talking about the town. . . . "

The first train steamed into town on July 16, 1872, and Dallas went crazy. As Robert Seay, a young lawyer recently arrived from Tennessee, wrote: "Men whooped, women screamed, or even sobbed, and children yelped in fright and amazement. As to that, there were some grown folks there who had never seen a railway train before, and I think the chugging of the log-burning furnace and the hissing of the steam startled them, a little. An estimated 5,000 to 10,000 people turned out to hear hours of self-congratulatory speeches by city leaders and railroad officials and to feast on free buffalo steaks.

The civic leaders also turned their sights on the Texas & Pacific Railroad, which had been chartered by Congress in 1871 to extend its line to San Diego. They planned the line along the 32nd Parallel, fifty miles south of Dallas. But a local legislator attached to the right of way bill a seemingly innocuous rider requiring the T&P to cross the H&TC within a mile of Browder Springs. It didn't mention, of course, that Browder Springs, south of town, was Dallas's water supply. (The site is now Old City Park.) When railroad officials learned this, they threatened to run the line south of the springs, so it would still miss Dallas. But Gaston kicked in 142 acres for right of way plus the ten for the station. The city came up with $200,000 in bonds and $5,000 in cash and offered to let the railroad run on Burleson Street, which would be renamed Pacific Avenue. The T&P reached Dallas in February 1873, just in time for a panic, or depression, that halted its growth for several years at the community of Eagle Ford, about six miles west of town.

A resident named Wood Ramsey wrote that when he came to Dallas in 1875, "The Union Depot building was a squatty, one-story structure. . . . The farmers, cowboys, Negroes, loafers and loungers who crowded the platform and opened a way for us to get from the train as it pulled up with a clanging bell, broke up into squads and leisurely gravitated back to the domino tables in the adjacent saloons from which the whistle of the locomotive had jerked them."

Within a year of the H&TC's arrival, between 750 and 900 new buildings were erected in the city, including a $75,000 courthouse. Dallas was virtually starting over; the wooden buildings downtown had been destroyed in 1860 by a fire that was blamed (falsely, many believe) on a slave revolt. The post-railroad boom brought the terminus merchants, so-called because they had followed the H&TC north, setting up stores in the railroad towns: Bryan,

Hearne, Calvert, Kosse, Bremond, Groesbeck, Corsicana, many were called the "Corsicana Crowd" once they reached Dallas.

The new arrivals, many of whom were Eastern European Jews, erected portable buildings with amazing speed. As the young lawyer Robert Seay wrote:

The merchants, professional men, gamblers and floaters who had followed the terminus all the way to the north moved from Corsicana to Dallas in a body. Up to that time the town had been confined to the courthouse square. The newcomers bought on the road now known as Elm Street, between Jefferson and Griffin, and began to set up their portable houses which in sections they had brought from Corsicana. Almost overnight they built a new town. It was all so so sudden and amazing that the natives could liken it to nothing but the fiction they had read in Arabian Nights. But to most of them it was woefully lacking in the pleasures that went with the perusal of Aladdin's performances, for it looked very much as if the railroad and the people who had come with it were bent on killing the old town . . . [T]he old town began to put up its dukes for a fight . . . but the town had started to wander from the square and there was no bringing it back—and by the time the towns had met at Jeffereson and Market, everybody had become friendly, for it was plain that after all the two towns were only one.

Some of the terminus merchants stayed to become major business and civic figures in Dallas. The Sanger brothers—Alex and Philip Sanger—and E. M. Kahn established successful department stores downtown. The Sangers settled in the Cedars, a fashionable neighborhood south of downtown.

Dallas did not become another Indianapolis. In many ways, it was a typical frontier settlement. In the 1870s, cattle were driven through downtown Dallas to cross the Trinity at the ford below Bryan's cabin. Buffalo were shot in the nearby countryside, and the town became a center for the trade in their hides. Amusements included several red-light districts, dance halls, beer halls and gardens, boxing matches, cockfighting, rat killing and an occasional bear baiting. J. H. "Doc" Holliday practiced dentistry in Dallas for three years before he was asked to leave town following a saloon shooting. The outlaw Belle Starr also spent time around Dallas, living in the community of Scyene, which is now part of the eastern suburb of Mesquite.

People kept pouring in. Historian Philip Lindsley wrote of the city in 1875: "The flood tide of emigration was now on. Every train on the Texas and Pacific Railway was literally packed with emigrants from the older states. In addition there were regular emigrant trains with special rates, and these overflowed with men, women and children."

In the 1870s, soon after the railroads came, the future Deep Ellum was a ragtag collection of pastures, cornfields, cattle and hog pens, restaurants, lodging houses and saloons. People went about armed, and gambling flourished at all hours. Cowboys whooped and fired their pistols as they rode up and down the unpaved streets—sometimes right into the saloons. Variety (vaudeville or burlesque) theaters featured scantily clad women, and alcohol and other drugs often heightened the patrons' fun.

Meanwhile, northeast of the city limits, another community was growing, one founded by freed slaves. It was referred to as "Freedmantown" in the city directories of the period; later, it became known as North Dallas. The intersection of Thomas Avenue and Hall Street became the heart of Freedmantown, whose growth, like that of the rest of the city, was fed by the railroads. The lines provided work for many black men and housed some of them and their families in narrow rent houses along the right of way south of Freedmantown. This strung-out community became known as Stringtown. The houses were called "shotgun houses" because, it was said, a shotgun shell fired through the front door would travel out the back without hitting anything (presuming, of course, that no one was unlucky enough to be standing in the way). South of downtown near the H&TC track was another black community, a sprawl of unpaved streets called the Prairie.

Black men also found jobs in the industrial area that grew up near the railroad junction, in planing mills, meatpacking plants, oil works, waste mills, and dairies. The black influx was fed, too, by the boll-weevil that began devastating the Texas cotton crop in the early 1890s. Some African Americans continued to pick cotton after moving to Dallas, waiting near the railroad station to be hired. Farmers, first in wagons, later in trucks, hauled laborers to fields around Dallas or farther into East or West Texas, a practice which continued until after World War II.

Many black women worked in white homes. Some lived with their families in servants' quarters, others in houses purchased by their employers, who deducted the mortgage payments from their pay. Thus, segregated housing emerged, though the city would not codify it into an ordinance until the early twentieth century.

Gradually, black businesses were established along Central Track, replacing the shotgun houses of Stringtown and some of the white-owned businesses. By the turn of the century, the pattern was set: Central Track was predominantly black; Elm Street was mostly white-owned, but catering to customers of both races. For blacks and whites alike, Dallas was a city of opportunity, and Deep Ellum, near the railroad station and relatively far from the main business district, was a place to get started.

BELLOC BREAKS A VOW

from *The Path to Rome*

Hilaire Belloc (1870–1953)

A poet, essayist, satirist, and historian, Hilaire Belloc—controversial during his time because of his view that Europe should be a "Catholic society"—is considered one of the greatest English writers of light verse. His works include The Bad Child's Book of Beasts *(1896), his widely read* The Path to Rome *(1902), and* Napoleon *(1922), among others. Belloc, with friend G. K. Chesterton, founded the* New Witness, *a weekly political paper, in which they idealized the politics of the Middle Ages and shunned modern political theories and market economies.*

In Como I bought bread, sausage, and a very little wine for fourpence, and with one franc eighty left I stood in the street eating and wondering what my next step should be.

It seemed on the map perhaps twenty-five, perhaps twenty-six miles to Milan. It was now nearly noon, and as hot as could be. I might, if I held out, cover the distance in eight or nine hours, but I did not see myself walking in the middle heat on the plain of Lombardy, and even if I had been able I should only have got into Milan at dark or later, when the post office (with my money in it) would be shut; and where could I sleep, for my one franc eighty would be gone? A man covering these distances must have one good meal a day or he falls ill. I could beg, but there was the risk of being arrested, and that means an indefinite waste of time, perhaps several days.... I had nothing to sell or to pawn, and I had no friends. The Consul I would not attempt; I knew too much of such things as Consuls when poor and dirty men try them. Besides which, there was no Consul. I pondered.

I went into the cool of the cathedral to sit in its fine darkness and think better. I sat before a shrine where candles were burning, put up for their private intentions by the faithful. Of many, two had nearly burnt out. I watched them in their slow race for extinction when a thought took me.

"I will," said I to myself, "use these candles for an ordeal or heavenly judgement. The left hand one shall be for attempting the road at the risk of illness or very dangerous failure; the right hand one shall stand for my going by rail till I come to that point on the railway where one franc eighty will take me, and thence walking into Milan—and heaven defend the right."

They were a long time going out, and they fell evenly. At last the right hand one shot up the long flame that precedes the death of candles; the contest took on interest, and even excitement, when, just as I thought the left hand certain of winning, it went out without guess or warning, like a second-rate person leaving this world for another. The right hand candle waved its flame still higher, as though in triumph, outlived its colleague just the moment to enjoy glory, and then in its turn went fluttering down the dark way from which they say there is no return.

None may protest against the voice of the Gods. I went straight to the nearest railway station (for there are two), and putting down one franc eighty, asked in French for a ticket to whatever station that sum would reach down the line. The ticket came out marked Milan, and I admitted the miracle and confessed the finger of Providence. There was no change, and as I got into the train I had become that rarest and ultimate kind of traveller, the man without any money whatsoever—without passport, without letters, without food or wine; it would be interesting to see what would follow if the train broke down.

The train rolled on. I noticed Lombardy out of the windows. It is flat. I listened to the talk of the crowded peasants in the train. I did not understand it. I twice leaned out to see if Milan were not standing up before me out of the plain, but I saw nothing. Then I fell asleep, and when I woke suddenly it was because we were in the terminus of that noble great town, which I then set out to traverse in search of my necessary money and sustenance. It was yet but early in the afternoon.

A JOURNEY

Edith Wharton (1862–1937)

Subtle, ironic novels of manners and social convention in fin-de-siecle New York brought fame to Edith Wharton. The House of Mirth *(1905) won her wide recognition, and she went on to pen more than fifty works, among them* The Age of Innocence *(1920), for which she won the Pulitzer Prize. Wharton was awarded the Cross of the Legion of Honor in 1915 by the French government for her services during World War I.*

As she lay in her berth, staring at the shadows overhead, the rush of the wheels was in her brain, driving her deeper and deeper into circles of wakeful lucidity. The sleeping car had sunk into its night silence. Through the wet windowpane she watched the sudden lights, the long stretches of hurrying blackness. Now and then she turned her head and looked through the opening in the hangings at her husband's curtains across the aisle. . . .

She wondered restlessly if he wanted anything and if she could hear him if he called. His voice had grown very weak within the last months and it irritated him when she did not hear. This irritability, this increasing childish petulance seemed to give expression to their imperceptible estrangement. Like two faces looking at one another through a sheet of glass they were close together, almost touching, but they could not hear or feel each other: the conductivity between them was broken. She, at least, had this sense of separation, and she fancied sometimes that she saw it reflected in the look with which he supplemented his failing words. Doubtless the fault was hers. She was too impenetrably healthy to be touched by the irrelevancies of disease. Her self-reproachful tenderness was tinged with the sense of his irrationality: she had a vague feeling that there was a purpose in his helpless tyrannies. The suddenness of the change had found her so unprepared. A year ago their pulses had beat to one robust measure; both had the same prodigal confidence in an exhaustless future. Now their energies no longer kept step: hers still bounded ahead of life, pre-empting unclaimed regions of hope and activity, while his lagged behind, vainly struggling to overtake her.

When they married, she had such arrears of living to make up: her days had been as bare as the white-washed schoolroom where she forced innutritious facts upon reluctant children. His coming had broken in on the slumber of circumstance, widening the present till it became the encloser of remotest chances. But imperceptibly the horizon narrowed. Life had a grudge against her: she was never to be allowed to spread her wings.

At first the doctors had said that six weeks of mild air would set him right; but when he came back this assurance was explained as having of course included a winter in a dry climate. They gave up their pretty house, storing the wedding presents and new furniture, and went to Colorado. She had hated it there from the first. Nobody knew her or cared about her; there was no one to wonder at the good match she had made, or to envy her the new dresses and the visiting cards which were still a surprise to her. And he kept growing worse. She felt herself beset with difficulties too evasive to be fought by so direct a temperament. She still loved him, of course; but he was gradually, undefinably ceasing to be himself. The man she had married had been strong, active, gently masterful: the male whose pleasure it is to clear a way through the material obstructions of life; but now it was she who was the protector, he who must be shielded from importunities and given his drops or his beef juice though the skies were falling. The routine of the sickroom bewildered her; this punctual administering of medicine seemed as idle as some uncomprehended religious mummery.

There were moments, indeed, when warm gushes of pity swept away her instinctive resentment of his condition, when she still found his old self in his eyes as they groped for each other through the dense medium of his weakness. But these moments had grown rare. Sometimes he frightened her: his sunken expressionless face seemed that of a stranger; his voice was weak and hoarse; his thin-lipped smile a mere muscular contraction. Her hand avoided his damp soft skin, which had lost the familiar roughness of health: she caught herself furtively watching him as she might have watched a strange animal. It frightened her to feel that this was the man she loved; there were hours when to tell him what she suffered seemed the one escape from her fears. But in general she judged herself more leniently, reflecting that she had perhaps been too long alone with him, and that she would feel differently when they were at home again, surrounded by her robust and buoyant family. How she had rejoiced when the doctors at last gave their consent to his going home! She knew, of course, what the decision meant; they both knew. It meant that he was to die; but they dressed the truth in hopeful euphemisms, and at times, in the joy of preparation, she really forgot the purpose of their journey, and slipped into an eager allusion to next year's plans.

At last the day of leaving came. She had a dreadful fear that they would never get away; that somehow at the last moment he would fail her; that the doctors held one of their accustomed treacheries in reserve; but nothing happened. They drove to the station, he was installed in a seat with a rug over his knees and a cushion at his back, and she hung out of the windows waving unregretful farewells to the acquaintances she had really never liked till then.

The first twenty-four hours had passed off well. He revived a little and it amused him to look out of the window and to observe the humors of the car. The second day he began to grow weary and to chafe under the dispassionate stare of the freckled child with the lump of chewing gum. She had to explain to the child's mother that her husband was too ill to be disturbed: a statement received by that lady with a resentment visibly supported by the maternal sentiment of the whole car. . . .

That night he slept badly and the next morning his temperature frightened her: she was sure he was growing worse. The day passed slowly, punctuated by the small irritations of travel. Watching his tired face, she traced in its contractions every rattle and jolt of the train, till her own body vibrated with sympathetic fatigue. She felt the others observing him too, and hovered restlessly between him and the line of interrogative eyes. The freckled child hung about him like a fly; offer of candy and picture books failed to dislodge her: she twisted one leg around the other and watched him imperturbably. The porter, as he passed, lingered with vague proffers of help, probably inspired by philanthropic passengers swelling with the sense that 'something ought to be done'; and one nervous man in a skull cap was audibly concerned as to the possible effect on his wife's health.

The hours dragged on in a dreary inoccupation. Towards dusk she sat down beside him and he laid his hand on hers. The touch startled her. He seemed to be calling her from far off. She looked at him helplessly and his smile went through her like a physical pang.

'Are you very tired?' she asked.

'No, not very.'

'We'll be there soon now.'

'Yes, very soon.'

'This time tomorrow—'

He nodded and they sat silent. When she had put him to bed and crawled into her own berth she tried to cheer herself with the thought that in less than twenty-four hours they would be in New York. Her people would all be at the station to meet her—she pictured their round unanxious faces pressing through the crowd. She only hoped they would not tell him too loudly that he was looking splendidly and would be all right in no time: the subtler sympathies developed by long contact with suffering were making her aware of a certain coarseness of texture in the family sensibilities.

Suddenly she thought she heard him call. She parted the curtains and listened. No, it was only a man snoring at the other end of the car. His snores had a greasy sound, as though they passed through tallow. She lay down and tried to sleep. . . . Had she not heard him move? She started up trembling. . . . The silence frightened her more than any sound. He might not be able to make her hear—he might be calling her now. . . . What made her think of such things? It was merely the familiar tendency of an overtired mind to fasten itself on the most intolerable chance within the range of its forebodings. . . . Putting her head out, she listened: but she could not distinguish his breathing from that of the other pairs of lungs about her. She longed to get up and look at him, but she knew the impulse was a mere vent for her restlessness, and the fear of disturbing him restrained her. . . . The regular movement of his curtain reassured her, she knew not why; she remembered that he had wished her a cheerful good night; and the sheer inability to endure her hears a moment longer made her put them from her with an effort of her whole sound-tired body. She turned on her side and slept.

She sat up stiffly, staring out at the dawn. The train was rushing through a region of bare hillocks huddled against a lifeless sky. It looked like the first day of creation. The air of the car was close, and she pushed up her window to let in the keen wind. Then she looked at her watch: it was seven o'clock, and soon the people about her would be stirring. She slipped into her clothes, smoothed her disheveled hair and crept to the dressing-room. When she had washed her face and adjusted her dress she felt more hopeful. It was always a struggle for her not to be cheerful in the morning. Her cheeks burned deliciously under the coarse towel and the wet hair about her temples broke into strong upward tendrils.

Every inch of her was full of life and elasticity. And in ten hours they would be at home!

She stepped to her husband's berth: it was time for him to take his early glass of milk. The window shade was down, and in the dusk of the curtained enclosure she could just see that he lay sideways, with his face away from her. She leaned over him and drew up the shade. As she did so she touched one of his hands. It felt cold. . . .

She bent closer, laying her hand on his arm and calling him by name. He did not move. She spoke again more loudly; she grasped his shoulder and gently shook it. He lay motionless. She caught hold of his hand again: it slipped from her limply, like a dead thing. A dead thing?

Her breath caught. She must see his face. She leaned forward, and hurriedly, shrinkingly, with a sickening reluctance of the flesh, laid her hands on his shoulders and turned him over. His head fell back; his face looked small and smooth; he gazed at her with steady eyes.

She remained motionless for a long time, holding him thus; and they looked at each other. Suddenly she shrank back: the longing to scream, to call out, to fly from him, had almost overpowered her. But a strong hand arrested her. Good God! If it were known that he was dead they would be put off the train at the next station—

In a terrifying flash of remembrance there arose before her a scene she had once witnessed in traveling, when a husband and wife, whose child had died in the train, had been thrust out at some chance station. She saw them standing on the platform with the child's body between them; she had never forgotten the dazed look with which they followed the receding train. And this was what would happen to her. Within the next hour she might find herself on the platform of some strange station, alone with her husband's body. . . . Anything but that! It was too horrible—She quivered like a creature at bay.

As she cowered there, she felt the train moving more slowly. It was coming then—they were approaching a station! She saw again the husband and wife standing on the lonely platform; and with a violent gesture she drew down the shade to hide her husband's face.

Feeling dizzy, she sank down on the edge of the berth, keeping away from his outstretched body, and pulling the curtains close, so that he and she were shut into a kind of sepulchral twilight. She tried to think. At all costs she must conceal the fact that he was dead. But how? Her mind refused to act: she could not plan, combine. She could think of no way but to sit there, clutching the curtains, all day long. . . .

She heard the porter making up her bed; people were beginning to move about the car; the dressing-room door was being opened and shut. She tried to rouse herself. At length with a supreme effort she rose to her feet, stepping into the aisle of the car and drawing the curtains tight behind her. She noticed that they still parted slightly with the motion of the car, and finding a pin in her dress she fastened them together. Now she was safe. She looked round and saw the porter. She fancied he was watching her.

'Ain't he awake yet?' he inquired.

'No,' she faltered.

'I got his milk all ready when he wants it. You know you told me to have it for him by seven.'

She nodded silently and crept into her seat.

At half-past eight the train reached Buffalo. By this time the other passengers were dressed and the berths had been folded back for the day. The porter, moving to and fro under his burden of sheets and pillows, glanced at her as he passed. At length he said: 'Ain't he going to get up? You know we're ordered to make up the berths as early as we can.'

She turned cold with fear. They were just entering the station.

'Oh, not yet,' she stammered. 'Not till he's had his milk. Won't you get it, please?'

'All right. Soon as we start again.'

When the train moved on he reappeared with the milk. She took it from him and sat vaguely looking at it: her brain moved slowly from one idea to another, as though they were stepping-stones set far apart across a whirling flood. At length she became aware that the porter still hovered expectantly.

'Will I give it to him?' he suggested.

'Oh, no,' she cried, rising. 'He—he's asleep yet, I think—'

She waited till the porter had passed on; then she unpinned the curtains and slipped behind them. In the semi-obscurity her husband's face stared up at her like a marble mask with agate eyes. The eyes were dreadful. She put out her hand and drew down the lids. Then she remembered the glass of milk in her other hand: what was she to do with it? She thought of raising the window and throwing it out; but to do so she would have to lean across his body and bring her face close to his. She decided to drink the milk.

She returned to her seat with the empty glass and after a while the porter came back to get it.

'When'll I fold up his bed?' he asked.

'Oh, not now—not yet; he's ill—he's very ill. Can't you let him stay as he is? The doctor wants him to lie down as much as possible.'

He scratched his head. 'Well, if he's really sick—'

He took the empty glass and walked away, explaining to the passengers that the party behind the curtains was too sick to get up just yet.

She found herself the center of sympathetic eyes. A motherly woman with an intimate smile sat down beside her.

'I'm real sorry to hear your husband's sick. I've had a remarkable amount of sickness in my family and maybe I could assist you. Can I take a look at him?'

'Oh, no—no please! He mustn't be disturbed.'

The lady accepted the rebuff indulgently.

'Well, it's just as you say, of course, but you don't look to me as if you'd had much experience in sickness and I'd have been glad to assist you. What do you generally do when your husband's taken this way?'

'I—I let him sleep.'

'Too much sleep ain't any too healthful either. Don't you give him any medicine?'

'Y—yes.'

'Don't you wake him to take it?'

'Yes.'

'When does he take the next dose?'

'Not for—two hours—'

The lady looked disappointed. 'Well, if I was you I'd try giving it oftener. That's what I do with my folks.'

After that many faces seemed to press upon her. The passengers were on their way to the dining car, and she was conscious that as they passed down the aisle they glanced curiously at the closed curtains. One lantern-jawed man with prominent eyes stood still and tried to shoot his projecting glance through the division between the folds. The freckled child, returning from breakfast, waylaid the passers with a buttery clutch, saying in a loud whisper, 'He's sick'; and once the conductor came by, asking for tickets. She shrank into her corner and looked out of the window at the flying trees and houses, meaningless hieroglyphs of an endlessly unrolled papyrus.

Now and then the train stopped, and the newcomers on entering the car stared in turn at the closed curtains. More and more people seemed to pass—their faces began to blend fantastically with the images surging in her brain. . . .

Later in the day a fat man detached himself from the mist of faces. He had a creased stomach and soft pale lips. As he pressed himself into the seat facing her she noticed that he was dressed in black broadcloth, with a soiled white tie.

'Husband's pretty bad this morning, is he?'

'Yes.'

'Dear, dear! Now that's terribly distressing, ain't it?' An apostolic smile revealed his gold-filled teeth. 'Of course you know there's no sech thing as sickness. Ain't that a lovely thought? Death itself is but a deloosion of our grosser senses. On'y lay yourself open to the influx of the sperrit, submit yourself passively to the action of the divine force, and disease and dissolution will cease to exist for you. If you could indooce your husband to read this little pamphlet—'

The faces about her again grew indistinct. She had a vague recollection of hearing the motherly lady and the parent of the freckled child ardently disputing the relative advantages of trying several medicines at once, or of taking each in turn; the motherly lady maintaining that the competitive system saved time; the other objecting that you couldn't tell which remedy had effected the cure; their voices went on and on, like bell buoys droning through a fog. . . . The porter came up now and then with questions that she did not understand, but somehow she must have answered since he went away again without repeating them; every two hours the motherly lady reminded her that her husband ought to have his drops; people left the car and others replaced them. . . .

Her head was spinning and she tried to steady herself by clutching at her thoughts as they swept by, but they slipped away from her like bushes on the side of a sheer precipice down which she seemed to be falling. Suddenly her mind grew clear again and she found herself vividly picturing what would happen when the train reached New York. She shuddered as it occurred to her that he would be quite cold and that someone might perceive he had been dead since morning.

She thought hurriedly: 'If they see I am not surprised they will suspect something. They will ask questions, and if I tell them the truth they won't believe me—no one would believe me! It will be terrible'—and she kept repeating to herself—'I must pretend I don't know. I must pretend I don't know. When they open the curtains I must go up to him quite naturally—and then I must scream! She had an idea that the scream would be very hard to do.

Gradually new thoughts crowded upon her, vivid and urgent: she tried to separate and retrain them, but they beset her clamorously, like her school children at the end of a hot day, when she was too tired to silence them. Her head grew confused, and she felt a sick fear of forgetting her part, of betraying herself by some unguarded word or look.

'I must pretend I don't know,' she went on murmuring. The words had lost their significance, but she repeated them mechanically, as though they had been a magic formula, until suddenly she heard herself saying: 'I can't remember, I can't remember!'

Her voice sounded very loud, and she looked about her in terror; but no one seemed to notice that she had spoken.

As she glanced down the car her eye caught the curtains of her husband's berth, and she began to examine the monotonous arabesques woven through their heavy folds. The pattern was intricate and difficult to trace; she gazed fixedly at the curtains and as she did so the thick stuff grew transparent and through it she saw her husband's face—his dead face. She struggled to avert her look, but her eyes refused to move and her head seemed to be held in a vice. At last, with an effort that left her weak and shaking, she turned away; but it was of no use; close in front of her, small and smooth, was her husband's face. It seemed to be suspended in the air between her and the false braids of the woman who sat in front of her. With an uncontrollable gesture she stretched out her hand to push the face away, and suddenly she felt the touch of his smooth skin. She repressed a cry and half started from her seat. The woman with the false braids looked around, and feeling that she must justify her movement in some way she rose and lifted her traveling bag from the opposite seat. She unlocked the bag and looked into it; but the first object her hand met was a small flask of her husband's, thrust there at the last moment, in the haste of departure. She locked the bag and closed her eyes . . . his face was there again, hanging between her eyeballs and lids like a waxen mask against a red curtain. . . .

She roused herself with a shiver. Had she fainted or slept? Hours seemed to have elapsed; but it was still broad day, and the people about her were witting in the same attitudes as before.

A sudden sense of hunger made her aware hat she had eaten nothing since morning. The thought of food filled her with disgust, but she dreaded a return of faintness, and remembering that she had some biscuits in her bag she took one out and ate it. The dry crumbs choked her, and she hastily swallowed a little brandy from her husband's flask. The burning sensation in her throat acted as a counter-irritant, momentarily relieving the dull ache of her nerves. Then she felt a gently-stealing warmth, as though a soft air fanned her, and the swarming fears relaxed their clutch, receding through the stillness that enclosed her, a stillness soothing as the spacious quietude of a summer day. She slept.

Through her sleep she felt the impetuous rush of

the train. It seemed to be life itself that was sweeping her on with headlong inexorable force—sweeping her into darkness and terror, and the awe of unknown days. Now all at once everything was still—not a sound, not a pulsation. . . . She was dead in her turn, and lay beside him with smooth upstaring face. How quiet it was!—and yet she heard feet coming, the feet of the men who were to carry them away. . . . She could feel too—she felt a sudden prolonged vibration, a series of hard shocks, and then another plunge into darkness: the darkness of death this time—a black whirlwind on which they were both spinning like leaves, in wild uncoiling spirals, with millions and millions of the dead. . . .

She sprang up in terror. Her sleep must have lasted a long time, for the winter day had paled and the lights had been lit. The car was in confusion, and as she regained her self-possession she saw that the passengers were gathering up their wraps and bags. The woman with the false braids had brought from the dressing room a sickly ivy plant in a bottle, and the Christian Scientist was reversing his cuffs. The porter passed down the aisle with his impartial brush. An impersonal figure with a gold-banded cap asked for her husband's ticket. A voice shouted 'Baig-gage express!' and she heard the clicking of metal as the passengers handed over their checks.

Presently her window was blocked by an expanse of sooty wall, and the train passed into the Harlem tunnel. The journey was over; in a few minutes she would see her family pushing their joyous way through the throng at the station. Her heart dilated. The worst terror was past. . . .

'We'd better get him up now, hadn't we?' asked the porter, touching her arm.

He had her husband's hat in his hand and was meditatively revolving it under his brush.

She looked at the hat and tried to speak; but suddenly the car grew dark. She flung up her arms, struggling to catch at something, and fell face downward, striking her head against the dead man's berth.

FROM *WHERE ANGELS FEAR TO TREAD*

E. M. Forster (1879–1970)

Considered one of the most important British novelists of the twentieth century, E. M. Forster wrote about the emotional and sensual deficiencies of English society. From Where Angels Fear to Tread *(1905) and* A Room with a View *(1908) to his masterpiece* A Passage to India *(1924), emotion pitted against social convention is a common theme. His short stories are collected in* The Celestial Omnibus *(1911) and* The Eternal Moment *(1928). Other Forster works of note are* The Longest Journey *(1907) and* Howard's End *(1910).*

They were all at Charing Cross to see Lilia off—Philip, Harriet, Irma, Mrs. Herriton herself. Even Mrs. Theobald, squired by Mr. Kingcroft, had braved the journey from Yorkshire to bid her only daughter goodbye. Miss Abbott was likewise attended by numerous relatives, and the sight of so many people talking at once and saying such different things caused Lilia to break into ungovernable peals of laughter.

"Quite an ovation," she cried, sprawling out of her first-class carriage. "They'll take us for royalty. Oh Mr. Kingcroft, get us footwarmers."

The good-natured young man hurried away, and Philip, taking his place, flooded her with a final stream of advice and injunctions,—where to stop, how to learn Italian, when to use mosquito-nets, what pictures to look at. "Remember," he concluded, "that it is only by going off the track that you get to know the country. See the little towns—Gubbio, Pienza, Cortona, San Gemignano, Monteriano. And don't, let me beg you, go with that awful tourist idea that Italy's only a museum of antiquities and art. Love and understand the Italians, for the people are more marvelous than the land."

"How I wish you were coming, Philip," she said, flattered at the unwonted notice her brother-in-law was giving her.

"I wish I were." He could have managed it without great difficulty, for his career at the Bar was not so intense as to prevent occasional holidays. But his family disliked his continual visits to the Continent, and he himself often found pleasure in the idea that he was too busy to leave town.

"Good-bye, dear every one. What a whirl." She caught sight of her little daughter Irma, and felt that a touch of maternal solemnity was required. "Good-bye, darling. Mind you're always good, and do what Granny tells you."

She referred not to her own mother, but to her mother-in-law, Mrs. Herriton, who hated the title of Granny.

Irma lifted a serious face to be kissed, and said cautiously, "I'll do my best."

"She is sure to be good," said Mrs. Herriton, who was standing pensively a little out of the hub-bub. But Lilia was already calling to Miss Abbott, a tall, grave, rather nice-looking young lady who was conducting her adieus in a more decorous manner on the platform.

"Caroline, my Caroline! Jump in, or your chaperon will go off without you."

And Philip, whom the idea of Italy always intoxicated, had started again, telling her of the supreme moments of her coming journey,—the Campanile of Airolo, which would burst on her when she emerged from the St. Gothard tunnel, presaging the future; the view of the Ticino and Lago Maggiore as the train climbed the slopes of Monte Cenere; the view of Lugano, the view of Como,—Italy gathering thick around her now,—the arrival at her first resting-place, when, after long driving through dark and dirty streets, she should at last behold, amid the roar of trams and the glare of arc lamps, the buttresses of the cathedral of Milan.

"Handkerchiefs and collars," screamed Harriet, "in my inlaid box! I've lent you my inlaid box."

"Good old Harry!" She kissed, every one again, and there was a moment's silence. They all smiled steadily, excepting Philip, who was choking in the fog, and old Mrs. Theobald, who had begun to cry. Miss Abbott got into the carriage. The guard himself shut the door, and told Lilia that she would be all right. Then the train moved, and they all moved with it a couple of steps, and waved their handkerchiefs, and uttered cheerful little cries. At that moment Mr. Kingcroft reappeared, carrying a footwarmer by both ends, as if it was a tea-tray. He was sorry that he was too late, and called out in a quavering voice, "Good-bye, Mrs. Charles. May you enjoy yourself, and may God bless you."

Lilia smiled and nodded, and then the absurd position of the footwarmer overcame her, and she began to laugh again.

"Oh, I am so sorry," she cried back, "but you do look so funny. Oh, you all look so funny waving! Oh, pray!" And laughing helplessly, she was carried out into the fog.

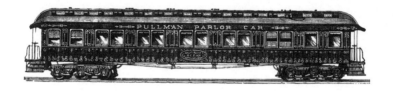

FROM *HOWARD'S END*

E. M. Forster (1879–1970)

Like many others who have lived long in a great capital, she had strong feelings about the various railway termini. They are our gates to the glorious and the unknown. Through them we pass out into adventure and sunshine, to them, alas! we return. In Paddington all Cornwall is latent and the remoter west; down the inclines of Liverpool Street lie fenlands and the illimitable Broads; Scotland is through the pylons of Euston; Wessex behind the poised chaos of Waterloo. Italians realize this, as is natural; those of them who are so unfortunate as to serve as waiters in Berlin call the Anhalt Bahnhof the Stazione d'Italia, because by it they must return to their homes. And he is a chilly Londoner who does not endow his stations with some personality, and extend to them, however shyly, the emotions of fear and love.

To Margaret—I hope that it will not set the reader against her—the station of King's Cross had always suggested Infinity. Its very situation—withdrawn a little behind the facile splendours of St. Pancras—implied a comment on the materialism of life. Those two great arches, colourless, indifferent, shouldering between them an unlovely clock, were fit portals for some eternal adventure, whose issue might be prosperous, but would certainly not be expressed in the ordinary language of prosperity. If you think this ridiculous, remember that it is not Margaret who is telling you about it; and let me hasten to add that they were in plenty of time for the train; and that Mrs. Munt, though she took a second-class ticket, was put by the guard into a first (only two seconds on the train, one smoking and the other babies—one cannot be expected to travel with babies); and that Margaret, on her return to Wickham Place, was confronted with the following telegram:

All over. Wish I had never written. Tell no one.
—Helen

But Aunt Juley was gone—gone irrevocably, and no power on earth could stop her.

DAWN

Rupert Brooke (1887–1915)

A promising and gifted English poet, Rupert Brooke died of septicemia off the coast of Skyros, Greece, while serving in the Royal Navy during World War I. Before his death, he published Poems *(1911) and* 1914 and Other Poems *(1915), which brought him immediate fame and was inspired by his 1913 to 1914 travels in the United States and New Zealand. The volume* Letters from America *was published posthumously (1916).*

Opposite me two Germans snore and sweat.
    Through sullen swirling gloom we jolt and roar.
We have been here for ever: even yet
    A dim watch tells two hours, two aeons, more.
The windows are tight-shut and slimy-wet
    With a night's foetor. There are two hours more;
Two hours to dawn and Milan; two hours yet.
    Opposite me two Germans sweat and snore. . . .

One of them wakes, and spits, and sleeps again.
The darkness shivers. A wan light through the rain
Strikes on our faces, drawn and white. Somewhere
A new day sprawls; and, inside, the foul air
Is chill, and damp, and fouler than before. . . .
Opposite me two Germans sweat and snore.

THE PREHISTORIC RAILWAY STATION

from *Tremendous Trifles*

G. K. Chesterton (1874–1936)

The prolific G. K. Chesterton became popular as a literary critic with the works Robert Browning *(1903),* Charles Dickens *(1906) and* The Victorian Age in Literature *(1913). As a fiction writer, he is best known for his* Father Browne *detective stories (1911–1935). After his conversion to Roman Catholicism in 1922, Chesterton wrote* St. Francis of Assisi *(1923),* Catholic Essays *(1929),* St. Thomas Aquinas *(1933) and other religious works.*

A railway station is an admirable place, although Ruskin did not think so. He did not think so because he himself was even more modern than the railway station. He did not think so because he was himself feverish, irritable, and snorting like an engine. He could not value the ancient silence of the railway station. "In a railway station," he said, "you are in a hurry, and therefore miserable"; but you need not be either unless you are as modern as Ruskin. The true philosopher does not think of coming just in time for his train except as a bet or a joke.

The only way of catching a train I have ever discovered is to miss the train before. Do this, and you will find in a railway station much of the quietude and consolation of a cathedral. It has many of the characteristics of a great ecclesiastical building; it has vast arches, void spaces, coloured lights, and, above all, it has recurrence or ritual. It is dedicated to the celebration of water and fire, the two prime elements of all human ceremonial. Lastly, a station resembles the old religions rather than the new religions in this point, that people go to it.

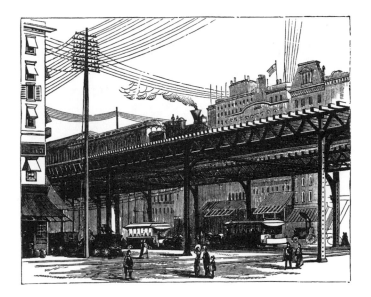

EVENING SONG

from *Mid-American Chants*

Sherwood Anderson (1876–1941)

Known for his use of vernacular language and a nontraditional writing style, Sherwood Anderson strongly influenced American short-story writing in the 1920s and '30s. The critically acclaimed Winesburg, Ohio *(1919), short sketches and tales about a Midwestern town and its hidden passions, established his reputation. First novels* Windy McPherson's Son *(1916) and* Marching Men *(1917) were published before he left the business world to pursue a career in fiction.*

Back of Chicago the open fields—were you ever there?
Trains coming toward you out of the West—
Streaks of light on the long grey plains?—many a song—Aching to sing.

I've got a grey and ragged brother in my breast—
That's a fact.

Back of
Chicago the open fields—were you ever there?
Trains coming from you into the West—
Clouds of dust on the long grey plains.
Long trains go West, too—in the silence

Always a song—
Waiting to sing.

MORNING EXPRESS

Siegfried Sassoon (1886–1967)

Wounded as an officer in World War I, Siegfried Sassoon wrote a series of volumes of powerful anti-war poems, including The Old Huntsman *(1917),* Counter-Attack *(1918) and* Satirical Poems *(1926).* Memoirs of George Sheraton, *a fictional autobiographical trilogy published separately (1928, 1930, 1936) put him in the public eye. Later in life he converted to Catholicism and wrote devotional poetry. His* Collected Poems: 1908–56 *was published in 1961.*

Along the wind-swept platform, pinched and white,
The travellers stand in pools of wintry light,
Offering themselves to morn's long, slanting arrows,
The train's due; porters trundle laden barrows.
The train steams in, volleying resplendent clouds
 of sun-blown vapour. Hither and about,
Scared people hurry, storming the doors in crowds.
 The officials seem to waken with a shout,
Resolved to hoist and plunder; some to the vans
Leap; others rumble the milk in gleaming cans.
Boys, indolent-eyes, from baskets leaning back,
 Question each face; a man with a hammer steals
Stooping from coach to coach; with clang and clack
 Touches and tests, and listens to the wheels.
Guard sounds a warning whistle, points to the clock
With brandished flag, and on his folded flock
Claps the last door: the monster grunts: 'Enough!'
Tightening his load of links with pant and puff.
Under the arch, then forth into blue day,
Glide the processional windows on their way,
And glimpse the stately folk who sit at ease
To view the world like kings taking the seas
In prosperous weather: drifting banners tell
 Their progress to the counties; with them goes
 The clamour of their journeying; while those
who sped them stand to wave a last farewell.

A LOCAL TRAIN OF THOUGHT

Siegfried Sassoon (1886–1967)

Alone, in silence, at a certain time of night,
Listening, and looking up from what I'm trying to write,
I hear a local train along the Valley. And "There
Goes the one-fifty," think I to myself; aware
That somehow its habitual travelling comforts me,
Making my world seem safer, homelier, sure to be
The same to-morrow; and the same, one hopes, next year.
"There's peacetime in that train." One hears it disappear
With needless warning whistle and rail-resounding wheels,
"That train's quite like an old familiar friend," one feels.

THE CICERONE

from *Cast a Cold Eye*

Mary McCarthy (1912–1989)

Mary McCarthy was part of the New York literati set and a drama critic for Partisan Review *from 1937 to 1945, and gained a reputation for her wit, intellect and acerbity. Her novels, among them* The Oasis *(1949),* A Charmed Life *(1955) and* The Group *(1963), established McCarthy as a world-renowned author. Her nonfiction works include the masterful* Venice Observed *(1956),* The Stones of Florence *(1959) and* Vietnam *(1967).*

When they first met him, in the wagons-lits, he was not so nervous. Tall, straw-colored, standing smoking in the corridor, he looked like an English cigarette. Indeed, there was something about him so altogether parched and faded that he seemed to bear the same relation to a man that a Gold Flake bears to a normal cigarette. English, surely, said the young American lady. The young American man was not convinced. If English, then a bounder, he said, adjusting his glasses to peer at the stranger with such impassioned curiosity that his eyes in their light-brown frames seemed to rush dangerously forward, like strange green headlights on an old-fashioned car. As yet, he felt no unusual interest in the stranger who had just emerged from a compartment; this curiosity was his ordinary state of being.

It was so hard, the young lady complained, to tell a bounder in a foreign country; one was never sure; those dreadful striped suits that English gentlemen wear . . . and the Duke of Windsor talking in a cockney accent. Here on the continent, continued the young man, it was even more confusing, with the upper classes trying to dress like English gentlemen and striking the inevitable false notes; the dukes all looked like floorwalkers, but every man who looked like a floorwalker was unfortunately not a duke. Their conversation continued in an agreeable rattle-tattle. Its inspiration, the Bounder, was already half-dismissed. It was not quite clear to either of them whether they were trying to get into European society or whether this was simply a joke that they had between them. The young man had lunched with a viscountess in Paris and had admired her house and her houseboat, which was docked in the Seine. They had poked their heads into a great many courtyards in the Faubourg St. Germain, including the very grandiose one, bristling with guards who

instantly ejected them, that belonged to the Soviet Embassy. On the whole, architecture, they felt, provided the most solid answer to their social curiosity; the bedroom of Marie Antoinette at the Petit Trianon had informed them that the French royal family were dwarfs, a secret already hinted at in Mme Pompadour's bedroom at the Frick museum in New York; in Milan, they would meet the Sforzas through the agency of their Castello; at Stra, on the Brenta, they would get to know the Pisani. They had read Proust, and the decline of the great names in modern times was accepted by them as a fact; the political speeches of the living Count Sforza suggested the table-talk of Mme Verdurin, gracing with her bourgeois platitudes the board of an ancient house. Nevertheless, the sight of a rococo ceiling, a great swaying crystal chandelier, glimpsed at night through an open second-story window, would come to them like an invitation which is known to exist but which has been incomprehensibly lost in the mails; a vague sadness descended, yet they did not feel like outsiders.

Victors in a world war of unparalleled ferocity, heirs of imperialism and the philosophy of the enlightenment, they walked proudly on the dilapidated streets of Europe. They had not approved of the war and were pacifist and bohemian in their sympathies, but the exchange had made them feel rich, and they could not help showing it. The exchange had turned them into a prince and a princess, and, considering the small bills, the weekly financial anxieties that attended them at home, this was quite an accomplishment. There was no door, therefore, that, they believed, would not open to them should they present themselves fresh and crisp as two one-dollar bills. These beliefs, these dreams, were, so far, no more to them than a story children tell each other. The young man, in fact, had found his small role as war-profiteer so distasteful and also so frightening that he had refused for a whole week to go to his money-changer and had cashed his checks at the regular rate at the bank. For the most part, their practical, moral life was lived, guidebooks in hand, on the narrow streets and cafés of the Left Bank—they got few messages at their hotel.

Yet occasionally when they went in their best clothes to a fashionable bar, she wearing the flowers he had bought her (ten cents in American money), they hoped in silent unison during the first cocktail for the Dr.-Livingstone-I-presume that would discover them in this dark continent. And now on the train that was carrying them into Italy, the European illusion quickened once more within them. They eyed every stranger with that suspension of disbelief which, to invert Wordsworth, makes its object poetical. The man at the next table had talked all through lunch to two low types with his mouth full, but the young man remained steady in his conviction that the chewer was a certain English baronet traveling to his villa in Florence, and he had nearly persuaded the young lady to go up and ask him his name. He particularly valued the young lady today because, coming from the West, she entered readily into conversation with people she did not know. It was a handicap, of course, that there were two of them ("My dear," said the young lady, "a couple looks so complete"), but they were not inclined to separate—the best jockey in a horse race scorns to take a lighter weight. Unfortunately, their car, except for the Bounder at the other end, offered very little scope to his imaginative talent or her loquacity.

But, as they were saying, Continental standards were mysteriously different; at the frontier at Domodossola a crowd gathered on the rainy platform in front of their car. Clearly there was some object of attraction here, and, dismissing the idea that

it was herself, the young lady moved to the window. Next to her, a short, heavy, ugly man with steel-rimmed spectacles was passing some money to a person on the platform, who immediately hurried away. Other men came up and spoke in undertones through the window to the man beside her. In all of this there was something that struck the young lady as strange—so much quiet and so much motion, which seemed the more purposeful, the more businesslike without it natural accompaniment of sound. Her clear, school-teacher-on-holiday voice intruded resolutely on this quarantine. "*Qu'est-ce que se passé?*" she demanded. "*Rien,*" said her neighbor abruptly, glancing at her and away with a single swiveling movement of the spectacled eyes. "C'est des amis qui recontrent des amis." Rebuffed, she turned back to the young man. "Black market," she said. "They are changing money." He nodded, but seeing her thoughts travel capably to the dollar bills pinned to her underslip, he touched her with a cautioning hand. The dead, non-committal face beside her, the briefcase, the noiseless, nondescript young men on the platform, the single laugh that had rung out in the Bounders' end of the car when the young lady had put her question, all bade him beware: this black market was not for tourists. The man who had hurried away came back with a dirty roll of bills which he thrust through the window. "Ite, missa est," remarked the young lady sardonically, but the man beside her gave no sign of having heard; he continued to gaze immovably at the thin young men before him, as though the transaction had not been digested.

At this moment, suddenly, a hubbub of singing, of agitated voices shouting slogans was heard. A kind of frenzy of noise, which had an unruly, an unmistakably seditious character, moved toward the train from somewhere outside the shed. The train gave a loud puff, "A revolution!" thought the young lady, clasping the young man's hand with a pang of terror and excitement; he, like everyone else in the car, had jumped to his feet. A strange procession came into sight, bright and bedraggled in the rain—an old woman in a white dress and flowered hat waving a large red flag, two or three followers with a home-made-looking bouquet, and finally a gray-bearded old man dressed in an ancient frock coat, carrying an open old-fashioned black umbrella and leaping nimbly into the air. Each of the old man's hops was fully two yards high; his thin legs in the black trousers were jackknifed neatly under him; the umbrella maintained a perfect perpendicular; only his beard flew forward and his coat-tails back; at the summit of each hop, he shouted joyously, "Togliatti!" The demonstration was coming toward the car, where alarm had given way to amazement; Steel Glasses alone was undisturbed by the appearance of these relics of political idealism; his eyes rested on them without expression. Just as they gained the protection of the shed, the train, unfortunately, began to move. The followers, lacking the old man's gymnastic precision, were haphazard with the bouquet; it missed the window, which had been opened for the lira-changing, and fell back into the silent crowd. The train picked up speed.

In the compartment, the young man was rolling on the seat with laughter; he was always the victim of his emotions, which—even the pleasurable ones—seemed to overrun him like the troops of some marauding army. Thus happiness, with him, had a look of intensest suffering, and the young lady clucked sympathetically as he gasped out, "The Possessed, The Possessed." To the newcomer in the compartment, however, the young man's condition appeared strange. "What is the matter with him?" the young man, deep in the depths of his joy, heard an odd, accented little voice asking; then the young lady's voice was explaining, "Dostoevski . . . a small political . . . a provincial Russian town." "But no," said the other voice, "it is Togliatti, the leader of *Italian* Communists who is in the next compartment. He is coming from the Peace Conference where he talks to Molotov." The words, *Communist, Molotov, Peace Conference*, bored the young man so much that he came to his senses instantly, sat up, wiped his glasses, and perceived that it was the Bounder who was in the campartment, and to whom the young lady was now re-explaining that her friend was laughing because the scene on the platform had reminded him of something in a book. "But no," protested the Bounder, who was still convinced that the young lady had not understood *him*. He appeared to come to some sort of decision and ran out into the corridor, returning with a Milanese newspaper folded to show an item in which the words, *Togliatti, Parigi, Pace* and *Molotov* all indubitably figured. The young lady, weary of explanation, allowed a bright smile as of final comprehension to pass over her features and handed the paper to the young man, who could not read Italian either; in such acts of submission their conversations with Europeans always ended. They had got used to it, but they sometimes felt that they had stepped at Le Havre into some vast cathedral where a series of intrusive custodians stood between them and the frescoes relating with tireless patience the story of the Nativity. Europeans, indeed, seemed to them often a race of custodians, didactic automatons who answered, like fortune-telling machines, questions to which one already knew the answer or questions which no one would conceivably ask.

True to this character, the Bounder, now, had plainly taken a shine to the young lady, who was permitting him to tell her facts about the Italian political situation which she had previously read in a newspaper. That her position on Togliatti was identical with his own, he assumed as axiomatic, and her dissident murmurs of correction he treated as a kind of linguistic static. Her seat on the wagons-lits spoke louder to him than words; she could never persuade him that she hated Togliatti from the left, any more than she could convince a guide in Paris of her indifference to Puvis de Chavannes. Her attention he took for assent, and only the young man troubled him, as he had troubled many guides in many palaces and museums by lingering behind in some room he fancied; an occasional half-smothered burst of laughter indicated to the two talkers that he was still in the Dostoevski attic. But the glances of tender understanding that the young lady kept rather pointedly turning toward her friend were an explanation in pantomime; his alarms stilled, the visitor neatly drew up his trousers and sat down.

They judged him to be a man about forty-two years old. In America he might have passed for younger; he had kept his hair, light brown and slightly oiled, with a ripple at the brow and a half-ripple at the back; his figure, moreover, was slim—it had not taken on that architectural form, those transepts, bows, and barrel-vaulting, that with Americans demonstrate (how quickly often!) that the man is no longer a boy but an Institution. Like the young lady's hairdresser, like the gay little grocer on Third Avenue, he had retained in middle age something for which there is no English word, something très mignon, something gentil, something joli garcon. It lay in a quickness and lightness of movement, in a certain demure swoop of lowering eyelids, in the play of lashes, and the butterfly flutter of the airy white handkerchief protruding from the breast pocket. It lay also in a politeness so eager as to seem freshly learned and in a childlike vanity, a covert

sense of performance, in which one could trace the swing of the censer and the half-military, half-theatrical swish of the altar-boy's skirts.

But if this sprightliness of demeanor and of dress gave the visitor an appearance of youthfulness, it also gave him, by its very exaggeration, a morbid appearance of age. Those quick, small smiles, those turns of the eye, and expressive raisings of the eyebrow had left a thousand tiny wrinkles on his dust-colored face; his slimness too had something cadaverous in it—chicken-breasted he appeared in his tan silk gabardine suit. And, oddly enough, this look of premature senility was not masculine but feminine. Though no more barbered and perfumed than the next Italian man, he evoked the black mass of the dressing-table and the hand-mirror; he reminded them of that horror so often met in Paris, city of beauty, the well-preserved woman in her fifties. At the same time, he was unquestionably a man; he was already talking of conquests. It was simply, perhaps, that the preservation of youth had been his main occupation; age was the specter he had dealt with too closely; like those middle-aged women he had become its intimate through long animosity.

Yet just as they had decided that he was a man somehow without a profession (they had come to think in unison and needed the spoken word only for a check), he steered himself out of a small whirlpool of ruffled political feelings and announced that he was in the silk business. He was returning from London, and had spent a week in Paris, where he had been short of francs and had suffered a serious embarrassment when taking a lady out to lunch. The lady, it appeared, was the wife of the Egyptian delegate to the Peace Conference, whom he had met—also—on the *wagons-lits*. There was a great deal more of this, all either very simple or very complicated, they were unable to say which, for they could not make out whether he was telling the same story twice, or, whether, as in a folk tale, the second story repeated the pattern of the first but had a variant ending. His English was very odd; it had a speed and a precision of enunciation that combined with a vagueness of grammar so as to make the two Americans feel that they were listening to a foreign language, a few words of which they could recognize. In the same way, his anecdotes had a wealth and circumstantiality of detail and an overall absence of form, or at least so the young lady, who was the only one who was listening, reported later to the young man. The young man, who was tone-deaf, found the visitor's conversation reminiscent of many concerts he had been taken to, where he could only distinguish the opening bars of any given work; for him, Mr. Sciarappa's stories were all in their beginnings, and he would interrupt quite often with a reply square in the middle, just as, quite often, he used to break in with wild applause when the pianist paused between the first and second movements of a sonata.

But at the mention of the silk business, the young man's eyes had once more burned a terrifying green. With his afflamed imagination, he was at the same time extremely practical. Hostile to Marxist theory, he was marxist in personal matters, having no interest in people's opinions, or even, perhaps in their emotions (the superstructure), but passionately, madly curious as to what people did and how they made their money (the base). He did not intend that Mr. Sciarappa (he had presented his card) should linger forever in Paris adding up the lunch bill of the Egyptian delegate's wife. Having lain *couchant* for the ten minutes that human politeness required, he sprang into the conversation with a question: did the signor have an interest in the silk mills at Como? And now the visitor betrayed the first signs of nervousness. The question had suggested knowledge that was at least second-hand. The answer remained obscure. Mr. Sciarappa did not precisely own a factory, nor was he precisely in the exporting business. The two friends, who were not lacking in common humanity, precipitately turned the subject to the beauty of Italian silks, the superiority of Italian tailoring to French or even English tailoring, the chic of Italian men. The moment passed, and a little later, under the pretense of needing her help as a translator, Mr. Sciarappa showed the young lady a cablegram dated London which seemed to be a provisional order for a certain quantity of something, but the garbled character of the English suggested that the cable had been composed—in London—by Mr. Sciarrappa himself. Nevertheless, the Americans accepted the cablegram as a proof of their visitor's *bona fides*, though actually it proved no more than that he was in business, that is, that he existed in the Italy of the post-war world.

FATHER AND THE GIRLS

from *The Short Stories of Katherine Mansfield*

Katherine Mansfield (1888–1923)

Katherine Mansfield is considered one of the founders of the modern short story, and she popularized experimental literary techniques. Born in New Zealand, she fled to London where she lived the life of a bohemian, engaging in sexual affairs with men and women. In a German Pension *(1911),* Bliss and Other Stories *(1920) and* The Garden Party, and Other Stories *(1922) were published prior to her death of tuberculosis. Much of her other work, including letters, journals, scrapbooks and short stories, was published posthumously by her second husband.*

At midday, Ernestine, who had come down from the mountains with her mother to work in the vineyards belonging to the hotel, heard the faint, far-away chuff-chuff of the train from Italy. Trains were a novelty to Ernestine; they were fascinating, unknown, terrible. What were they like as they came tearing their way through the valley, plunging between the mountains as if not even the mountains could stop them? When she saw the dark, flat breast of the engine, so bare so powerful hurtled as it were towards her, she felt a weakness; she could have sunk to the earth. And yet she must look. So she straightened up, stopped pulling at the blue-green leaves, tugging at the long, bright-green, curly suckers, and with eyes like a bird stared. The vines were very tall. There was nothing to be seen of Ernestine but her beautiful, youthful bosom buttoned into a blue cotton jacket and her small, dark head covered with a faded cherry-coloured handkerchief.

Chiff-chuff-chaff. Chiff-chuff-chaff, sounded the train. Now a wisp of white smoke shone and melted. Now there was another, and the monster itself came into sight and snorting horribly drew up the little, toy-like station five minutes away. The railway ran at the bottom of the hotel garden which was perched high and surrounded by a stone wall. Steps cut in the stone led to the terraces where the vines were planted. Ernestine, looking out from the leaves like a bright bird, saw the terrible engine and looked beyond it at doors swinging open, at strangers stepping down. She would never know who they were or where they had come from. A moment ago they were not here; perhaps tomorrow they would be gone again. And looking like a bird herself, she remembered how, at home, in the late autumn, she had sometimes seen strange birds in the fir tree that were there one day and gone the next. Where from? Where to? She felt an ache in her bosom. Wings were tight-folded there. Why could she not stretch them out and fly away and away?

THE LITTLE GOVERNESS

from *The Short Stories of Katherine Mansfield*

Katherine Mansfield (1888–1923)

Oh, dear, how she wished that it wasn't night-time. She'd have much rather travelled by day, much much rather. But the lady at the Governess Bureau had said: "You had better take an evening boat and then if you get into a compartment for 'Ladies Only' in the train you will be far safer than sleeping in a foreign hotel. Don't go out of the carriage; don't walk about the corridors and be sure to lock the lavatory door if you go there. The train arrives at Munich at eight o'clock, and Frau Arnholdt says that the Hotel Grunewald is only one minute away. A porter can take you there. She will arrive at six the same evening, so you will have a nice quiet day to rest after the journey and rub up your German. And when you want anything to eat I would advise you to pop into the nearest baker's and get a bun and some coffee. You haven't been abroad before, have you?" "No." "Well, I always tell my girls that it's better to mistrust people at first rather than trust them, and it's safer to suspect people of evil intentions rather than good ones. . . . It sounds rather hard but we've got to be women of the world, haven't we?" It had been nice in the Ladies' Cabin. The stewardess was so kind and changed her money for her and tucked up her feet. She lay on one of the hard pink-sprigged couches and watched the other passengers, friendly and natural, pinning their hats to the bolsters, taking off their boots and skirts, opening dressing-cases and arranging mysterious rustling little packages, tying their heads up in veils before lying down. Thud, thud, thud, went the steady screw of the steamer. The stewardess pulled a green shade over the light and sat down by the stove, her skirt turned back over her knees, a long piece of knitting on her lap. On a shelf above her head there was a water-bottle with a tight bunch of flowers stuck in it. "I like travelling very much," thought the little governess. She

smiled and yielded to the warm rocking.

But when the boat stopped and she went up on deck, her dress-basket in one hand, her rug and umbrella in the other, a cold, strange wind flew under her hat. She looked up at the masts and spars of the ship black against a green glittering sky and down to the dark landing stage where strange muffled figures lounged, waiting; she moved forward with the sleepy flock, all knowing where to go to and what to do except her, and she felt afraid. Just a little—just enough to wish—oh, to wish that it was daytime and that one of those women who had smiled at her in the glass, when they both did their hair in the Ladies' Cabin, was somewhere near now. "Tickets, please. Show your tickets. Have your tickets ready." She went down the gangway balancing herself carefully on her heels. Then a man in a black leather cap came forward and touched her on the arm. "Where for, Miss?" He spoke English—he must be a guard or a stationmaster with a cap like that. She had scarcely answered when he pounced on her dress-basket. "This way," he shouted, in a rude, determined voice, and elbowing his way he strode past the people. "But I don't want a porter." What a horrible man! "I don't want a porter. I want to carry it myself." She had to run to keep up with him, and her anger, far stronger than she, ran before her and snatched the bag out of the wretch's hand. He paid no attention at all, but swung on down the long dark platform, and across a railway line. "He is a robber." She was sure he was a robber as she stepped between the silvery rails and felt the cinders crunch under her shoes. On the other side—oh, thank goodness!—there was a train with Munich written on it. The man stopped by the huge lighted carriages. "Second class?" asked the insolent voice. "Yes, a Ladies' compartment." She was quite out of breath. She opened her little purse to find something small enough to give this horrible man while he tossed her dress-basket into the rack of an empty carriage that had a ticket, Dames Seules, gummed on the window. She got into the train and handed him twenty centimes.

"What's this?" shouted the man, glaring at the money and then at her, holding it up to his nose, sniffing at it as though he had never in his life seen, much less held, such a sum. "It's a franc." You know that, don't you? It's a franc. That's my fare!" A franc! Did he imagine that she was going to give him a franc for playing a trick like that just because she was a girl and travelling alone at night? Never, never! She squeezed her purse in her hand and simply did not see him—she looked at a view of St. Malo on the wall opposite and simply did not hear him. "Ah, no. Ah, no. Four sous. You make a mistake. Here, take it. It's a franc I want." He leapt on to the step of the train and threw the money on to her lap. Trembling with terror she screwed herself tight, tight, and put out an icy hand and took the money—stowed it away in her hand. "That's all you're going to get," she said. For a minute or two she felt his sharp eyes pricking her all over, while he nodded slowly, pulling down his mouth: "Ve-ry well. Trrrès bien." He shrugged his shoulders and disappeared into the dark. Oh, the relief! How simply terrible that had been! As she stood up to feel if the dress-basket was firm she caught sight of herself in the mirror, quite white, with big round eyes. She untied her "motor veil" and unbuttoned her green cape. "But it's all over now," she said to the mirror face, feeling in some way that it was more frightened than she.

People began to assemble on the platform. They stood together in little groups talking; a strange light from the station lamps painted their faces almost green. A little boy in red clattered up with a huge tea wagon and leaned against it, whistling and flicking his boots with a serviette. A woman in a black alpaca apron pushed a barrow with pillows for hire. Dreamy and vacant she looked—like a woman wheeling a perambulator—up and down, up and down—with a sleeping baby inside it. Wreaths of white smoke floated up from somewhere and hung below the roof like misty vines. "How strange it all is," thought the little governess, "and the middle of the night, too." She looked out from her safe corner, frightened no longer but proud that she had not given that franc. "I can look after myself—of course I can. The great thing is not to—" Suddenly from the corridor there came a stamping of feet and men's voices, high and broken with snatches of loud laughter. They were coming her way. The little governess shrank into her corner as four young men in bowler hats passed, staring through the door and window. One of them, bursting with the joke, pointed to the notice Dames Seules and the four bent down the better to see the one little girl in the corner. Oh dear, they were in the carriage next door. She heard them tramping about and then a sudden hush followed by a tall thin fellow with a tiny black moustache who flung her door open. "If mademoiselle cares to come in with us," he said, in French. She saw the others crowding behind him, peeping under his arm and over his shoulder, and she sat very straight and still. "If mademoiselle will do us the honour," mocked the tall man. One of them could be quiet no longer; his laughter went off in a loud crack. "Mademoiselle is serious," persisted the young man, bowing and grimacing. He took off his hat with a flourish, and she was alone again.

"*En voiture. En voiture!*" Some one ran up and down beside the train. "I wish it wasn't night-time. I wish there was another woman in the carriage. I'm frightened of the men next door." The little governess looked out to see her porter coming back again—the same man making for her carriage with his arms full of luggage. But—but what was he doing? He put his thumbnail under the label Dames Seules and tore it right off and then stood aside squinting at her while an old man wrapped in a plaid cape climbed up the high step. "But this is a ladies' compartment." "Oh, no, Mademoiselle, you make a mistake. No, no, I assure you. Merci, Monsieur." "*En voiture!*" A shrill whistle. The porter stepped off triumphant and the train started. For a moment or two big tears brimmed her eyes and through them she saw the old man unwinding a scarf from his neck and untying the flaps of his Jaeger cap. He looked very old. Ninety at least. He had a white moustache and big gold-rimmed spectacles with little blue eyes behind them and pink wrinkled cheeks. A nice face—and charming the way he bent forward and said in halting French: "Do I disturb you, Mademoiselle? Would you rather I took all these things out of the rack and found another carriage?" What! that old man has to move all those heavy things just because she . . . "No, it's quite all right. You don't disturb me at all." "Ah, a thousand thanks." He sat down opposite her and unbuttoned the cape of his enormous coat and flung it off his shoulders.

The train seemed glad to have left the station. With a long leap it sprang into the dark. She rubbed a place in the window with her glove but she could see nothing—just a tree outspread like a black fan or a scatter of lights, or the line of a hill, solemn and huge. In the carriage next door the young men started singing "*Un, deux, trois.*" They sang the same song over and over at the tops of their voices.

"I never could have dared to sleep if I had been alone," she decided. "I *couldn't* have put my feet up or even taken off my hat." The singing gave her a queer little tremble in her stomach and, hugging herself to stop it, with her arms crossed under her cape, she felt really glad to have the old man in the carriage with her. Careful to see that he was not looking she peeped at him through her long lashes. He sat extremely upright, the chest thrown out, the chin well in, knees pressed together, reading a German paper. That was why he spoke French so funnily. He was a German. Something in the army, she supposed—a Colonel or a General—once, of course, not now; he was too old for that now. How spick and span he looked for an old man. He wore a pearl pin stuck in his black tie and a ring with a dark red stone on his little finger; the tip of a white silk handkerchief showed in the pocket of his double-breasted jacket. Somehow, altogether, he was really nice to look at. Most old men were so horrid. She couldn't bear them doddery—or they had a disgusting cough or something. But not having a beard—that made all the difference—and then cheeks were so pink and his moustach so very white. Down went the Herman paper and the old man leaned forward with the same delightful courtesy: "Do you speak German, Mademoiselle?" "*Ja, ein wenig, mehr als Französisch,*" said the little governess, blushing a deep pink colour that spread slowly over her cheeks and made her blue eyes look almost black. "*Ach, so!*" The old man bowed graciously. "Then perhaps you would care to look at some illustrated papers." He slipped a rubber band from a little roll of them and handed them across. "Thank you very much." She was fond of looking at pictures, but first she would take off her hat and gloves. So she stood up, unpinned the brown straw and put it neatly in the rack beside the dress-basket, stripped off her brown kid gloves, paired them in a tight roll and put them in the crown of the hat for safety, and then sat down again, more comfortably this time, her feet crossed, the papers on her lap. How kindly the old man in the corner watched her bare little hand turning over the big white pages, watched her lips moving as she pronounced the long words to herself, rested upon her hair that fairly blazed under the light. Alas! how tragic for a little governess to possess hair that made one think of tangerines and marigolds, of apricots and tortoise-shell cats and champagne! Perhaps that was what the old man was thinking as he gazed and gazed, and that not even the dark ugly clothes could disguise her soft beauty. Perhaps the flush that licked his cheeks and lips was a flush of rage that anyone so young and tender should have to travel alone and unprotected through the night. Who knows he was not murmuring in his sentimental German fashion: "*Ja, es ist eine Tragödie!* Would to God I were the child's grandpapa!"

"Thank you very much. They were very interesting." She smiled prettily handing back the papers. "But you speak German extremely well," said the old man. "You have been in Germany before, of course?" "Oh no, this is the first time"—a little pause, then—"this is the first time that I have ever been abroad at all." "Really! I am surprised. You gave me the impression, if I may say so, that you were accustomed to travelling." "Oh, well—I have been about a good deal in England, and to Scotland, once." "So. I myself have been in England once, but I could not learn English." He raised one hand and shook his head, laughing. "No, it was too difficult for me. . . . 'Ow-do-you-do. Please vich is ze vay to Leicestaire Squaare.'" She laughed too. "Foreigners always say . . ." They had quite a little talk about it.

"But you will like Munich," said the old man. "Munich is a wonderful city. Museums, pictures, galleries, fine buildings and shops, concerts, theatres, restaurants—all are in Munich. I have travelled all over Europe many, many times in my life, but it is always to Munich that I return. You will enjoy yourself there." "I am not going to stay in Munich," said the little governess, and she added, shyly, "I am going to a post as governess to a doctor's family in Augsburg." "Ah, that was it." Augsburg he knew. Augsburg—well—was not beautiful. A solid manufacturing town. But if Germany was new to her he hoped she would find something interesting there too. "I am sure I shall." "But what a pity not to see Munich before you go. You ought to take a little holiday on your way"—he smiled—"and store up some pleasant memories." "I am afraid I could not do that," said the little governess, shaking her head, suddenly important and serious. "And also, if one is alone . . ." He quite understood. He bowed, serious too. They were silent after that. The train shattered on, baring its dark, flaming breast to the hills and to the valleys. It was warm in the carriage. She seemed to lean against the dark rushing and to be carried away and away. Little sounds made themselves heard; steps in the corridor, doors opening and shutting— a murmur of voices—whistling . . . Then the window was pricked with long needles of rain . . . But it did not matter . . . it was outside . . . and she had her umbrella . . . she pouted, sighed, opened and shut her hands once and fell fast asleep.

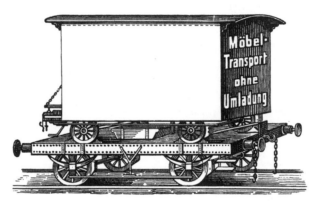

WORK GANGS

from *Smoke and Steel*

Carl Sandburg (1878–1967)

Recognized as one of America's greatest poets, Carl Sandburg initially attracted attention in Harriet Monroe's Poetry *magazine. His reputation as a poet was established with his earlier volumes, including* Cornhuskers *(1918) and* Smoke and Steel *(1920). In 1950, his* Complete Poems *won the Pulitzer Prize. Sandburg won another Pulitzer for the last four volumes of a six-volume biography of Abraham Lincoln, and he wrote his first work of fiction,* Remembrance Rock *(1948), at the age of seventy.*

Box cars run by a mile long.
And I wonder what they say to each other
When they stop a mile long on a sidetrack.
Maybe their chatter goes:
I came from Fargo with a load of wheat up to the danger line.
I came from Omaha with a load of shorthorns and they splintered my boards.
I came from Detroit heavy with a load of flivvers.
I carried apples from the Hood River last year and this year bunches of bananas from Florida; they look for
me with watermelons from Mississippi next year.

Hammers and shovels of work gangs sleep in shop corners
when the dark stars come on the sky and the night watchmen walk and look.
Then the hammer heads talk to the handles,
then the scoops of the shovels talk,
how the day's work nicked and trimmed them,
how they swung and lifted all day,
how the hands of the work gangs smelled of hope.
In the night of the dark stars
when the curve of the sky is a work gang handle,
in the night on the mile long sidetracks,
in the night where the hammers and shovels sleep in corners,
the night watchmen stuff their pipes with dreams—
and sometimes they doze and don't care for nothin',
and sometimes they search their heads for meanings, stories, stars.
The stuff of it runs like this:
A long way we come; a long way to go; long rests and long deep sniffs
For our lungs on the way.
Sleep is a belonging of all; even if all songs are old songs and the
Singing heart is snuffed out like a switchman's lantern with the oil
Gone, even if we forget our names and houses in the finish, the secret of sleep is left us, sleep belongs to all,
sleep is the first and last and best of all.

People singing; people with song mouths connecting with song hearts;
People who must sing or die; people whose song hearts break if there is no song mouth;
these are my people.

FROM *THE GREAT GATSBY*

F. Scott Fitzgerald (1896–1940)

Credited with chronicling the Jazz Age, novelist and short-story writer F. Scott Fitzgerald is considered one of the greatest authors of the twentieth century. Characteristics of his own life—heavy drinking, madness and expatriation—are some of the themes prevalent in his novels, which include the instant successes This Side of Paradise *(1920),* The Great Gatsby *(1925),* Tender is the Night *(1934) and* The Last Tycoon *(1941).*

One of my most vivid memories is of coming back West from prep school and later from college at Christmas time. Those who went farther than Chicago would gather in the old dim Union Station at six o'clock of a December evening, with a few Chicago friends, already caught up into their own holiday gaieties, to bid them a hasty good-bye. I remember fur coats of the girls returning from Miss This-or-That's and the chatter of frozen breath and the hands waving overhead as we caught sight of old acquaintances and the matchings of invitations: "Are you going to the Ordways'? the Herseys'? the Schultzes'?" and the long green tickets clasped tight in our gloved hands. And last the murky yellow cars of the Chicago, Milwaukee and St. Paul railroad looking cheerful as Christmas itself on the tracks beside the gate.

When we pulled out into the winter night and the real snow, our snow, began to stretch out beside us and twinkle against the windows, and the dim lights of small Wisconsin stations moved by, a sharp wild brace came suddenly into the air. We drew in deep breaths of it as we walked back from dinner through the cold vestibules, unutterably aware of our identity with this country for one strange hour, before we melted indistinguishably into it again.

That's my Middle West—not the wheat or the prairies or the lost Swede towns, but the thrilling returning trains of my youth, and the street lamps and sleigh bells in the frosty dark and the shadows of holly wreaths thrown by lighted windows on the snow. I am part of that, a little solemn with the feel of those long winters, a little complacent from growing up in the Carraway house in a city where dwellings are stilled called through decades by a family's name. I see now that this has been a story of the West, after all—Tom and Gatsby, Daisy and Jordan and I, were all Westerners, and perhaps we possessed some deficiency in common which made us subtly unadaptable to Eastern life.

HOMESICK BLUES

from *Collected Poems*

Langston Hughes (1902–1956)

An important literary figure from the Harlem Renaissance, Langston Hughes won critical acclaim for his poem "The Negro Speaks of Rivers" (1921), though its vernacular language infuriated some black critics who accused Hughes of demeaning the African-American community. His first book, The Weary Blues *(1926), was followed by* Not Without Laughter *(1930),* The Ways of White Folks *(1934),* Shakespeare in Harlem *(1942), and* Simple Speaks His Mind *(1950), among others. He wrote numerous plays as well as the lyrics for the Kurt Weill opera* Street Scene *(1947). Hughes won the Harmon Gold Medal for Literature in 1931 and was the recipient of a Guggenheim Fellowship for creative work in 1935.*

De railroad bridge's
A sad song in de air.
De railroad bridge's
A sad song in de air.
Ever time de trains pass
I wants to go somewhere.

I went down to de station.
Ma heart was in ma mouth.
Went down to de station.
Heart was in ma mouth.
Lookin' for a box car
To roll me to de South.
Homesick blues, Lawd,
'S a terrible thing to have.
Homesick blues is
A terrible thing to have.
To keep from cryin'
I opens ma mouth an' laughs.

PENNSYLVANIA STATION

from *Collected Poems*

Langston Hughes (1902–1956)

The Pennsylvania Station in New York
Is like some vast basilica of old
That towers above the terrors of the dark
As bulwark and protection to the soul.
Now people who are hurrying alone
And those who come in crowds from far away
Pass through this great concourse of steel and stone
To trains, or else from trains out into day.
And as in great basilicas of old
The search was ever for a dream of God,
So here the search is still within each soul
Some seed to find that sprouts a holy tree
To glorify the earth—and you—and me.

BEDBUG EXPRESS

from *Orient Express*

John Dos Passos (1896–1970)

Hailed as the best novelist of his day, John Dos Passos revealed in his early works a perception and emotion that was unexcelled. His first novel, Three Soldiers *(1921), which deals with socially conscious postwar disillusionment, put him on the literary map. He became better known with* Manhattan Transfer *(1925), and even more popular with the 1937 trilogy* USA.

Ce n'est pas serios," the tall Swede had said when he and I and an extremely evil-looking Levantine with gimlet-pointed whiskers had not been allowed to go down the gangplank at Batum. "Ce n'est pas serios," he had said, indicating the rotting harbor and the long roofs of the grey and black town set in dense pyrites-green trees, and the blue and purple mountains in the distance, and the Red Guards loafing on the wharf, and the hammer and sickle of the Soviet Republic painted on the wharf-house. The last I saw of him, he was still standing at the end of the gangplank, the points of his stand-up collar making pink dents in his thick chin, shaking his head and muttering, "Ce n'est pas serios."

I thought of him when, accompanied by a swaggering interpreter and by a cheerful man very worried about typhus from the N. E. R., I stood in front of the Tiflis express waving a sheaf of little papers in my hand, passes in Georgian and in Russian, transport orders, sleeping-car tickets, a pass from the Cheka and one from the Commissar for Foreign Affairs of the Republic of Adjaria. The Tiflis express consists of an engine, three huge unpainted: sleepers, and a very gaudy sun-cracked restaurant-car. One car was reserved for civil officials, one for the military, and one for the general public. So far it was extremely serious, but the trouble was that long before the train had drawn into the station it had been stormed by upwards of seven thousand people, soldiers in white tunics, peasant women with bundles, men with long moustaches and astrakhan caps, speculators with pedlars' packs and honest proletarians with loaves of bread, so that clots of people all sweating and laughing and shoving and wriggling, obliterated the cars, like flies on a lump of sugar. There were people on every speck of the roof, people hanging in clusters from all the doors, people on the coal in the coal-tender, people on the engine; from every window protruded legs of people trying to wriggle in. Those already on board tried to barricade themselves in the compartments, and with surprising gentleness tried to push the newcomers out of the windows again. Meanwhile the east-bound American ran up and down the platform, dragging his hippopotamus suit-case, streaking sweat from every pore and trying to find a chink to hide himself in. At last recourse had to be had to authority. Authority gave him a great boost by the seat of the pants and shot him and his suitcase in by a window into a compartment full of very tall men in very large boots, six of the seven soldiers who occupied his seat were thrown out, all hands got settled and furbished up their foreign languages and sat quietly sweating waiting for the train to leave.

Eventually after considerable circulation of rumours that we were not going to leave that day, that the track was torn up, that a green army had captured Tiflis, that traffic was stopped on account of the cholera, we started off without the formality of a whistle. The train wound slowly through the rich jade and emerald jungle of the Black Sea coast towards tall mountains to the northeast that took on inconceivable peacock colours as the day declined. In the compartment we nibbled black bread and I tried to juggle French and German into a conversation. Someone was complaining of the lack of manufactured articles, paint and women's stockings and medicine and spare parts for motor-cars and soap and flat-irons and tooth-brushes. Someone else was saying that none of those things were necessary. "The mountains will give us wool, the fields will give us food, the forests will give us houses; let every man bake his own and spin his own and build his own; that way we will be happy and independent of the world. If only they would not compromise with industrialism. But in Moscow they think, if only we get enough foreign machinery the revolution will be saved; we should be self-sufficient like the bees."

Strange how often they speak to you of bees. The order of sweetness of a hive seems to have made a great impression on the Russians of this age. Again and again in Tiflis people talked of bees with a sort of wistful affection, as if the cool pungence of bees were a tonic to them in the midst of the soggy bleeding chaos of civil war and revolution.

By this time it was night. The train was joggling its desultory way through mountain passes under a sky solidly massed with stars like a field of daisies. In the crowded compartment, where people had taken off their boots and laid their heads on each other's shoulders to sleep, hordes of bedbugs had come out of the stripped seats and bunks, marching in columns of three or four, well disciplined and eager. I had already put a newspaper down and sprinkled insect powder in the corner of the upper berth in which I was hemmed by a solid mass of sleepers. The bedbugs took the insect powder like snuff and found it very stimulating, but it got into my nose and burned, got into my eyes and blinded me, got into my throat and choked me, until the only thing for it was to climb into the baggage rack, which fortunately is very large and strong in the Brobdingnagian Russian trains. There I hung, eaten only by the more acrobatic of the bugs, the rail cutting into my back, the insect powder poisoning every breath, trying to make myself believe that a roving life was the life for me. Above my head I could hear the people on the roof stirring about.

At about midnight the train stopped for a long while at a station. Tea was handed round, made in great samovars like water-tanks; their fires were the only light; you could feel that there was a river below in the valley, a smell of dry walls and human filth came up from some town or other. Huge

rounded shoulders of hills cut into the stars. Enlivened by the scalding tea, we all crawled into our holes again, the bunches of people holding on at the doors reformed, and the train was off. This time I went very decently to sleep listening to the stirring of the people on the roof above my head, to the sonorous rumble of the broad-gauge wheels and to a concertina that wheezed out a torn bit of song now and then in another carriage.

In the morning we look out at a silver looping river far below in a huge valley between swelling lion-coloured hills. The train casts a strange shadow in the morning light, all its angles obliterated by joggling, dangling figures of soldiers; on the roofs are the shadows of old women with baskets, of men standing up and stretching themselves, of children with caps too big for them. On a siding we pass the long train of the second tank division of the Red Army; a new-painted engine, then endless box-waggons, blond young soldiers lolling in the doors. Few of them look more than eighteen; they are barefoot and scantily dressed in canvas trousers and tunics; they look happy and at their ease, dangling their legs from the roofs and steps of box-waggons and sleepers. You can't tell which are the officers. Out of the big club-car decorated with signs and posters that looks as if it might have been a diner in its day, boys lean to wave at the passing train. Then come flat trucks with equipment, then a long row of tanks splotched and striped with lizard green. "A gift of the British," says a man beside me. "The British gave them to Denikin, and Denikin left them to us."

Our train, the windows full of travel-grimed faces and the seats full of vermin, gathers speed and tilts round a bend. The sight of the green tanks has made everybody feel better. The man beside me, who used to be a banker in Batum and hopes to be again, exclaims fervently: "All these words, Bolshevik, Socialist, Menshevik, have no meaning any more. . . . Conscious of it or not, we are only Russians."

THE EXPRESS

Stephen Spender (1909–1995)

An exponent of the "new writing" of the 1930s, Spender wrote poetry, essays, plays and criticism through-out his sixty-year career. Among his books are The Backward Son *(1940),* Collected Poems, 1928–1985 *(1985) and* Dolphins *(1994). In his later career he was known less for his poetry than for his criticism and association with the reviews* Horizon *(1940–41) and* Encounter *(1953–67).*

After the fist powerful plain manifesto
The black statement of pistons, without more fuss
But gliding like a queen, she leaves the station.
Without bowing and with restrained unconcern
She passes the houses which humbly crowd outside,
The gasworks and at last the heavy page
Of death, printed by gravestones in the cemetery.
Beyond the town there lies the open country
Where, gathering speed, she acquires mystery,
The luminous self-possession of ships on ocean.
It is now she begins to sing—at first quite low
Then loud, and at last with a jazzy madness—
The song of her whistle screaming at curves.
Of deafening tunnels, brakes, innumerable bolts.
And always light, aerial, underneath
Goes the elate metre of her wheels.
Steaming through metal landscape on her lines
She plunges new eras of wild happiness
Where speed throws up strange shapes, broad curves
And parallels clean like the steel of guns.
At last, further than Edinburgh or Rome,
Beyond the crest of the world, she reaches night
Where only a low streamline brightness
Of phosphorus on the tossing hills is white.
Ah, like a comet through flame she moves entranced
Wrapt in her music no bird song, no, nor bough
Breaking with honey buds, shall ever equal.

A CRASH ON THE TRANS-SIBERIAN RAILWAY

Peter Fleming (1890–1976)

Author, explorer and brother of James Bond-creator Ian Fleming, Peter Fleming wrote numerous popular books in the 1930s documenting his travels in China, Mongolia, Japan and Brazil. His most acclaimed work, News from Tartary: A Journey from Peking to Kashmir *(1936), describes his hike with author Ella Maillart from China to India. Prior to enlisting as an officer in WWII, he worked for the* Times *of London. During the 1950s, Fleming wrote mainly about the British Empire, including* The Siege at Peking *(1959), about the Boxer Rebellion.*

There was a frightful jarring, followed by a crash. . . .

I sat up in my berth. From the rack high above me my heaviest suitcase, metal-bound, was cannonaded down, catching me with fearful force on either knee-cap. I was somehow not particularly surprised. This is the end of the world, I thought, and in addition they have broken both my legs. I had a vague sense of injustice.

My little world was tilted drunkenly. The window showed me nothing except a few square yards of goodish grazing, of which it offered an oblique bird's eye view. Larks were singing somewhere. It was six o'clock. I began to dress. I now felt very much annoyed.

But I climbed out of the carriage into a refreshingly spectacular world, and the annoyance passed. The Trans-Siberian Express sprawled foolishly down the embankment. The mail van and the dining-car, which had been in front, lay on their sides at the bottom. Behind them the five sleeping-cars, headed by my own, were disposed in attitudes which became less and less grotesque until you got to the last, which had remained, primly, on the rails. Fifty yards down the line the engine, which had parted company with the train, was dug in, snorting, on top of the embankment. It had a truculent and naughty look; it was defiantly conscious of indiscretion. . . .

There she lay, in the middle of a wide green plain: the crack train, the Trans-Siberian Luxury Express. For more than a week she had bullied us. She had knocked us about when we tried to clean our teeth, she had jogged our elbows when we wrote, and when we read she had made the print dance tiresomely before our eyes. Her whistle had arbitrarily curtailed our frenzied excursions on the wayside platforms. Her windows we might not open on account of the dust, and when closed they had proved a perpetual attraction to small, sabotaging boys with stones. She had annoyed us in a hundred little ways: by spilling tea in our laps, by running out of butter, by regulating her life in accordance with Moscow time, now six hours behind the sun. She had been our prison, our Little Ease. We had not liked her.

Now she was down and out. We left her lying there, a broken, buckled toy, a thick black worm without a head, awkwardly twisted: a thing of no use, above which larks sang in an empty plain.

If I know Russia, she is lying there still.

DELIVERANCE

from *The Only Poet Short Stories*

Rebecca West (1892–1983)

Dame Rebecca West (the pseudonym of Cicily Fairfield) began her career as a journalist for feminist and suffragist publications, and later served as a literary critic and political writer for American and British journals. Black Lamb and Grey Falcon *(1941), considered her masterpiece, was part travelogue, and part political analysis, examining the precarious balance of politics in Yugoslavia at the eve of World War II. West's novels include* The Return of the Soldier *(1918),* The Thinking Reed *(1939) and* Birds Fall Down *(1966).*

One autumn evening a woman in her early forties walked along the platform of the Terminal Station in Rome and boarded a wagon-lit in the Paris Express. She sat down on the made-up bed in her compartment, took off her small, perfect, inconspicuous hat, and looked about her with an air of annoyance. It was a long time since she had travelled by rail, and she had been pushed to it against her will, because there had not been a seat free on any of the planes leaving Rome that day or the next. But this was the least of her worries, and she wasted no time on it, but set about arranging her passport and her tickets in order to have them ready when the wagon-lit attendant arrived. This required close scrutiny, for although she was a Frenchwoman named Madame Rémy, another impression was conveyed by her passport, her tickets and the labels on her luggage, and she had to remind herself what that impression was, for only a few hours before she had been yet a third person.

Such inconsistencies, however, never made her nervous. They were unlikely to be noticed because she herself was so unnoticeable. She was neither tall nor short, dark nor fair, handsome nor ugly. She left a pleasant impression on those she met in her quiet passage through the world, and then these people forgot her. She had no remarkable attributes except some which were without outward sign, such as a command of six languages and an unusually good memory.

When the door opened, Madame Rémy had not quite finished getting her papers out of a handbag which had more than the usual number of pockets and flaps in it, and some very intricate fastenings. Without raising her head, she asked the attendant to wait a moment, in her excellent Italian, which, just for verisimilitude, had a slight Florentine accent. Then, as he did not answer, she looked up sharply.

She had only time to remark that he was wearing not the uniform of a wagon-lit attendant but a dark grey suit with a checked blue muffler, and that his pale face was shining with sweat. Then the door banged between them. She did not follow him, because she was as highly disciplined as any soldier, and she knew that her first concern must be with the tiny ball of paper which he had dropped in her lap. When she had unrolled it she read a typewritten message: "A man is travelling on this train under orders to kill you." She rolled it up again and went into the corridor and stood there, looking out at the crowds on the ill-lit platform. It would have been unwise to leave the train. A clever man with a knife, she calculated, could do his work among the shadows and get away quite easily. Several times she had to step back into her compartment, to get out of the way of passengers who were coming aboard, and at these, if they were male, she looked with some interest. She was standing thus, looking up with a noncommittal glance, neither too blank nor too keenly interested, at a tall man in a tweed overcoat and wondering if he were so tall as to be specially memorable, and therefore ineligible as an assassin, when she heard shouts from the platform.

The tall man came to a halt, and she crushed past him and stood beside him, looking out through the wide corridor window at a scene still as a painted picture. Everybody was motionless, even the porters with their luggage barrows, while four men made their way back to the platform gates, at a quiet and steady pace, two in front, and two behind who were walking backwards. Their faces were darkened by masks, and all held revolvers which they pointed at the crowd. The man beside Madame Rémy made a scandalized and bluff noise which told her that he was not an assassin, and at that moment the train began to move. He went on his way to his compartment and left Madame Rémy standing alone at the window, waiting to see what had happened at the end of the platform. But she saw nothing unusual till the train was leaving the station behind it and sliding out into the open evening. Then her eye was caught by the last iron pillar that held up the platform roof. A man was embracing it as if it were a beloved woman to whom he was bidding farewell. His suit was dark grey; and as he slid to the ground and toppled over and fell face upward, it could be seen that he was wearing a checked blue muffler.

Madame Rémy went back to her compartment and said a prayer for his soul. She looked at her hands with some distaste, because they were shaking, and took the little ball of paper out of her bag and read the message again. This was not because she feared she had forgotten it, or thought she had overlooked any of its implications, but because it interested her as a technician to see if there were any distinguishing marks in the typefaces which recalled any typed letters that she had received before. Then she thought of all the things it would be sensible to do, such as ringing for the attendant and showing him the message, out in the corridor, in front of some open door, in the hearing of some other passenger, preferably a woman, and she decided to do none of them.

She said aloud, "I am a lucky woman." Leaning back her head against the cushions, she repeated, "How very lucky I am."

There had seemed no way out of the wretchedness that was all around her. She was under no illusion as to the reason why the doctor she had consulted in Rome concerning a slight but persistent symptom had begged her to go into hospital for an X-ray examination the next day, and had urged her, when he found she was resolved to go back to Paris, not to let one day pass after she got there without

seeking a surgeon. The thing was in her father's family, and she was familiar with its method of approach.

She was, moreover, in financial difficulties to which there could be no end. She had loved her dead husband very much, so much that she felt that she could deny nothing to the child of his first marriage. But Madeleine was sullen and unaffectionate, had early insisted on marrying a worthless young man and had three children already and might have more; and her only remarkable characteristic was a capacity for getting into debt without having anything to show for it in purchased goods. Madame Rémy really did not see how she could meet this last crop of bills without selling either the few jewels remaining to her, which were those she wore so constantly, except when she was on duty, that they seemed part of her body, or her little house in Passy, where she had spent all her married life. In either case it would be a joyless sacrifice, for Madeleine had nothing of her father in her.

Also, it was evident to Madame Rémy that her long-standing friendship with Claude was over. Just before she left Paris she had heard again the rumour that he was going to marry the Armenian heiress, and his denial had left her in no doubt that they were going to part before very long, perhaps even without tenderness. That would take from the last five years of her life the value which she had believed made them remarkable. She had always thought that she had taken up her peculiar work because she and a distinguished member of the French Foreign Office had fallen in love with each other, and that had made it a romantic adventure. But now she suspected that a member of the French Foreign Office had had a love affair with her because she had an aptitude for a certain peculiar kind of work; and though she recognized that even if this were so, Claude had formed some real affection for her, and that she owed him gratitude for much charming companionship, she knew that she would never be able to look back on their relations without a sense of humiliation. Even her work, in which she had hoped to find her main interest as her life went on, would now be darkened in her mind by association with a long pretence, and her own gullibility. There was nothing at the end of her journey except several sorts of pain, so if the journey had no end there was no reason for grief.

When she had worked it out to her final satisfaction she found that the wagon-lit attendant was standing in front of her, asking for her tickets and passport. She gave them to him slowly, feeling a certain sense of luxury, because his presence meant her last hope of life, and she was not taking it. They wished each other good night, and then she called him back, because it had occurred to her that it would be hardly fair if he had to go without his tip in the morning just because she was dead. Agents were trained never to make themselves memorable by giving more or less than the standard tip, and she acted according to habit, but regretted it, for surely the occasion called for a little lavishness. As she explained to him that she was giving him the tip in case they were rushed at the other end she noted his casual air. He was evidently to be the second-last man she was to see, not the last.

Once she was alone, she burned the message in her washbasin, and pulled up the window blind so that she could look at the bright villages and the dark countryside that raced by. She thought of the smell of anaesthetics that hangs about the vestibules of clinics, and she thought of the last time she had met Madame Couthier in the Champs Elysées and how Madame Couthier had looked through her as if they had never been at school together, and how it

had turned out that Madeleine had run up a huge bill with young Couthier, who was finding it hard to make his way as an interior decorator. She thought of an evening, just before she had heard the rumour about the Armenian heiress, when Claude had driven her back from dinner at Ville-d'Avray, and she had rested her head against his shoulder for a minute when the road was dark, and had kissed his sleeve. Claude and she were the same age, yet she felt hot with shame when she remembered this, as if she had been an old woman doting on a boy.

She pulled down the blind, and began to make very careful preparations for the night. Her large case was on the rack, and she did not care to ring for the attendant and ask him to move it for her, lest somebody else should come in his stead and the attack be precipitated before she was ready for it. But she was obliged to get it down, because she had packed in it her best nightgown, which was made of pleated white chiffon. For a reason she had never understood she had always liked to carry it with her when she went on a specially dangerous enterprise; and now she saw that it had been a sensible thing to do. It was very pleasant to put it on after she had undressed and washed very carefully, rubbing herself down with toilet water, as she could not have a bath. After she had made up her face again and recoiffed her hair, she lay down between the sheets. Then it occurred to her that she had not unpacked her bedroom slippers, and she made a move to get out of bed before she realized that she need not take the trouble.

She turned out the big light in the compartment ceiling, and left on only the little reading lamp at the head of her bed. She had not locked the door. Her careful toilette had made her tired: and indeed she had been working very hard for some days preparing all the papers that were now safe in her embassy.

She thought of Madeleine and Claude, and bleakly realized that she had no desire to see either of them ever again. She tried to remember something pleasant, and found that for that she had to go back to the days when her husband was alive. It had been delightful when he came back in the evenings from his office, particularly at this very time of year, in the autumn, when he brought her sweet-smelling bouquets of bronze and gold chrysanthemums, and after tea they did not light the lamps, and sat with the firelight playing on the Japanese gilt wallpaper. It had been delightful, too, when they went for holidays in Switzerland and skied in winter and climbed in summer, and he always was astounded and pleased by her courage. But dear Louis was not at the end of her journey. There was nothing waiting for her there but Madeleine and Claude, and the smell that hangs about the vestibules of clinics.

The train slowed down at a station. There were cries, lurchings and trampings in the corridors, long periods of silence and immobility, a thin blast on a trumpet; and the train jerked forward again. That happened a second time, and a third. But still the man who was travelling under orders did not come to carry them out.

Madame Rémy turned out the reading lamp and prayed to the darkness that he might hurry; and then for a little, retreating again from the thought of Madeleine and Claude to the memory of her husband, she passed into something nearly a dream. But she was fully awake as soon as someone tried the lock of the door with a wire. It was as if a bucket had been emptied over her, a bucket filled, not with water, but with fear. There was not a part of her which was not drenched with terror. She disliked this emotion, which she had never felt before except in a slight degree, just as much as added to the zest of an enterprise. To escape from this shuddering abasement she reminded herself that she wanted to die, she had chosen to die, and she sat up and cried, "Entrez! Entrate!"

The door swung open, and softly closed again. There followed a silence, and, feeling fear coming on her again, she switched on the light. It was a relief to her that the man who was standing with his back to the door did not wear the uniform of a wagon-lit attendant, and that he was the sort of person who would be selected for such a mission. He was young and lean and spectacled, and wore a soft hat crushed down over his brows and a loose greatcoat with the collar turned up, in a way that she tenderly noted as amateurish. It would be very hard for him to get away from the scene of a crime without arousing suspicion. There was also a sign that he was the man for whom she was waiting, in the woodenness of his features and his posture. He knew quite well that what he was doing was wrong, and to persuade himself that it was right, he had had to stop the natural flow of not only his thoughts and feelings but his muscles.

Yet he made no move to commit the violent act for which this rigidity had been a preparation. Simply he stood there, staring at her. She thought "Poor child, he is very young" and remained quite still, fearing to do anything which might turn him from his resolution. But he went on staring at her. "Is he never going to do it?" she asked herself, wondering at the same time whether it was a cord or a knife that he was fingering in the pocket of his greatcoat. It occurred to her that with such a slow-moving assailant she had still a very good chance of making a fight for her life and saving it. But then there came to her the look of surgical instruments on a tray, the whine that came into Madeleine's voice when she spoke of the inevitability of debt, and the fluency, which now recalled to her a conjurer's patter, of Claude's lovemaking; and she was conscious of the immense distance that divided her from the only real happiness she had ever known. She flung open her arms in invitation to the assassin, smiling at him to assure him that she felt no ill will against him, that all she asked of him was to do his work quickly.

Suddenly, he stepped backwards, and she found herself looking at the door with a stare as fixed as his own. She had made an absurd mistake. This was simply a fellow passenger who had mistaken the number of his compartment, and all the signs she had read in his appearance were fictions of her own mind, excited by the typewritten message. It was a disappointment, but she did not allow it to depress her. When she thought of the man in the dark grey suit with the checked blue muffler, sliding down the pillar and turning over as he reached the ground, it was as a child might think of an adult who had made it a promise. She contemplated in sorrow and wonder the fact that a stranger had given up his life because he wished her well, and switched out the light and again said a prayer for him into the darkness. Then, although she had no reason to suppose that the man who was traveling under orders would come sooner or later to carry them out, she grew drowsy.

"What, not stay awake even to be assassinated?" she muttered to her pillow, and laughed, and was swallowed up by sleep, deep sleep, such as had often come on her at the end of a long day on the mountains.

The next morning a spectacled young man wearing a soft hat and a loose greatcoat, who had made his way back to Rome while the sun came up, stood in a hotel room and gave a disappointing report to his superior.

He said, "Madame Rémy was not on the train. It was all a mistake. There was one woman who answered to the description, and I went into her compartment, but I found she was quite a different sort of person. She was not at all haggard and worn; indeed, she looked much younger than the age you gave me, and she was very animated. And though we know that if Ferrero found Madame Rémy on the train he must have warned her, this woman was not at all frightened. She had left her door unlocked, and when she saw me she showed no fear at all."

"Indeed," he said gloomily, "she was evidently a loose woman. Though she was in bed her face was painted, and her hair was done up as if she were going to a ball, and it was really quite extraordinary—she even stretched out her arms and smiled at me. I think," he asserted, blushing faintly, "that if I had cared to stay in her compartment I would have received quite a warm welcome."

His superior expressed an unfavourable opinion regarding the morals of all bourgeois women, but had his doubts, and made certain enquiries. As a result the spectacled young man was doomed not to realize what was at that time his dearest ambition, for he was never given another chance to commit a political assassination. He regretted this much less than he would have owned. Even then, standing in the golden sunshine of a Roman morning, he was not really disturbed because the night had been so innocent.

At that moment Madame Rémy was sitting in the restaurant car of the Paris Express, eating breakfast. She could have had it brought to her in her compartment, but she had felt a desire to have it where the windows were wider and she could see more of the countryside. Her first pot of coffee had been so good that she had ordered a second, and she was spreading the butter on a roll, smiling a little, because it seemed so absurd that after such a night she should have awakened to find herself suddenly freed from the wretchedness that had hung about her for so long. Certainly she had lost none of her troubles; but they no longer appalled her. There came to mind the names of several among her friends who had survived serious operations. As for Madeleine's debts, if nobody paid them it might help the poor silly child to grow up; and the wisest thing, even the loyallest thing, for her stepmother to do was to keep the jewels and the house that Louis Rémy had given her and leave them intact to Madeleine's children. It might well be true that she could no longer support the desperate nature of her present work, but there was no need for her days to be idle, for the great dressmaker, Mariol, had always had a liking for her and had more than once offered her a post in his business. And there was no need for her to think of Claude. If she wanted to think of someone who was not there any more, she could remember Louis.

Some other names occurred to her: the names of people who had not survived operations. But they cast no darkness on her mind; she was conscious only of a certain grandeur, and they went from her. For all her interest was given to looking out of the window at what she was seeing again only because of some inexplicable carelessness on the part of those who were usually careful.

Now the train was running toward the mountains, and was passing through a valley in the foothills.

There were cliffs, steel-grey where the sun caught them, dark blue in the shadow, rising to heights patterned with the first snows, glistening sugar-white under the sharp blue sky. At the foot of the cliffs a line of poplars, golden with autumn, marked the course of a broad and shallow river racing over grey shingle; and between the river and the railway track was a field where a few corn shocks, like dried, gesticulating men, were still standing among some trailing morning mists. Across this field, through the mists, an old man in a dark blue shirt and light blue trousers was leading a red cart, drawn by two oxen the colour of the coffee and milk in her cup. Deliberately the two beasts trod, so slowly that they seemed to sleep between paces, so dutifully that if they were dreaming it must be of industry. There was nothing very beautiful in the scene, yet it was wonderful, and it existed, it would go on being there when she was far away.

As the train met the mountains and passed into a tunnel, she closed her eyes so that she could go on seeing the cliffs and the snow and the poplars, the man and his cart and his oxen. Amazed by what the world looked like when one had thought it lost and had found it again, she sat quite still, in a trance of contentment, while the train carried her on to the end of her journey.

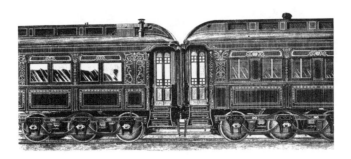

CHAPTER 12: NO TRAIN TONIGHT

from *Grand European Expresses: The Story of the Wagon-Lits*

George (Henry Sandham) Behrend (1922–)

A true lover of locomotives, British freelance writer George Behrend has written extensively about luxury trains. He describes this romantic form of travel in the books Pullman in Europe *(1962),* Channel Silver Wings *(1972),* History of Trains de Luxe *(1982) and* The Orient Express: A Century of Railway Adventures *(1988).*

Shall I ever forget him, that hall porter in the Hotel Grande Bretagne? One of those men whose life is one vast mass of complicated commissions, arrangements and pleasantries; who speak about six languages; whose excursion facilities are always better than those of the travel agents, and who can fix anything, or so the ignorant traveller is led to believe. Surrounded by a number of underlings whom they treated in an off-hand and peremptory manner, hall porters were personages of whom even the managements were shy.

This particular porter differed from most of those found in every large hotel in all the capitals of Europe, because he made no effort to conceal his nationality behind a bluff cosmopolitanism. He was Greek and proud of it: 'No train tonight', he shouted in a curious accent, both hands raised in a manner unconsciously identical with that of a British shunter creating an emergency stop.

The startled passengers paused uncertainly in the lobby, their bags packed, some even at that moment being carried by the porter's underlings to a waiting taxi. Something must be wrong, for such emotional behaviour was usually reserved for double-crossing dragomen; his deferential obsequity had suddenly deserted him.

"Pourquoi?" he lapsed suddenly into French, shrugging his shoulders and spreading out his hands. *"Je ne sais pas, on me telephone de la gare . . . Accident . . . no train tonight,"* he said again finally, triumphantly, with a wicked smile, for of course the departing passengers had already tipped him and would now have to do so again.

It was not possible to find out anything more, nor to do anything else but have dinner in Le Petit Palais, as the hotel also called itself. After dinner it was announced that a goods train had become derailed, blocking the line at Thermopylae. There would, assuredly, be a train tomorrow.

By going down next morning to the Wagons-Lits office in Constitution Square, before its doors opened, it was possible to steal a march on the other passengers, who cheerfully believed their reservations to be in order. To spend yet another night in Athens, simply in order to return to England via Budapest and Vienna was considered impractical; the tickets had to be altered to the Simplon-Orient Express.

In those days telegraph charges were high and always paid by the passengers; luckily only one wire to Belgrade was necessary. In view of the circumstances two single berths were sold at second-class prices, but not before the other two English, staying in the hotel, had entered the office. While waiting for the wire to arrive, it was entertaining to watch their faces. Angrily they demanded to know why they had to come to the office at all: where were their reservations? That they had booked berths on a Wednesday and had not got any for Thursday was utterly beyond them. The idea that only two through sleeping cars per day were permitted by the Yugoslav Railways was not only incomprehensible, it was intolerable, stupid, foreign—Yugoslav in fact (fortunately they did not say Greek). So, if they could not go on Wednesday because the incompetent Greeks—"it was a landslide, madam"—could not stop their trucks from falling off the line, they would go on Thursday; two double berths please. What? Full? What about these people here? They had taken the last two, had they? Well, what was going to be done about it? Berths in the Berlin car? But they did not want to go to Berlin! What did they think they were—Nazis?

The agent respectfully suggested that they might be able to change into the Istanbul-Calais Car, avoiding a change at Paris. Should he enquire if there was room? Yes, by all means. What was he waiting for? The agent made out a chit for two telegrams, to Sofia and Trieste.

The allocation of berths in the Grand European Expresses was one of the more closely guarded secrets of the Company. In the through cars various cabins are held by different agencies along the line for intermediate passengers.

So at the same hour on the same evening, the passengers found themselves once more in the hotel lobby, and soon afterwards were locked for safety in the station waiting-room to await the arrival of the Simplon-Orient Express from Piraeus. The cars came up from the port in charge of the Greek cleaners, who handed them over to the French and German conductors at Athens Station. There were four cars, but it was the two teak ones at the front of the train that attracted attention, for in place of the familiar brass letters screwed into the cant rail they bore the Company's title in Greek; one was an R3 third-class car for Salonika, the other an R class car for Istanbul via Alexandropolis. Next to them were the blue and gold coaches, and right at the rear another teak car of Wagons-Lits, smoke pouring from its kitchen chimney.

Dinner would be served as soon as the train started: but this the train did not do. The passengers were settled on board, their hand luggage stowed by the cleaners. The conductor, refusing to allow anyone out, himself got down on to the platform to chat with a Greek, perhaps the owner of the room in which he lodged during the day's brief respite from six nights' continuous travelling. At the head of the train, beyond the ordinary carriages, a massive 2-10-0 was outlined against the clear moonlight of the early December night. It whistled rather mournfully, crowing in quasi-American style.

The conductor was evidently used to late starting:

he continued to talk to his friend as if starting on a thousand-mile journey across Europe was the last thing he was about to do. Suddenly the train rushed out of the station; the short cut-off and the five pairs of driving wheels gave it a quick and quiet getaway. The conductor had ignominiously to run after his car and jump on to the running board; with a wry smile, he fastened the latch bolts the door from the inside.

The best thing about traveling in the Simplon-Orient Express in this direction was that the food and the dining cars gradually became superior. This teak dining car came off at Amfiklia, after serving soup, risotto with shell fish, mutton pilaf, sauté potatoes and beans, cheese and fruit. The Naousa red wine went down well with the mutton, but the cheese was rather strong, as was the Turkish coffee and Ouzou. The menu was hand-written in Greek and French in the usual Wagons-Lits style.

Before the first war Wagons-Lits only ran one dining car in Greece. This was a narrow-gauge service on the Peloponnesus Railway and was suspended in November 1915. The sleeping car to Salonika from Nis was a Serbian Division service.

The journey from Athens to Salonika is one succession of climbs and descents; one could hear the hard working of the engine, the echoing whistle in the tunnels, or the sudden wheezing of the brakes. Stops were frequent and long, but next morning, at about 8 a.m., the Simplon-Orient Express was passing between Mount Olympus and the sea, in the neighbourhood of Platamona. Here the railway is more level than the road, and as recently as 1960 it became necessary to stop trespassers, in particular Grecian beauties in bathing costumes, walking out with their beaux. One of these young ladies so captivated a passing driver with her good looks that he ran into the train in front!

Thessaloniki Station is a terminus: normally there

was a twenty-minute delay here but the express was late. It arrived at 8.25 a.m., and left again at 8.30. Presumably it was frequently late in arriving at the frontier, and the unaccustomed haste was an effort to show the Greek flag. Another massive 2-10-0 of the same class came on at the rear of the train, pushing another teak dining car, which belonged to the now defunct Yugoslav Division of the Company, that also worked some narrow-gauge cars.

Breakfast was continental style. Moreover the crew did not allow the passengers to linger as it was apparently essential to clear the car before reaching Idomeni, the frontier. No doubt the fuss was partly due to the crew being Yugoslav and their French was somewhat limited. The train, which had been pursuing its leisurely way up the Axios Valley and passed through a gorge at the back of the Salonika plain, now stopped at a small Macedonian village where soldiers came aboard. Their grey field uniforms and swarthy unshaven faces distinguished them from the soldiers in the neighbouring village, who had brown uniforms. They all looked as though the passage of the express was an unwarranted intrusion, from which they would retire to sleep until the passage of the returning express in the evening, when perhaps some incautious travellers would provide the wherewithal for the evening's drinking; the Macedonian frontier was reminiscent of the Irish border with the Six Counties. With a flourish, the C. E. H. 2-10-0 snorted off into a siding, and from the single track main line a diminutive J. D. Z. Henschel 2-6-2 backed on in its place. The C. E. H. 2-10-0 was still on its siding when the train left, for no doubt it also had all day in which to turn and go back from Djevjelija to Idomeni, to await the evening train.

For the whole morning the landscape was one long sea of mud; in fact only three motor cars were passed during the entire day. At this time of year there were no nude damsels bathing in the Varda, as the Axios calls itself in Yugoslavia, where the conductors at one time had instructions to pull down the blinds!

Shortly before 1 p.m. the train arrived at Skoplje; here the engine was replaced by another of the same class, and the exchange provided the only chance to stretch one's legs, although the train stopped frequently for a few moments elsewhere along the line. Since the new line has been built to Kraljevo, the old station has been abandoned and trains for Nis have to reverse out of the new station built on the new line back to the junction.

After Skoplje there was luncheon of hors d'oeuvres, pork and odd-tasting pastry, and very local cheese. Yugoslav mineral water tasted most peculiar; Dalmatian Riesling was no thirst quencher either, but its tippling qualities were enhanced by the fatigue of the journey.

There was something soothing in the rumbling of the train as the wheels clicked over the short rails, the background music to the flamboyant luxury of the sleeping car, which seemed the more ostentatious by contrast with the primitive countryside. The struggling peasants, who ploughed through the mud, tending their cows and goats, or who now and then struggled with their chickens and bundles in or out of the ancient wooden carriages up in front, seemed at variance with the rest of the train. Here was something set apart, unworldly almost; even the conductor, dozing on his seat at the end of the corridor, seemed some sort of extra-terrestrial being, although, descending to the track at every major stop, he seemed to know everyone along the line. The splendid isolation of first-class travel, lolling on the regal plush, one's head against the antimacassar, one's feet in carpet slippers, with nothing to do, is completed when even kings must wait for one to pass; and in a passing loop in the neighbourhood of Ristovac the south-bound Simplon-Orient Express waited, with an extra sleeper, in which King George of Greece was known to be travelling privately.

As it grew dark the train rolled into Nis. The dining car and the ordinary coaches were shunted off, to run on in the slow train to Belgrade. The main train was delayed in coming from Dimitrovgrad on the Bulgarian frontier; it could be heard a long time before it arrived, for the line curves right round into Nis, necessitating a reversal. For this reason the Direct Orient Express today divides at Crveni Krst, reached by a new spur built since the war.

At Nis the Simplon-Orient Express changed its appearance. No longer was it made up of railway carriages. There were seven steel sleeping cars, a steel diner and two Wagons-Lits fourgons. The dining car was based at Trieste and worked through from Svilengrad, the Bulgarian frontier with Greece. Headed by a huge black German Pacific, the whole express roared off through the night, at twice its former speed, while an elegant dinner was served by the Italian *brigade*. The rolls were Bulgarian, the wine was Yugoslav, but the spaghetti and the meat were unmistakably Italian, as was the *gelati* that had travelled in the refrigerated compartment successfully to Svilengrad and back. The bill did not bear either the Company's title or any other heading; it was divided into squares and stated only, in Yugoslav and French, that it should be attached in case of complaint. Through the glass partition the sleeping-car conductors from Paris, Calais, Berlin and Ostend could be seen having dinner together.

Having turned in early, with the intention of watching the shunting operations at Belgrade from the advantageous position of a single berth compartment, it was distressing to wake up at one o'clock in the morning at Vinkovci, where the Bucharest portion of the Simplon-Orient Express was attached. There was thick snow at Zagreb and Ljubljana, where water squirted from a dozen leaks in the hose pipe which was filling the dining car tanks.

An expansive 'meat breakfast' was served before Rakek, at that time the Yugoslav frontier. The train descended the steep hill to Postumia (Pivka), and on the way Mussolini's *Alpini* were much in evidence. At Postumia his militiamen climbed aboard the train while the J. D. Z. engine came off and an F. S. electric engine took its place.

After two days and two nights on the train from Trieste to Svilengrad and back the crew were relaxing in the diner before being relieved. The journey from Postumia took little more than an hour. I had an unquenchable thirst and demanded a bottle of Fiuggi as soon as the frontier was passed. The chef de brigade gave me a look I can remember even after twenty-five years; but the Fiuggi was produced, and so was an enormous piece of blank paper for sales in Italy, which had to be made out specially to account for it.

At Trieste the dining car was taken off during the forty minutes' wait that elapsed in the station. When the new dining car appeared, with a different crew, it proved to be the same vehicle; it remained in the train all the rest of the day.

During lunch the engine was changed at Cervignano from electric back to steam, but owing to the short time (about seven minutes) spent in Venice, it was not possible to see what sort was used. Lunch was delicious, particularly the Gorgonzola cheese, which was very different from those evil-smelling fabrications proffered with such a flourish in the Balkan dining cars.

The line from Trieste goes inland. Only at Mestre does it come down to the water's edge, to cross the causeway to Santa Lucia Station at the back of

Venice, where all trains have to reverse. A single *sandolo* was all the water traffic visible. Sandolos today are notably lacking, their place taken by innumerable motor boats. A large 4-6-2 of the 691 class was waiting at Venice to take over the train to Milan, across the great Lombardy plain through so many historic places—Padua, Vicenza, Verona, Brescia. There were plenty of interesting trains on this part of the journey, ranging from the 740 class 2-8-0 goods engines to the 640 Moguls on the secondary line trains. The ubiquitous 835 0-6-0 tank engines sometimes hauled branch trains of four-wheeled open-ended carriages, and were much in evidence as the Simplon-Orient Express wove its way into Milano Centrale, that monumental station, the largest in Europe, where black-shirted Fascists strutted up and down.

The station was bursting with uniforms—Carabinieri, militia-men, railway officials and Wagons-Lits staff. The latter renewed the ice boxes and the food supplies and removed the empties from the Simplon-Orient's diner. The authorities took great interest in the passengers, who were only in Italy for a day; but outwardly all was calm, serene, benevolent. At Milan, where the train reversed for the last time, two 685 class 2-6-2 engines were attached for the steep climb to Domodossola. Many more passengers had come aboard, and in the carrozza-ristorante dinner was almost ready. One could follow the train's progress on the map in the corridor, alongside the customs *carnet* for the carriage.

The dinner was very Italian. Clear soup, ravioli, steak tortellini, belpaese cheese, fruit and cassata. Finally a cappuccino instead of the thick Turkish coffee, and a Strega to go with it. The train roared through Gallerate, but later stopped at Arona and Stresa, where Lago Maggiore matched the colour of the sleepers, a dark and dirty blue. The train ran ever more slowly as it climbed into the Alps. It is a difficult pull up to Domodossola, but nothing to the climb from there up to Iselle, at the mouth of the Simplon Tunnel. The F. S. did not electrify the whole line until 1951, and because of the many spiral tunnels and cramped space at Iselle, the Swiss have for years operated the Italian line from Domodossola onwards.

At Domodossola one could hear the slam of the carriage examiner's hammer, and I so far forgot Mussolini and all his works as to lean out to see if the wheel-tapper was a Swiss. On the down platform, standing in the light of a lamp standard, something moved, and looking more closely to my horror I saw an officer leveling a revolver straight at me. The first phase that one learns in Italian—*E pericoloso sporgersi*—took on a new and harsher meaning. Scarcely had I pulled down the blind and assumed a position of feigned sleep when there was a discreet but peremptory tap on the door. The conductor, troubled, entered with an Italian officer, who snapped something about passport. *"Inglese,"* I heard the conductor say, and then "Athene-Londra." The officer tried to make me understand without response, and then they mercifully withdrew.

The chronic whirring of the Westinghouse electric pump on the Swiss engine was as balm to the nerves, and the heavy roar of the train inside the 12-mile Simplon Tunnel restored the feeling of closeted serenity. The train stopped with a jerk at Brig, where there was more tramping up and down the corridor—no doubt the frustrated Italian was telling his Swiss colleague about the incident. Soon those comforting bells heralded the dparture down the Rhône valley to Lausanne, where the dining car came off, to await the arrival of the Simplon-Orient Express from Paris.

Dijon was reached at 4.27 a.m. in those days, and

here yet another dining car was attached to serve breakfast. This voiture-restaurant was a new one. The smell of fresh paint and of the shiny leather tip-up seats was quite different from the Italian car, which had movable chairs and brass fittings, instead of anodized metal work. The French car worked back to Dijon in an ordinary train, which was why it had fifty-six seats instead of forty-two chairs. The sense of speed was reflected in the echoing roar through its saloons, like a hundred flushing toilets.

After breakfast the conductor came round with passports and tickets, enquiring if English passengers wished to move along the corridor into the Calais car. But it was quicker to drive across Paris to catch the Golden Arrow rather than trundle round the Ceinture in the Simplon-Orient car, which avoided the Gare du Nord but arrived after the Pullman train, for it stopped at Etaples on the way.

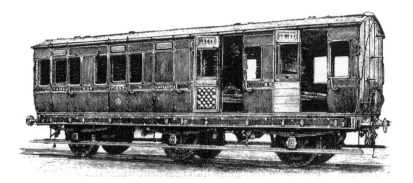

FLIPPING THE MEAT TRAIN

from *American Heritage* Magazine

Dale Wasserman (1917–)

Dale Wasserman ran away from home at the age of fourteen and lived a hobo life for the next five years. Ultimately arriving in Hollywood, he became a playwright and screenwriter, author of such screenplays as The Vikings *(1955) and* Cleopatra *(1963). He also dramatized Ken Kesey's* One Flew Over the Cuckoo's Nest *for Broadway. He has won several awards for his long-running musical* Man of La Mancha.

I picked up my first clue at a cocktail reception. Over my shoulder, hearing an enthusiastic discussion, I realized that I was eavesdropping on a group of several youngish to middle-aged men and one woman who were comparing their exploits in an activity that was illegal, hazardous, and, to me, utterly astonishing. As they chattered on, it became clear that they were members of an organization whose hobby, if I could believe my hearing aid, was riding freight trains.

I inquired and found it to be true: There is a generation of prosperous hobohemians whose drug of choice is flipping freight trains in emulation of the vanished hobo. Riding the rails has become a recreational kick. Well-fed baby boomers are taking trips on the high iron. Further, there are books of instruction, which recommend clothing and equipment suitable for flipping freights, and equipment suitable for flipping freights, and a number of how-to manuals. Among the most comprehensive is Duffy Littlejohn's Hopping Freight Trains in America. This book is wonderful. An amazement. All 360 fact-crammed pages of it. "Why ride freight trains?" asks Duffy. And answers, "Riding the rails is the last pure red-blooded adventure in North America."

Furthermore, he lists "The 100 Commandments of Riding the Rails," a compendium of everything the hobohemian might need to know, from how to find the freight yards to how to jump off a moving train. Particularly fascinating is the section devoted to the equipment considered necessary for the New Age hobo: a backpack of nylon or another synthetic material, "not over 26 pounds when fully packed"; blankets of a certain weight and texture; toilet paper, absolutely; warm clothing of precise specification and surprising cost; and bottled water.

My amazement rose from the fact that back in the days when hoboes were an established underclass, I was there. Living the life, the real thing, *sans* all equipment but the clothing on my back and a three-inch pocketknife. From the age of 14 to 19, embracing all adolescence, I was a hobo, homeless and surviving day to day in a life that for all its horrors could also engender astonishing delights. Only now do I realize that I may be one of the last of the *echt* hoboes, and I am therefore driven to speak in their behalf.

In taking to the Road, one entered distinguished company. Jack London was a hobo, though held in low esteem since he made only one trip and thereafter made a book and a big deal of it. Upton Sinclair hoboed, as did John Dos Passos, Walt Whitman, Mark Twain, John Steinbeck, and Zane Grey. So did Vachel Lindsay, Robert W. Service, John Fante, and Bret Harte. Harry Kemp made a career as the "tramp poet," as did W. H. Davies, and one must grant that their credentials were authentic. Jack Kerouac's were not; he belonged to the suborder of Hoboes-Vicarious. Clark Gable rode the rails, as did Robert Mitchum (Mitchum and I compared Road notes at our first meeting) and Frank Capra, Melvin Belli, Supreme Court Justice William O. Douglas, and a host of others.

In the rigid order of the Road that was, a hobo ranked high. It must be understood that he was not a tramp. A tramp might be a thug, a jackroller, a punch-drunk boxer, or a yegg on the lam. The Road, among its other attractions, was a refuge from the law.

Nor was a hobo a bum. A bum hung out on Chicago's West Madison Avenue and panhandled the stem. In the hobo jungles he might be seen squeezing Sterno Canned Heat through an old sock to extract the grain alcohol. Hoboes disdained tramps, felt nothing warmer than pity for bums, and avoided both.

For what defines the hobo is that he *worked*. The great majority of hoboes (at least until the Depression struck) were skilled at a host of occupations. Lumberjacks, cigar-rollers, woodchoppers, construction stiffs, fruit and vegetable pickers, barley buckers, short-order cooks, merchant mariners . . . name it, and there were hoboes who could do it. They wouldn't do it for long, however. The Road was home; other domiciles were temporary.

In looking back, I realize that I can claim affinity with Lavengro and the Romany Rye, with Jim Tully and Huckleberry Finn, with Ishmael and Thor Heyerdahl and Casanova and Randle P. McMurphy and Johnny Appleseed and Don Quixote and Fry Pan Jack and the Cheyenne Kid and all the men and women, fictional and historical, who ran away from home and never looked back.

On the rare occasion that I mention my time on the Road, people invariably ask, "But wasn't it dangerous?"

Yes. Extremely. If I tend to forget, I am reminded by the bullet scar on my right leg, a memento of shots fired by a town clown in Anniston, Alabama. A seam on my right eyebrow recalls a cosh slammed against my head by a yard bull (railroad cop) in Wyoming. My floating ribs are adrift from their original anchorage. A scar across the back of my hand recalls . . . odd, I can't remember.

The population of the Road itself numbered many who were dangerous to others. There were prison escapees and ex-cons. Lunatics were common.

One learned to keep a wary distance, to wake instantly from sleep and hit the ground running, especially if one was a "gaycat," a young apprentice like me. Also dangerous were the jockers, men seeking "punks" among the young to whom they offered protection, often in exchange for sexual favors.

But most dangerous of all were the trains themselves. There were precise techniques for flipping a freight and for the even more hazardous move, dropping off. Thousands of Road kids were killed or injured; there are no statistics numbering those who fell beneath the wheels. One may extrapolate from the figures of one railroad alone, the Missouri Pacific, which from 1930 (the year I started jumping freights) to 1932 recorded 330 trespassers killed and 682 seriously injured.

And yet. As though "normal" danger was too tame, we Road kids sought more. Status on the Road was awarded according to which trains one had ridden. It wasn't enough to ride and survive the red ball—express-freights, which, after all, started and stopped at conservative speeds and lumbered along at a mere 30 to 50 miles per hour. There were passenger trains, and there were crack passenger trains that offered one mere seconds to catch and no safe place to ride and which braked so sharply there was no way to drop off until they had stopped in the glare of the station lights.

On such trains there were only certain places it was possible to ride. Each spot had its virtues, each its hazards. The blind baggage, the space between a locomotive's tender and the mail or baggage car at the head end, was a favorite. On the other hand, if the crew discovered you there, they'd think nothing of booting you off at 80 miles an hour. Riding between any other cars could be done if one were able to survive the muscle ache from clinging to a single ladder rung beside the bumpers, plus the wind that worked always to tear one loose, plus the buffeting from cinders and stones churned up by suction from the roadbed. And there were the battery boxes, usually empty, beneath some coaches. A person might crawl into one if it could be done unobserved and, if young and limber, huddle in its claustrophobic murk to ride in safety. But there was the chance of the outside latch's being closed, deliberately or accidentally, wereupon one was privileged to die in darkness; battery boxes, like refrigerator cars, had no inside handles.

In hobo jungles one could garner fascinating information of trains even more prestigious to ride than the crack passenger flyers, the Silk Train from the West Coast for instance, carrying valuable cargo destined for New York and escorted by armed guards who were privileged to shoot on sight. I should like to claim that I rode it. I scoped it, certainly, but, having observed the gimlet-eyed men with rifles, found it too intimidating to approach. I heard claims by other 'boes that they'd ridden the Silk Train but concluded that there were no fewer liars on the Road than in the square life.

The Meat Trains were famous. They were "contract runs," rolling nightly at high speed from Sioux Falls to Chicago, carrying beef carcasses that *had* to be there by dawn. The cars that made up the "consist" were neither special nor adapted to the breakneck velocity. The Meat Train carried no empties. It made no scheduled stops. Its violence of motion made it impossible to ride the bumpers. Strictly suicide, warned the older 'boes.

I was determined to ride it.

I am dozing on and off in a swale amid infinite Iowa corn rows, close by the crossing of two railroads. The tracks, shining by moonlight, intersect at precise right angles. I wear a beret, a light jacket, and two pairs of Frisco jeans as a cloth sandwich to guard against early-morning chill.

In the far distance, a locomotive whistles. Instantly I'm awake and listening. One short: a train signaling that it's about to stop. The glow of a headlight, the engine coming on at speed; yes, on the Northwestern's tracks, precisely where it should be. Brakes scream, steel on steel, as the hogger hits the air and the train pauses just short of the junction. But it's a pause, not a stop, and the whistle immediately sounds two long blasts, the highball, meaning "We go!" and it's rolling again.

In the few seconds available, my eyes canvass the train in dismay. I'd expected reefers (refrigerator cars) with room for a 'bo to ride up top where the open hatches would at least provide windbreaks or, better still, allow him to drop down into an empty ice compartment. But these aren't reefers, they're ordinary boxcars, and for a moment I think, "It's the wrong train." Then I realize: beef carcasses not iced but simply loaded in boxcars at a huge savings in cost but demanding speed, speed! if they're to get to the packinghouse before nature renders them rotten.

I've waited a fraction too long; the train is already under way, crossing the frogs. Nothing for it but to board where I can.

Running alongside until I'm moving almost as fast as the train, I make my play, hooking on to the ladder at the front end of a car, perhaps the tenth in the string. My foot finds a stirrup. There I cling until I catch my breath. I climb halfway up the side of the car—and stop.

Something wrong!

I feel it, a squirming of a powerful muscle against my left thigh and, although incredulous, realize that it must be a *snake*, that while I was sleeping, a snake crawled between the two pairs of jeans I am wearing. Are there rattlesnakes in Iowa? Copperheads?

Panic strikes. I kick free of the ladder, hanging on by my hands, swinging wildly, slamming my body against the side of the boxcar to dislodge the terrifying thing that is clinging to me. Finally it loses its grip. I catch a glimpse as it falls: almost three feet long, glistening darkly in the moonlight.

When the panic subsides, I consider dropping off but, looking down at the ties spinning away, realize that the train is already rolling too fast. There's no choice. I'm going to have to deck it, ride the top.

The runway on top is three boards wide, about 20 inches overall. I'd like to be many cars farther back, but it's impossible to navigate the rocking deck, so I have to settle for lying prone, my head toward the locomotive, where of necessity it must take the brunt of sparks, smoke, and cinders spewing from the smokestack.

The train accelerates. It's rolling, I guess, at close to 90 miles an hour. Not unusual for a passenger hotshot but very much so for boxcars, which never were designed for that speed. The car beneath me is bucking, pitching, yawing, jerking violently from side to side. I grip the edges of the runway, sure I'm leaving fingerprints embedded in its coarse, weathered wood. Not enough; I dig sneakered feet into the space between runway and car top, finally anchored at both ends though still deafened and buffeted by hurricane-force wind.

Now I know why nobody rides the Meat Train.

An infinity later I realize that the train is slowing down, that it's rolling placidly through the freight yards of suburban Chicago.

A new problem: how to get off. My hands are claws. My muscles ache. My kidneys feel as though I'd finished 10 tough rounds in the ring. I crawl to the ladder on hand and knees, make my way down, shakily, and plant my feet in the stirrup. I drop off the train in the way I've learned from watching brakemen do it, opposite the "natural" way, back foot first, leaning backward so that if you fall, you fall away from, not into, the wheels. I do it nicely too, but overstrained muscles give way, and I hit the cinders, rolling.

But alive. And I've ridden the Meat Train. I am now a hobo cum laude.

How does one attain the profession of hobo? A town called Estherville in northern Iowa; the Rock Island Line ran through it. Few trains actually *stopped* in Estherville, but many came thundering through. They came out of the horizon, emerging from a sea of corn rows. The locomotive was black, its round face topped by a single blazing eye that grew enormous as it approached. I would shrink from the juggernaut's passage, trapped between fascination and fear. Occasionally my vigil would be rewarded by a condescending wave from the cab as a train rolled ground-shakingly past. In this even, delirium! Engineers were royalty, as pilots on the Mississippi had been in Mark Twain's day.

Estherville ended with the death of my parents and the dealing out of my siblings like a poker hand to relatives or to orphanages. Undisciplined, secretive, and almost entirely unschooled, at the age of 14 I was shipped to a family member in Blunt, South Dakota.

Blunt was a town of 400 and well named. I lasted less than a month there, conniving with a friendly truck driver to escape. So it happened that in the middle of a hot summer night in the year 1930 I dropped off a truck in South Dakota's capital, Pierre, not knowing quite where I was, much less where I might be going.

I'd arrived at a no man's land between freight yards and the river. To the left were a few, a very few lights in the town, seen across a spidery maze of railroad tracks. To the right was the Missouri, a deeper darkness of slow-moving water. The wail of a locomotive's whistle approached from the east. A lovely sound, the *only* sound on this summer's night: one short cry, then dying to a disconsolate silence. I knew what that meant: Days of hanging out at the Rock Island depot were paying off. The engineer was signaling "down brakes."

On the river, no traffic in sight; on the track, a freight train. An easy choice. I made for the tracks, swung up onto the sill of one of the boxcars. Soon the train jolted into motion, and from the depths of the car I'd chosen came an irritated voice: "Get in or get out, yuh damn fool, 'less yer waitin' fer the f—in' door tuh cut yer f—in' legs off."

Thank you, Professor, for my first Road lesson. There were to be more, and in general I accepted instruction gratefully. The train rolled. I sat cross-legged on the floor of my car, watching America flow by, feeling happy, feeling anonymous, feeling *free*.

I eventually went to sleep and woke to bright sunlight in Chadron, Nebraska, and with the help of a friendly switchman caught a red ball freight heading for the Rocky Mountains, Hong Kong, Istanbul, and Ouarzazate, all of which I reached in due course.

No one knows the origin of the word *hobo*, but it had to be invented for a cast of wanderers who lucked into a mode of travel that existed for one century and never will again. Without trains there could have been no hoboes. Traveling was the essence, and the 250,000-mile railroad system of North America offered a unique means.

It was perilous, it was delightful, it was brutal and exalting, and above all it was romantic. Millions of adolescent boys dreamed of becoming hoboes, and thousands upon thousands of them did. It took guts, courage, and imagination. Any lapse and the results could be devastating. Consider this account, for instance, by the poet W. H. Davies from his *Autobiography of a Super-Tramp*, a book that opens with a laudatory preface by no less a hobo manqué than George Bernard Shaw: "Taking a firmer grip on the bar, I jumped, but it was too late, for the train was now going at a rapid rate. My foot came short of the step, and I fell, and, still clinging to the handle bar was dragged several yards before I relinquished my hold. And there I lay for several minutes, feeling a little shaken, whilst the train swiftly passed on into the darkness.

"Even then I did not know what had happened, for I attempted to stand, but found that something had happened to prevent me from doing this. Sitting down in an upright position, I then began to examine myself, and now found that the right foot had been severed from the ankle."

Compassionate railroad workers found Davies and saved his life. The chances of being maimed were multiple, but nothing deterred all those boys (myself among them) who, in the words of Thomas Wolfe, were "burning in the night." There were an estimated quarter-million of them riding freights at the height of the Depression.

The Depression accounted for the fact that the Road belonged no longer to the young but to the dispossessed of all ages, no longer the life of those who'd chosen but of those who'd been deprived of any choice at all. They swarmed onto the freight trains, husbands, wives, children, in futile search for work, for a welcoming community, for an unlikely offer of food, friendship, compassion. Estimates of the numbers of homeless on the road at the depth of the Depression reached one million . . . two million. The truth is, no one knows.

I fear I may have given the impression that hoboing was an unending round of danger, discomfort, and anomie. Well, yes. But it offered so much more. Independence. Freedom, like none other on earth. Unexpected pleasures, astonishing sights. Ecstasy even, and the joy of wonders previously known only from rumor or from books.

Nor in the course of my travels did I neglect education. In the library of a small town, I would select two books, slip them under my belt at the small of my back, read as I rode, and slip them back into the stacks of another library in another town far down the line, where I would "borrow" two more. I thus acquired a substantial, if incoherent, fund of knowledge that, together with experience, became my total education.

I have danced with joy on the decks of freight trains laboring though the High Sierra in the time of snow, intoxicated by beauty, and yelled with jubilation at the swoops of whitened valleys and sculptured peaks fresh-born or still in the process of parturition, if reckoned in geologic time. The stars were close about my ears.

There was exhilaration in going over the Sierra Nevada, even factoring in the cold, the ominous snow tunnels, the steel-straining labors of a nearly mile-long freight. I was in awe of the giant engines that pulled, pushed, and powered this numbing tonnage several times daily. They were cab-front Malletts, one of the largest and most powerful locomotives on earth, and there were three to a train. They were god-like, but, like most gods, they had alarmingly human characteristics. One could *feel* their muscles straining at the task; one could *hear* it in the huff-chuff, huff-chuff, of their exhaust. When at rest, on a sidetrack, for instance, they coughed and panted in a unique pattern not to be mistaken for that of any other locomotive. Now, at this moment, I can hear it in my head.

Of all the gifts of hobodom, however, the sweetest and most dangerous is the freedom, that most abused word in the lexicon. To the wanderer alienated from society, it has precise and profound implications, fulfilling the sense of the Camus phrase *terrible freedom*.

As a hobo I was free of family pressures and responsibility—and free to endure the absence of support in the rites of passage enjoyed by a "normal" member of society. I was free of moral and behavioral restraints and free of the social accommodations that make living among one's fellow folk possible. I was free of sexual education or modulation,

and free to suffer the consequences in tainted relationships for decades to follow.

I found freedom marvelous, joyous, wing-spreading. I found it crippling, dangerous, and lonely.

Now I'm sixteen, slight but wiry, wearing my black beret, Frisco jeans, and a ready grin. I am a gaycat, Road-wise, a real slim-jim. Unfortunately, I've misremembered the distinction between carefree and careless.

On a humid summer's evening, with soft dark rain falling in a railroad town between Rawlins and Rock Springs, Wyoming, I've spotted a road hog waiting on a siding, its lights and numbers up, ready to roll.

Now I'm strolling along, canvassing the cars of the red ball freight it will be hauling, checking for empties. A tall man, wearing a straw Stetson with a rolled brim, steps out from between two cars and beckons with his left hand: Come closer.

It's too dark to see what he's holding in his other hand. A gun? On the chance that it is, I check my first instinct, which is to run.

I'm reassured by the tall man's eyes. They're brown, they're friendly. No danger signals. Nor in his voice when he speaks; concern, rather, and courtesy. In a soft Texas accent the tall man asks, "Headin' out?"

"Yup."

"On this train?"

"I was figuring."

The tall man nods, his manner almost mournful. "Y'all know you're on railroad property?"

I tense up. Run? But what's concealed in his right hand?

"I wasn't fixing to steal anything."

"Said you was. Said you was goin' to steal a ride on this here train."

"Well, I never figured that flipping a ride on a

freight—"

I don't see it coming. Only know a blinding flash of light, cold and scintillating. And a clang in my head followed by a fast, nauseating vibration.

I'm lying on the ground. I raise my eyes to see, at last, the implement in the tall man's right hand. Not a gun, a billy club perhaps fashioned from a sawed-off table leg. The fog clears from my eyes, and I can see more clearly now, can even make out the dull gray plug of metal at its business end. The billy has been cored with a half-pound of lead. Yard bull's trick.

The pain has not yet reached its apex. What I feel is shame, shame in the stupidity of not recognizing danger while there was a chance to avoid it.

The soft Texas voice, solicitous: "Y'all listenin'?"

I summon up a whisper. "Yes, sir."

"Want you should pay note t' this."

I see it coming, and there's not one damn thing I can do about it. There's time, even, to note the steel capping of the yard bull's boots as I am kicked, with precise aim, in the center of my ribs. I feel them crack and give. Breath is driven out, and now the pain is no longer shy; it washes over in a blinding wave, and to my own shame I cry out, "All *right*," as though it will interdict the beating. Through a mist I hear the warm, solicitous voice, "Kin yuh git up?" and I gasp, "No . . . no . . . ," with an irrational expectation that now hostilities will cease, friendship be declared, and my wounds tended.

"Git up or take the next one in the nuts." The voice is no more emphatic than before, but I know it doesn't piss around, it *means* it.

I struggle to my feet. The effort costs, a price paid in pain, in waves of nausea, in shame and fury.

The yard bull faces me away from the tracks, south toward the empty hills. "Start walkin'," he says. "And *keep* walkin'."

The night has fully settled in by now, the soft drizzle persisting. I stumble on, unseeing, sick with pain. The rain stops. A few stars appear, even a blur of moon. The night seemingly has no end. Yet after an eternity or two there's the beginning of light.

I am out of sight of anything man-made, town, railroad, anything at all. Nothing but great, undulating hills. I'm aware principally of thirst.

The nightmare begins. It will last three, possibly four days. Hunger . . . one can live with hunger for a long time. But thirst . . . thirst is not passive. Thirst *demands*.

Mirages now. This one's lovely. I am in the green shade of northern Wisconsin, place of my birth, and all the little mouths of my body drink endlessly of the cool, clear water flowing over me. A coyote preaches a sermon from a pulpit of bones. A Lakota boy of my own age takes me by the hand and leads me for a while but callously abandons me when I am unable to match his pace.

Now one quite extraordinary: At the foot of the hillock on which I have sat down to die, a column of tarantulas is passing. They march in military order; they have leaders, scouts, flankers, and they set a brisk pace.

Ridiculous. Still, these great hairy spiders have a destination.

I find the strength to rise and follow, vision fixed on the tail of the column. I am unconscious of how far I've gone or how the terrain is changing around me. Then the spiders have disappeared; they have changed into sheep. *Sheep*? I lift my eyes to see, silhouetted, the blocky figure of a man. Surely another mirage. But soon I'm being administered small sips of water.

It's dark, and there's a huge black pot simmering on a small fire, and the sheepherder, grinning affably with squarish teeth set in a dark-skinned face, hands me a wooden bowl of mutton stew and speaks to me, but I think my ears or brain have been affected, for the language is a jumble of sounds. Later I learn that the man and the language are Basque.

I eat, drink water, and sleep long hours in a fleece-lined bedroll in the shadow of the shepherd's wagon. The broken ribs are painful, but they're healing (never set, they'll be forever crooked). A scar across my right eyebrow will be a further reminder, and I have suffered sunstroke.

One day I'm on my feet, expressing shame at having so imposed on a stranger. The Basque seems to feel no imposition; indeed he has enjoyed the break in his isolation. But I insist, and he draws on the ground a map of sorts. There is a highway to the south and west, half a day's walk.

Were the spiders really there? Months later I consult an encyclopedia and learn that tarantulas do, on occasion and for reasons unknown, assemble and move en masse to a new location. So they might have been real.

Or possibly not.

By 1940 the day of the hobo had ended—in its pre-recreational mode, that is. As for me, restless and rootless, I have continued to avoid a fixed address. I have been true to hoboism in my fashion.

Post-Road there was a time of living on the rooftops of office buildings in Los Angeles. With the confidence of ignorance, having landed in a revolutionary theater group wholly by accident, I embarked upon producing, directing, and acting in a propaganda form we'd now call street theater. The Federal Theater Project hired me as a director but gave me no plays to direct; in the resulting vacuum I taught myself theatrical lighting and thereafter designed lighting for such eminent dance companies as Martha Graham, Myra Kinch, the Ballets Russes, and, finally, Katherine Dunham, with whom I toured the world. Our headquarters were in Haiti, where we planted the entire menagerie of dancers, singers, and musicians on the old Maria-Paulette Buonaparte Leclerc plantation.

The impresario S. Hurok engaged my services, sending me to stage and light his multicultural attractions in Java, Japan, Africa.

Back in New York I made the only truly courageous decision of my life: At the age of 33, unburdened by education and ignorant even of the rules of grammar, I decided that I would try to become a writer. I would give myself one year to learn to write and to make a living at it. The year ended with the sale of a story I'd written, barely within my deadline.

Whereupon I turned to what I knew best, theater. It was television's golden age (though in truth much of it was leaden). I was not yet, if ever, a good writer, but I had one distinct advantage over my colleagues: Theater was embedded in my instincts. Indeed, it was all I really knew. My first play for television took an award as top TV play of the year. Many more plays and awards were to follow.

And still I had no fixed abode. *Man of La Mancha* (originally a television play) was written in a mountainside cabin overlooking Lake Maggiore, in the Ticino. I wrote *The Vikings* in Denmark, in the shadow of Kronborg Castle. *One Flew Over the Cuckoo's Nest* was hammered out in a disreputable hotel in Jamaica, preceded by one conference with Ken Kesey, the novel's author. As it happened, we never discussed the problems of dramatization, instead comparing notes on lumber camps we'd worked and jails in which we'd been temporarily domiciled.

I never stopped traveling, never fixed on a "permanent" address, even as the funds to make that possible came in.

I own a clock that every hour on the hour plays recording of a steam locomotive getting under way, its bells clanging "Clear the track," gut-straining for power, drive wheels spinning until they grip the rails, at length conquering the inertia of a half-million tons of loaded cars, sounding its whistle across a vanished past.

FROM *TENDER IS THE NIGHT*

F. Scott Fitzgerald (1896–1940)

A ride in a train can be a terrible, heavy-hearted, or comic thing; it can be a trial flight; it can be a prefiguration of another journey, just as a given day with a friend can be long, from the taste of hurry in the morning up to the realization of both being hungry and taking food together. Then comes the afternoon with the journey fading, and dying, but quickening again at the end.

FROM A TRAIN WINDOW

from *Collected Poems*

Edna St. Vincent Millay (1892–1950)

Edna St. Vincent Millay was one of the most celebrated poets of her era, and she was admired for her bohemian lifestyle as well as her verse. Her first volume, Renascence, *appeared in 1917, followed by* Second April *(1921) and Pulitzer Prize-winning* The Harp Weaver *(1923). Millay's later volumes, considered inferior to her earlier work, include* Fatal Interview *(1931),* Conversations at Midnight *(1937) and* Make Bright the Arrows *(1940).*

Precious in the light of the early sun the Housatonic
Between its not unscalable mountains flows.
Precious in the January morning the shabby fur of the cat-tails by the stream.
The farmer driving his horse to the feed-store for a sack of cracked corn
Is not in haste; there is no whip in the socket.

Pleasant enough, gay even, by no means sad
Is the rickety graveyard on the hill, Those are not cypress trees
Perpendicular among the lurching slabs, but cedars from the neighbourhood,
Native to this rocky land, self-sown. Precious
In the early light, reassuring
Is the grave-scarred hillside.
As if after all, the earth might know what it is about.

FROM *SISTER OF THE ROAD:*
THE AUTOBIOGRAPHY OF BOX CAR BERTHA

Box-Car Bertha (Bertha Thompson) (ca. 1900–?)

Bertha Thompson took to the road in adolescence, and during the next fifteen years became a hobo, a member of a gang of shoplifters and a prostitute in a Chicago brothel. She eventually settled down and became a research worker in a New York social services bureau.

So I knew that he was tired of me, or had another woman, or both, and when I told him that I was going away we were both relieved.

A week later Ena, her poet lover and I got a ride with a sister of one of the men in Mr. Schroeder's office as far as Alton, Illinois, and from Alton got an empty box car with two men hoboes on a midnight freight.

It was a bumpy ride, full of scrapings and stoppings at every little jerk-water town in Illinois. Toward morning a brakie found us, but we gave him fifty cents apiece to shut him up. We ran into only one woman on this trip, but her story was worth all the discomfort we had. She and two tall, lanky southern male hoboes, all of them drawling in their talk, got on towards morning when we stopped and switched about in a little spot. The brakie had tipped us off that we had about an hour's wait, and we had gotten out to stretch ourselves. As it was getting light we walked around the quiet streets and up past the little red brick store buildings and the courthouse square that then had hitching posts around it. When we got back in our box car we found the girl and the two men there before us.

Her name was Virginia Hargreaves. She was thin, raw-boned, rather attractive in her overalls and heavy boy's sweater. Her husband had left her and she had attached herself to the two older men hoboes and was trying to make Chicago where a girlfriend of hers had a job in a "house." She said the two men had helped her all the way from Alabama. Part of the time they had come in box cars, part of the time on the road hitch-hiking. They had hustled food for her and in return she had given them what sex expression they wanted. She was pretty cynical about men generally. After the train got rolling she told me how she lost her husband on her first hobo trip, on her wedding night.

Virginia was seventeen and had lived all her life in a small Georgia town. Hargreaves was the son of a farmer who had been dispossessed. They scraped together five dollars, bought a marriage license, gave the preacher fifty cents to marry them, and immediately after the ceremony hopped on a freight train intending to spend their honeymoon with relatives in Alabama.

When they got on the freight it was already moving, so they climbed up the ladder and got on top of an empty. It started to rain and soon poured down. They decided to swing down from the top and jump inside, a feat quite common among hoboes and sisters of the road.

Hargreaves held on to his wife's hands while she swung over the roof of the car and let her body down. She was in overalls. As her legs began to descend a pair of arms took hold of them and helped her into the car. Her husband attempted to follow her, but the train had gained speed and was jerking so badly that he was afraid he couldn't make it. He put one leg down slowly, then yelled after her, "I can't do it. I'll falloff!" He swung back and flattened himself on the top of the car, holding the sides for support. Hanging over the edge, he looked inside the car. What he saw made him wild. The arms that had helped his wife down belonged to a male hobo and were now around Virginia, struggling with her. But Hargreaves wasn't man enough to make another attempt to do anything about it. He simply lay there and watched while the hobo raped his wife.

The train thundered on a hundred miles through the mountains. Finally, when they came near a small town and the train slowed down to about twenty miles an hour, the hobo jumped off. When the train stopped, Hargreaves climbed down to his wife. He was beside himself with rage.

"You had no business leaving me on top of the

car," he shouted. "It was your fault. You sure as hell can beat it. I'm going back."

And he did.

Virginia and her men were willing to risk the railroad dicks in Chicago, but Ena's poet had been picked up twice in the yards there, so we got off the train when it slowed up in Berwyn and rode into the city on a street car. We had sent our baggage on by American Express and walked through the Loop to get it on Randolph Street. Ena's poet suggested we go over to the Near North Side close to the Dill Pickle Club and Bughouse Square. Here we found a little three-room house-keeping apartment with two beds, and proceeded to settle down and look around.

Girls and women of every variety seemed to keep Chicago as their hobo center. They came in bronzed from hitchhiking, in khaki. They came in ragged in men's overalls, having ridden freights, decking mail trains, riding the reefers, or riding the blinds on passenger trains. They came in driving their own dilapidated Fords or in the rattling side-cars of men hoboes' motorcycles. A few of them even had bicycles. They were from the west, south, east and north, even from Canada. They all centered about the Near North Side, in Bughouse Square, in the cheap rooming houses and light housekeeping establishments, or begged or accepted sleeping space from men or other women there before them. Some of them had paid their own way on buses or passenger trains but arrived broke to panhandle their food or berths with men temporarily able to keep them. A few had been stowaways on Lake boats, and I remember one who said she stowed away on an airplane from Philadelphia. Not a few of them had their ways paid by charity organizations believing their stories that they had relatives here who would keep them.

On arrival most of them were bedraggled, dirty, and hungry. Half of them were ill. There were pitiful older ones who had been riding freights all over the country with raging toothaches. In Chicago they got themselves to clinics, and although they couldn't get any dental work done free they could usually get the old snags of teeth taken out. Some were obviously diseased, and most of them were careless about their ailments unless they had overwhelming pain.

The bulk of these women, and most all women on the road, I should say, traveled in pairs, either with a man to whom by feeling or by chance they had attached themselves, or with another woman. A few had husbands and children with them. There were a number traveling with brothers. Now and then there was a group of college girls. A few women traveled about with a mob or gang of men. These were of the hard-boiled, bossy type, usually, who had careless sex relations with anyone in their own group, and who, therefore, never had to bother to hunt for food or shelter. I do not remember, during the first years, seeing many pairs of lesbians come in off the road together, but of course they are common now, women who are emotionally attached to each other, even though, on the road, or while they stop, they give their sex to men or to other women in exchange for food, transportation, and lodging.

These women were out of every conceivable type of home. But even that first summer I could see what I know now after many years, that the women who take to the road are mainly those who come from broken homes, homes where the father and mother are divorced, where there are step-mothers or step-fathers, where both parents are dead, where they have had to live with aunts and uncles and grandparents. At least half the women on the road are out of such homes.

Many others, I have found, are graduates of

orphan asylums. Shut up and held away from all activity, such girls have dreamed all their childhoods about traveling and seeing the world. As soon as they are released they take the quickest way to realizing their dreams, and become hoboes. Not a few are out of jails and institutions, choosing the road for freedom, the same way, regardless of hardship. Among these are actually many paroled from institutions for the feeble-minded and insane.

During my years in and out of Chicago I talked to hundreds of these women. How they managed without money on the road always fascinated me. Many worked from time to time. Some were typists, some file clerks, and carried with them recommendations from companies they had worked for. I knew one that first summer who was a graduate nurse. The only thing she carried with her on the road was a conservative looking dress which she could put on when she wanted to register for a job. She'd stay on a case, or a couple of cases, until she got a little money again, and then she'd pack the good dress away and go out on the road in trousers, hitch-hiking.

The bulk of the women on the road made no pretense of working, however, even when they stayed for weeks or even months, as they do in Chicago or any other big center. I have already explained how they get by, by begging, stealing or hustling, or with help from the welfare agencies.

Today, of course, all over the country there are state relief stations, federal transient bureaus, travelers' aid offices, but in the earlier days the missions and the private charities would help transients, especially women. Some of the girls made a specialty of all the words and attitudes that went with "being saved," and used them all successfully to get the watery soup and the coffee and bread that were put out by rescue missions in the name of the Lord. Some of them made up circumstantial stories of

their Jewish ancestry (being Irish) and got emergency help from Jewish agencies. Or they manufactured Roman Catholic backgrounds (being Jewish) and got help from Catholic missions. Others had acquired the language of various lodges and fraternal organizations and in the name of fathers and brothers and uncles who were Masons, Moose, Woodmen, Kiwanians, they were given food or clothes or money for transportation.

But the great group of hobo women practiced none of these tricks. Most of them weren't clever enough. Instead they begged from stores and restaurants; from people on the road or on the city sidewalks. A lot of them didn't bother to beg rooms. If the weather was good they slept in the parks with the men, or alongside them, cleaning up in the morning in the toilets of the libraries or other public buildings. And on the Near North Side there were dozens of people in studios and rooming houses who would let any of them in for a bath or clean-up.

One of the roughest, toughest and smuttiest flats we used to gather in was Tobey's. Tobey ran a bootleg joint on Hill Street, near the elevated, and this side of hell there was no worse conglomeration of human beings. Tobey was a rebel and a freethinker. He was tough and vulgar, a vicious, crooked, frightful sort of man. The vile, filthy language that he spouted, and the degrading way in which he handled his women were almost unspeakable, but I doubt if any aristocratic apartment of a wealthy bachelor in town attracted such a varied assortment of brains and talent as did Tobey's lousy flat.

Many of the best known labor leaders, the ones who not only believed in, but practiced, violence, came to his place for a loud drink, and quite a number of distinguished professors and literary men could be found there often. The poets, the real ones whose books did something for the community, came often.

I shall never forget the first night that Lucille Donoghue, the wife of the star reporter, Terry Donoghue, brought me to Tobey's. The place was stuffy and crowded with half-drunken men and soused women. Two of the "heavy men" (burglars) I met that night were killed by policemen soon after.

I despised Tobey, with his heavy jaw and penetrating eyes, the moment I laid eyes on him. He leered at me, and attempted to put his dirty hand under my dress before he had talked with me five minutes. About twelve o'clock two cabs stopped in front of the place, and a group of actors and newspaper men came in. Among them was Earl Ford, who was playing in *The Front Page*, and some of the stars from *My Maryland*.

There was no piano, but there was music. There was no modesty or decency, but there was genuine intellectual activity. I was amazed at how clearly the drunken, brutal Tobey could think. After Earl Ford downed a pint of "moon," he recited part of *The Ballad of Reading Gaol*. I left the party with a bunch of actors. Ena refused to leave, and when her poet attempted to drag her out, Tobey broke a china cuspidor over his head.

In practically every large city that I have visited, except those in the South, I found hobo colleges, unemployed councils, and radical forums that were run especially for the hoboes and the unemployed. They were nothing new to me. But the most interesting of them all was the one in Chicago, located in an old bank building at Washington and Desplaines Streets. The director was a physician, and the superintendent was John Bums, the Bughouse Square speaker I have already mentioned. For months I attended the meetings regularly. There were three each day, one at ten in the morning, the others at three and eight in the evening.

The staff at Hobo College was drawn from many walks of life some of which had nothing to do with hoboing. It was here that I not only heard but met Richard Bennett, the actor. He made a delightful and humorous speech and invited the whole audience to come to his play. We all loved him in *They Knew What They Wanted*, and after the play we all ganged into his dressing room and had a grand time. Mary McCormic sang for us at the College, and afterwards gave the superintendent fifty dollars and sent him out to buy food for the crowd. Gilda Gray, the dancer, and her husband and publicity man came over and danced and sang for us. Her husband got a taxi and brought us some wonderful cakes from the swellest baker in town and a whole milk can full of steaming coffee.

There were a good many authors at the College. Jim Tully came and made an arrogant speech. He was short, ferocious and red-headed, with a very dramatic manner. He brought with him Daniel Hennessy, a newspaper man who had written several good books on hoboes for the Haldeman Julius Little Blue Books. Professor Nels Anderson, author of *The Hobo*, and several other textbooks on sociology, also spoke to us. He had a strong, rugged, purposeful face and a rare way of telling a funny story, but the thing I remember most about him was a certain sweetness and tolerance that showed in his lips and in his voice as he talked of conditions on the road and of the things he and we had done and were then doing. Professor Edwin Sutherland, author of a splendid book on criminals, also gave us a fine talk.

Besides these men we heard some of the most-noted professors and sociologists in America, Professor E. A. Ross, of Madison, Professor E. W. Burgess, of the University of Chicago, and Professor Herbert Blumer, secretary of the American Sociological Society. Professor Blumer was a former college football star, large and dominating in body but with scholarly eyes and quietness of manner.

I am mentioning all these illustrious names to make it quite plain that the hoboes are not a bunch of dumb ignoramuses, and that they have an interest in and capacity for good lectures and for worthwhile intellectual food. Besides having the finest type of teachers, the most profound professors, and the ablest adult educators come to Hobo College, the students themselves, the hoboes, became able to think and talk more clearly. By far the most brilliant teachers and the most inspiring speakers who taught at the College belonged to us and came from the life we knew. One of these was Franklin Jordan, the man who later became "my heart."

GARE DU MIDI

from *Collected Poems*

W. H. Auden (1907–1973)

One of Britain's best-known poets, Wystan Hugh Auden was among a young group of British writers who sought to modernize poetry. His first volume, Poems *(1930), was followed by thirteen more volumes of verse. He was the editor of the* Oxford Book of Light Verse *(1938) and collaborated with friend Christopher Isherwood on* Journey to War *and the plays* The Dog Beneath The Skin *(1935) and* The Ascent of F6 *(1936). From 1956 until 1961, Auden was the professor of poetry at Oxford. He was awarded the National Medal for Literature in 1967.*

A nondescript express from the South,
Crowds round the ticket barrier, a face
To welcome which the mayor has not contrived
Bugles or braid: something about the mouth
Distracts the stray look with alarm and pity.
Snow is falling. Clutching a little case,
He walks out briskly to infect a city
Whose terrible future may just have arrived.

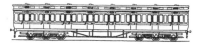

FROM *L'AMERIQUE AU JOUR LE JOUR*

Simone de Beauvoir (1908–1986)

Along with colleague and lover Jean Paul Sarte, Simone de Beauvoir was considered one of the leading exponents of existentialism. She taught philosophy until dedicating herself to writing in 1943. In 1949, she published the celebrated Le Deuxieme Sexe (The Second Sex), *on the oppressed state of women in western society, which became a battle cry for the feminist movement during the second half of the twentieth century. Popular in Europe and the United States,* La Vieillesse *(1970; known as* The Coming of Age*) examines how various cultures treat their elderly. Her novels include* All Men are Mortal *(1946) and* The Blood of Others *(1946). The following excerpts come from journal entries documenting her 1947 lecture tour of American colleges published in* L'Amerique au jour le jour (America Day by Day).

The newspapers cover a press conference held by George Marshall, in which he declares that he's opposed to any kind of disarmament. Furthermore, today is the start of the trial of Eisler, the number one communist leader, accused of conspiracy against the government, contempt of Congress, tax fraud, and passport falsification. Willingness to go to war is asserted; the persecution of the Reds goes on.

This evening I must give a lecture at Vassar College. For the first time I enter Grand Central Station, that huge building whose tower dominates Park Avenue. It reminds me of the lower floor of Rockefeller Center: restaurants, cafés, lunchroom; drugstore; telephone; bookstores; vendors selling flowers, cigars, and candy; hair salons; shoe-shine stands. Stairways everywhere. There are waiting rooms, a hall where they sell tickets, black porters with red caps. But nothing suggests the presence of the trains hidden underground.

It's the first time I'm taking a train. I stand for a moment in front of a door that opens ten minutes before departure: a corridor descends to the lower floor. I enter a coach. The train car doesn't look like any French train car but rather like the inside of an automobile. The air is, of course, overheated. In the central corridor, vendors of magazines, ice cream, Coca-Cola, candy, and sandwiches pass up and down. Café au lait is also served in cardboard cups. The train plunges into an underground tunnel; it emerges between New York's apartment houses at third-floor level. It follows Park Avenue, whose splendor has faded and which is now just a wretched boulevard crossing the Puerto Rican section. Then it crosses the Bronx. To my left, I glimpse the Cloisters perched on its hill. Now the train follows the Hudson. Today I can hardly believe that New York has the same latitude as Naples. The Hudson is frozen; the snow swirls in a thousand patterns on the ice. The cold has not discouraged the pigeons; they gather on the frozen surface. On the other side of this vast skating rink, the empty hills surprise me— so close to one of the world's capitals, and so forsaken.

Poughkeepsie is the first small American town I've seen. Under the snow, with its wooden houses and its cheerful streets, it reminds me of a winter sports resort. The houses scattered along the sides of the white roads have the artificial look of chalets in Mégève. How peaceful to leave New York! The car stops in front of a sumptuous villa; this is my hosts' house. Hall, living rooms, library, dining room, spacious rooms in a sort of medieval style that at once evokes a "deluxe" inn and a monastery. My room is as white and peaceful as the snowy countryside. It invites illness; you might wish for a slight fever so that you could really enjoy the silence and the freshness of the walls and curtains. About a hundred meters from here, a turreted gate opens onto the campus, which is a large plot of virgin country with hills and woods. Between the medieval-style buildings, which are dormitories, libraries, and laboratories, I meet college girls in ski clothes carrying skis on their shoulders. They go hesitantly down a little slope that wouldn't faze a French beginner. I'm taken to visit the gymnasium; there's a dance class going on. In blue shorts with bare legs, the students balance on their tiptoes. In the blue water of the swimming pool others swim rhythmically under the eye of a teacher who knits as she watches them. In the library they seem so comfortable and free: they read, curled up in deep armchairs or sitting cross-legged on the floor, scattered through little rooms by themselves or gathered together in large halls. Through the bay windows, you can see the trees, the snow. How I envy them. But I must have tea with the French teachers of the college, then dinner with them at my hosts' house. It's the sort of carefully prepared meal you'd eat at a well-kept family pension—no cocktails or wine. Two male professors are invited, but the atmosphere is clearly feminine; there's something soft and quaint about it. I discover here the same spirit of caution as in our lycée classrooms, but it has been aggravated among these exiled French people by their concern for their country's reputation; a critical remark about the teaching of philosophy at the Sorbonne is enough to make them raise their eyebrows.

February 25

When I awoke yesterday morning, it was in an endless desert of pink stones. I spent the whole day in the bar with magnificent bay windows that allowed the desert to invade the train. In Albuquerque, the afternoon sun was burning-hot. On the platform, Indians with braids were selling rungs and little multicolored moccasins. In the garden of the beautiful Mexican-style hotel, tourists sitting in rocking chairs watched the train travelers, who watched them back. I knew I would return at leisure to these regions in a few weeks, so I felt no regret as I saw the great plateaus of flaming color and the Indian shacks disappear. It was still desert while I slept. But at dawn, when I pull back the curtain, the scenery has changed. A gray fog fills the damp prairies and the trees; in the distance the hills are a blur against a muggy sky. This is how I've entered California. The name is almost as magical as "New York." It's the land of streets paved with gold, of pioneers and cowboys. Through history and movies it's become a legendary country that, like all legends, belongs to my own past.

I'm burning with impatience. This time I'm not arriving as a tourist in a land where nothing is meant for me; I'm coming to see a woman friend who happens to be living in a land everyone says is marvelous. It's perhaps even stranger to feel expected in an unknown place than to prepare yourself to disembark without help. I don't know what awaits me, but someone knows. The sea, orange juice, mountains, flowers, whiskeys—I'm not going to encounter them and try to possess them; they will be given to me. Someone is waiting for the right moment to present them to me as a gift. They already are a gift; and in my heart I feel the anxiety and greed of childhood Christmas Eves.

The fog lifts a little. I see long, shady avenues of palm trees and quiet houses surrounded by fresh lawns. The train stops at a little suburban station—Pasadena. For another half hour, we roll through the outlying suburbs cut out of the shapeless countryside, and the train goes underground. Los Angeles. A black employee unfolds three folding steps, which connect the train car to the ground. I am on the deserted platform, then in a corridor, and finally in the hall where N. [Nathalie ("Natasha") Sorokine Moffatt, a close friend] is waiting for me.

Translated by Carol Cosman, 1999

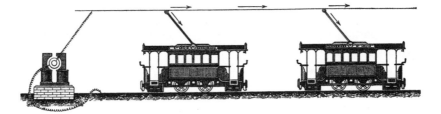

FROM *IN SEARCH OF SOUTH AFRICA*

H. V. Morton (1892–1979)

Renowned for a series of "In Search of" travel books, such as In Search of Ireland *(1930) and* In Search of London *(1951), Henry Canova Vollam Morton was considered an expert on the British Isles. He was a prolific author, sometimes writing two books a year, and served as a journalist for various newspapers, positions that took him to the Middle East, Spain and South America. Morton also wrote several books on biblical places and people, including* In the Steps of St. Paul *(1936),* Women of the Bible *(1940),* In the Steps of Jesus *(1953) and* In Search of the Holy Land *(1979).*

It was a train of great splendour and finer than any train at present running in Europe, and as fine as the best the United States can boast. It was a train of blue sleeping-coaches and restaurant cars, each coach, even each compartment, air-conditioned, as I discovered when I found it possible to raise or lower the temperature by moving a little chromium switch above the bed.

South African railways, airways, harbours, and all forms of public transport are owned by the State. The guards, restaurant-car attendants, and the coloured men who make up the beds at night, are a good advertisement for the Union, for they are the most polite public servants you will find in a day's march. The railways are unusual, because their rolling-stock of normal size does not run upon the European gauge of four feet, eight and a half inches, but on a narrower gauge of three feet, six inches. This gauge has been dictated by the enormous distances to be covered and by the mountainous character of the Cape and Natal, and the example has been followed by most of the railways in Africa.

I went along to the observation car after lunch. We were now running through a country of clear-cut distances, broken by low ridges and detached koppies, or hills. Cattle grazed and horses cropped the thin grass that grew on the parched soil. The red roads ran for miles beside the track and then struck off across country to the sky.

Certain little things, not necessarily the most important things or the most characteristic, fix themselves in the mind of a traveller in his first moments of exploration and remain there for ever. I knew I should always remember the Free State when I saw the queer, undulating flight of the widow bird. Out of the mealie-fields, or maize as we call it, these small finches rose into the sunlight, carrying the absurd black streamer of a tail which the male birds grow in the mating season; hampered by this impediment, they would undulate and flutter until they seemed hardly air-borne, and would sink, it would seem gratefully, to earth a few yards away. An agile boy, I thought, would surely be able to catch these gay, preposterous little birds in his hands while they were on the wing.

Then I saw a sight which, of all the things to be encountered upon a road, is essentially South African: I saw red oxen yoked two by two, drawing a wagon, and in front walked a small half-naked black boy, while a native in a blanket who might have been his father walked beside the wagon and seemed to be singing or shouting to the oxen as he walked. The train sped on. There was a horseman on the road. Far away a farmer's car was speeding like a comet, drawing a tail of red dust across the landscape.

We came to a line of blue gum trees and a station. In the shade of the trees were American cars, Cape carts, and wagons. Upon the platform was a crowd of white South Africans and black South Africans. They were on the same platform, but on different parts of it. The natives had collected at the far end, near the locomotive, where they knew the "natives only" coaches would be; the Europeans were together elsewhere. There were station benches and lavatories labelled for black or white, and thus I learnt again the first lesson of South Africa: that there is a white South Africa and a black South Africa.

Another interesting feature of this railway station, and of all stations in the Union, was its interest in altitude, for beside the name of the station was printed its height above the distant ocean. I saw that we were four thousand feet above sea level.

Away we went into the sunlight and the wide spaces of the veld, and I looked at this country and knew that its attraction is twofold: its colour, which is the red of the roads, the green and gold of the grass, and the blue of the distance, and its resemblance to the sea; for the eye is constantly roving to the horizon as it does at sea, searching and probing into the distance and finding there refreshment, peace, and freedom. So we ran south on our long way to Cape Town, into the heart of a burning afternoon.

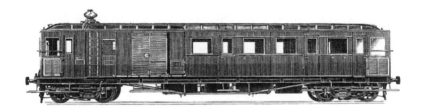

WATCHING THE TRAINS GO BY

from *The Fascination of Railways*

Roger Lloyd (1901–1966)

Roger Lloyd is a British writer and the author of Railwayman's Gallery.

The curious but intense pleasure that is given to many people by the watching and the study of railway trains, their engines, and the detail of their organization is both an art and a mystery. It is an art because the pleasure to be had is exactly proportionate to the informed enthusiasm one puts into it. It is a mystery because, try as one will, it is impossible to explain to others exactly in what the pleasure consists. The connection between the sight of a railway engine and the quite deep feeling of satisfaction is very real for multitudes of people but it eludes rational analysis. You can perhaps say what it is about railways you enjoy most: but if somebody asks you why you should get any pleasure at all from what is no more than a handy method of conveying your person and your goods from one place to another, you can say, "Just because it is so," and then you have nothing further to add to that bald and very unconvincing remark. The pleasure of railway watching cannot be explained, but it can perhaps be communicated, and it can certainly be shared.

Generally "this strange madness," as somebody centuries ago accused Petrarch of possessing because he liked to travel about Europe more than to stay at home, is caught young; and once caught it is rarely lost while life lasts. My own memory, peering backwards through the years and cleaving the mists of time, comes to its terminus in 1915 with a little boy of ten or eleven who was much given to haunting the railway station at Whitchurch. It was the Shropshire Whitchurch where our home was. Unlike all the half-dozen other Whitchurches in England, the Shropshire Whitchurch is a place of considerable railway importance. It lies on the main line from North West to South West, between Crewe and Shrewsbury. From it the old Cambrian Railway,

later of course part of the Great Western, takes its beginning, curves away to the right, and goes meandering sedately along its single track through the Welsh valleys. There is also a branch line from Whitchurch to Chester with a very few trains each way a day, all of which travel rather after the manner of an elderly tortoise. In those days they were mostly hauled by the old North Western 0-6-0 "Cauliflowers", which panted furiously all the way and at night treated the beholder to grand firework displays.

Whitchurch station was incredibly ugly. But it was a good place for small boys all the same. It had two admirable features. The main line from Manchester and Liverpool to Shrewsbury and Hereford was very busy, and it was dead straight for a long way both north and south of the station. Trains which did not stop there did not hesitate either. They moved. Sixty miles an hour was slow dawdling for them. The other feature was an iron footbridge north of the station. It had lattice work sides, so that a small boy could look through the holes and down at the track underneath. To this bridge I regularly made my pilgrimage. That is to say I made it as regularly as I could contrive. But those were the days of the governess-cum-nurse era of social history. A child did not go for walks by himself. He was taken for walks; and there is a vast difference. My mother, who loathed everything to do with trains, rationed me. She would put up with the bridge once a week and for half an hour at a time; but the governess, though hating it just as thoroughly, was more pliable. She could be edged skilfully in the required direction on many of the occasions when we had really set out to walk in quite another.

Once on top of that bridge a rather murky but for me a most real heaven lay all about. If no trains were coming through there was the shunting in the Yard to watch. But trains were very frequent and they generally came very fast indeed, rushing at the bridge with a great roar, and crashing under it with a roll of thunder. I would stick my head as far through the iron lattice work as it would go and try to look right down the chimney. I never could, of course, but for long after there was a highly satisfactory smell of sulphur, and flying smuts which descended on one's clothes, and the tail lamp vanishing fast into the distance. To that bridge also I owe the fact that I discovered the right way to look at a freight train. It must be viewed from above the track, for then you can see what all the open wagons contain, and lose yourself in a maze of pleasant speculation about the extraordinary variety of goods which one freight train takes, and make guesses about where a particular wagon has come from and where it is bound.

Those of course were the days of the old "North Western", the L. N. W. R. The trains were of mixed coaching stock, half of them the purple-brown and white of the North Western, and half the brownish red (as I think it was in those days) of the great Western. The engines were mostly 4-4-0's, "Precursors" and "George V's", with the former heavily predominating. They seem very small now, and when the trains had more than a dozen coaches they often had to be double-headed; but small or not they could undoubtedly move. To be on the bridge as they fled beneath it was to savour in full measure the thrill of that speed. The one disadvantage was that there was no chance to read the engine's name as she flew under one's feet, nor yet the number of the engine shed to which it belonged, for that, painted on a white enamel circular tag, was then screwed to the lintel of the cab room and could be seen only from behind. Most of

the engines which took the expresses through Whitchurch belonged to Crewe or Manchester, while the slow trains were mostly drawn by Shrewsbury engines. But occasionally you got one from the Camden shed. There was moreover a special treat to be had sometimes, for the authorities at Crewe were fond of using the line to Shrewsbury to put new engines through their paces, so that if you were very lucky indeed you might get a sight of the prototype of a new class of engine—the very first "Claughton" perhaps—before anybody even at Euston had seen her. To learn these details you had to be on the station itself, and escorts were only forthcoming with difficulty. But from time to time somebody would feel kind and take me there; and sometimes there were guests to be met or seen off, and it could usually be arranged that these visits lasted longer than the strict requirements of the matter in hand.

It is now thirty-five years since I stood on Whitchurch station and I have never been there since. Yet I am surprised at how much I remember about it, and how much detail the slightest twitch of the cord of memory recalls. There was room in the station for three trains to stand at a time, for one of the two platforms was an island. A short spur led away from this platform to the tiny engine shed. It was not more than fifty yards away and it opened towards the platform, though you could never see more than a yard inside for there murk and darkness reigned. They kept not more than two or three engines there, an old North Western "Jumbo" perhaps and a couple of small tank engines, all with built-up chimneys. But there was always just the one engine of great resplendence. This was the Cambrian Railway's pride and joy, a new and gleaming 4-4-0. This particular engine used to take out the train for Machynlleth Junction which left somewhere about 4.30 in the afternoon. On the other side of the station was a short bay. The local to Chester always left from there—generally three elderly and grimy six-wheel coaches with an exceedingly decrepit "Cauliflower" at its head.

Whitchurch was a North Western station. The great Western did not take over till Shrewsbury, and the Cambrian was allowed to use Whitchurch by courtesy rather than by right. This naturally did not much delight the Cambrian men, and their dependence and poor relation status was well rubbed into them. I had much sympathy for them then and still have. The Cambrian never had a high reputation for speed or punctuality, and most of its engines and rolling stock looked as if they had been bought cheap off the nearest scrap heap. However they did have their one crack engine and train, and this was the 4.30 from Witchurch, which I have already mentioned. Unfortunately for them it was timed to run in connection with a train from Manchester and Liverpool to Bristol which was due at Whitchurch at about 4.20. That train was not seldom late: sometimes it was three hours late. On these occasions the station authorities used to hold back the Cambrian, whereupon the driver used to protest vigorously in Welsh. No doubt the authorities deeply regretted the unfortunate necessity . . . and all the rest of the formula. But the trouble was that hey always looked as though they were really rather pleased, and they grinned broadly as they gave the message, "The 4.20's running 40 minutes late, so you'll have to wait". There were groans from the guard, floods of vehement Welsh from the driver, and broad grins from the North Western men. On the whole Whitchurch was no bad station for a child to be initiated into the fascination of train watching. It offered plenty of variety—the one real criterion of excellence in a station—and a good

deal of human interest. But it ws a bit hard on my mother and the governess.

Still, I was all the time finding something worth much fine gold—a lifelong source of delight and fascination—and perhaps my mother realized that. If she did, I know very well she would have counted herself amply repaid for any boredom I made her suffer. A hobby which lasts as long as life does and odes not stale as years pass, and which can be pursued at any time and with negligible cost is at the least a subsidiary secret of joy. . . .

In Mr C. S. Lewis's brilliant book, *The Screwtape Letters*, the chief of the tempters, Screwtape, turns on his subordinate Wormwood, because Wormwood has allowed his human charge to be converted to Christianity at a deeper level than before and that at a time when Wormwood seemed to be doing rather well in his effort to edge him off the road that leads to God and into the road that leads to Hell. With diabolic prescience Screwtape puts his finger on what was the beginning of Wormwood's failure. He had actually allowed his charge to indulge a simple pleasure.

How can you have failed to see what a *real* pleasure was the last thing you ought to have let him meet? Didn't you foresee that it would kill by contrast all the trumpery which you have been so laboriously teaching him to value? . . . The man who truly and disinterestedly enjoys any one thing in the world, for its own sake, and without caring twopence what other people say about it, is by that very fact forearmed against some of our subtlest modes of attack.

The pleasure of watching trains comes under the definition. That it is of no particular use to anybody does not in the least matter. We are not all Utilitarians or Pragmatists. The point is that it is satisfying and innocent, and it is morally good in the sense that it healthily occupies the mind, and so becomes a subsidiary and indirect cause of that self-forgetfulness which is at the root of all virtue. So the mothers whom we have bored when children are not without their reward.

FROM *THE BIG BOXCAR*

Alfred Maund (1923–)

Alfred Maund has published numerous stories, edited union newsletters, held editorial posts on the New Orleans Times-Picayune *and the* Louisville Courier-Journal, *and participated in southern labor and civil rights movements. While* The Big Boxcar *(1957) was praised in the North for its honest portrayal of the South, it was reviled by much of the southern press for vilifying whites.*

The train was moving slow—just as Sam had seen it do when he was hitching Jess the mule on many a morning at plowing time. The dawn sun shone splashy red like a pullet egg, and the soil was brown-wet as a man could ask. But Sam wasn't looking at things from behind a mule's ass. He climbed aboard, just him and a bundle, saying goodbye to Lauderdale County, Mississippi. Heading North.

Sam made the sixth in the boxcar. And though he was a country man who never left his house of birth more than thirty miles any direction, he knew it bad for six black men to be coveyed close like this. One Negro boy a policeman finds can beg and crawl and get off with a kick and a cussing. But more, and white policemen reach for their guns, and Negroes together don't want to be the first to kneel. Death and bloodshed.

The others in the car knew it, too, Sam could tell by their eyes, but his was the only open car he could have caught on. They must have appreciated that, because they didn't speak; they sliced him a share of their slim chance without a word.

The car was too shadowed to make out people plain, but from a sneaky look-around Sam decided they weren't of a party. Each had made his own choice; each had his private trouble.

They rolled along in quiet an hour or more. Sam watched the land, from habit's sake, and saw it spread out like a picnic blanket, all colors and lumps. At one place somebody had eat his fill and left just toothpick pine and clay gulleys the color of spilled catsup. He'd eat his fill and gone. More than one had got his belly full and gone. Then one big pasture, miles long, green—green like good pea soup with cows floating around like salted crackers—*there* somebody was eating still. He played the food game a long time, comparing what he saw to a holiday meal, because he

wanted to give his leaving day a happy feel. What was more, all that outside was the same as that he'd left behind and he had to make it seem new so he could feel he was on his way.

A fine field, just dug up, came by, black and deep, like chocolate cake. Like a cake. Sam laughed at his own smartness, until smack beside the rails was a shanty made into a house out of an old cotton storehouse. It gave him a sore turn. He knew every crack in that red-sided two-roomer which had a ramp running down one side instead of a porch, and could guess within four-five how many rats there was; it was the spit-image of the home he'd left. Two little children stood on the ramp, waving their hands— little rag-tags pumping halloos at every car that passed. They smashed his picnic mood.

What are we but ants among the feast, we Negroes? We are the feasters' joke that makes their food taste better even while they fuss and tread us under foot. Just ants! Sam thought all this, and hot with the thought he leapt up and stuck his head out and waved back to the kids. He knew it a foolish thing to do, to risk an unfriendly eye. But he wanted to say "Look at me! Look at me!" to those kids and point the way a man must go when he's grown. He made a big wave, even if inside he couldn't tell whether he was leaving them behind or they were leaving him.

"Sit down, fool!" a big voice said. Sam sat, scrunched back in a corner of the car, all to himself. The floor was hard and damp. Spilled grain ate through his jeans like buckshot. Nothing happened for a while until the train made a turn that let more sun into the car, turning the shadow to mustard-gray.

Then, like a fat old hen getting off the nest, one of the people across from Sam stirred himself and stood up. He moved to the center of the car and started dusting himself, showing off his black-stripe suit.

Sam was impressed by the wooly white felt the man had on; except for some patches of grease stain it was razor-sharp. The man was baggy built, but he held his back stiff and his belly out, and his bottom lip and eyebrows drooped like they were weighing a bale of important plans. He scuffed around in a circle, rocking more than the train called for. He reminded Sam of a honky-tonk owner he had seen once, so to himself Sam named him Good-Rocking Poppa, for the fun of it.

"Who's got an old blanket?" Good-Rocking Poppa said suddenly, like a general calling for a horse. Nobody gave reply. He wrinkled his flat nose up and down and lit a cigar that wasn't more than half used. "Now look here, gentlemen," he said again. "I'm a gambling man of more than usual luck. It wasn't bad luck brought me here, it was good. They was watching all the Pullmans and buses." He gave them a minute to guess who *they* was. "I still got luck to burn, and I was wondering if any of you sports wanted to try put out the fire." He held out his hand, and sitting on the palm was a pair of dice. He flipped one up in the air and caught it, then hunched there waiting.

"I got a blanket and a mite of risking money," a real short fellow said, moving up like he was on hands and knees. He slung a gray blanket to the floor and started unknotting a handkerchief he pulled out of his blue jeans. Old Shorty looked more like a bull pup than a gambler; he didn't appear to have anything he could afford to risk, either. That handkerchief knot was real tight. Sam guessed he wanted to make some money bad, and he thought it a sorry thing for a country man to think he could make money that way.

Another fellow drifted up and waited while Good-Rocking Poppa, like a man uprooting thistle bushes, smoothed out the blanket with his feet. This new one was real drifty. His face turned three-four shades of light gray while Sam looked at him, and he didn't seem to have any eyes. If it hadn't been for his slick red shirt inside his city suit, Sam felt he might not have seen him at all. Between those two, Shorty was going to get chopped even shorter, for sure.

"Anybody else?" Poppa asked, all scorn. Nobody stirred. But when the three gambling men humped down to their knees to start their game, the rest of the passengers slid up on their haunches to watch better. They let Shorty have first shot with the dice. He was nervous, but was trying hard not to let his nerves show. "What with this train," he said, "this is sure a painless game. Just hold out your hand and that old locomotive will do your rolling for you. Except I don't want no boxcars, for sure."

"How much you betting?"

"Five and one-two-three. Eight cents. Start out small and win it all, a fellow told me. And he must have known what he said, because at Zac's Place— that's in Hattiesburg—he used to play by the hour, and he wasn't nothing but a turpentine-tapper like me, getting two dollars a day wages."

"Shoot, man, shoot."

Shorty shot. He didn't roll boxcars. He rolled snake-eyes. Poppa and the Spook sucked mocking wind through their teeth as they took away his coins, but Shorty didn't blink. "It's funny I had to come this far to meet these dice just when they was ready to do that," he mumbled, wondering-like. He peered at them in his hand like they were baby chicks he was trying to tell the sex of. "Think of all the times they been flung out. How come they couldn't have been flung just one more time before I got them? I bet a dime." He did better on the next roll—one point better. He made a three. The other two hissed even louder. "Don't take it too hard, son," Good-Rocking Poppa said. "All good hands start with craps." Shorty smiled like Poppa had really meant to wish him well, and he said, "These mules done run off with me so far that I don't know which would be the most trouble—to let 'em go and walk back, or try to get 'em to carry me home. Since I still got a hand on the reins, I guess I'll ride. Twenty cents."

He was green as grass, that Shorty. He put his pennies down on that blanket with sweetness and trust, like it was a church collection box. The amount he fished up left his handkerchief purse flat. Poppa drew in deep on his cigar and blew big-shot smoke. The Spook sat curled up on his spine like a snake. Shorty shoveled out the dice and spaded up the same one and two he had caught before. He kept his smile, but he wasn't able to talk. He dabbed at his nose with his empty handkerchief. Sam didn't like to see that kind of thing happen to a man.

"Or-or-or," old Poppa laughed. "Out of ammunition? Well, maybe we can talk some about bartering when the cash gets low all around. You," he asked the Spook, "you going to take up the hammer?" The Spook laid out a couple of dollar bills and the coins he had won from Shorty and took the dice. Poppa matched his money. Then the Spook half stood up and began to take a bath with the dice. He rubbed them under his arms, behind his neck, even between his legs before he twisted around and let them go with his back turned to them. He made a seven. It was good for Good-Rocking Poppa that the Spook made a seven, Sam said to himself. He didn't like for a country man to be cheated, and he hadn't believed until then that those dice could roll a seven. If it hadn't turned out to be so, Poppa would have given Shorty his money back. At an ordinary time this would have seemed none of Sam's business, but leaving home and being alone makes a man draw up in himself all ready to pop like a spring.

"Well, well, the licorice whip hit a lick," Poppa joshed. "How much you bet now?" "Let it ride," the Spook whispered. Poppa stopped smiling, but shoveled bills out quick enough. The Spook wound up and delivered another seven. He rippled with inside laughter then whispered lower than before: "I bet it all." Poppa puffed, and with a mean motion had to dig in his pocket for money to cover the bet. He slapped down greenbacks, one by one, like a man who's not going to put up with this for long.

The Spook did his stuff with the dice, even more fancy than before, but pooped out a nine. His face went the color of a catfish's belly, and as he tried to make the point everything went into slow, like a movie-picture stunt Sam saw one time of a man diving into a tank of water. "Come on, man, get with it or get off it." Good-Rocking Poppa pushed him, but he rushed not a jot. Twist, bend, quiver, push—but all he rolled was five, three, ten, six. Old percentage had him and he was sweating. He rolled, but this time, most astonishing, one of the dice tripped on his finger and flew out through the open boxcar door. Gone.

Poppa jumped up. "Aheh! Aheh!" he blew through his nose. The Spook made for to take his money back, but Poppa stomped at his hand. "It slipped. But I didn't lose," the Spook squeaked. "I want my money. I didn't lose."

"It slipped, hah? Well, go fetch that dice! Go fetch it! I'll guard the money till you come back. Hah, yes, I'll keep while you fetch. Fetch!" Poppa pounced and caught the collar of the spook's nice red shirt. He pulled him down flat on his back and was dragging him for the door, however much the Spook twisted and grabbed.

He had him to the edge when a fellow in dungarees jumped up and said, "Stop that foolishment. I don't want to go to jail for none of your penny-nickel monkeyshines." This man didn't say it loud, but the scuffle stopped because it wasn't a man, but a woman in dungarees. What with the nighttime darkness, nobody had noticed before. She was pretty; hard but pretty. Her face was little darker than a peach, her hair lay flat and shiny black, with bangs across her forehead. She didn't yield to any man, Sam knew, the way her lean cheekbones and jaw stuck out to make an anvil for her slant eyes to flash on. And now he knew she was a woman, the points of her body stuck out against the blue rough clothes real ripe and ready. Everyone gazed like bird dogs around a bitch in springtime. The Spook slipped loose but didn't move far; he just sat and watched, too.

Poppa caught his wits the quickest. "Why sure, ma'am," he said smooth. "I guess this man accidental threw away that dice, after all. Take your money back," he purred to the Spook. "Just what you put up *at first*, that is. And leave down a dollar to pay me for that lost dice."

Sam didn't like Poppa's tipping his big white hat and hitching at his pants high and mighty. "If there is money being given back," he said, "then he should get his back, too." Sam pointed to Shorty, and Shorty looked up with Christmas eyes. Poppa popped air through his lips. He disliked this pushing in when he was trying to make up to the Woman, but he couldn't tell right off how tough Sam was.

The Woman looked at Sam, too, and he felt fire start inside. But he didn't think she could like him; he turned his thoughts to getting set for a fight for his fellow country man's interests. Then the Woman said, "I think the little guy ought to have his dough," and Poppa had to give in. He made it clear it was a favor to her and used it as excuse to pass his hand across her back. Sam wanted to hit him, then thought that would be foolish and watched instead while Shorty

put his nickels and pennies back in his handkerchief.

But Poppa's hot pants wouldn't allow peace to last. He scraped about, spreading his coat on the floor to make a seat for the Woman. She smiled and sat. He strutted in front of her, and with a hocus-pocus motion started rolling up one of his pants legs slow. Sam couldn't help staring, nor could the rest. He had a big black whiskey bottle stuck against his leg with adhesive tape. He snickered and pointed for her to undo it. She took one strip and pried it loose from his fat flesh real easy until she got near the end and then she popped it off with a snap. "Damn!" Poppa yelled and flapped up and down. The other passengers laughed and jeered. He started to cloud, but the Woman smiled up at him and said sweet, "It was stuck." He let her work at the other strip and just bit hard on his cigar when she popped him again.

When he sat close beside her and uncorked the bottle, it was too much for any man to stand. The raw teasing smell of that booze pulled Sam's nose until his stomach stretched and shivered. And when he looked to the bottle he saw Good-Rocking Poppa slobbering to lay hands on the Woman.

A fellow who had stayed quiet in the back until then jumped up and started a speech. He couldn't stand it any longer, either, Sam could see, and even before Sam measured him, if he had said "Let's throw that fat bastard off the train," Sam would have helped him do it. But he was a very young man, a pious man with some schooling, his words showed. This Teacher-Man said, "It is not right we should divide up like this. We are all going the same direction and sharing the same danger. Let's amuse each other with stories and fellowship. With a friendly drink or two, we could make a good party." This was mighty weak argument. Teacher-Man, tall and skinny, with two kinky shingles of hair balanced on his head, looked foolish in his prayer-meeting clothes, smiling a big horse-tooth smile.

The other men all nodded and backed him up, though, hoping against hope old Poppa would take the bait. He did not. "I appreciate your sentiments," he said syrup-smooth, "but I ain't got but this small fifth not even full. It wouldn't even start a party, and if I passed it around nobody would have sup enough to do them good. Besides, I'm faced with a situation that calls for stimulants." He clamped a hand on the Woman's thigh to show off what he meant by his last remark. Sam studied her to see what she might be thinking of this, but she had had some mileage, her, and the little lines that give away thoughts had rubbed off some time since.

"You all want to have a party?" Shorty spoke up. He could have been pushed off the train himself for being so stupid if he had not toddled over to a cardboard box that held his goods and come back with a gallon fruit jar that sparkled with the prettiest brown moonshine Sam ever saw. He set it down like a birthday cake, saying, "My uncle gave me this for to offer any policeman who might catch me." Shorty sure surprised Sam. He was going to sit there with his jailhouse insurance tucked away and going thirsty, no matter how much Good-Rocking Poppa taunted; but when he finally understood that others were yearning bad, he offered his jar up. He was a country man, all right.

Everybody gathered, squatting to each side of Poppa and the Woman. Poppa held his bottle close to him and grumbled: "I bet that stuff strikes them blind." But he was shamed and his rooster wings

were trimmed. "We going to tell stories?" Shorty asked when he handed the jar to Teacher-Man to start off the drinking. Teacher-Man looked blank, but had the wit to take a swig before looking blank again. Nobody had meant to tell stories. That was only talk for pushing Poppa.

"Didn't they teach you in school, ladies first?" the Woman asked of Teacher-Man, making him jump and slosh the whiskey in rushing it to her. She took a man-sized swallow and a second; Sam knew she had asked for the fruit jar, instead of taking from Poppa's black bottle, in order to show where her sympathy was. But when she passed the jar to Sam, and he wasn't the next one to her, he didn't know what she meant. She said then, "Now how about some happy stories to kill the hours?"

"Why sure," Teacher-Man agreed. He scratched his head. "Why don't we each in turn tell all about ourselves?" That was a bad idea. Nobody wanted to meet head-on with their pasts; everybody was running from it. The party fell so quiet that the only sound was of the whiskey trickling down a man's throat and splashing on his bottom rib. They scrunched uncertain and uncomfortable, like ants on the land, until the Woman said, "I'd rather hear stories about white people. There's a lot of interesting things about white people." She giggled deep and mean. Before Sam could separate one white man he knew and not confuse him with the others, Good-Rocking Poppa had took over. "I got a lively story to tell," he said. And after he had fiddled with lighting his cigar he told his story.

THE OLD GREAT WESTERN

from *Great Western Steam*

W. A. Tuplin (1902–1975)

W. A. Tuplin was a British mechanical engineer and Professor of Applied Mechanics at the University of Sheffield, who wrote extensively about trains and train engineering. His works, such as British Steam Since 1900 *(1969),* Great Western Saints and Sinners *(1971),* Great Northern Steam *(1971), and* Great Western Power *(1975), explored the history of railroads in Britain.*

For the student or the lover of the locomotive, the Great Western [was] unique. At the end it had not the largest locomotives in Great Britain, nor the fastest trains, nor the British railway-speed record, but the locomotives associated with these distinctions all owed much to Swindon practice, which had been developed, not for the purpose of breaking records, but simply to meet anticipated operating needs with certainty and economy.

We who find fascination in examining the form and details of locomotives and their ability to do their work have had in Swindon a treasure indeed. We have seen a whole railway system laid on the broad 7 ft. gauge and upon in established a standard of railway speed that was barely equalled in the subsequent century. We have seen the gaunt shapelessness of many of the engines of that era replaced by pretty elegance in the time of Dean who nevertheless kept ahead of traffic needs. We have seen his beautiful single-wheelers moving swan-like with no visible means of propulsion on the level lines of Brunel's Great Way Round, the sturdy "Dukes" pounding with flashing cranks up the steep banks of the West Country and an endless variety of saddle-tanks working hard in every sphere.

We have seen the Swindon engine take on quite different forms devised by Churchward for power and speed, with hints from the New World and the Old. With tapered, domeless boiler, copper-capped chimney, thirty-inch stroke and gun-shot blast, they stood out from all else in Britain and gradually we came to find them everywhere on Great Western metals.

We have seen them fly through Reading with screaming whistle, purring chimney and nimbly whirling rods on to the great sweeping curves of the Thames Valley and so to Bristol or West Wales. We have seen the west-bound "Riviera" in full flight behind a ten-wheeler gleaming in green paint, copper and brass, held in to an easy "seventy" through the sylvan country of the Somerton cut-off. We have seen them battle swiftly across Sedgemoor despite Atlantic-born gales of wind and rain and at other times flit at ease along the sun-scorched front at Dawlish, gathering strength for the climb to Dainton.

On seaside branches in the west, we have ridden with scurrying "forty-fives" and we have heard the mighty blasts of "thirty-ones" in sulphurous murk beneath the Severn. The "Stars", "Castles" and "Kings" have taken us from Paddington to Volverhampton with a rollicking zest that Euston never knew, and lesser Sindon lights have completed our journeys to the northern corner of Great Western territory. Behind "Bulldogs" and "forty-threes" we have traversed the Vale of Edeyrnion and skirted the Mawddach estuary on the way to the Cambrian coast, while "Dean goods" and "forty-eights" have taken us along the valley of the romantic Wye. Everywhere we have heard the hard dry cough of the industrious "panniers" on branch-lines or dock-sides with passengers, coal or freight. They have toiled in dust and heat in London sidings, prowled on obscure byways in the Balck Country, and burrowed chimney deep into blizzard-swept snowdrifts high up on Arenig Fawr.

On nights when fog made even walking hazardous we have travelled at speed behind Great Western drivers confident of a siren-call and a brake-application on the approach to any caution signal. In the brilliance of high summer we have crossed from Brecon to Neath with the engine whistling to arouse sheep prone on the unfenced mountain track.

As a background to these railway experiences we noticed the spread of the Churchward standard classes, their multiplication in replacement of older types, the demonstrations of their quality on their own lines and others, and we came gradually to realize that in them the Stephenson locomotive had been brought to ultimate refinement. Commonsense compromise between theoretical ideals and practical possibilities had produced at Swindon a unique family of standard engines unsurpassed anywhere in fitness for purpose.

Shall we ever again see such distinction on rails? We fear; we doubt; we can scarcely hope.

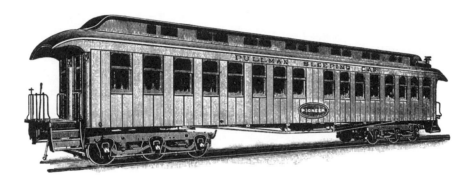

SPARTAN'S ODYSSEY

from *The New York Times Magazine*

Russell Baker (1925–)

Russell baker is best known for his columns in The New York Times, *some of which are collected in* An American in Washington *(1961) and* Poor Russell's Almanac *(1971). He is also the author of two memoirs—*Growing Up *(1982) and* The Good Times *(1989).*

That summer we took the boys out west by train. Easterners still said "out west" in those days when they meant Arizona, Utah, Colorado. I suppose nobody says it now, except old-timers too set in their ways to change. Nowadays, when every place is the same place, old-timers who remember when America was many different places are probably the only people who find remote territory remarkable enough to be spoken of with the awe implicit in "out west."

Anyhow, out west is where we headed by train. Even then, you could fly there in the time it takes to drink a couple of soda pops and eat a bad meal, but the point of the trip was the train.

It was obvious that it would soon be impossible to cross the country by train, and it seemed important for the children to experience that trip, because they were going to be around well into the 21st century, and it would be good for the country to have a few old galoots—as they would then be—who could remember what America felt like when it was a vast continental land mass. So we took a Pullman from Washington to Chicago. Two air-conditioned bedrooms with the dividing partition removed was luxury, compared to the Conestoga wagons in which the real old-timers made the trip in the genuine, authentic old days, as I must have told the boys somewhere near Harpers Ferry, since by that time I would have taken two martinis, thereby reaching the state where I have always enjoyed telling the young what soft lives they lead.

In those days the boys still listened respectfully to lectures deploring the decline of the Spartan spirit in America, for they were still in short pants and could be easily sent to bed for interrupting with sarcastic questions about whether Conestoga wagons carried ice cubes and martini pitchers.

In those days—ah, what a long time ago—marti-nis were still drunk by fancy people, a lot of whom also still smoked cigarettes. I could tell that transcontinental train travel couldn't last much longer, but I did not foresee the martini's decline or its astonishing replacement by cheap jug wine, which in those days was the mainstay of that hopeless class of rummies called "smokehounds."

After a night on the B. & O., we changed trains at Chicago. And there was time to take the boys outside to let them feel their feet sink into the gummy asphalt, because the streets were melting in that awful Chicago August heat. And to tell them Jan Morris's story of the stranger arriving in the city, asking what kind of place it was, and being told "Mister, Chicago ain't no sissy town."

And to tell them about the Saint Valentine's Day massacre, which gave me a chance to lecture on how soft modern American gangsters had become. In the evening, we rolled out across the prairie and felt ourselves engulfed by the continental immensities.

The dining car was all gleaming white linen, heavy silverware, ice tinkling in the glasses, real food odors coming from the kitchen, and afterward we sat in the darkened dome car and watched the lightning from distant storms bombard the flat black earth, just as it does in movies about bad weather on distant planets.

And of course, we actually were on a distant planet: this strange, by us mostly unexplored planet Earth, in the area called America, on a vast prairie hardly less alien to us than the surface of Jupiter, in a time that would have been inconceivable to the old-timers with their wagons, horses, slow-poke oxen.

I let up on the boys about all this. Didn't tell them about the Mormons pulling those heavy carts behind them all the way from the Mississippi to the Great Salt Lake, or about grasshopper plagues, the cattle turned to ice by the blizzards, the leather hinges on sod shanties—O Pioneers! Children can get America into their bones if you move them across it not too fast and let them see and feel for themselves. You don't have to pound this kind of thing into a child; you have to let it take him by surprise.

Then the mountains. My god, the mountains! The beauty of them! Out on the horizon they are a vision of grandeur that, like the 50 billion stars over the Grand Canyon on a clear moonless night, makes a human, perhaps even a very young human, realize how infinitesimally inconsequential a human must be.

I like to think that a child who has seen those stars and those mountains will ever after, surely without ever understanding why, understand that it is important to strive but absurd to strut.

After three days we left the train, in Albuquerque. Three days is a fast trip across America, except when compared to what the jets do, and what the jets do is wipe America out of your consciousness, out of your bones, marrow and blood.

In Albuquerque we rented a car and set out across the desert, and I made the boys listen to the Apache Lutheran Hour on the radio. That was 20 years ago, just a few weeks before every place became the same place.

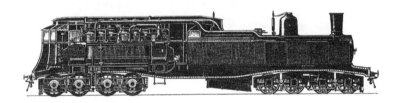

IN THE MIDDLE OF THE JOURNEY

from *The Overcrowded Barracoon*

V. S. Naipaul (1932–)

The writer V. S. Naipaul was born in Trinidad to Indian immigrants and educated at Oxford in England. His books ae often peopled with characters that frequently exemplify a rootlessness that parallels his own. His work ranges from travel writing, such as The Middle Passage *(1962), to novels, such as* A House for Mr. Biswas *(1961), to autobiographical writings, including* The Enigma of Arrival *(1987) and* A Way in the World *(1994).*

Coming from a small island—Trinidad is no bigger than Goa—I had always been fascinated by size. To see the wide river, the high mountains, to take the twenty-four-hour train journey: these were some of the delights the outside world offered. But now after six months in India my fascination with big is tinged with disquiet. For here is a vastness beyond imagination, a sky so wide and deep that sunsets cannot be taken in at a glance but have to be studied section by section, a landscape made monotonous by its size and frightening by its very simplicity and its special quality of exhaustion: poor choked crops in small crooked fields, undersized people, undernourished animals, crumbling villages and towns which, even while they develop, have an air of decay. Dawn comes, night falls; railway stations undistinguishable one from the other, their name-boards cunningly concealed, are arrived at and departed from, abrupt and puzzling interludes of populousness and noise; and still the journey goes on, until the vastness, ceasing to have a meaning, becomes insupportable, and from this endless repetition of exhaustion and decay one wishes to escape.

To state this is to state the obvious. But in India the obvious is, overwhelming, and often during these past six months I have known moments of near-hysteria, when I have wished to forget India, when I have escaped to the first-class waiting room or sleeper not so much for privacy and comfort as for protection, to shut out the sight of the thin bodies prostrate on railway platforms, the starved dogs licking the food-leaves clean, and to shut out the whine of the playfully assaulted dog. Such a moment I knew in Bombay, on the day of my arrival, when I felt India only as an assault on the senses. Such a moment I knew five months later, at Jammu, where the simple, frightening geography of the country becomes plain—to the north the hills, rising in range after ascending range; to the south, beyond the temple spires, the plains whose vastness, already experienced, excited only unease.

Yet between these recurring moments there have been so many others, when fear and impatience have been replaced by enthusiasm and delight, when the town, explored beyond what one sees from the train, reveals that the air of exhaustion is only apparent, that in India, more than in any other country I have visited, things are happening. To hear the sounds of hammer on metal in a small Punjab town, to visit a chemical plant in Hyderabad where much of the equipment is Indian-designed and manufactured, is to realize that one is in the middle of an industrial revolution, in which, perhaps because of faulty publicity, one had never really seriously believed. To see the new housing colonies in towns all over India is to realize that, separate from the talk of India's ancient culture (which invariably has me reaching for my lathi), the Indian aesthetic sense has revived and is now capable of creating, out of materials which are international, something which is essentially Indian. (India's ancient culture, defiantly paraded, has made the Ashoka Hotel one of New Delhi's most ridiculous buildings, outmatched in absurdity only by the Pakistan High Commission, which defiantly asserts the Faith.)

I have been to unpublicized villages, semi-developed and undeveloped. And where before I would have sensed only despair, now I feel that the despair lies more with the observer than the people. I have learned to see beyond the dirt and the recumbent figures on string beds, and to look for the signs of improvement and hope, however faint: the brick-topped road, covered though it might be with filth; the rice planted in rows and not scattered broadcast; the degree of ease with which the villager faces the official or the visitor. For such small things I have learned to look: over the months my eye has been adjusted.

Yet always the obvious is overwhelming. One is a traveller and as soon as the dread of a particular district has been lessened by familiarity, it is time to move on again, through vast tracts which will never become familiar, which will sadden; and the urge to escape will return.

Yet in so many ways the size of the country is only a physical fact. For, perhaps because of the very size, Indians appear to feel the need to categorize minutely, delimit, to reduce to manageable proportions.

"Where do you come from?" It is the Indian question, and to people who think in terms of the village, the district, the province, the community, the caste, my answer that I am a Trinidadian is only puzzling.

"But you look Indian."

"Well, I am Indian. But we have been living for several generations in Trinidad."

"But you look Indian."

Three or four times a day the dialogue occurs, and now I often abandon explanation. "I am a Mexican, really."

"Ah." Great satisfaction. Pause. "What do you do?"

"I write"

"Journalism or books?"

"Books".

"Westerns, crime, romance? How many books do you write a year? How much do you make?"

So now I invent: "I am a teacher."

"What are your qualifications?"

"I am a BA."

"Only a BA? What do you teach?"

"Chemistry. And a little history."

"How interesting!" said the man on the Pathankot-Srinagar bus. "I am a teacher of chemistry too."

He was sitting across the aisle from me, and several hours remained of our journey.

In this vast land of India it is necessary to explain yourself, to define your function and status in the universe. It is very difficult.

If I thought in terms of race or community, this experience of India would surely have dispelled it. An Indian, I have never before been in streets where everyone is Indian, where I blend unremarkably into the crowd. This has been curiously deflating, for all my life I have expected some recognition of my difference; and it is only in India that I have recognized how necessary this stimulus is to me, how conditioned I have been by the multiracial society of Trinidad and then by my life as an outsider in England. To be a member of a minority community has always seemed to me attractive. To be one of four hundred and thirty-nine million Indians is terrifying.

A colonial, in the double sense of one who had grown up in a Crown colony and one who had been cut off from the metropolis, be it either England or India, I came to India expecting to find metropolitan attitudes. I had imagined that in some ways the largeness of the land would be reflected in the attitudes of the people. I have found, as I have said, the psychology of the cell and the hive. And I have been surprised by similarities. In India, as in tiny Trinidad, I have found the feeling that the metropolis is elsewhere, in Europe or America. Where I had expected largeness, rootedness and confidence, I have found all the colonial attitudes of self-distrust.

"I am craze phor phoreign," the wife of a too-successful contractor said. And this craze extended from foreign food to German sanitary fittings to a possible European wife for her son, who sought to establish his claim further by announcing at the lunch table, "Oh, by the way, did I tell you we spend three thousand rupees a month?"

"You are a tourist, you don't know," the chemistry teacher on the Srinagar bus said. "But this is a terrible country. Give me a chance and I leave it tomorrow."

For among a certain class of Indians, usually more prosperous than their fellows, there is a passionate urge to explain to the visitor that they must not be considered part of poor, dirty India, that their values and standards are higher, and they live perpetually outraged by the country which gives them their livelihood. For them the second-rate foreign product, either people or manufactures, is preferable to the Indian. They suggest that for them, as much as for the European "technician", India is only a country to be temporarily exploited. How strange to find, in free India, this attitude of the conqueror, this attitude of plundering—a frenzied attitude, as though the opportunity might at any moment be withdrawn—in those very people to whom the developing society has given so many opportunities.

This attitude of plundering is that of the immigrant colonial society. It has bred, as in Trinidad, the pathetic philistinism of the renonçant (an excellent French word that describes the native who renounces his own culture and strives towards the French). And in India this philistinism, a blending of the vulgarity of East and West—those sad dance floors, those sad "western" cabarets, those transistor radios tuned to Radio Ceylon, those Don Juans with letter jackets or check tweed jackets—is peculiarly frightening. A certain glamour attaches to this philistinism, as glamour attaches to those Indians who, after two or three years, in a foreign country, proclaim that they are neither of the East nor of the West.

The observer, it must be confessed, seldom sees the difficulty. The contractor's wife, so anxious to demonstrate her Westernness, regularly consulted her astrologer and made daily trips to the temple to ensure the continuance of her good fortune. The schoolteacher, who complained with feeling about the indiscipline and crudity of Indians, proceeded, as soon as we got to the bus station at Srinagar, to change his clothes in public.

The Trinidadian, whatever his race, is a genuine colonial. The Indian, whatever his claim, is rooted in India. But while the Trinidadian, a colonial, strives towards the metropolitan, the Indian of whom I have been speaking, metropolitan by virtue of the uniqueness of his country, its achievements in the past and its manifold achievements in the last decade or so, is striving towards the colonial.

Where one had expected pride, then, one finds the spirit of plunder. Where one had expected the metropolitan one finds the colonial. Where one had expected largeness one finds narrowness. Goa, scarcely liberated, is the subject of an unseemly inter-State squabble. Fifteen years after Independence the politician as national leader appears to have been replaced by the politician as village headman (a type I had thought peculiar to the colonial Indian community of Trinidad, for whom politics was a game where little more than PWD contracts was at stake).

To the village headman India is only a multiplicity of villages. So that the vision of India as a great country appears to be something imposed from without and the vastness of the country turns out to be oddly fraudulent.

Yet there remains a concept of India—as what? Something more than the urban middle class, the politicians, the industrialists, the separate villages. Neither this nor that, we are so often told, is the "real" India. And how well one begins to understand why this word is used! Perhaps India is only a word, a mystical idea that embraces all those vast plains and rivers through which the train moves, all those anonymous figures asleep on railway platforms and the footpaths of Bombay, all those poor fields and stunted animals, all this exhausted plundered land. Perhaps it is this, this vastness which no one can ever get to know: India as an ache, for which one has a great tenderness, but from which at length one always wishes to separate oneself.

THE KALKA MAIL FOR SIMLA

from *The Great Railway Bazaar: By Train through Asia*

Paul Theroux (1941–)

Paul Theroux published his first novel, Waldo *(1966), after a stint with the Peace Corps in Africa. In 1968, he took a teaching position in Singapore where he wrote and published three more novels. Among his most notable works are* The Great Railway Bazaar *(1975), which documents a four-month trip though Asia, and* The Mosquito Coast *(1982), which was nominated for an American Book Award and made into a film.*

In spite of my disheveled appearance, it was thought by some in Delhi to be beneath my dignity to stand in line for my ticket north to Simla, though perhaps this was a tactful way of suggesting that if I did stand in line I might be mistaken for an Untouchable and set alight (these Harijan combustions are reported daily in Indian newspapers). The American official who claimed his stomach was collapsing with dysentery introduced me to Mr. Nath, who said, "Don't sweat. We'll take care of every thing." I had heard that one before. Mr. Nath rang his deputy, Mr. Sheth, who told his secretary to ring a travel agent. At four o'clock there was no sign of the ticket. I saw Mr. Sheth. He offered me tea. I refused his tea and went to the travel agent. This was Mr. Sud. He had delegated the ticket-buying to one of his clerks. The clerk was summoned. He didn't have the ticket; he had sent a messenger, a low-caste Tamil whose role in life, it seemed, was to lengthen lines at ticket windows. An Indian story: and still no ticket. Mr. Nath and Mr. Sud accompanied me to the ticket office, and there we stood ("Are you sure you don't want a nice cup of tea?") watching this damned messenger, ten feet from the window, holding my application. Bustling Indians began cutting in front of him.

"Now you see," said Mr. Nath, "with your own eyes why things are so backwards over here. But don't worry. There are always seats for VIPs." He explained that compartments for VIPs and senior government officials were reserved on every train until two hours before departure time, in case someone of importance might wish to travel at the last minute. Apparently a waiting list was drawn up every day for each of India's 10,000 trains.

"Mr. Nath," I said, "I'm not a VIP."

"Don't be silly," he said. He puffed his pipe and moved his eyes from the messenger to me. I think he saw my point because his next words were, "Also we could try money."

"*Baksheesh*," I said. Mr. Nath made a face.

Mr. Sud said, "Why don't you fly?"

"Planes make me throw up."

"I think we've waited long enough," said Mr. Nath. "We'll see the man in charge and explain the situation. Let me do the talking."

We walked around the barrier to where the ticket manager sat, squinting irritably at a ledger. He did not look up. He said, "Yes, what is it?" Mr. Nath pointed his pipe stem at me and, with the pomposity Indians assume when they speak to each other in English, introduced me as a distinguished American writer who was getting a bad impression of Indian Railways.

"Wait a minute," I said.

"It is imperative that we do our utmost to ensure—"

"Tourist?" said the ticket manager.

I said yes.

He snapped his fingers. "Passport."

I handed it over. He wrote a new application and dismissed us. The application went back to the messenger, who had wormed his way to the window.

"It's a priority matter," said Mr. Nath crossly. "You are a tourist. You have come all this way, so you have priority. We want to give favorable impression. If I want to travel with my family—wife, small children, maybe my mother too—they say, 'Oh, no, there is a *tourist* here. Priority matter!'" He grinned without pleasure. "That is the situation. But you have your ticket—that's the important thing, isn't it?"

The elderly Indian in the compartment was sitting cross-legged on his berth reading a copy of *Filmfare*. Seeing me enter, he took off his glasses, smiled, then returned to his magazine. I went to a large wooden cupboard and smacked it with my hand, trying to open it. I wanted to hang up my jacket. I got my fingers into the louvered front and tugged. The Indian took off his glasses again, and this time he closed the magazine.

"Please," he said, "you will break the air conditioner."

"This is an air conditioner?" It was a tall box the height of the room, four feet wide, varnished, silent, and warm.

He nodded. "It has been modernized. This carriage is fifty years old."

"Nineteen twenty?"

"About that," he said. "The cooling system was very interesting then. Every compartment had its own unit. That is a unit. It worked very well."

"I didn't realize there were air conditioners in the twenties," I said.

"They used ice," he said. He explained that blocks of ice were slipped into lockers under the floor—it was done from the outside so that the passengers' sleep would not be disturbed. Fans in the cupboard I had tried to open blew air over the ice and into the compartment. Every three hours or so the ice was renewed. (I imagined an Englishman snoring in his berth while at the platform of some outlying station Indians with bright eyes pushed cakes of ice into the lockers.) But the system had been converted: a refrigerating device had been installed under the blowers. Just as he finished speaking there was a whirr from behind the louvers and a loud and prolonged whoosh!

"When did they stop using ice?"

"About four years ago," he said. He yawned. "You will excuse me if I go to bed?"

The train started up, and the wood paneling of this old sleeping car groaned and creaked; the floor shuddered, the metal marauder-proof windows clattered in their frames, and the *whooshing* from the tall

cupboard went on all night. The Kalka Mail was full of Bengalis, on their way to Simla for a festival, the Kali *puja*. Bengalis, whose complexion resembles that of the black goddess of destruction they worship, and who have the same sharp hook to their noses, have the misfortune to live at the opposite end of the country from the most favored Kali temple. Kali is usually depicted wearing a necklace of human skulls, sticking her maroon tongue out, and trampling a human corpse. But the Bengalis were smiling sweetly all along the train, with their baskets of food and neatly woven garlands of flowers.

I was asleep when the train reached Kalka at dawn, but the elderly Indian obligingly woke me up. He was dressed and seated at the drop-leaf table, having a cup of tea and reading the *Chandigarh Tribune*. He poured his tea into the cup, blew on it, poured half a cup into the saucer, blew on it, and then, making a pedestal of his fingers, drank the tea from the saucer, lapping it like a cat.

"You will want to read this," he said. "Your vice president has resigned."

He showed me the paper, and there was the glad news, sharing the front page with an item about a Mr. Dikshit. It seemed a happy combination, Dikshit and Agnew, though I am sure Mr. Dikshit's political life had been blameless. As for Agnew's, the Indian laughed derisively when I translated the amount he had extorted into rupees. Even the black-market rate turned him into a cut-price punk. The Indian was in stitches.

In Kalka two landscapes meet. There is nothing gradual in the change from plains to mountains: the Himalayas stand at the upper edge of the Indo-Gangetic plain; the rise is sudden and dramatic. The trains must conform to the severity of the change; two are required—one large roomy one for the ride to Kalka, and a small tough beast for the ascent to

Simla. Kalka itself is a well-organized station at the end of the broad-gauge line. Between the Himalayas and Kalka is the cool hill station of Simla on a bright balding ridge. I had my choice of trains for "the sixty-mile journey on the narrow gauge: the toy train or the rail car. The blue wooden carriages of the train were already packed with pilgrims—the Bengalis, nimble at boarding trains, had performed the Calcutta trick of diving headfirst through the train windows and had gotten the best seats. It was an urban skill, this somersault—a fire drill in reverse—and it left the more patient hill people a bit glassy-eyed. I decided to take the rail car. This was a white squarish machine, with the face of a Model T Ford and the body of an old bus. It was mounted low on the narrow-gauge tracks and had the look of a battered limousine. But considering that it was built in 1925 (so the driver assured me), it was in wonderful shape.

I found the conductor. He wore a stained white uniform and a brown peaked cap that did not fit him. He was sorry to hear I wanted to take the rail car. He ran his thumb down his clipboard to mystify me and said, "I am expecting another party."

There were only three people in the rail car. I felt he was angling for *baksheesh*. I said, "How many people can you fit in?"

"Twelve," he said.

"How many seats have been booked?"

He hid his clipboard and turned away. He said, "I am very sorry."

"You are very unhelpful."

"I am expecting another party."

"If they show up, you let me know," I said. "In the meantime, I'm putting my bag inside."

"It might get stolen," he said brightly.

"Nothing could please me more."

"Wanting breakfast, sahib?" said a little man with a push-broom.

I said yes, and within five minutes my breakfast was laid out on an unused ticket counter in the middle of the platform: tea, toast, jam, a cube of butter, and an omelette. The morning sunlight struck through the platform, warming me as I stood eating my breakfast. It was an unusual station for India: it was not crowded, there were no sleepers, no encampment of naked squatters, no cows. It was filled that early hour with the smell of damp grass and wildflowers. I buttered a thick slice of toast and ate it, but I couldn't finish all the breakfast. I left two slices of toast, the jam, and half the omelette uneaten, and I walked over to the rail car. When I looked back, I saw two ragged children reaching up to the counter and stuffing the remainder of my breakfast into their mouths.

At seven-fifteen, the driver of the rail car inserted a long-handled crank into the engine and gave it a jerk. The engine shook and coughed and, still juddering and smoking, began to whine. Within minutes we were on the slope, looking down at the top of Kalka Station, where in the train yard two men were winching a huge steam locomotive around in a circle. The rail car's speed was a steady ten miles an hour, zigzagging in and out of the steeply pitched hill, reversing on switchbacks through the terraced gardens and the white flocks of butterflies. We passed through several tunnels before I noticed they were numbered; a large number 4 was painted over the entrance of the next one. The man seated beside me, who had told me he was a civil servant in Simla, said there were 103 tunnels altogether. I tried not to notice the numbers after that. Outside the car, there was a sheer drop, hundreds of feet down, for the railway, which was opened in 1904, is cut directly into the hillside, and the line above is notched like the skidway on a toboggan run, circling the hills.

After thirty minutes everyone in the rail car was asleep except the civil servant and me. At the little stations along the way, the postman in the rear seat awoke from his doze to throw a mailbag out the window to a waiting porter on the platform. I tried to take pictures, but the landscape eluded me: one vista shifted into another, lasting only seconds, a dizzying displacement of hill and air, of haze and all the morning shades of green. The meat-grinder cogs working against the rack under the rail car ticked like an aging clock and made me drowsy. I took out my inflatable pillow, blew it up, put it under my head, and slept peacefully in the sunshine until I was awakened by the thud of the rail car's brakes and the banging of doors.

"Ten minutes," said the driver.

We were just below a wooden structure, a doll's house, its window boxes overflowing with red blossoms, and moss trimming its wide eaves. This was Bangu Station. It had a wide complicated verandah on which a waiter stood with a menu under his arm. The rail-car passengers scrambled up the stairs. My Kalka breakfast had been premature; I smelled eggs and coffee and heard the Bengalis quarreling with the waiters in English.

I walked down the gravel paths to admire the well-tended flower beds and the carefully mown lengths of turf beside the track; below the station a rushing stream gurgled, and signs there, and near the flower beds, read NO PLUCKING. A waiter chased me down to the stream and called out, "We have juices! You like fresh mango juice? A little porridge? Coffee-tea?"

We resumed the ride, and the time passed quickly as I dozed again and woke to higher mountains, with fewer trees, stonier slopes, and huts perched more precariously. The haze had disappeared and the hillsides were bright, but the air was cool and a fresh breeze blew through the open windows of the rail car. In every tunnel the driver switched on orange lamps, and the racket of the clattering wheels increased and echoed. After Solon the only people in the rail car were a family of Bengali pilgrims (all of them sound asleep, snoring, their faces turned up), the civil servant, the postman, and me. The next stop was Solon Brewery, where the air was pungent with yeast and hops, and after that we passed through pine forests and cedar groves. On one stretch a baboon the size of a six-year-old crept off the tracks to let us go by. I remarked on the largeness of the creature.

The civil servant said, "There was once a *Saddhu*—a holy man—who lived near Simla. He could speak to monkeys. A certain Englishman had a garden, and all the time the monkeys were causing him trouble. Monkeys can be very destructive. The Englishman told this *saddhu* his problem. The *saddhu* said, 'I will see what I can do.' Then the *saddhu* went into the forest and assembled all the monkeys. He said, 'I hear you are troubling the Englishman. That is bad. You must stop; leave his garden alone. If I hear that you are causing damage I will treat you very harshly.' And from that time onwards the monkeys never went into the Englishman's garden."

"Do you believe that story?"

"Oh, yes. But the man is now dead—the *saddhu*. I don't know what happened to the Englishman. Perhaps he went away, like the rest of them."

A little farther on, he said, "What do you think of India?"

"It's a hard question," I said. I wanted to tell him about the children I had seen that morning pathetically raiding the leftovers of my breakfast, and ask him if he thought there was any truth in Mark Twain's comment on Indians: "It is a curious people. With them, all life seems to be sacred except human life." But I added instead, "I haven't been here very long."

"I will tell you what I think," he said. "If all the people who are talking about honesty, fair play, socialism, and so forth—if they began to practice it themselves, India will do well. Otherwise there will be a revolution."

He was an unsmiling man in his early fifties and had the stern features of a Brahmin. He neither drank nor smoked, and before he joined the civil service he had been a Sanskrit scholar in an Indian university. He got up at five every morning, had an apple, a glass of milk, and some almonds; he washed and said his prayers and after that took a long walk. Then he went to his office. To set an example for his junior officers he always walked to work, he furnished his office sparsely, and he did not require his bearer to wear a khaki uniform. He admitted that his example was unpersuasive. His junior officers had parking permits, sumptuous furnishings, and uniformed bearers.

"I ask them why all this money is spent for nothing. They tell me to make a good first impression is very important. I say to the blighters, 'What about *second* impression?'"

"Blighters" was a word that occurred often in his speech. Lord Clive was a blighter and so were most of the other viceroys. Blighters ask for bribes; blighters try to cheat the Accounts Department; blighters are living in luxury and talking about socialism. It was a point of honor with this civil servant that he had never in his life given or received *baksheesh*: "Not even a single paisa." Some of his clerks had, and in eighteen years in the civil service he had personally fired thirty-two people. He thought it might be a record. I asked him what they had done wrong.

"Gross incompetence," he said, "pinching money, hanky-panky. But I never fire anyone without first having a good talk with his parents. There was a blighter in the Audit Department, always pinching girls' bottoms. Indian girls from good families! I warned him about this, but he wouldn't stop. So I told him I wanted to see his parents. The blighter said his parents lived fifty miles away. I gave him money for their bus fare. They were poor, and they were quite worried about the blighter. I said to them, 'Now I want you to understand that your son is in deep trouble. He is causing annoyance to the lady members of this department. Please talk to him and make him understand that if this continues I will have no choice but to sack him.' Parents go away, blighter goes back to work, and ten days later he is at it again. I suspended him on the spot, then I charge-sheeted him."

I wondered whether any of these people had tried to take revenge on him.

"Yes, there was one. He got himself drunk one night and came to my house with a knife. 'Come outside and I will kill you!' That sort of thing. My wife was upset. But I was angry. I couldn't control myself. I dashed outside and fetched the blighter a blooming kick. He dropped his knife and began to cry. 'Don't call the police,' he said. 'I have a wife and children.' He was a complete coward, you see. I let him go and everyone criticized me—they said I should have brought charges. But I told them he'll never bother anyone again.

"And there was another time. I was working for Heavy Electricals, doing an audit for some cheaters in Bengal. Faulty construction, double entries, and estimates that were five times what they should have been. There was also immorality. One bloke—son of the contractor, very wealthy—kept four harlots. He gave them whisky and made them take their clothes off and run naked into a group of women and children doing *puja*. Disgraceful! Well, they didn't like me at all and the day I left there were four *dacoits* with knives waiting for me on the station road. But I expected that, so I took a different road, and the blighters never caught me. A month later two auditors were murdered by *dacoits*."

The rail car tottered around a cliffside, and on the opposite slope, across a deep valley, was Simla. Most of the town fits the ridge like a saddle made entirely of rusty roofs, but as we drew closer the fringes seemed to be sliding into the valley. Simla is unmistakable, for as *Murray's Handbook* indicates, "its skyline is incongruously dominated by a Gothic Church, a baronial castle and a Victorian country mansion." Above these brick piles is the sharply pointed peak of Jakhu (8000 feet); below are the clinging house fronts. The southerly aspect of Simla is so steep that flights of cement stairs take the place of roads. From the rail car it looked an attractive place, a town of rusting splendor with snowy mountains in the background.

"My office is in that castle," said the civil servant.

"Gorton Castle," I said, referring to my handbook. "Do you work for the Accountant General of the Punjab?"

"Well, I *am* the A. G.," he said. But he was giving information, not boasting. At Simla Station the porter strapped my suitcase to his back (he was a Kashmiri, up for the season). The civil servant introduced himself as Vishnu Bhardwaj and invited me for tea that afternoon.

The Mall was filled with Indian vacationers taking their morning stroll, warmly dressed children, women with cardigans over their saris, and men in tweed suits, clasping the green Simla guidebook in one hand and a cane in the other. The promenading has strict hours, nine to twelve in the morning and four to eight in the evening, determined by mealtimes and shop openings. These hours were fixed a

hundred years ago, when Simla was the summer capital of the Indian empire, and they have not varied. The architecture is similarly unchanged—it is all high Victorian, with the vulgarly grandiose touches colonial labor allowed, extravagant gutters and porticoes, buttressed by pillars and steelwork to prevent its slipping down the hill. The Gaiety Theatre (1887) is still the Gaiety Theatre (though when I was there it was the venue of a "Spiritual Exhibition" I was not privileged to see); pettifogging continues in Gorton Castle, as praying does in Christ Church (1857), the Anglican cathedral; the viceroy's lodge (Rastrapati Nivas), a baronial mansion, is now the Indian Institute of Advanced Studies, but the visiting scholars creep about with the diffidence of caretakers maintaining the sepulchral stateliness of the place. Scattered among these large Simla buildings are the bungalows—Holly Lodge, Romney Castle, The Bricks, Forest View, Sevenoaks, Fernside—but the inhabitants now are Indians, or rather that inheriting breed of Indian that insists on the guidebook, the walking stick, the cravat, tea at four, and an evening stroll to Scandal Point. It is the Empire with a dark complexion, an imperial outpost that the mimicking vacationers have preserved from change, though not the place of highly colored intrigues described in *Kim*, and certainly tamer than it was a century ago. After all, Lola Montez, the *grande horizontale*, began her whoring in Simla, and the only single women I saw were short red-cheeked Tibetan laborers in quilted coats, who walked along the Mall with heavy stones in slings on their backs.

I had tea with the Bhardwaj family. It was not the simple meal I had expected. There were eight or nine dishes: *pakora*, vegetables fried in batter; *poha*, a rice mixture with peas, coriander, and turmeric; *khira*, a creamy pudding of rice, milk, and sugar; a kind of fruit salad, with cucumber and lemon added to it, called *chaat*; *murak*, a Tamil savory, like large nutty pretzels; *tikkiya*, potato cakes; *malai* chops, sweet sugary balls topped with cream; and almond-scented *pinnis*. I ate what I could, and the next day I saw Mr. Bhardwaj's office in Gorton Castle. It was as sparely furnished as he had said on the rail car, and over his desk was this sign:

I am not interested in excuses for delay;
I am interested only in a thing done.
— Jawaharlal Nehru

The day I left I found an ashram on one of Simla's slopes. I had been interested in visiting an ashram ever since the hippies on the Teheran Express had told me what marvelous places they were. But I was disappointed. The ashram was a ramshackle bunga-low run by a talkative old man named Gupta, who claimed he had cured many people of advanced paralysis by running his hands over their legs. There were no hippies in this ashram, though Mr. Gupta was anxious to recruit me. I said I had a train to catch. He said that if I was a believer in yoga I wouldn't worry about catching trains. I said that was why I wasn't a believer in yoga.

Mr. Gupta said, "I will tell you a story. A yogi was approached by a certain man who said he wanted to be a student. Yogi said he was very busy and had no time for man. Man said he was desperate. Yogi did not believe him. Man said he would commit suicide by jumping from roof if yogi would not take him on. Yogi said nothing. Man jumped."

" 'Bring his body to me,' said yogi. Body was brought. Yogi passed his hands over body and after few minutes man regained his life."

" 'Now you are ready to be my student,' said yogi. 'I believe you can act on proper impulses and you have shown me great sincerity.' So man who had

been restored to the living became student."

"Have you ever brought anyone to life?" I asked.

"Not as yet," said Mr. Gupta.

Not as yet! His guru was Paramahansa Yogananda, whose sleek saintly face was displayed all over the bungalow. In Ranchi, Paramahansa Y. had a vision. This was his vision: a gathering of millions of Americans who needed his advice. He described them in his *Autobiography* as "a vast multitude, gazing at me intently" that "swept actorlike across the stage of consciousness . . . the Lord is calling me to America . . . Yes! I am going forth to discover America, like Columbus. He thought he had found India; surely there is a karmic link between these two lands!" He could see the people so clearly, he recognized their faces when he arrived in California a few years later. He stayed in Los Angeles for thirty years, and, unlike Columbus, died rich, happy, and fulfilled. Mr. Gupta told me this hilarious story in a tone of great reverence, and then he took me on a tour of the bungalow, drawing my attention to the many portraits of Jesus (painted to look like a yogi) he had tacked to the walls.

"Where do you live?" asked a small friendly ashramite, who was eating an apple. (Simla apples are delicious, but, because of a trade agreement, the whole crop goes to Poland.)

"South London at the moment."

"But it is so noisy and dirty there!"

I found this an astonishing observation from a man who said he was from Kathmandu; but I let it pass.

"I used to live in Kensington Palace Gardens," he said. "The rent was high, but my government paid. I was the Nepalese ambassador at the time."

"Did you ever meet the queen?"

"Many times! The queen liked to talk about the plays that were on in London. She talked about the actors and the plot and so on. She would say, 'Did you like *this* part of the play or *that* one?' If you hadn't seen the play it was very difficult to reply. But usually she talked about horses, and I'm sorry to say I have no interest at all in horses."

I left the ashram and paid a last visit to Mr. Bhardwaj. He gave me various practical warnings about traveling and advised me to visit Madras, where I would see the real India. He was off to have the carburetor in his car checked and to finish up some accounts at his office. He hoped I had enjoyed Simla and said it was a shame I hadn't seen any snow. He was formal, almost severe in his farewell, but, walking down to Cart Road, he said, "I will see you in England or America."

"That would be nice. I hope we do meet again."

"We will," he said, with such certainty I challenged it.

"How do you know?"

"I am about to be transferred from Simla. Maybe going to England, maybe to the States. That is what my horoscope says."

ZAMBEZI EXPRESS

from *Great Railway Journeys of the World*

Michael Wood (1948–)

Journalist, historian and filmmaker, Micahel Wood is best known for his BBC and PBS documentaries, particularly the enormously popular "Great Railway Journeys of the World" series (1979). His more recent works include In Search of the Dark Ages *(1981),* In Search of the Trojan War *(1987),* Art of the Western World *(1989),* In the Footsteps of Alexander the Great: A Journey from Greece to Asia *(1997) and* Conquistadors *(2001), all of which became television series.*

The train's name recalls the luxurious Blue Train from Victoria Station which, in the twenties and thirties, transported passengers overnight from the chilly, fog-dim streets of London to the palm-lined promenades of the Riviera. It is this train that Henry Green's fog-shrouded characters hope to board in his 1939 novel *Party Going*, and Agatha Christie used it as a setting in *The Mystery of the Blue Train*. South Africa's Blue Train has the same sort of cachet, with the difference that it is itself a destination just as much as either of its termini. It first went into service in 1939, replacing an earlier luxury train, the steam-powered Johannesburg-Cape Town Union Limited. It carries its passengers in considerable comfort from the suburban ease of Cape Town to the wild beauty and drama of the Zambezi River and Victoria Falls—and, looked at the other way, from the interior of the continent to the last point of land at the Cape and the meeting of two mighty oceans.

"It ignores the outside world. At a sedate forty miles an hour it transports its pampered passengers smoothly and soundlessly behind windows tinted with pure gold to keep down the glare."

In the autumn of 1979 I went to southern Africa in the privileged position of a journalist and traveller. I was to retrace Cecil Rhodes' railway route from Cape Town to Victoria Falls, from the mother city of the whites in Africa to Lobengula's indaba tree. The railway had been Rhodes' dream, part of a strip of British Empire red right up Africa. He it was who financed the push to the Zambezi in the 1890s, where (having disposed of Lobengula, king of the Matabele) he founded a country and named it after himself: Rhodesia. My journey, then, was his: into the heart of Africa.

And what a time to do it! That November Rhodesia was teetering on the edge. Fifteen years after a UDI which was intended to inaugurate 1000 years of white supremacy, the illegal and racialist regime of Ian Smith had very rapidly come face to face with History. For eight years now the black nationalists of the Patriotic Front had been fighting a full-scale guerilla war against the white settlers to win back the land seized by Rhodes in the 1890s. Declaring themselves Lobengula's heirs by proxy, they consulted the spirit mediums of the people; they swore their oaths on the dead freedom fighters of the failed revolt of 1897; they had even determined that their new country would bear the name Zimbabwe, after the great stone city which is the supreme architectural achievement of the ancient black races of Rhodesia (an achievement which hard-line whites denied them). Now, despite heavy losses, the Patriotic Front controlled much of the countryside. And now, around the conference table at Lancaster House in London, they were negotiating with the British government and the Smith regime to obtain a free election.

The war had already displaced hundreds of thousands of people into protected villages and the black townships around Salisbury. A quarter of a million more had fled to refugee camps in Botswana, Zambia and Mozambique, where they were living in destitution. A million head of cattle had been lost. There was devastation, disease and malnutrition. When I set off on 16 November from Cape Town, the war was still being fought while the PF talked. It might be over by the time I reached the Falls. If it ended, where would that leave South Africa, Rhodesia's chief ally, and their illegally held colony in Namibia, where another guerilla war was increasing in severity? And if talks broke down, would war eventually engulf the whole of southern Africa, drawing in all Rhodesia's neighbours? Such thoughts gave me a sharp sense of anticipation at the start of the journey. Whatever happened, the next weeks would be unrepeatable.

Cape Town 16 November 1979. "You must take the Blue Train," everyone said, "it's the most luxurious train in the world." That had never struck me as a reason to travel. Quite the reverse, in fact: I always seem to have chosen the most eccentric and decrepit ways of getting to places. But South Africa is a land of the most violent contrasts, and somehow with its vaunted luxury the Blue Train seemed an appropriate way to begin this venture into the interior.

Twice a week the Blue Train runs the thousand miles from the Cape to Pretoria. In the old days it used to meet the Union Castle liners, and it preserves that vanished air of pre-war gentility. It is a diesel train with absolute self-confidence. It ignores the outside world. At a sedate forty miles an hour it transports its pampered passengers smoothly and soundlessly behind windows tinted with pure gold to keep down the glare. There is a private suite with lounge and bathroom; a bar in whose leafy corner one might see a bridge class in progress; a pince-nez *maître d'hôtel* whose fastidious regard would do credit to Claridges. This, in short, is a train on which travel itself is the destination.

The first hours of the journey pass through the fertile, temperate plains of Cape Province with their vineyards and oak trees in the lee of the grandiose spurs and fairy tale peaks of the Drakenstein. This was the heartland of the original Dutch settlers of the seventeenth century, who built their farms in the delectable valleys around Paarl and Stellenbosch. Their descendants—Afrikaners, Africans, as they call themselves—have formed the ruling elite in South Africa since 1948. It was they who regularised forms of racial separation already practised in British colonies south of the Zambezi into apartheid, the total separation of black and white races. Of course they are now a state under siege. If not yet physically, then certainly spiritually.

You would not know it from the wealth and self-confidence of the Blue Train's clientele. To them events beyond the Limpopo are a mote in the mind's eye. But at the lunch table Willem de Clerc, a tenth-generation Afrikaner who farms near Paarl, shook his head sadly: "We are not a strange people, we are a very human people, but they thought they could change the world. This is a reformed society. Like the English revolution, or the communists, or the Jacobins in France, they thought a political system could provide all the answers in human life. It's like Hamlet—you know how that ends—the bodies piling up around him."

A state under siege. At Paarl there are three massive, pale-coloured granite boulders, like debris from some planetary ice age. The largest is a mile in circumference. A mile! It was named Paarl, "pearl," in 1657 by an early Dutch settler who thought it glistened like a pearl in the sunshine after rain. On the top, reaching far into the blue sky, is the Taalmonument, the Language Monument. "It symbolises the origin and development of our language here over the three hundred years," said my lady companion in the cocktail bar. "We say that Afrikaans is '*n Perel van Groot Waarde*,' a pearl of great worth," she added. In what other country could you find a monument to a language erected by the people who speak it? You might expect it to have been erected in the heroic days of the nineteenth-century struggles with the British, or maybe in 1948. But no. It was built in 1975. When you become hated by most of your fellow citizens in the world, you have to define very clearly what it is you are fighting for.

The route which the train now follows is the route by which the whites penetrated into the interior, first by ox carts through a precipitous and almost trackless mountain terrain, on the trail of the transhumant Bantu; later by the railway tracks which were laid up the Hex River in the late 1870s and early 80s, rising from the orchards of Worcester (750 feet above sea level) to the top of the pass at nearly 3600 feet, higher than the summit of Table Mountain.

The Blue Train climbs the Hex River Pass by an extraordinary series of curves, some only 100 yards in diameter, so that at one point the front and rear of the train are parallel to each other, going in opposite directions! At the top there is a spectacular view of the 7000-foot peak of the Matroosberg on the one hand, and stretching back below us the rich vineyards of the Hex valley. Then, within a couple of hours, there is a dramatic change in the landscape. We enter a wilderness like nowhere else on earth. The Great Karroo, the Hottentot "Land of Thirst."

Into this "worn-out emaciated land without soil or verdure" (as a nineteenth-century traveller put it) the Afrikaners made their Great Trek in the 1830s, away from the British overlords of the Cape to find a new promised land. They called it New Eden: a land of baked wastes broken by sills of ancient rock and protruding kopjes blazing hot by day and cold, black, starry brilliant by night. Here hardy farmers of Dutch and British stock still make their living from this intransigent soil, scratching fertile oases in an immensity of scrub. Treeless, dun-coloured and crumbling, the soil of the Karroo comes alive only infrequently when the rain makes gullies run with water and a carpet of red and blue flowers springs overnight, as from nowhere. But in some places in the Karroo there has been no rain now for three years.

Life cannot be viewed through gold windows. At five o'clock the Blue Train stopped at Touws River to change engines. I decided to get off there, to see something of the people who live by the track. From the conditioned air of the Blue Train I stepped on to the platform and into a sunlight that falls like a heavy weight on the head and shoulders; the eyes narrow with the glare; the air is dry and hot and smells of the surrounding mountains, of gorse and (is it?) thyme. No one else gets off. The Blue Train's doors hiss shut, and soon its last coach disappears in the heat haze in front of the red hills towards Lainsburg.

The familiar images of the Karroo: the wind pump, the white farmhouse with its cluster of pepper trees out of sight of its neighbours' chimney smoke. A perpetual frontier country; a drought-stricken land where the landlords make their money from sheep or nothing. The Afrikaners are fond of saying that their oldest tradition is their feel for the land, and out here everything has a biblical simplicity: the throat-cutting of the sheep for the owner's monthly gift to the workers; the weekly hand-outs of water, meal, coffee and sugar; the poverty of the workers themselves, most of them itinerant, earning thirty or forty Rand a month; their stoical resignation.

"We hope the Lord will help us so that life gets better than it is now," Maria said to me, sturdy wife of a deaf mute farm hand, "then I might like the Karroo. As it is, we have to work in the Karroo because only some bosses understand my husband: it's the bosses here who know him. I've no choice. I've three children still at school. I must stay here now. He's my legal husband. If I'd been alone I would have gone somewhere else. It may be better for my children. White people we've worked for say I bring them up well. My daughter wants to be a welfare worker. The boy wants to be a carpenter. The baby—he's nine—says he will work on the railways. They earn good money there."

Here too is the larger-than-life figure of Oom Dan, the "old boss," the foreman who rules this farm with a paternal iron rod for the absentee landlord.

"The workers I treat like children, they look on me as their father. I've told them that they can call me 'meneer,' *Mr.* Van Vuuren, but they have always called me 'baas' and now they want to call me 'oubaas.' They prefer that. I don't work with them any more, but I go with them wherever they go. Where they work, I sit with them. When they go to the veld they want me with them. Ask them. They'll tell you they haven't got a 'radio.' They need me because I am their 'radio'. . . . As for the life here in the Karoo, I never go to town. Take me to a town, take me away from the farm, and within two months you can bury me."

Above Dan Van Vuuren's living-room door there is a portrait of D. F. Malan, the nationalist architect of apartheid. I suppose his compatriots would consider Oom Dan a typical Afrikaner countryman—the man who knows sheeps, who knows the veld; a red-necked bull of a man, devout and intolerant, hard as nails; the ruler of his roost. Such were the original Trekkers, one imagines, hard-bitten frontiersmen building their society on traditional Afrikaner virtues—self sufficiency, a refusal to kow-tow to outside authority, Old Testament fundamentalism and a belief in the divinely ordained supremacy of white over black.

In the next few days I wound my way slowly through the center of the republic. First from Touws River up to Ladismith on a delightful slow train which starts at two in the morning and can take up to eight hours to do eighty miles. It is an old "24" class built at the Hyde Park Works of the North British Locomotive Company in Glasgow, a smart little branch line engine which chugs slowly up and down this one line twice a week. A pleasant life for a train, I suppose. Its job is to ferry workers to the vineyards of the Ladismith valley, to carry supplies to isolated farms in a region with no made-up roads, and to bring domestic water to tiny, one-horse halts in the long dry season. The locals call the train Makadas. I could not discover why. "Muck and dust" someone suggested (plausible enough). "Make a dash" said another (surely not?).

The train was already two hours late by the time dawn came up over Hondewater. But on the Makadas time has no meaning. The traveler must simply sit back on his wooden seat and watch the splendid sunrise touch the far-off tips of the Oudtshoorn range with gold. Then, as the still morning air becomes warmer, listen to the explosive whoosh of steam echoing in the crags of the Little Karoo. On this train a local farmer responded memorably to my comments on the efficiency of the service.

"Well, this is an old-fashioned system for sure," he said, "but so are we. Diesel is surely not fitting with our mountains. We've just got to have this steam locomotive." Later on in the journey I would understand his remark.

The Makadas stops at Ladismith. The line was never driven through to Oudtshoorn to join up with the coastal route and the Indian Ocean. The last station on the Oudtshoorn side of the mountains is called Protem, "so far." But, in fact, it goes no farther. Ladismith was thus left at the end of the line and nobody goes there today. So, to return to the main line north you must either go back from Ladismith the way you came, or you can cut through the Seven Weeks Pass under "Magic Mountain" and back by road to Lainsburg.

From Lainsburg it is possible to take any number

of trains through the desert northwards. One, the Trans-Karroo Express, is still pulled by steam engines, the 15Fs. Some of these are "stars," kept in immaculate condition by their crews with whitened wheel rims and cab roofs, coloured number plates, burnished pipes and personal brass emblems: an eagle, a horse, a star. In South Africa the railways are the biggest employers and among the best. Pride in the locomotive is expected and fostered.

At Beaufort West, on the way to De Aar, we are overhauled by a Garratt steaming free at full speed, charging north with no load. "We are lending several of them to the Rhodesians," the conductor said in a confidential tone in answer to my question, "diesels too, and technicians." A black smudge of smoke hung over the horizon to the north long after the engine had whirled frantically out of sight.

De Aar is not a place you would visit for the fun of it. Central rail junction of the republic, like Crewe and Swindon it is an out-and-out railway colony. It stands in the middle of a hot, howling wilderness, said an early traveller, and it stands there simply because of the railway. Here the main lines go north and south, east and west, carrying minerals, the arterial wealth of South Africa: iron ore, copper, manganese. The distances are terrific: the eight o'clock evening train from De Aar to Windhoek in Namibia, 800 miles away, takes two days. The railyards are all smoke, grime and coal dust, with hundreds of steam locomotives and thousands of black and coloured workers to service them. These people live in townships which are literally on the other side of the tracks. For them there is a curfew in the white town.

In De Aar it is easy to see why steam has survived in South Africa. The republic has no natural oil deposits of its own. But it does have ample coal. And an almost limitless supply of cheap African labour to maintain the labour-intensive steam locomotives.

Cleaning and greasing, but not driving—there are no black drivers in South Africa—white railwaymen do that. "An old-fashioned system," said the man on the Makadas. And this is why.

I travelled the next 150 miles to Kimberley on the footplate of one of the giant freight trains going north. The two coupled class 25 giants, *Maria* and *Jennifer*, whose names belie their devastating power, pour columns of black smoke hundreds of feet into the air as they roar at 50 mph past the kopjes of the northern Karroo. Here the landscape is a vivid orange desolation, a place of mirages. This line from De Aar to Kimberley is the steam buff's paradise. Thirty freights a day pull up the long incline to Krankhuil huffing and puffing, shooting unburned coal into the sky. We pass mineral trains going south ("We're pulling it out of Namibia as fast as we can," someone would later tell me in Kimberley); moving north we saw armaments: for Namibia, Rhodesia, who knows?

We cross the Orange River, the historic dividing line between the original Boer republics and the British imperial possessions in Cape Province. In fact we do not enter the Free State here but skirt its southwestern edge, reminding us that the British built this railway to outflank the Boers, via Kimberley through Bechuanaland and on to Rhodesia. While the crew boil their coffee on the end of a rod thrust into the furnace, we pass over the Modder River where the British suffered a humiliating disaster in the Boer War, and then on to Kimberley past a reassuring litany of English and Dutch country stations: Chalk Farm, Heuningneskloof, Spytfontein, Wimbledon—names for an Afrikaner John Betjeman to conjure with.

Kimberley. Those backwoods republics across the Orange and the Vaal rivers might have remained quietly in their inhospitable landscape and never made their mark on history had it not been for the accident of the discovery of mineral wealth: diamonds in Kimberley in 1869, and the subsequent finds of gold on the Witwatersrand in Transvaal in 1887. The conflicts by which the British tried to dominate the Boers and control this wealth—the Boer Wars—have been the determining factors in the politics of South Africa ever since.

Kimberley bears few signs of the rush now. But this was where Rhodes, then Prime-Minister of the Cape, made his fortune, signing the biggest cheque ever for the rights to the main mine, the Big Hole. This is what enabled him to finance the construction of a railway 1000 miles to the Zambezi, to found Rhodesia, and to conceive his kingmaking visions of a southern African federation. The Big Hole is his monument. A pit of Babel. It is silent now, filled with water. Like a meteorite crater gouged in the veld, it goes down a thousand feet. "When I'm in Kimberley," said Rhodes, "I often go and sit on the edge of the mine and reckon up the value of the diamonds and the power they conferred. Every foot of that blue ground means so much power."

History has passed Kimberley by. Rhodes' company, De Beers, still have their head office here, but their operation has moved elsewhere, to the Joburg gold reef and the new diamond mines of Botswana. Kimberley just sits and swelters with its wild west sidewalks, waiting for the one blessing of the African summer, the torrential downpour which comes here punctually every day at five and leaves the awnings streaming, main street aflood with a momentary monsoon.

The go-getters have got up and gone. But behind them is left a strange flotsam. It is a sight you might have seen in the days before the rush—a handful of poor white prospectors, men and women, licensed by De Beers to hand-sieve for loose diamonds in the stony hills above the Vaal river. The temperature is 114 degrees, but men like Lou Bothes still work here as he has for fifty years. An archetypal prospector, Lou lives in the same hut he has had for all that time. At seventy-three he still puts in a full day of backbreaking toil in a claim hole with no corner of shade. He still dreams of finding the big one (and after all, the Cullinan itself was a loose diamond, missed by the diggers).

It is a strange world, the diggers' world. Ruled by dreams, omens and superstitions. It is considered bad luck to have women on a claim; they abandon it altogether if they find a snake in it. Men in white shirts are a good sign, so are dreams of silver fish, of "dog diamonds" and especially sheep's heads. A diggers' legend here at Noitgedacht has it that the biggest diamond of all will be the shape of a sheep's skull. The sheep's skull drives them on. . . .

In the bar while a pianist played "My Way" Craig was holding forth in front of the girl we'd met on the train. He was depressed because a convoy car had been hit and four men killed near Vic Falls. Tomorrow while Graham and I rode an armed freight, he would be in a convoy.

"Look, man," he said. "I guarantee we will get hit: no way we will not get hit tomorrow." He still had his Rhodesian-made replica of a short Israeli tommy gun: "I'll sit up front tomorrow, next to the driver, 'cos if the 'ters attack I'll want to spray 180 degrees, and if you boys are in the front seat I don't want to have to blow your effing heads off, man." Suddenly I was glad I was going to be on the footplate.

Next morning in the yards at Thompson Junction by Wankie I boarded the footplate of class 15a number 395, a Beyer-Garratt bound for the Falls with a cargo of coking coal for Zambia and Zaire. On the plate with me was a soldier, Bruce (a real gentleman, quiet, dignified), and the three-man crew, the furnace being hand-stoked. Graham was in the guards van with the guard and two black troopers of the Rhodesian army ("trust them with my life," whispered Bruce). The most exhilarating journey of my life began at about 10.00 on 13 December, the day after Soames' arrival. The war was still going on. The previous night in Thompson Junction a shunter had been wounded and a train sprayed with bullets. In Wankie town a policeman had been killed. None of us really knew what to expect.

There are a dozen little halts between TJ and the Falls. Now they are deserted. One by one we passed them, Sambawizi, Nashome, Lobangwe, and not a sign of life at any of them. At midday we stopped at Matetsi to take on water and rake out the fire box. The previous day I had visited the military command for permission to go to Matetsi, and I knew that it lay in the heart of a guerilla zone. When we got there we found the army post sandbagged in at the river crossing. There was a small radio station behind high wires, and the water tank. Two men had been killed here last week. Bruce tied a bandana round his forehead to keep the sweat out of his eyes. The driver's mate perched on top of the engine and swung the gantry pipe round to the boiler, while Graham and the troops fanned out facing the silent bush. The sun was really hot by now, and the burning ash showering out of the fire box made it impossible to stand near the locomotive. The bush was invitingly green and shady, but Bruce said the paths were booby-trapped. I sat down on the rails until it was time to climb back aboard.

On the last stretch, the thirty miles to the Falls, we touched fifty miles an hour through beautiful broken country, vivid green bush with rocky gulleys traversed by water courses. Some trees were covered with blossom, others dotted with red fruit; there were baobabs, palms, and some trees which looked like oaks, elms and chestnuts. *Et in Arcadia ego!* Momentarily all thoughts of war receded. Then, at about five miles distance, we saw the tell-tale cloud of spray beginning to be distinguishable from the clouds. Exactly what Livingstone had seen in 1855.

We came in sight for the first time of the columns of vapour, appropriately called "smoke," rising at a distance of five or six miles, exactly as when large tracts of grass are burned in Africa. Five columns now arose, and bending in the direction of the wind . . . the tops of the columns at this distance appeared to mingle with the clouds.

We sped into the Falls zone past the wire fences of the minefield, under the blockhouse with its oil drums and sandbags on the road bridge checkpoint. Victoria Falls was then a defended zone—a "protected village" for whites, as it were. Ironic to think of the white hoteliers and shopkeepers huddled round the Falls for safety. When the Falls were first discovered by Livingstone, no natives were found to be living within a radius of ten miles, as if respectful of its primordial force.

Vic Falls Station: neat, well-kept, overflowing with bougainvillaea and jacarandas, flower-boxes and mimosa. The white sign says Cape Town 2651 k/m, Beira 1534 k/m. Engine 395 wheezed to a halt. We staggered on to *terra firma* black-faced, unburned coal in our hair, hot, shaky and exhilarated. The journey was almost over.

The railways reached the Falls in 1904, and the tourist industry rapidly followed to make the most of the scene. The Edwardian Falls Hotel, where I was booked in, still preserves the old style: huge electric fans swishing in the dining-room: be-fezzed waiters, misanthropic monkeys munching mangoes in the palm court, bougainvillaea, mosquito nets, barbecues, sundowners, planters punch, marimba bands, tribal dancing, tea, toast and marmalade, egg and bacon. And always the roar of the Falls, invisible from the hotel but for the smoke merging with the sky above Rhodes' railway bridge.

The place was virtually deserted. Tourism was by now non-existent. Not surprising really, for there were only two ways of getting there now the trains didn't run: either you careered by convoy from Wankie, guns at the ready, or you took an old Viscount from Bulawayo and twisted down like a falling leaf from the cloud cover in tight circles on to the airstrip, constantly veering away from the Zambian side to cut down the risk of SAM missiles and sniper fire. Such precautions were taken everywhere after a Viscount was hot down over Kariba.

That evening before dinner the station master drove me up the Zambezi to the edge of the minefield. Gingerly, for after dark hippos walk the river road. We passed three big American-style motels, all deserted, musty, mildewed in the humid tropical air, their carpeted dance floors the haunt of snakes and insects. The Elephant Hills casino lay empty, hit by a stray SAM missile from Zambia. At sunset impala teemed at the water hole, temporarily returned to Africa.

We walked down to the river. The Zambezi looked like a great dark ocean. Harry picked up strange husks and fruit and told me how they grew. About to retire, he was weary and could not disguise the bitterness he felt about the fall of his country. He would not stay in Rhodesia if the PF won. I reflected that after all these years of war, the white Rhodesian nationalists lived in what was to all intents and purposes a police state. All their news was censored, for example. They had never heard Robert Mugabe speak! Harry shrugged and looked at me as if I was personally responsible for the Lancaster House sell-out, as he called it. We stood silent there in the forest like the characters in the Conrad novel, confronted by the stillness of the forest "with its ominous patience, waiting for the passing of a fantastic invasion."

There remained one last walk to complete the journey. The curfew lasted till 6 A. M., but I went down to the Falls at five to savour the moment. Dawn here rises over Zambia right behind Rhodes bridge, shooting streams of sunlight through the cascades and forming rainbows in the water vapour, above you, below you and all around you. One of the few places on earth, perhaps, where you actually can be over the rainbow! By the gorge the rain forest grows out of itself, tangled creepers and saplings pushing through the sodden trunks of their dead progenitors: a mulch of rotten bark and leaves dotted with red aloes and dozens of orange butterflies. Wild animals are here too, warthogs, impala, gazelles, though all retire at dawn. In this fantastic moment I felt the ecstasy of a rain king, but my reverie was broken by the muffled boom of a landmine.

"Usually game, sometimes a 'ter," said Craig when I got back for breakfast. "The elephants break down the fences. Sometimes you get a whole herd of impala blowing themselves to pieces."

Rhodes' graceful bridge still spans the Zambezi gorge, four hundred feet above the swirling maelstrom of the Boiling Pot. It was built by the Cleveland Bridge and Engineering Company of Darlington in 1903–4, prefabricated and pre-erected on their premises before being shipped out to Africa. The railway reached the Falls in 1904, and the bridge itself was opened the next spring. By then Rhodes had been dead three years. He had asked that the bridge be built so close to the Falls that the spray would wet the carriage windows. It does, I am told. But in December 1979 the only trains to pass over the bridge were Zambian, picking up our load of coal and maize. Like everyone else I was forbidden even to step on the bridge. In December 1979 this was the front line in Africa.

Over the gorge the Zambian frontier post surveyed us with binoculars. Had it not been for the war, I could have crossed the bridge and followed Rhodes' route northwards through Livingstone to Lusaka, Dar-es-Salaam, Mombasa, Nairobi, Lake Victoria, Kampala, Rejaf, then eleven days by boat to Juba and back on the train at Khartoum, Wadi Halfa, Aswan and Cairo. Rhodes' dream never actually became reality, though you can still travel 6500 of the 8000 miles by rail. Maybe I'll do it one day.

Now it all seems so long ago. The Blue Train still carries its cosseted passengers from the Cape to Pretoria. But steam is to end on the line from De Aar to Kimberley. The South African government has announced plans to give Soweto full city status and its own university; so Derek and Lucky will no longer be "temporary." Mafeking is no more. Rhodesia is now Zimbabwe, and Rhodesia Railways are the National Railways of Zimbabwe. You can travel once more by passenger train to Victoria Falls.

It is hardly a hundred years since the Falls were first seen by a white man. "A scene so lovely," Livingstone said, "that it must have been gazed on by the angels in their flight." In that time the tide of white colonialism has advanced and receded. It may already be too late for South Africa to respond to that tide. Like the Falls themselves the current of history is remorseless, unswerving and deaf to persuasion.

KAAMOS, THE DARKEST TIME OF THE YEAR

from *Northern Nightbook*

Kirsti Simonsuuri (1945–)

Finnish-born Kirsti Simonsuuri is a professor of comparative literature at Helsinki University. She has also held positions at Harvard and Columbia Universities, and served as director of the Finnish Archaeological Institute of Athens. Her works include Homer's Original Genius *(1979),* Portrait of a Man *(1992) and* Akropolis *(1999).*

In the cold. The cold that nips, the dark that is pitch-dark, tarry. I jam myself into a steaming-hot train carriage. It is morning.

How can you tell. How can the people discern. Somebody must have informed them that it is seven o'clock in the morning, that it is time to undo the sandwich bags, to eat the bread quietly nibbling, and to peel an orange.

The metal tube dashes into the North. But how can you tell, there is no movement, for the black windows reflect only what there is inside the tube, dull strangers darkly dressed, on garish green seats. An amazingly singular-looking people with Indian features and thin blond hair.

They are as if transported somewhere, unwilling beings.

When the day breaks, vast expanses open. Nowhere is bleakness deeper than here. The grain-fields are textiles, rough tow cloth, and above them hangs a grey gossamer, a rickety sky. What is visible is only a tiny fraction of what there is. The measure of frustration, as if the thin light visible above the horizon on a winter's day would try to suppress the real light.

All this must be learned again much more attentively than I could have foreseen. Behind language, there is something gigantic, monstrous, consolidated, the existence of which I could not imagine before.

Beyond Ylivieska there is only Oulu. When we arrive there, the day has brightened, and darkened again.

There is a long platform, immeasurable, its one end reaches north and its other end south. I stand there with my suitcase. My feet trample the whiteness, the snow squeals under my boots. I do not want to leave right away.

The city is bare. It is like a newly slaughtered skin that has been turned over, the wrong side up, so that all the veins and the dried bits of innards gleam on its surface. Lights flash as if in an amusement park, deserted by its patrons.

FROM ZEPHYR: TRACKING A DREAM ACROSS AMERICA

Henry Kisor (1940–)

Critic and newspaper editor based in Chicago, Kisor is the recipient of numerous journalism awards and was a finalist for the Pulitzer Prize in Criticism (1981). His more recent books include What's that Pig Outdoors?: A Memoir of Deafness *(1990) and* Flight of the Gin Fizz: Midlife at 4,500 Feet *(1997).*

The *California Zephyr* follows not the route of the first transcontinental railroad, the Union Pacific line from Omaha across upper Nebraska through Wyoming and Utah, but that of a comparative Johnny-come-lately. What it lacks in historical primacy, however, the Rio Grande makes up for in staggering beauty, and it has a pungent historical flavor of its own.

After the Civil War Coloradans had lobbied mightily for the transcontinental breakthrough to be built through their state, but the Union Pacific opted for the much easier route through the low mountain passes of southern Wyoming. In 1872, three years after the historic linkup of the westward-building Union Pacific and the eastbound Central Pacific at Promontory, Utah, the new Denver & Rio Grande Railroad drove south along the Front Range to Colorado Springs and Pueblo, aiming to follow the Rio Grande River to El Paso, Texas, then cross the stream and head for Mexico City. After skirmishing with the Santa Fe Railway over access to mountain passes near New Mexico, the Rio Grande gave up its lofty goal of spanning Texas and Mexico and instead pushed west through the spectacular Royal Gorge of the Arkansas River, finally reaching Utah in 1882.

The Rio Grande originally was a narrow-gauge line, its rails standing three feet apart instead of everybody else's four feet, eight and one-half inches. The only economical way to throw a railroad around the cliffs and over the chasms of the rugged Rockies to the precious metals within was to employ comparatively cheap narrow-gauge tracks under short cars and small locomotives that could handle tight curves and steep grades. A narrow-gauge railroad, the saying went, could "curve on the brim of a sombrero," and by the 1880s a large network of "baby railroad" crisscrossed the Colorado Rockies.

At the same time, however, the Rio Grande needed to carry the standard cars of other railroads, and began converting some of its through lines to dual-gauge track. By 1890 its main line from Denver through the Royal Gorge to Ogden, Utah, had been converted to standard gauge. When the precious-metal mines petered out, so did the "baby railroad" lines, rapidly abandoned after World War II. Surprisingly heavy traffic kept open the narrow-gauge branch between Durango and Silverton in the southwestern corner of the state until 1979, when the Rio Grande sold it to a private operator who still runs it as a tourist railroad.

The *California Zephyr* departs Denver not on the original Rio Grande tracks of the nineteenth century but those of an entirely different railroad, born in 1902 as the Denver, Northwestern & Pacific. It was the brainchild of a farsighted but underfunded Denver banker named David Moffat, who decided to build a railroad connecting Salt Lake City with the Burlington Route, which had merged its way into Denver by 1882. He aimed his line west from Denver through the forbidding Front Range of the Rockies, in 1905 surmounting 11,680-foot Rollins Pass hard by 13,260-foot James Peak. The line was so high and so rugged it was easily choked by snow, and during the bitter winter of 1904–5 it had to be shut down for several months when its new rotary plow became snowbound.

The next summer, Moffat ran out of money when his railroad reached Hot Sulphur Springs in northwestern Colorado. In 1912 the "Moffat Road" was reorganized as the Denver & Salt Lake Railroad, which staggered only a few miles farther west, to Craig. It never reached Salt Lake City but struggled along through snowstorms, tunnel collapses, bankruptcy and strikes until 1922. That year the city of Denver and the state of Colorado at last recognized the importance of Moffat's railroad to the development of the northwestern part of the state, and passed a bill that funded the boring of a six-mile-long tunnel under Rollins Pass, ensuring the railroad's survival.

At the time it opened in 1928, the Moffat Tunnel was the longest railroad bore in North America; only the 7.2-mile Cascade and Flathead Tunnels on the Burlington Northern in Washington and Montana, and the 9.1-mile Mount Macdonald Tunnel on the Canadian Pacific in British Columbia, are longer. The circuitous twenty-three-mile-long journey over Rollins Pass had taken five hours; the tunnel, crossing the Continental Divide at more than nine thousand feet, cut the time to ten minutes. Not long after, the Rio Grande swallowed the Denver & Salt Lake.

Much later, in 1971, when Amtrak took over most of the nation's remaining long-distance passenger trains, the Rio Grande was one of the few holdouts. The maverick railroad's official reason was that it believed the grandeur of its Rockies scenery might attract enough passengers for it to turn a profit operating a daily train between Denver and Salt Lake City. The real reason was that management thought two Amtrak trains each day would interfere with the profitable running of freight trains on the single-track mainline. If the Rio Grande could keep its segment of the *Zephyr* operating between Denver and

Salt Lake City, Amtrak would stay away. The Rio Grande believed, as did many observers at the time, that Amtrak had no future and the *Zephyr* could easily be dropped in a few years.

And so the Rio Grande renamed its share of the streamliner the *Rio Grande Zephyr*, and kept it going. Meanwhile, Amtrak rerouted what was left of the Burlington and Western Pacific train over the faster, less scenic, more northerly Overland Route—the Union Pacific Railroad main line north from Denver to Cheyenne, Wyoming, thence west to Ogden, Utah, bypassing Salt Lake City—and renamed it the *San Francisco Zephyr*. Amtrak's train also mounted the Sierra Nevada over the shorter and more direct Southern Pacific line rather than the slower and prettier Western Pacific route. The new route cut the total mileage of today's Amtrak *California Zephyr* run from 2,525 to 2,416.

By 1982—when Amtrak had demonstrated that it was here to stay—the *Rio Grande Zephyr* had become so popular, winning free and favorable publicity from Europe to Japan, that the Rio Grande faced a hard decision. Fine as the train was, the *Zephyr's* cars were reaching the end of their serviceable life and needed to be replaced. The only way to avoid doing so was to reverse the decision of 1971, and Amtrak immediately rerouted its Superliner *Zephyr* across Colorado.

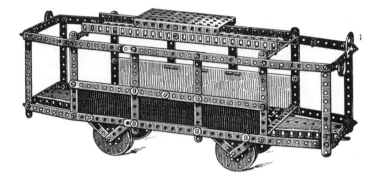

THE MAN WHO STOPPED TRAINS

from *Dix Contes et Nouvelles Fantastiques*

François Barcelo (1941–)

Montreal native François Barcelo left a career in advertising to pursue his dream of becoming a writer. His first two novels, Agénor, Agénor, Agénor et Agénor *and* La Tribu, *were published in 1981. He has written numerous children's books, including* Premier Boulot pour Momo de Simro *(1998) and* Pince-nez, le Crabe en Conserve *(1999). His more recent novels include* Cadavres *(1998) and* Chiens Sales *(2000). In 1999, Barcelo won the Grand Prix littéraire de la Montérégie for his complete works.*

By the time he had reached his thirty-fifth birthday, Gonzague Gagnon had given up trying to discover paranormal powers within himself.

Of the first half of his life, only two years and six months remained. Surely then the months and the years would begin to whiz by as quickly as the kilometres after he was halfway through his run.

The morning of his birthday, Gonzague Gagnon laced on his running shoes, determined to make an assault on a goal he had set long ago: to run ten kilometres in thirty-five minutes on his thirty-fifth birthday. For many years he had made similar goals: thirty-two minutes at thirty-two, thirty-three minutes at thirty-three years, and so on. He'd never succeeded. But as the years went by, the goal became easier. And last week he had managed to run the distance in thirty-six minutes.

It was six o'clock in the morning, which meant that he had two hours in which to run his ten kilometres, walk back, take a shower and go down to work.

It was a beautiful morning and Gonzague Gagnon congratulated himself once more on being born in May, rather than having been conceived in the spring and then born in November or December, like most of the villagers. He ran the first two kilometres at an easy pace, to make sure his legs were warmed up. Then he lengthened his stride and began to speed up. He reached the one-third stake three minutes later. As always, he began to feel a bit out of breath. But if he wanted to get in under thirty-five minutes, he couldn't slow down, even though every step seemed to drag.

From a distance, Gonzague Gagnon saw the St. Nicol River. Just on the other side he would find the five-kilometre marker. But his legs were growing heavy. Should he slow down and risk not doing his ten kilometres in thirty-five minutes? Or maintain or even accelerate his pace, and risk not finishing?

A far-away rumbling attracted his attention. It was the passenger train. It gave a long whistle and Gonzague Gagnon couldn't resist the temptation to turn his head, even though he knew he would lose a fraction of a second.

The train was quickly catching up to him, along the railway track that ran parallel to the road.

It was always the same train, no doubt always with the same passengers and the same conductor.

Once more Gonzague Gagnon looked ahead. The wooden bridge that straddled the St. Nicol River was now at most a hundred feet away.

At that moment Gonzague Gagnon realized that he had not tried to exercise his powers on anything mechanical. Why had he always tried to move tables, chairs and other immobile objects? Was it not mobile things like cars, trucks or trains that he— Gonzague Gagnon, apprentice mechanic—would be the most likely to affect?

He glanced to the right. The train was about to draw up level with him and would soon begin to cross the metal railway bridge upstream from the wooden one.

"Stop," said Gonzague Gagnon.

He had spoken in an undertone, for fear of appearing ridiculous. But even if the train had had ears and hadn't been making so much noise, it could hardly have heard him from such a distance.

Nevertheless the train braked. Its wheels locked and screeched, sending up great showers of sparks. Then the engine stopped, just a few turns of the wheel form the metal bridge.

Gonzague Gagnon also came to a halt, a few steps from the wooden bridge.

Out came the engineer and the brakeman, gesturing wildly, the former shouting abuse apparently directed at the latter. They leaned over the track, inspected the wheels, then climbed back up. The train started up again, advancing slowly and with caution. Gonzague Gagnon watched as it gathered speed and pulled away.

He forgot his running. "I can stop trains," he said to himself over and over again as he walked back home. But upon due reflection, he had to conclude that the experiment was not conclusive.

He waited impatiently for the train to appear again the following week. Just as it was on the point of crossing the St. Nicol River, he said, as he had the last time, "Stop." And the train stopped.

For several weeks that summer, Gonzague Gagnon took great pleasure in commanding the train to stop and watching the engineers leap frantically onto the track. Each time, the locomotive carried more inspectors, more mechanics, more people whom Gonzague Gagnon guessed to be specialists of all kinds, from places farther and farther away, from positions which were more and more exalted.

The authorities had a length of the track replaced. Nothing changed. In the village people began to talk about a curse, about a haunted railway track. When they brought the subject up with Gonzague Gagnon he smiled but said nothing.

Finally, when a team came to demolish the old metal bridge in order to replace it with a new one, Gonzague Gagnon told himself that he had gone too far. The authorities were delighted that the new bridge had solved the problem of the inexplicable stoppages of the train, even if the stoppages themselves remained unexplained.

"Today my life is half over," Gonzague Gagnon realized one fine December morning.

He brushed his teeth and put on his tights and his tracksuit, taking special care to slide into place a lit-tle handkerchief folded in four. It kept the cold from a particularly sensitive part of his anatomy.

His usual road was well ploughed, but with a base of slippery ice that encouraged caution. For this reason, Gonzague Gagnon was unable to achieve his goal of thirty-seven-and-one-half minutes at thirty-seven-and-one-half years of age. "That pleasure will be for my thirty-eighth birthday." He came to this conclusion philosophically, though his recent failures might have led him into bitterness. For a long time he had been convinced that eventually it would be easy to run the ten kilometres in the number of minutes equal to his age. But age was weakening him, and each year he needed more than an extra minute to run his distance.

On this particular morning he ran without any precise goal, without pushing himself, with no purpose other than enjoying the outdoors and feeling the harmonious working of his thirty-seven-and-a-half-year-old body.

He was even taking pleasure in musing that since he had now reached the middle of his life, the rest would be easy and full of excitement. Soon he would be two-thirds of the way through, then three-quarters. Never again would he be as bored as he had been between the third and the halfway mark.

Approaching the halfway point, the St. Nicol River, he ran easily though without great speed. He was getting ready to cross the wooden bridge when he noticed a black silhouette against the frozen white bank of the river.

He slowed down. Sitting on a log, waving a short rod above a hole in the ice, someone was fishing in the river.

The fisherman suddenly raised his eyes towards him, as though he had sensed his presence.

Gonzague Gagnon stopped short. The fisherman

was a woman. He had seen women fish before, but a woman fisherman alone, on the river—he had never seen that.

He decided to go closer and crossed the ditch at the edge of the road, aware of the snow working its way into his shoes. He advanced with difficulty, sinking to mid-thigh with each step.

Soon he was on the river. The wind had swept it clean of snow. The woman watched as he came near. He saw that she was beautiful. That frightened Gonzague Gagnon. He wanted to turn back. But what would she think after having seen him come towards her? That he was afraid?

Of course he was afraid. More and more afraid as the woman became more and more beautiful. What was he going to say to her?

He stopped a few steps away from her.

"Hello," he said.

"Hello."

"Are they biting?"

She didn't reply. Gonzague Gagnon only needed to look at the fish that surrounded her on the ice—ten perch and two pike. The most recently caught still flopped about before freezing and dying—or dying and freezing.

For a few moments he stood still, watching her. Suddenly the woman jerked her rod. Then she stood up and pulled out a beautiful perch, wriggling through the hole. Gonzague Gagnon moved forward to take the fish off the hook.

"I can do it," said the woman, removing her gloves.

Gonzague Gagnon stepped back. He would have liked to spend the day there, not speaking, just watching her. But he felt he should speak. He searched for a subject of conversation that would be interesting or, better still, would make him interesting.

"I'm a runner," he finally said.

"So it seems."

He ought to have added that he was an apprentice mechanic. But for the first time in his life, he was ashamed of his trade. Not that it suddenly seemed too humble. But too ordinary. Doubtless every village in the world had at least one apprentice mechanic, and maybe there were hundreds in the city that this woman came from—it seemed certain that she came from a city.

Again Gonzague Gagnon made his silent search for something to say. Then there was a faint trembling in the air, hardly noticeable.

"It's the train," thought Gonzague Gagnon, pricking up his ears.

In fact the trembling had become a deep and faraway rumbling.

"It's the passenger train," said Gonzague Gagnon.

The woman nodded her head distractedly. All of her attention was on the tip of her fishing rod, which she was shaking in brief staccato bursts.

Gonzague Gagnon turned to watch the train. It was now visible, and rapidly growing larger.

"I can stop trains," he said.

Immediately he regretted having spoken. The woman had given him a look that was both incredulous and indifferent, as if he were insane.

"I'm going to show her," he said to himself. And then, aloud: "You'll see."

But suddenly he feared that his power might have weakened with the passage of time. He ran towards the railway track, to be closer to the train.

A second doubt seized him: what if the young woman found his ability to stop trains absolutely useless? Would he not be more sure of impressing her if at the same time he demonstrated his courage?

He climbed the embankment and positioned himself on a railway tie, facing the train. The train was only about a hundred metres away. Gonzague Gagnon could feel the track vibrating beneath his feet. He waited a few seconds. Then he crossed his arms and closed his eyes.

"Stop," he said in a firm voice, loud enough for the young woman to hear.

The screeching of the wheels was enough to shatter his eardrums—but the noise reassured him of his power. The train came to a stop so close that he felt the heat of the engine on his cheeks.

He opened his eyes and looked towards the woman. She was still there, standing up, a black silhouette in the middle of her circle of fish. She was too far away for him to be able to see if she was watching him. But how could she not?

Voices drew his attention.

"This hasn't happened for years," Gonzague Gagnon heard one rough voice say.

A moment later he was facing two men in overalls.

"What are you doing?" the larger of the two asked him.

"I just wanted to stop the train," stammered Gonzague Gagnon.

"You think you're funny?" the big man asked.

The smaller of the two said nothing, but threw a punch at Gonzague Gagnon's nose. This tiny fellow was a former boxing champion, which explains how Gonzague Gagnon was literally lifted from the earth. He flapped his arms in the air, expecting to land on the railway track or roll down the embankment.

But he was so close to the bridge that he fell into the river, in a place where the ice was thin.

He was immediately snatched up by the current. He tried to use his nails to grasp the rough surface of the ice above him: but the current was too strong. Then he said to himself that it would be better to let go and hold his breath: the open river wasn't far away and a fit man like himself had only to let himself be carried along under the ice until he was in the clear.

He stayed on his back in the water, pushing with his palms against the ice to make himself go more quickly.

He saw a long shadow across the ice and at the end of this shadow two darker patches. This must be the woman, he thought. How he should tell her not to worry, that he would be back soon. But he reminded himself that he was under water. So he kept his mouth closed tight even though his lungs were beginning to burn. A few seconds later he decided to swallow just a little water, because that would be less painful than continuing to hold his breath.

Through the ice he saw the shadows of the great willow trees that flanked the river. He thought that he would soon be safe.

After that he saw nothing more.

"Impossible," he thought. "I am only half-way through my life."

When spring came Gaston Gagnon, who was religious, nailed a crossbar onto the stake which, on the other side of the river, had marked the half-way point of Gonzague Gagnon.

Translated by Matt Cohen

ADELAIDE TO ALICE SPRINGS

Chapter 3 from *Train to Julia Creek: A Journey to the Heart of Australia*

Scyld Berry (1954–)

A journalist with the Sunday Telegraph of London, Scyld Berry has traveled in India, Australia and North Yemen to cover cricket matches. These journeys have provided him with the material for his books like Cricket Wallah: With England in India, 1981–1982 *(1982),* The Observer on Cricket *(1987),* Cricket Odyssey *(1988) and* 100 Great Bowlers *(1989).*

As Australia does not have an overwhelming interest in its past I think it's appropriate that the memory of these Afghan pioneers should have been perpetuated in the name of the train from Adelaide to Alice Springs, the Ghan. Exactly when the name stuck—whether it originated in the anecdote about an Afghan passenger stopping to pray beside the track at Oodnadata in 1923, or in the fact that the construction trains going up to William Creek in the 1880s were half full of Afghans—can never be established and it hardly matters. It is "the Ghan" and always will be, even the new standard-gauge version of it which has been running since 1980 via Tarcoola.

Perhaps inevitably, the new Ghan is to the old Ghan what the New English Bible is to the King James: modernised but lacking in mystery. It wasn't so much the drifting sand which made a journey on the old Ghan eventful, or the bushfires, or the occasional derailment, or the wild camels that had to be shunted off the line, or the plagues of grasshoppers and ants which at times swarmed so thickly that the rails were too slippery to grip. "It was the clouds you had to watch out for," a former driver told me, "you always had to keep an ear and eye out for them." The old Ghan ran along some creek beds that drained into Lake Eyre, and over flimsy bridges spanning others, and when the rain began torrential flash-floods would come down so suddenly that there might be no chance to avoid the on-coming rush. The best a driver could do was wait on higher ground till the flood subsided. Thus the Ghan was often delayed a week, sometimes for several weeks, once for three months; 200 passengers had to be air-lifted from the carriage roofs by helicopter in 1963; but few passengers complained, for none of them expected the old Ghan to keep to its schedule on worn-out narrow-gauge track.

The new Ghan is efficient and regular, as efficient and regular as it is unexciting. Not only in the matter of gauge has the route been standardised: it is now like a modern train journey anywhere else in sealed, air-conditioned carriages, having no more contact with the landscape it passes through than if the countryside were a cinema screen outside the window. You leave Adelaide in the morning, set off from Port Pirie in the afternoon and wake up next morning not far out of Alice Springs. Perhaps the surprising and wonderful thing is that the anachronism of the old Ghan actually lasted until the 1980s.

The crew on board the new Ghan still recalled the old one fondly on the evening I travelled north from Adelaide; I think most of them, even the younger men, would have gladly gone back to it. "When we left home in Pirie on a Monday," said one gaunt old hand, "we used to say, 'See you Friday'. But you never knew which Friday it might be—the next, the one after or a month later. It was even worse before they built a standard-gauge line up to Marree in 1957 as it could take a couple of hours to do fifteen miles on the old narrow-gauge through Quorn. Then we crossed the platform in Marree to the Ghan proper and the fun began.

"I started as a waiter in the buffet car, which meant that after leaving Marree on a Monday night we served breakfast, lunch and dinner on the Tuesday and breakfast on the Wednesday morning before reaching Alice—if everything went to schedule, that is. We brought all the tucker up from Pirie for the journey there and back, but there wasn't a 'frig on the Ghan until the sixties, just blocks of ice which used to melt after a couple of days until we could get some more in Alice.

"We had two big coal-burning stoves in the kitchen and the cook had to be up at four-thirty, chopping up old tomato crates for wood to get 'em going and put the steaks on. It was that smoky in there we used to call him Al Jonson, and every trip someone had to climb on to the roof to clean the chimney out."

Old Hand stopped to refresh himself. His beer can was wrapped in one of the white napkins left in our dining-car.

"I reckon it sometimes reached 150° in that kitchen. You couldn't wear a collar and tie in there, just a tee-shirt and handkerchief round your neck. Of course you weren't allowed a beer because railway rules said you could never drink on board—but they'd roll a five-gallon keg on all the same at Quorn. The inspector would get on there too but he'd never find it in that kitchen, that's how good they were at hiding it."

When Old Hand started in the fifties the carriages came from Germany and had Rhine castles painted all over their interiors. They didn't have any air-conditioning, just a canvas water-bag at the end of each carriage from which to take a drink. Some of the diesel engines brought in about then came from Germany too, and he said they had the same sort of engine as the old U-boats. Later they built some carriages in Port Augusta which had battery-operated air-conditioners in the lounge-car and dining-car, but even then the dust and rain still came in round the window frames and passengers in the morning had their faces covered in grime.

"I had to go round every morning with hot water, for washing and shaving in, with a couple of watering cans like you have in your garden. 'Have a shave this morning, sir?' I used to say. Had to do the shoes as well, which they left in a box outside the compartment door. I'd clean 'em if there was two bob inside; if there wasn't I'd leave 'em or put a bit of black polish on if they were brown ones.

"After breakfast I had to go round selling sweets and things down the train. There'd be two or three first-class and a couple of second-class carriages, and at the back you used to get all the old stockmen and boongs [Aborigines]. One day when I was sixteen I went into the last carriage to sell my minties and one of 'em says to me: 'Have a drink, go on, have a drink, lad!' And he was drinking metho—methylated spirits. I ran out of there with one hand on my wallet and the other on my minties and didn't dare go back.

"It was hot in summer all right, 1400 in the water-bag, and the winds were freezing in winter: I reckon that was the worst part of it. But the floods were all right, something different; they made it into a regular mystery tour. We were never near starving or anything like that because these old bombers would come overhead as slow as possible and drop a load of canvas bags, which would burst and scatter meat and vegies all over the roof. The old boongs round Oodnadatta used to have a field-day then, picking up all the stray tucker.

"I've seen water thirty feet deep and quarter of a mile wide at the Alberga Bridge and several times we were stuck at Finke River. They built concrete pillars for a new bridge there, and—no bullshit—it collapsed the first time it flooded: a bloody great mallee was swept down, the water banked up behind and I reckon it must have undermined the whole bridge. We had to spend three days there once, waiting for the water to go down. Whenever we were stuck at the Finke we bought all the tucker out of the store and all the drink out of the pub, and the railway had to pay. That's why it never made any money—paying passengers' meals for a week or two instead of the scheduled couple of days."

The conductor came round, and Old Hand wrapped the napkin more tightly round his can so that railway regulations wouldn't be seen to be broken. The dining-car had long since emptied after the evening meal. The new Ghan, locked and sealed, hurried over its concrete-sleepered rails.

"After a while of these bridges being washed away," he resumed, "they'd build the line straight through the water-courses. The trouble was that diesels can only go through two or three inches of water because if it gets into your traction motors you're in strife, whereas steam engines could be taken as far under water as they'd go. At least Lake Eyre never gave us much trouble, although I've seen waves coming over us like if you were by the sea. But then it started drying up and the dead fish were something—until the pelicans came along.

"For water we used to stop at William Creek, Edwards Creek, Finke River—anywhere we could water up. When we stopped at William Creek everyone climbed over the fence and went to the pub where they were supposed to sign the book saying they were bona fide travellers, though nobody did. And when the Ghan pulled out, if you were a bit tardy you had to run after it—which was all right, no worries, except if you happened to be carrying a dozen cans.

"By the time we reached Alice I reckon eighty per cent of the bloody township would be waiting to see the Ghan come in. They treated us like kings in those days—walking round amongst the stockmen in our black trousers, and white shirts—'bringing civilisation to the outback', we used to call it. There must have been less than 5,000 people in Alice in those days. Now it's all changed. I don't think I've seen anywhere in the last twenty years that has changed so much as Alice."

But it wasn't called Alice Springs when the first train arrived there—a mere five hours late—in 1929. That name was only applied to the nearby telegraph station. The township itself was known as Stuart until 1933, when the name of Alice Springs was given to the whole settlement to avoid confusion—and a soft feminine name for this oasis between two masculine-sounding deserts, the Gibson and the Simpson, has created a uniquely romantic appeal.

It is being cashed in on. When the number of legalised casinos in the whole of Australia was four, two of them were in Alice Springs. And it is the tourist centre for Ayers Rock, 200 miles away, frequently said to be the greatest monolith in the world but in fact not even the biggest in Australia. "Come to Ayers Rock and watch its many moods from your air-conditioned room or at our slide evenings," the brochures suggest. "In the morning depart from Sunset Strip for a climb to the top of the Rock, sign your name in the visitors' book at the top, and explore the many caves sacred to the Aborigines. And try our Dreamtime Tours!"

OF TIME AND THE TRAIN

from *The New York Times*

Virginia Van Der Veer Hamilton (1921–)

Virginia Van Der Veer Hamilton was a staff writer for the Associated Press during World War II. Much of her contemporary writings focus on her native Alabama. She profiled the Supreme Court Justice in the biography Hugo Black: The Alabama Years *(1972), which was followed by* Alabama: A History *(1977) and* Seeing Historic Alabama *(1982).*

In the early 1940s, with gas severely rationed and commercial aviation unequal to the demands of wartime, I and millions of other Americans aged 20 to 40 moved about the country by train. What a pity that Thomas Wolfe, that bard of train travel, did not live to chronicle an entire generation packed into trains; men in khaki, navy or white bound for leaves or new assignments, others in civilian clothing being transported from plow to machine; thousands of young women like myself, in demure dresses, shoulder-length hair restrained by snoods, heading for jobs vacated by men; a few adventurous women parading in the drab brown skirts and jackets of Wacs or the spiffier blue outfits of Waves.

At major holidays, all of us at once, or so it seemed, jammed aboard the trains, perched on suitcases in the aisle or stood all night or even rode in the dangerous open space between cars to return briefly to familiar surroundings from which war had wrenched us. In summers, these trains converted their steam into an early form of air conditioning. On occasion, however, this process continued to produce heat, whereupon we forced open the windows to admit blasts of humid air along with fine black cinders.

With the ebullience of youth, we transformed these tests of endurance into high adventure: singing (laments like "I'll Never Smile Again" or a nonsensical ballad like "Mairzy Doats"), joking, flirting, eating the stale sandwiches hawked on station platforms, consuming gallons of Coke. For white passengers accustomed to the highly structured society of the South, the all-coach train between Birmingham and New York proved a democratic experience, albeit temporary. I once spent an entire overnight journey in conversation with the young ensign on the next suitcase, a scion of wealth and privilege in my hometown, who I, an offspring of improvident gentry; would never otherwise have met.

My wartime journeys took place aboard the Southerner. I don't remember ever hearing anyone remark on the name of this train. To travelers from the north, the Southerner seemed to promise exotic sights. To us natives, such a designation seemed entirely suitable although we might have taken umbrage at the invasion of a train christened the Northerner.

Despite the romantic implications of its name, the Southerner followed tracks laid down with profit rather than scenery in mind. J. P. Morgan had created the Southern Railway in the late 19th century to help divest the South of timber, coal, iron ore and minerals, and to deliver the yarns and coarse cotton cloth of the Carolina Piedmont to the finishing houses of the East.

Originating in New Orleans, the Southerner whipped through Mississippi's pine barrens and the western edge of Alabama's Black Belt, navigated the smoky haze emitted by Birmingham's steel mills, dawdled in Atlanta, then, after nightfall, moaned and hooted its way through the Piedmont of the Carolinas and Virginia, past towns as empty as deserted stage sets; occasionally coming upon what Wolfe described as "the thrilling, haunting, white-glazed incandescence of a cotton mill"; sometimes pulling alongside another train occupied entirely by khaki-clad men. What a torrent of eloquence those troop trains would have evoked from Wolfe!

More than four decades after these journeys, I await another train northbound from Birmingham. The Southerner is no more, but Amtrak operates its longtime companion, the Crescent, its name hinting at the fleshpots of New Orleans. As it approaches, I see that the Crescent is propelled by a workaday diesel instead of one of the smoke-belching Pacific steam engines, green trimmed in gold, that were the pride of the Southern line. On the platform, knots of people are absorbed in the rituals of farewell. But the roles of the 40's seem reversed: now the younger generation is seeing its elders aboard.

As the journey unfolds, I am struck by evidence of further change. Gone are the Jim Crow cars that always headed up the trains of the 40's. No heavy curtain separates blacks from whites in the dining car; now races mingle in club car and diner as if it had never been otherwise. Plastic, in the form of dishes, tablecloths, napkins and yellow roses, has displaced glass, china, cotton and nature. Microwaved steaks and eggs have succeeded the Spanish omelets and corned-beef hash of memory. However Amtrak is not wholly oblivious to tradition: its menu still boasts of "old-fashioned French railroad toast" and coyly suggests that "on certain trains" grits may be substituted for home fries.

But the route through the Piedmont is as drab as ever, cruelly revealing the South's enduring poverty: Kudzu, not yet green, grips expanses of this infertile clay like a gray hairnet. Clearings beside the tracks reveal scruffy pine trees, shacks, trailers and rainbow-hued jumbles of what had once been automobiles. In the era when my choice of a car was limited to a black Ford or a dark green Ford, and in years when no cars rolled off American assembly lines, what might I have sacrificed for an automobile such as one of these rusting models in its prime?

By contrast with sitting all night on a suitcase, I consider my roomette a marvel. In an enclosure 4 feet by 6 feet, I am provided with washbasin, toilet, tiny closet, a small enclosure opening into the aisle in case my shoes need shining, mirrors, reading light, night light, eyeglasses case, armchair or bed and—greatest treasure of all—privacy. I am

separated from fellow travelers by a door as well as the traditional curtain. No matter that disrobing requires the agility of a contortionist; in the skies above, only presidents and potentates rate luxuries like these.

But I find it impossible to sleep while hurtling feet first toward my destination, especially on a train that stops at least once an hour. Never mind. Wolfe, drinking, roistering or thrashing about in his berth, stored up vivid images for *Of Time and the River* on the passage from midnight to dawn over this route: a little "moving-picture theater . . . that one small cell of radiance, warmth and joy" in a dark Carolina town; a black station attendant toiling to pull a heavy truck loaded with baggage, the landscape of Virginia, "dreaming in the moonlight."

Through my window, I observe the cotton mills and lumberyards of Wolfe's era but I also see newer plants that produce plastic roses, nuclear power or nylon pantyhose. And neon billboards proclaiming theme parks, auto speedways and the electronic ministry. Who would have dreamed of such eventualities in the days when a woman's rarest possession was a pair of silk stockings?

As we cross the Potomac, the porter knocks to offer a plastic cup of coffee. It is still the case that most train attendants are black. But white jackets have been replaced by snappy red vests or tunics; the deferential "yes ma'am" has given way to amiable breeziness. My requests meet with an almost unvarying response. I would like a bucket of ice. "No problem!" An extra blanket. "No problem!" A morning paper. "No problem!" More coffee. "Sure. No problem!"

I am surprised, however, that this porter is a female. Lots of women work on trains nowadays, she informs me, explaining cheerily: "This is the 80s, honey."

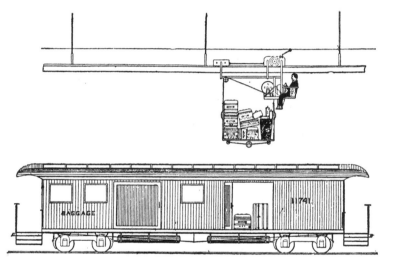

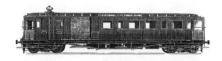

FROM *NIGHT TRAIN TO TURKISTAN:* MODERN ADVENTURES ALONG CHINA'S ANCIENT SILK ROAD

Stuart Stevens

Stuart Stevens is the founder of a political advertising firm, a novelist and travel writer. His most notable work, Night Train to Turkistan: Modern Adventure's Along China's Ancient Silk Road *(1988), documents his and three friends' travels along the legendary trade route to re-create a trek taken by 1930s writers Peter Fleming and Ella Maillart. The comical* Feeding Frenzy: Across Europe in Search of the Perfect Meal *(1997) relates his adventures dining at nearly thirty of Europe's Michelin three-star restaurants in just under a month.*

Chapter One

From the beginning it was a silly idea, without the slightest utilitarian purpose or merit. This, of course, I liked.

The scheme was to retrace Peter Fleming and Ella Maillart's 1935 journey from Beijing to India via Kashgar. Their's was a preposterous trip made by the most unlikely of companions. A young English aristocrat from a family of notable eccentrics teamed with a decidedly down-to-earth Swiss woman who was a member of the Swiss national sailing team. That they happened to be traveling through the area farthest from any ocean on the face of the earth seemed in complete keeping with the tone of the venture. Fleming was in a rush to get back to England in time for the grouse-hunting season; Maillart could have, as she put it, "spent her life learning more about Chinese Turkistan and its people." To Fleming—who once dissuaded a friend from beating up an incompetent native guide in Brazil by pointing out how rude it was to hit your butler—a life in Turkistan would have been a sentence.

Both wrote books about the adventure; Peter Fleming's 1936 *News From Tartary* was a trans-Atlantic hit, confirming his position as a literary leader of a post-World War I generation gone travel mad. Ella Maillart—or Kini, as everyone called her—titled her book *Forbidden Journey*. It made her a celebrity, one of the few women to participate in the travel-writing craze.

The big question, naturally, was whether the two were lovers. That and what sort of gun Fleming should have taken with him:

Sirs: It is difficult to comprehend the foolishness of setting across Asia on foot armed only, as we are to believe Mr. Peter Fleming was, with a defective .44 and a .22 sporting rifle. The "Times" would have done well to present their Special Correspondent with a proper .256 Mannlicher. Had Mr. Fleming been called upon, as he had reason to believe he might, to shoot himself out of a tight corner, his childish .22, which he refers to lovingly as a "rook" rifle, would hardly have served his purposes well.

Respectfully,
Mr. T. B. Money-Coutts

Sirs: I wonder how those who look on a .22 as a childish toy would like to make a target of the plump part of their own back view at 100 yards—or even 150—for a good .22 cartridge.

Lieutenant-Colonel G. A. Anson

This was all very serious stuff for *Times'* readers; the topic dominated the avidly read letters section for months after Fleming's account of the trip appeared in the spring of 1936. The other question, the sexual one, regrettably never made it into print. (Though it's true that when King Edward shocked the world in the summer of '36 by slipping off to the Mediterranean on a pleasure yacht with Mrs. Simpson, a trip around which rumors of nude sunbathing swirled, the press duly noted that everyone on board was reading *News From Tartary*.)

That Fleming and Maillart were traveling at all together was an acute embarrassment to both. His last book had been titled *One's Company*; her's was *Turkistan Solo*. Each revered the idea of "going it alone" and had substantial literary capital invested in their images of lone voyagers. In *One's Company*

Fleming had even gone to the trouble to give an overelaborate description of the joys of a party of one:

> It is easy enough for one man to adapt himself to living under strange and constantly changing conditions. It is much harder for two. Leave A or B alone in a distant country, and each will evolve a congenial *modus vivendi*. Throw them together, and the comforts of companionship are as likely as not offset by the strain of reconciling their divergent methods. A likes to start early and halt for a siesta; B does not feel the heat and insists on sleeping late. A instinctively complies with regulations, B instinctively defies them. A finds it impossible to pass a temple, B finds it impossible to pass a bar. . . .

For Fleming and Maillart, though, even traveling alone was no good if they weren't headed someplace strange and exotic, the more difficult to get to the better. "The trouble about journeys nowadays is that they are easy to make but difficult to justify," Fleming wrote in his introduction to *Tartary*. "The earth, which once danced and spun before us as alluringly as a celluloid ball on top of a fountain in a rifle-range, is now a dull and vulnerable target." But trying to make it from Peking to India across Chinese Turkistan was a challenge that even in the horribly modern era of the mid-1930s, could capture the imagination of a restless traveler.

In January of 1935, Fleming and Maillart both washed up in Peking after long journeys—solo, of course—through the East. Each was ready to return to Europe, and each had the rather absurd notion of traveling overland through Western China into India. Depending on the exact route, it was a 3,500-to-5,000-mile trip across the sort of territory boys' adventure stories relished labeling "barren and inhospitable." They were headed toward Xinjiang province, "the last home of romance in international politics," Fleming wrote. "Intrigue, violence, and melodrama have long been native to the Province . . . The Province is at the best of times difficult of access, being surrounded on three sides by mountain ranges whose peaks run well over 20,000 feet and on the fourth side by the Gobi and the wastes of Mongolia." In difficulty and length, the journey had a striking resemblance to the Long March led by Mao Zedong in 1934. Ninety thousand troops started; twenty thousand finished.

"As a matter of fact, I'm going back to Europe by that route," Fleming announced to Maillart in Peking. This was after she had confided her idea of crossing Turkistan on the way back to Europe. "You can come back with me if you like."

"I beg your pardon," she answered, "it's my route and it's I who will take you, if I can think of some way in which you might be useful to me."

You had to like this pair.

Chapter Eight

Leaving Xi'an is not an easy thing to do. Fleming and Maillart reluctantly hitched rides with a convoy of trucks that "did not look as if they would leave the next day; they did not look as if they would ever move again." This proved to be painfully close to the truth.

For us it should have been easy. All we had to do was buy a train ticket to Xinning, pack our bags, and leave.

No, no, no.

The CITS office will sell train sleeper tickets to foreigners—but only three or more days in advance.

This would make sense if it were a matter of reserving space, needing to contact another city to verify availability, any of those sorts of logical processes. What happens in practice, however, is that you request your ticket properly ahead of your departure date, and then on the day you are scheduled to leave, a member of the CITS staff bicycles over to the train station and tries to buy a ticket.

But no matter. There is no need to go through CITS. Anyone can do the same thing—bicycle over to the train station and buy a sleeper ticket.

At least that's the theory.

Let me describe the Xi'an train station. There is a main building of crumbling brick facing a typically massive dirt courtyard laced with broken glass and bits of masonry, generally the sort of effect induced by a moderate artillery bombardment. Since this courtyard is always jammed with people moving at panic speed-the only time Chinese seem to be in a hurry is at train stations and then they are *always* in a hurry-the dust kicked up is extreme.

Encircling the courtyard and station building is a stone wall about eight feet high strung with barbed wire. Whether this wall is intended to keep people out or in, I can't say. The gates in this wall are cleverly concealed on either side. Just finding them for the first time takes a good half-hour of questioning and hunting.

Inside the station, the scene resembles the World Cup soccer riot a few years ago in Belgium, the one the British press headlined KILLER PANIC. At waist height, the walls are riddled with windows slightly bigger than those on a largish birdhouse.

These are the ticket windows.

Each window sells tickets only for certain precise and limited circumstances—such as non-express trains leaving on Mondays for Xinning. Another window will handle tickets for Tuesday. Another entire series of windows exists for express trains.

And overnight trains. None of these are marked or arranged in order. To discover the designated purpose of each window, one waits in line. And waits and waits.

But the ticket windows inside the station are only part of the story. Sprinkled at random outside the station, some even outside the walls, are more ticket windows, each with a specific function.

There is nothing more complicated than buying a soft-sleeper berth. The reason for this is that soft-sleeper compartments are the most expensive and there seems to be a prevalent opinion in China that the more money you spend the more difficult everything should be.

To buy a soft-sleeper berth you must first find the window that exists for no other purpose than selling soft-sleeper tickets to foreigners. Since there are no other foreigners around and any non-foreigner, i.e. Chinese, has never needed such a ticket window, finding this exact window takes hours.

In fact, the proper window is *behind* the train station, an utterly ingenious location as it is invariably the last place one would look. Be warned it is only open two hours a day. But when it is open and you lean down to fit your face directly over the tiny window and explain, trying not to cough as the attendant blows smoke at you, what it is you want, the attendant, taking a while to transfer a particularly persistent hunk of mucous from his lungs to your feet, will issue you a little piece of colored tissue paper. This is cause for great celebration until you realize it is not actually a ticket. This flimsy bit of tissue merely verifies the fact that you are a real foreigner. That's all. Trying not to think why this might ever have been in question, you must proceed with your little toilet paper scrap to the actual ticket window.

If you can find it.

ROLLING HOME FOR CHRISTMAS: RIDING AMTRAK IN THE 1980s

from *Lands End catalog 24, 1988*

Eric Zorn (1958–)

Eric Zorn is a columnist for the Chicago Tribune *and co-author, with Joel Kaplan and George Papajohn,* *of* Murder of Innocence: The Tragic Life and Final Rampage of Laurie Dann, the Schoolhouse Killer *(1990).*

There is nothing to see out the window of the train but visions of the girl, of the family, and of Christmas.

Pfc. Ken Worthington is coming home from the Army for the first time. Night has fallen across the Illinois prairie, and a train they call "The California Zephyr" is rolling west across America fully loaded with passengers, presents, and holiday hopes.

"It's going to be like the old movies," says Private Worthington, passing time in a window seat in the club-car lounge. "You know, when the soldier gets off the train and his girl and his folks are waiting for him? It's going to be the ultimate."

He is 25 years old. He was working on the family farm in Roseville, Illinois, earlier this year when he decided he "wanted a different way of life," he says.

He left his girlfriend, Jenelle, and four siblings, and ended up stationed in San Antonio at Fort Sam Houston.

"Homesickness hits a lot of guys hard in the Army," he says, not talking about himself, exactly, but sort of. He flew up from Texas and caught the train in Chicago's Union Station. He is in uniform, on two week's leave, having a Coke, getting nervous and, now, less than 100 miles from home. It is the Saturday before Christmas and nearly all of the more than 400 passengers on the California Zephyr are headed home in one manner of speaking or another.

Debbie Perryman has lived in Little Rock, Arkansas, for many years, but home for her is still the family home in Denver where she is taking her husband, Rick, and daughter Emily, 7, for the holidays. The national rail network is now so thin that the Perrymans have had to go the long way around the farm belt and are now even further from their destination than they were when they left Little Rock.

"We wanted family time for just the three of us," says Rick Perryman, who is sitting on the arm of a chair in the club-car lounge and has his arm halfway around Debbie. "We can read. We can sightsee. We can get right back into the heart of this country."

"The train is so nostalgic," says Debbie. "And Christmas is such a nostalgic holiday."

She is a 1st grade teacher and speaks with a professionally honed enthusiasm. "You fly, you miss it all," she says. "This is an adventure, like a cruise."

The lounge is halfway back in the 14-car, quarter-mile-long train. A woman in a red vest stands at a counter in the middle and sells snacks and drinks. The windows are huge, curling into a partial dome on the roof of the car, but at night they reveal only what the imagination supplies.

"We'll go to services in the church I was brought up in," says Debbie Perryman, anticipating the holidays. "And, of course, we'll have to have oyster stew on Christmas Eve. It's an old tradition that I'm trying to break. I detest it."

"My family never experienced me being gone for so long," says Private Worthington. The train is running 20 minutes behind schedule and he knows people are already waiting for him at the station in Galesburg, Illinois, "It was a dramatic blow when I left."

In the next couple of days, he says, he and his neighbors will drive around in a pickup truck, caroling from door-to-door. "Then we'll have a bonfire," he says. "We used to have what they call barn dances, but they don't do so much dancing anymore. Now they're just get-togethers."

Down the line, the old-fashioned Amtrak station in Galesburg buzzes with the anticipation of those waiting to get on and of those waiting to meet loved ones. When Ken Worthington steps onto the platform, at first he cannot see anyone he recognizes. He can't hide his disappointment. He hitches his bag and trudges toward the station.

But then, from out of the darkness. . . .

He is home again. Jenelle is waiting. And behind him the train lurches and rolls away.

Dana Meyer is writing a short story.

"It's kinda dumb," she says. "Kinda hard to explain. I write a lot of morbid, depressing, horrible types of things. This one is about someone following someone down a street."

She is a junior in high school, sandy haired, coltish, eager. Her friends in Mobile, Alabama, have given her a blank, clothbound book to write in during the family train trip to visit relatives in the San Francisco area.

But the writing is not going well. The joyous spirit of the holidays has made it difficult for Dana's muse to sustain a dark mood.

"Christmas is special, the whole day," she says, casually draping a hand over the book to hide what she has written. "It's not what you get, it's the event itself. For our family it ties in with the train trip. Flying is too quick; we don't like it. The journey is just as important as the destination."

She is an actress in school and seems to have a gift for talking in quotes.

"I'll give you more," she says. "I love the train because you meet people. When I was 6, I met a lady on a train from India in full Indian dress. She said she was a princess. She said that I was a fascinating person."

Paul Michels hasn't taken a train trip since World War II, when he rode a troop transport from North Carolina to Washington, D. C., standing the whole way.

He and his wife, Agnes, now live in Rhinelander, Wisconsin, way up there, and are headed west to spend Christmas in Fort Collins, Colorado, with their two daughters and their 11-year old grandchild.

"We hardly know her, " says Agnes of her grandchild. Agnes is wearing a black sweater with a sparkling Christmas tree pendant on it. She and Paul are in chairs facing the window, keeping an eye out for the occasional small town with multi-colored lights.

"In Rhinelander," says Paul, "people have really gone all out. You see thousands of lights on houses."

Many holiday traditions in the Michels family are fluid, as they are for most families that are scattered geographically. Some years the girls come back to Rhinelander. Other years Paul and Agnes celebrate with their son, who still lives near home.

But every year, no matter what, family members always eat rutabagas with dinner on Christmas Eve.

Little Emily Perryman has written 13 letters to Santa Claus, each of them different. "The one thing that came up in all of them is that she wants a My Little Pony Perm Shop," says her father.

"With a Little Pony," adds Emily, a forward and wide-eyed child. She climbs around on her parents while they sit and talk, and the California Zephyr blows across the Mississippi River into Iowa.

"I was trying to explain to Emily about all the farmland we've been seeing out the window," says Debbie Perryman. "These people are feeding the United States. We're going through the breadbasket of America."

Rick Perryman, who is an executive with a power company in Arkansas, expresses more interest in the small towns and backyards he has seen. "You see the old taverns," he says. "Not bars, taverns. Every old neighborhood has its own tavern. So peaceful. So neighborly."

Emily says, frankly, she preferred the first train— the one the family took from Little Rock to Chicago. On that train, people in the club lounge sang Christmas songs. On this train, people in the lounge are silently watching the movie

"Mannequin," which has just started showing on TV sets at either end of the car.

Emily and Debbie get up to take a walk. Rick stays behind.

"Santa's going to bring her that My Little Pony Perm Shop," he says in confidence. "Plus more than she can imagine."

Agnes Michels gets sad when she thinks of trains. When she was a young woman in the Upper Peninsula of Michigan, and working as a telephone operator, she and the other local girls would go down to the station to see the boys off to war.

"That whistle would blow and everyone would cry," she says.

But the train also brought young Paul Michels back from the war. The two then met in a dairy bar where Paul says with a wink, he had actually had gone to hunt up an old girlfriend. Someone introduced him to Agnes instead. Forty years ago.

"Hard work, that's the secret," says Agnes.

"Hard work and compromise," says Paul.

"For example, usually he makes the decisions," says Agnes. "But making this train trip was my idea. Good idea I had, huh?"

She nudges him gently and he nods.

In the dining car, John Cahall has ordered the vegetarian entrée, pasta shells stuffed with ricotta cheese and splashed with marinara sauces.

Vegetarianism is part of the Indian philosophy of Vedanta, which he is studying at a small rural school in Pennsylvania. He is traveling across the country to be with his brother and his brother's family in Ukiah, California, 100 miles north of San Francisco.

"I'm not a big Christmas person," he says. "It's no big deal to me. It's probably because of emotional hangups from childhood."

Cahall is 46 but looks at least 10 years younger. His hair falls to the top of his shoulders in back, he wears wire-rimmed glasses, and he carries a knapsack around the train.

He grew up on a dairy and tobacco farm in Ohio but ended up in San Francisco, where he worked for the city in a senior citizens escort program. But eventually he was so drawn to Vedanta that he signed up for a three-year intensive course of study.

He had planned to do some good reading on the train, but so far, he says, he's mostly been relaxing and looking out the window. He's been aboard since last night and will not reach his destination for almost two more days.

"I like riding the train," he says, a hedge in his voice. "I have gotten discouraged a few times. But I guess I'm just not real crazy about flying."

"Safety seems to be the big reason people ride with us," says Amtrak porter Robert Brooker. He is reading a paperback potboiler called Rainbow Drive as the passengers in his coach sprawl across their seats in the comical attitudes of sleep.

It is nighttime on the California Zephyr. The movie is over in the lounge car and stops are now more than an hour apart as the Great Plains spread out to either side of the tracks.

"A woman passenger last week took her own survey to see why people would ride the train," says Brooker. "I don't remember the percentages, but the reasons were safety, cost, convenience, scenery, and love of the railroad. The railroad still has a peculiar mystique and fascination for some people."

Holidays are always busy and crowded on Amtrak, says Brooker, who quit a job as a restaurant maitre d' four years ago and joined the railroad to help get over a painful divorce. But despite the crowds this time of year, passengers are in a good mood.

He, too, is in a good mood. He, too, is headed home for the holidays. His four children and three grandchildren are waiting for him in Los Angeles.

"The last one was born November 12," he says. "I haven't seen him yet. I'm dying to see him."

Sleep? No. Ron Patterson cannot possibly.

"I get all wound up," he says. "I get overwhelmed with it all."

He says he has not slept since getting on the train in Culpepper, Virginia, yesterday afternoon. He and his wife and daughter are going to Portland, Oregon, to see his in-laws, and this will be the first Christmas in his 39 years that he will be away from Virginia.

He is in the club car on the lower level of the train, knocking back Budweisers with a kid named Scott Hohenshell from Omaha.

Hohenshell has gone by the nickname "Cricket" ever since he learned how to make cricket noises in junior high study hall. He demonstrates the noises repeatedly, to the evident distraction of the people up ahead in the club car who are having a loud argument about presidential politics.

"I've been trying to catch some city lights," says Patterson. He carries a portable radio to try to pick up some country music, but the bright orange earphone pads are sitting uselessly on his collar. "There's just not that much out here," he says.

Fifteen members of his wife's family will gather in Portland to feast and exchange presents. Patterson is hoping for snow "to make it feel like a traditional Christmas," but the forecast for the Pacific Northwest is not promising.

Cricket chirrups. At the other end of the car in a dense cloud of cigarette smoke, a big round guy in a military-style uniform that is not really a military uniform brags loudly to a circle of strangers about an expensive lighter he once owned.

The train crosses the Missouri River and rolls into Omaha. Some dude in an honest-to-goodness authentic relic of a leisure suit cackles that Nebraska

women are the most wonderful women of all. For an awkward moment, his remark kills the conversation.

"My fault," says Robert Brooker, the porter. He is talking about his divorce. The reading lamp above his seat in the dark coach looks like a spotlight on him.

"But neither of us ever remarried," he says. "So every year at Christmas we get together with the family. It's like nothing ever happened. The kids really love it."

Christmas Eve will be at their son's house in sub-urban Los Angeles. They will open a few presents and have a quiet dinner.

"I haven't been to church on Christmas Eve for a long time, but I think I'm going to take my mother this year," he says. "She's 86. There aren't too many Christmases left for her."

The next day they will travel a few miles to their daughter's house, where they will have a major feed and open the rest of their presents.

Brooker rides the California Zephyr for six straight days when he leaves home. "You've got a lot of time out here to ponder life's problems," he says. "Sometimes you get a few of its answers."

Ron Patterson did doze off there for about two hours during the night. Then he woke up Shirley and Nikki, their 5-year old, for breakfast. His watch said 6 A. M. but the train had crossed time zones and it was actually 5 A. M., an hour before the dining car opens.

"Man," he says later. "Come Monday I am going to be ready to be off this train for a while."

Nikki Patterson has made several little friends in the coach where Ron and Shirley have reserved seats. They play together while one of the parents keeps an eye on the group. A sense of community is building among the long-haul coach passengers who by now, half an hour from Denver, are nodding at each other when they pass in the aisles.

There is less familiarity among the first-class passengers, squirreled away in tiny sleeping compartments for which they have paid a premium of up to $200 each. The train is generally cheaper than flying if you don't get a sleeper, but it can take its toll in other ways.

"I just never could sleep in a moving car or anything," says Ron Patterson, who has reached the delicate state of fatigue where conversation begins to slide lazily here and there. "I've been that way all my life."

He is a groundskeeper on a private estate in Orange County, Virginia, and Shirley drives a school bus part time. They are getting Nikki a Barbie doll for Christmas. Ron has bought Shirley a diamond ring, but it is still on lay-away at the store.

"Lordy, Lordy, Rick is 40," sings Emily Perryman, nervous energy getting the best of her as the California Zephyr creeps the last mile toward the Denver train station. These words were written in icing on her father's last birthday cake and they have remained deeply etched in her memory.

"That's right, dear," says Debbie Perryman, somehow still euphoric after 33 hours on the train. She and Rick have packed up their sleeping compartment and seem almost as excited as their daughter to meet the family at the platform.

It has been Rick Perryman's first train ride. "I wouldn't have taken this trip any other way," he says. "It's been its own minivacation. We paid about what we would have to take an airplane, but we got more for our money this way."

When Debbie sees her mother and father waving on the platform, she looks happy enough even to eat oyster stew.

Agnes Michels slept the night reclined in an aisle seat and covered by her winter coat. But she is fresh, with new lipstick on, when the California Zephyr finally stops in Denver.

Granddaughter Allison is right there to greet her and Paul. The family embraces at more or less the same time that the Perrymans fall into delightful hugs with their family, bags and suitcases flying.

"Oregon!" shouts Debora Burd. She does not mean to shout, only she has earphones on and has been singing along loudly to a cassette tape of bluegrass music. "Dad is in Pendleton and we'll probably spend Christmas with my grandmother."

She takes off the headphones and turns off the tape player. "My train music," she explains. She has retreated to the lower half of the coach where she has found a door with an open window to lean out. The clean, cool mountain air blows her hair back.

"Last year, I met a guy from Paonia on the train," she says. "It was a railroad rendezvous. We drank a lot of beers and had a lot of fun. I was hoping it might happen again."

Burd is 31 and studying marketing at the Community College of Denver. She and two younger sisters are gathering at the family home for a quiet holiday celebration in honor of her grandmother, who is deaf, blind, and suffering from a variety of other ailments.

"I think it will be a sad Christmas," she says. "But I want Grandmother to be happy. If we can distract her from her discomfort for just a little while, it will be a good Christmas, I guess."

The skies are not cloudy so the lounge car has turned into a viewing salon. No seats available.

Dana Meyer, the short story writer, is curled up in a chair composing in a neat hand.

Insomniac Ron Patterson sits facing his wife who, to his annoyance, had a wonderful night's sleep.

John Cahall has taken a break from Indian philosophy and is reading *The Denver Post*.

And Trevor Copeland, a 16-year-old from

Paragould, Arkansas, has fallen into a rambling discussion about Stephen King's horror novels with Mike Range, a college football quarterback from suburban Chicago.

Copeland is traveling with his parents and two sisters to Colfax, California, where some 25 members of his extended family are having their biggest family reunion in a decade. "Dad's the only one of us who's ever been on a train before," he says.

Range is headed to Salt Lake City, where his parents have just moved. He now lives with his grandparents in his Mom and Dad's old house.

"It's weird," he says, contemplating the concept of "home" in this context.

The train cautiously follows the grade along the Fraser River toward Granby, and the young men lean forward against the glass to watch water dance in the half-frozen rapids. To accompany the scenery, Amtrak has piped in orchestral versions of popular hit songs, with string parts as sweet as the strawberry pancake topping at breakfast.

Copeland turns and says to Range, "Did you know that Stephen King once wrote books under the name Richard Bachman?

But of course he does.

Mary Lou Phillips has been interviewed before. Just last week, in fact, she was featured as the "Cook of the Corner" in the *Jefferson County Bee and Herald*, with a special focus on her Calico Beans Casserole.

"Oh, we love Christmas," she says. "We think it's a great time of year."

It is lunchtime in the dining car, and she and her husband, Robert, are both eating hamburgers because Robert is a cattle farmer and it's a question of professional loyalty.

Robert Phillips is an arresting sight in his red flannel shirt and his striped overalls. The couple—parents of six, grandparents of 10—are travelling to Pocatello, Idaho, from their home in rural southeast Iowa.

"The kids get together every year to buy us a gift," says Mary Lou. "One year it was wrist watches. One year it was a set of dishes. One year it was an exercise bike—we don't use that. And this year it's this trip."

They will spend Christmas in Idaho with their daughter and her family, whom they haven't seen in two years.

Robert Phillips flew for the U.S. Air Force in Europe during World War II, but has not flown since and will not fly now. "I still have the ulcers," he says. "The train is good enough for me."

"We've been watching the view and eating caramel corn," says Mary Lou, who works in a factory that builds washing machine parts while her husband tends to 90 cows and 5 bulls. "I brought along some magazines, but I haven't even read them yet."

Moses Green, a dining car waiter, regularly passes through some of the most magnificently scenic country in the world, the American Rockies. But he has never gotten off the train to look around.

"Someday," he says, "I should do it."

Today, though, Green's mind is on a different vacation—his upcoming visit home to Manning, South Carolina, where he will spend Christmas with his parents, four brothers, four sisters, aunts, uncles, and a variety of other relations.

"We always get a big pig, cut him in the middle and barbeque him in the yard," Green says. Green has worked for Amtrak for four years. He now lives in the rough Uptown neighborhood of Chicago, but gets back south once a year. His work schedule will take him Christmas Eve back to Chicago, where he will hop another train as a passenger and arrive home on Christmas Day.

"Some people on the crew make a lot of friends," he says, stopping to talk during a lull between meals.

"I tend not to socialize so much. My life is really off the train."

Nothing you can see from the windows of the lounge car can eclipse the beauty of the love between Hud Hudson and Tara Hughes. He is 23. She is 22. They are going back home to Boise, Idaho, with brand new, golden wedding rings on their left hands. Actually, they are not married yet. Not until two days after Christmas. "But we didn't want to lose the rings," says Hughes, almost apologetically.

They are graduate students at the University of Rochester in New York state, he in philosophy, she in English literature. They went to the same high school and have been dating for four years.

It seems like they have been on the train for four years, too. Actually, their trip is 38 hours, which is a long time to sit up in a coach car.

"I'm antsy," says Hughes. She will be wearing an old, ivory-colored bridesmaid's dress for the wedding ceremony, which will be simple and conducted in her parent's home.

Hudson will wear a suit. "This will be the most special Christmas ever," he says. "There will be the joy of our two families together and at least three big dinners."

He is concentrating in school on Spinoza's influence on Kant. She is focusing on 19th Century British novels. Right now, they are not making a lot of money.

"This trip home is our gift to each other and also our honeymoon," says Hudson.

Neither of them are quite used to wearing wedding bands yet. They are always playing with them, twirling them and looking at them.

Nighttime again on the California Zephyr.

Mary Lou and Robert Phillips are enjoying maybe their fifth nap of the day.

Moses Green is almost done with work and is listening to Nancy Wilson tapes while he helps count up the day's receipts in the dining car.

Tara Hughes and Hud Hudson have flopped their tray table down and are playing cards at their seats.

The TV in the lounge has crackled to life and is showing "White Christmas," which begins at almost the exact moment that a light snow begins to fall outside the train.

And the California Zephyr sweeps on through the Utah night, cleaving the flurries and leaving a trail of joy. It is headed to many, many different places, but, really, to only one place—Home.

LOVE-LETTERS FROM THE TRAIN

from *Off the Rails: Memoirs of a Train Addict*

Lisa St. Aubin de Teran (1953–)

After publication of her first novel, The Long Way Home (1983), which won the Somerset Maugham Award, Lisa St. Aubin de Teran was named one of Britain's twenty best young novelists by the London Times. *Her second novel, the autobiographical Slow Train to Milan (1983), won the John Llewellyn Rhys Memorial Prize. Teran's latest title, The Palace (2000), takes place in nineteenth-century Venice.*

Milan to Genoa
August 1987

Dear Robbie,

. . . Even the train seems strange, and my veil is no protection. I keep it on because it is a present from Venice, a transparent carnival hat that cannot mask the numbness of your departure. It is night-time at Milan Central, and the train is already nearly full of people elbowing their way along the corridors, oblivious of Mussolini's grandiose legacy. I am glad to leave the grey city; sorry to leave the invisible wake of your plane somewhere on the outskirts of Italy's industrial wasteland.

If there are to be any seats, they will always be in the very first carriage. I know this, but have ignored it, hoping against hope for an entire compartment in which to entomb the nothingness I feel without you. My suitcase is heavy and my feeling of approaching depression heavier. All around me, strains of English filter through. Many of the people who pass me have come from the airport, arriving as you left. I feel half-tempted to fall into conversation, to explain that my love has gone away and I must travel back to Liguria alone now. But I let them pass, until I find, at last, an empty place, for six, disguised by dim light. I heave my luggage on to the rack and remove my hat, feeling a faint sense of betrayal in so doing. Its black plumes are like a magnet.

The train continues to fill. I miss you. I have six hours of travel ahead, like six hours of a wake. (The Mars bar in my handbag has melted.) The train pulls silently along the platform. I prepare to feel tragic, adjusting myself on the brown vinyl to do so. The emptiness beside me is due, I now realize, entirely to the absence of any light. You have gone to a funeral; I have stayed to go home and wind up the summer. The stillness of Venice is still in my hair. We have

decided to settle there. Plans gel like the perfect hold of so many television ads. I miss you, but for once there is nothing tragic in your leaving beyond the dazed sadness of parted lovers.

I sit in solitary state, daydreaming of the lapis lazuli you love. Every day I can wake up, and, rising on one elbow, see the lapis lazuli of the gulf of Levanto and feel secure in its small waves fringing the hem of my premeditated passion. Without you, I would go over the precipice. If I drink three bottles of spumante I will also go over the precipice because the path to Raguggia is dark and dangerous. At several points there are drops of over a hundred feet. There are marks over the small bridge where the Irishman has wrenched away the path with his falling. Beer and bravado have rechristened him the pathbreaker. Three days ago he was found nearly drowned in a pool of his own sweat on a train to Brescia. Even Paddie, the gold filigree of our cloth, has gone, flown back to London to pour beer on the troubled waters of miscreant computers.

Raguggia is a synonym for inaccessability. Every day, for months, we have trekked through its vine-yard along the winding track that dies at its door. The moon has become crucial, not because of any Cancerian elements, but merely because every two weeks out of four it lights the precipitous path that leads us home: when there is a full moon there are no bruises.

The passengers are double stacked in the corridor, and, as though by some prearranged signal, five of them storm the darkness of my compartment. One by one, they look at me with misgiving, as though remembering a collective French lesson when they heard, "Why does the sun never set on the British Empire? Because God doesn't trust an Englishman in the dark." Or an Englishwoman; and why isn't the light on? One by one they fiddle with the switch over the door, and one by one they retire into the twilight of their seats.

Every morning I will watch the morning glories flower on the terrace over the sea. I planted the seeds and coaxed the spindly stems to twist and spiral in the excessive heat and relative drought of that veran-dah. The sight of each new blue flower gives me a physical pleasure; when there are no azure trumpets on display I feel a sense of failure and inadequacy, as though the day were incomplete, half its hours trun-cated, its air removed. As the train grinds through the darkness, I think about the morning glories, with their thin flowers more ephemeral than butterflies, lasting only a few hours and then dying before mid-day. They too are shades of lapis lazuli, shades of you.

My journey finishes off the evening and drags through the night. There are no connections. My choices seem to have whittled themselves down to arriving at Levanto at two a.m. and sleeping on the beach with my luggage and the mosquitoes, or hop-ing that Fernando has returned from Finland. I phone from Genova Principe, fighting off drunkards as I do so. Fernando replies, and I am saved from the insects, and the indignity of being "caught" on the beach. In Levanto, I am a respectable person, a figure of some renown, poised and elegant in the Cafe Roma. There is an air of mystery around us; we have been adopted, accepted in our eccentricity, and the town has closed a little to enclose us, protectively, like the sides of an oyster shell around a strange-coloured pearl.

So I make my way from Genova Principe, which is both a great station and a great circus of human dregs, to Fernando's flat in its turret of a castellated mansion on a hill overlooking the port. The taxi winds up the road, corkscrewing through dubious streets to what he obviously finds a dubious destina-tion. I have told the driver that it is near the Jesuit

seminary, but that, it seems, is no recommendation. After I leave the taxi there are hundreds of steep stone steps through half-ruined terrace gardens. Were it not nearly midnight, I would succumb to my gardener's urge and pull some of the goose-grass off the roses.

The route from Genova Principe is my route. I do not own it, but I feel as though I do. Once it led only as far as Sestri Levante, but in the last two years, by a process of osmosis, I have moved along the track to Levanto. I have incorporated all the extra names from Deiva Marina to Bonossola into my vocabu-lary, and each small station has become as familiar to me as the names of my own children. Occasionally I confuse one with another, but this seems like a nat-ural mistake, and, again, one that I make with the names of my young heirs. Beyond Levanto there are five more stations, the Cinque Terre, and these too have become a familiar part of my litany. I always pass them with pleasure, and, like so many places, I know them best from the rails. . . .

Florence to Siena
September 1987

Dear Robbie,

. . . Between the trips, and the night wanderings, and the meanderings, I return to Legnaro, to Liguria and Raguggia. Gradually the bare house is furnished and draped and filled with books, pictures, china and bric-a-brac, all carried from London, Victoria, by courtesy of British Rail and its European counter-parts. From Levanto station, the massive trunks are hauled to Legnaro by truck, or, with the smaller ones, in the convertible back seat of the Legnaro school taxi-cum-private car. From there, the carriage of chattels degenerates into the stations of a ludi-crous cross, dragging and heaving and lugging things to Raguggia. There are many pairs of unwilling hands to help, and by the end of the first month anyone arriving after the perilous crossing of brooks and vineyards would find a cluttered den, locked in its very private valley. My floating stock of trunks came out of the railway depots and borrowed cantinas, and went to Raguggia. A new batch was bought specially, and by pilfering the castle in Norfolk which had been my base until then, at least for my more cumbersome treasures, Raguggia began to have a settled air about it. So settled, in fact, that I am beginning to look around for somewhere else to decamp to for next year.

To this end, I studied my little bible, *I treni principali*, and set off for Siena. I have waited a long time to recognise the charms of Tuscany, partly, I suppose, because it is so widely recognised already. Sensitive English people go to Tuscany, as a matter of course, just as, in the past, impoverished younger sons went into the Church. So many people have extolled its virtues to me, that I have developed a stubborn prejudice against it, just as I do about films. If enough people say to me, "You must see such and such a film," I will wait years before I do. (Admittedly, I do eventually sneak into some out of the way cinema and watch the piece in question, but I am, as you know, wary of being in the swim of fashion. Whether this is through a fear of not being able to get out of it, and being condemned to a life of 'in' things and plastic, or whether it is just pig-headedness on my part, I do not know.)

Be that as it may, I, too, have discovered Tuscany. (In Venezuela, when someone does something of the kind, they call it discovering tepid water, or rediscovering America.) I wander in the landscape of the Madonna of the Rocks, entranced. Then, like my vicariously related Granny Mabel on her world cruise, I shut my cabin window with an unspoken 'seen it' and came back to Raguggia. Like so many others, I have come to love Tuscany, but my love lacks passion.

Last year, in the platonic phase of our affair, we sat in the Piazza della Signoria in Florence, with the Uffizi to our left and the fountain to our right and a couple of tumblers of brandy, and you pointed out a tall window like a studio northlight across the square, and chose it for a potential studio. In those days, adding my infatuation on to my natural vagueness, I didn't take in the detail of much that was said to me. Instead, I would spend hours at a time gazing at the picture made by your face, the frame of your dark wavy hair, and your brocade waistcoat, daydreaming of outrageous futures and lost in admiration for your looks (which I found Byronic, though better featured and less fat). Now that you are gone, I make a point, when I visit Florence, of sitting in the same bar in the same square, trying to make of myself an honorary Florentine so that at such time as the easel and canvas move there, I, too, will be prepared. . . .

WHISTLIN' THROUGH DIXIE

from *The Saturday Evening Post* (Jan.–Feb. 1990)

Marda Burton

Author Marda Burton writes for the New Orleans Times-Picayune *on topics such as luxury travel, restaurants and the Southeast. Her work has been published in numerous magazines and newspapers throughout North America. She was also a member of the Executive Board of The Pirate's Alley Faulkner Society and named Travel Writer of the Year in 1988.*

They didn't just wish they were in Dixie—they lived the American South on a charter train that ran from Appalachian uplands to Gulf shore waters.

In Alabama, if you're past a certain age, the lonesome, mournful wail of a train whistle is somewhere in your soul, calling up the good old days before five-and-dime became five dollars. Rare is the native who doesn't remember his first train ride or won't relate it in misty-eyed, minute detail to anyone who will listen.

Although passenger trains are almost extinct, virtually all of Alabama seems still in love with the rails. Tracks at every whistle stop are dotted with restored depots full of memorabilia. Benches hold old-timers who can recount tales of the legendary feats of railroad men and the Depression days when rail-riding hobos camped out under trestles and marked by secret signs the doorposts of homes with hospitable kitchens.

Nostalgia flourished in Alabama last May, as dignitaries, famous natives, and just plain citizens crisscrossed the state for seven hot, bright days on the Alabama Reunion Special. Gov. Guy Hunt, a one-time farm boy, reminisced, "When I was little, we'd go 60 miles just to ride a train, and there's still nothing like it."

Townspeople turned out in force to meet the Special on its 900-mile odyssey, a joint venture of the Norfolk Southern and CSX railroads along with the First Alabama Bank. Every stop was Americana personified: marching bands, performers, festivals, speeches, balloons, parades. Ignoring the sweltering Southern sun, people waited at crossings and lined tracks that hadn't carried passenger trains in more than a decade. In the village of Childersburg, one local historian was moved to observe, "This is the biggest crowd of people to gather in Childersburg since Grover Cleveland came through on a whistle-stop tour in July of 1884!"

Those riding the one-time excursion train had a unique platform from which to glimpse yesterday's set pieces, from Opelika's covered bridge to Bay Minette's North Baldwin Quilters. Although the Special pulled into the urban centers of Huntsville, Birmingham, Montgomery, and Mobile with appropriate fanfare, the small towns stole the show. Sheffield gave the Special a rousing send-off at its renovated depot, which is now the Right Track Restaurant/Museum, replete with railroad memorabilia and Southern home cooking.

In the green highlands of north Alabama, Decatur, Ft. Payne, Attalla, and Gadsden came into view, as well as larger cities, Huntsville and Birmingham. As the train approached the outskirts of Birmingham, the actress and author Fannie Flagg, honorary train-master, excitedly waved to fans waiting at the old Irondale Café, the focus of her latest novel, *Fried Green Tomatoes at the Whistle Stop Café.*

Several covered bridges enhance this scenic area of the state, notably in Blount County around Oneonta and in Gadsden's Pioneer Museum at Noccalula Falls Park.

Further down the line, past the vast cotton and soybean fields of the Black Belt—so named because of its rich soil—more monuments to the stagecoach of modern travel awaited in Tuscaloosa, whose handsome Victorian station still welcomes two passenger trains per day, and Bessemer and Selma, both of which have turned their old landmarks into museums. In Calera, Heart of Dixie Railroad Museum volunteers, who also played host on the Special, are rebuilding 40 pieces of rolling stock for a working railroad and a nine-acre park.

Halfway between Birmingham and the capital

city, Montgomery, Clanton makes an excellent overnight stop with two motels, and an old caboose and section house housing chamber of commerce offices and a mini-museum. In Montgomery, grand, looming Union Station has new life as Bludau's Restaurant. The station is the focus of extensive riverfront development that includes a historical restoration, Old Alabama Town. Out from town, an extraordinary new cultural park with green and rolling terrain encompasses two imposing edifices housing an art museum and the acclaimed Alabama Shakespeare Festival.

Hustling on down the track, the Special ended its historic journey in azalea-clad Mobile. Along the way, visitors saw Pike Pioneer Museum in Troy; the U.S. Army Aviation Museum at Fort Rucker near Ozark; Landmark Park in Dothan, also known for its

National Peanut Festival; the restored depot in Evergreen; and Bay Minette's 1904 train station, used in the filming of *Close Encounters of the Third Kind*.

The long ride was over, not far from the ancient swamps and cypress forests of Alabama's Gulf Coast. Nearby beckoned the playground of Alabama: Mobile Bay's Eastern Shore and its old-style, gentrified ambience; Dauphin Island, totally unspoiled and connected by ferryboat to Mobile; and Gulf Shores, an upscale beach resort that combines wide beaches and condominiums with an old-time back bayou flavor.

The 1989 Reunion Special is history, but travelers can enjoy Alabama's diverse landscape and lifestyle any time of year. Even in the colder weather of January and February, ice and snow almost never make the scene. But even if they did, that wonderful Alabama hospitality would warm visitors' hearts.

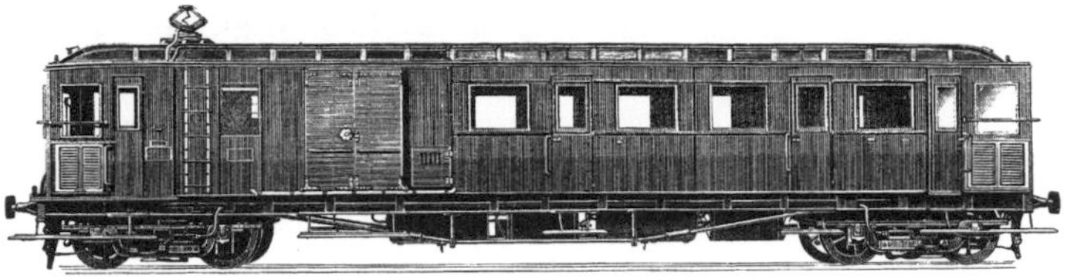

PASSAGES: THE LAKE SHORE LIMITED

Chapter 1 from *Making Tracks: An American Rail Odyssey*

Terry Pindell (1946–)

Terry Pindell covered 30,000 miles during 1988, when he took off a year from teaching to travel all of Amtrak's thirty-one lines. He chronicled the journey in Making Tracks: An American Rail Odyssey *(1990). For his second book,* Last Train to Toronto: A Canadian Rail Odyssey *(1991), Pindell headed north for a similar trek. His latest book,* A Good Place to Live: America's Last Migration *(1995), is based on his travels in the United States.*

While most Americans across the land are settling down with their popcorn and soft drinks, hero sandwiches, or pizza and beer in warm little gatherings before the flickering glow of the video hearth for the Super Bowl, I am waiting for a train to Chicago in the drafty hole in the wall that passes for the Amtrak station in Springfield, Massachusetts. When the cavernous old station was abandoned during Amtrak's 1981 budget cuts, the new station was literally carved into the Boston & Albany's east-west granite overpass at street level. Though the station serves a growing class of business commuters to New York, inside I still have to ask the ticket agent behind the wired-glass partition to release the electrically operated lock to the restroom.

A freight thunders overhead and the waiting travelers stir in their plastic airport-style bucket seats. There are two black mothers with children crawling over them, a trio of professorial types intensely declaiming in tweed, two college girls gushing in whispers, an elderly black man behind a *New York Post*, an irritable bearded father with his wife and two docile small girls, a nervous teenage couple huddling conspiratorially, and a friendly husky fellow listening to the Super Bowl on a Sony Walkman who once a month takes the train from Buffalo to visit his girlfriend in Hartford. "If I can wait a month to get it," he says, "I can sure as hell wait out a train ride and save some bucks over airfare." Earlier on a weekday, there would be more of the briefcase set commuting to New York, but at this hour on Sunday evening, these are long-distance passengers.

The station resembles nothing so much as an inner-city bus station, but to rural central New Englanders, it is a gateway to America. Springfield is the northernmost extension of Megalopolis, the supercity that runs northeastward from Washington.

Here there are buildings over six stories, an international airport, an intersection of interstates, the NBA Hall of Fame, big-city crime, and, best of all, an Amtrak station that connects with west and south. Springfield today is still a frontier crossing, just as it was three hundred years ago when the first expedition went up the Connecticut River to scout the area that became Keene.

I see the ticket agent take the call alerting him to the imminent arrival of our train and head up the stairs to the platform ahead of the announcement. Outside the frigid February air contends with the warm grumble of an idling locomotive with a few passenger cars attached to it, a scene that often greets the traveler at even the smaller stations on the line. That train is never the one you're going on, but it whets the appetite. On the siding two tracks away from the platform a Conrail diesel releases its air with a gasp and begins backing toward a line of empty flatcars while two trainmen chug coffee straight from the thermos on its front platform.

The teenage couple has followed me outside and neck joylessly in the shadows. I can hear the girl sobbing and asking if she can call her mother from Chicago. The boy is good to her: of course she can call; she can call right now and they can go back home if she wants to. But she rallies: "No, we're goin' for it—California—aren't we? Can't go back now."

I scan the nearest track to see if anyone has left a penny to be flattened as a souvenir for a subsequent traveler as we used to do on the tracks of my grandfather's Gulf, Mobile & Ohio in Bloomington, Illinois, but find only bare track and the usual scattering of candy wrappers, soda cans, odd twisted pieces of metal, hanks of cable, bolts, and nondescript lumpy detritus on the scummy ties. I place a penny on the rail, and then feel the burst of excitement I have been waiting for. As if in response to my invocation of the charm on the rail, a headlight gleams over a rise a mile away and slowly grows as the Boston section of the *Lake Shore Limited* drifts in.

For nearly a century, crossing the continent by rail served as a prerequisite rite of initiation before one could earn the title of "well-traveled American." That tradition was inaugurated on May 23, 1870, when members of the Boston Board of Trade made the first transcontinental rail passage in George Pullman's *Hotel Express*, a year after the driving of the golden spike which finally linked the coasts with steel. The trip was recorded by journalist W. R. Steele, who printed twelve issues of the *Trans-Continental* during the journey on a printing press carried in the baggage car. Editor Steele reported that a crowd of thousands gathered at South Station for the train's departure. In a flight of eloquence, he compared the conductor's "All aboard for San Francisco" to the "Yes" of Helen of Troy, to the "nod of a Belgian peasant to Napoleon" and the opening dots of the first transatlantic cablegram.

Tonight, a far more modest occasion, my goal is California too, over much of the same route as that first passage of steel-riders. Just two years ago this night I saw my father conscious for the last time as we watched the Super Bowl in the intensive-care room at the Lahey Clinic near Boston. In my own flight of fancy, I imagine him twenty years earlier boarding this train's forebear to journey by rail to his home town, Bloomington, Illinois, one last time after the death of his father. Already I feel part of something that generations of Americans have shared since early pioneers realized that they were possessed of a continent for a country. But I'm not going to stop with Bloomington or San Francisco; I mean to ride until I've seen it all.

On board, the *Lake Shore Limited* is crowded, and warm and stuffy, despite the cold outside. I notice a number of passengers fiddling with radios and earphones trying vainly to pick up the Super Bowl inside the stainless-steel car. Once we are underway, the conductor comes on the PA to announce that the *Lake Shore Limited* is on time for Albany, Buffalo, Cleveland, Toledo, and Chicago. He continues with a commentary on the progress of the game, which he has tuned in on the train's radio; he will update his report periodically.

As the train picks up speed in the yards of West Springfield, I spot the teenage runaways across the aisle from my seat. The boy has just finished spiking a can of Coke with a little bottle of rum he carries hidden in his pack and sees that I have caught him in the act. "Gimme a break—it's a long ride," he says.

I takes several tries at conversation before I can convince them that I'm not bent on hassling them, but finally Tom Grover and Jane Demaris share with me a few pieces of their story. They're both sixteen and have been dating since their first year in high school. Tom's parents are divorced, and he's lived with a friend's family for a year. "Nobody's going to miss me—it's Jane's family that's the problem." They want eventually to get married, but her father doesn't approve.

"We're not eloping," she urges. "We're going to California, where Tom's gonna work and we'll get our own start. Then we'll come back and get married after we've shown my dad that we can make it."

Jane's dad has been outspoken about his disdain for Tom: "You'll never earn what my daughter deserves . . . you aren't half the man I planned to give her to." Tom explains that in southern California he'll get a good construction job and Jane will work at a McDonald's or something. People have told them that you can do that in America today—just split and head for a new place to work.

I ask them why they are taking the train. Jane answers that it's pretty cheap, they don't have much money, and her dad happens to be a train buff. This is how he would do it.

They've never been on a train before, so they join me for a stroll to check it out. The Boston section of the *Lake Shore Limited* is a short train; when it meets and is joined to the New York section at Albany it will be a long one. At this point the consist—that is, the collection of engines and cars that forms a train—includes one F-40 engine, a baggage car, a sleeper, two coaches, and the lounge or bar car. We sit down in the lounge car—beer for me, unspiked Coke for the kids—and I survey the patrons' destinations: Syracuse, Buffalo, Cleveland, Detroit, several to Chicago, and one to Denver. "Looks like we're the long hitters here," I tell the kids.

"Yeah. Our friends think we're crazy, and there's something about how I could get in trouble because of Jane's age, but it doesn't matter. We just gotta do it," says Tom. "Where you headed?"

"Home to New Hampshire—by way of San Francisco, Los Angeles, and New Orleans."

"You're crazy too. Why don't you fly?"

"Because I want to see America."

It may be that television, with events like the Super Bowl, is the bond that unites and defines America today. The jury is still out on whether or not this is a positive expression of a great nation's identity, but there is no question that the thing that begat and bonded a new kind of national community on this continent was the railroad.

True, America didn't invent the railroad, and her early history was shaped more by her seafaring exploits than by the tentative experiments with rails out of Charleston and Baltimore and between Albany and Schenectady. When, in the 1830s, the prototypical Baltimore & Ohio established regular railroad service as a viable form of transportation, the railroad was still subordinate to water transport. Those early short roads linked seaports to nearby rivers, and even the great Pennsylvania Railroad began merely as a series of links over the ridges of the mountains to connect the network of canals in the Alleghenies.

But the steel link between America's railroads and her destiny and identity was inevitable. Here was a nation expanding to a three-thousand-mile width and populated by a people bound and determined to subdue and make use of every mile of it. The sea routes were expensive and slow and could link only the coastal edges. The canals and rivers could not leap mountain ranges and ultimately lost their continental promise when the dream of a Northwest Passage died. Americans saw their future in the great overland trails: the Cumberland, the Santa Fe, the Oregon, the California. These links were tenuous and frail as long as they depended on beast-drawn Conestoga wagons and Concord stagecoaches. But the iron horse would require much the same necessities as the flesh-and-blood steed: water, attainable grades, outposts for service, and a reason for taking people and freight to a particular place. Only when trains began to run on tracks laid on the routes of those trails could the nation begin to achieve its passage to maturity.

By the Civil War, railroads were fixtures in the east, so much so that they were partly responsible for making that war the first of the world's devastating modern conflicts. It wasn't just that American sectional rivalry demanded more hate and bloodshed; it was also the railroads' ability to bring larger numbers of troops to the field of battle in less time: more guns and more bodies to fall.

Despite damages to tracks and delays in building

programs it caused, the Civil War ultimately assisted the progress of the railroads. Railroading changed the face of the land, the towns and cities, the business world, and the life-style of people as no other invention had since the wheel. Folks who were oblivious to ways in which other aspects of the industrial revolution were changing their world seized upon the highly visible railroad as the object of righteous outrage. It was largely the Civil War's demonstration of the national need for physical union that overcame this opposition, because the railroads were the one entity that could fulfill that need.

The railroads created the melting pot, too. It wasn't just that waves of immigrants worked for the railroad; the railroads actively recruited homesteaders throughout the world and brought them to settle the vast spaces they served. So the railroads also created the west. The generations that responded to Horace Greeley's "Go west, young man" did so on the steel rails to the sunset.

No other entity so united the frontier and the industrial revolution, pluralism and mobility, freedom and unity. No other symbol so concretely embodied the national Manifest Destiny during America's rush into her century. And yet today, within one generation, the memory fades into a curious obscurity, like the rusted tracks one stumbles upon with surprise amid weeds and brush behind abandoned warehouses on the forgotten side of town.

As the squealing rails announce the tight curves of the Massachusetts Berkshires, the Super Bowl is already history around the orange Formica tables of the bar car, and the kids have gone back to snuggle in their coach seats. At the booth nearest the bar, three young men with the look of a trendy rock band have been asking questions about the game; they don't seem to know what it is. One has his hair cropped burrishly short and wears a weathered green leather jacket; the other two sport spiked hair and T-shirts with obscure logos.

All three have that slightly strange look of foreigners, and indeed Joe Fitzpatrick, Michael Mynihan, and Gary O'Leary are illegal aliens. They are the last of a group of seven that came to America from Ireland last year. "There's no work in Ireland," explains Joe. "All the young people back there want to come here for work, even the rock stars," he adds in reference to U-2, a popular rock group whose leader hails from Joe's hometown of Bray.

It's apparently easy if you don't mind being illegal. All you need is a letter from family or employers saying you're on vacation for three weeks. Joe claims that 160,000 applied for such visas last year; only forty-nine were turned down. He's been hassled a few times by immigration officials. "But I show the lady at the office a new letter from home. She shakes her head and says she sees letters like this all the time but always gives me an extension."

Despite the $8 an hour they could earn installing Sheetrock in Boston versus the $3.80 they'd earn back home if they could find a job, four of their group got homesick and returned to Ireland. "But no me," says Joe. "I'm never goin' back—not as long as I can send my mother more in a month than I could earn altogether in Bray." The remaining three are traveling to Albany to meet up with some friends who came over a couple of years ago.

After a few beers I become accustomed to the strong Irish accent and a barroom intimacy prevails. Joe has mixed feelings about his extra-legal status in America. On the one hand, he gets an adolescent charge out of being "a bit of an outlaw." That status has already netted him certain social benefits, including a shocking sexual offer from the first girl he met in a Boston nightclub, who delivered on the promise in somebody's unlocked car and then disappeared into the night wishing him, "Welcome to America." "But it's not fair really. The immigration quotas favor Hispanics over Irish, but I speak English. I work hard, I have dozens of American relatives, and I won't end up on welfare. I just don't get it."

Yet, restrictive immigration quotas or no, Joe has no doubt that he will someday be a legal U.S. citizen one way or another. "Back home everybody has relatives who came to America. You take it for granted—it's an option that's just there when things don't work out well at home. Isn't that how this whole country was built?"

Joe wants to introduce me to another young European he met boarding the train in Boston. We make our way to the next coach, where we find Franz, staring out the window of the darkened car. Franz is an Austrian rock guitarist, though in his blue serge suit and Reaganesque pompadour he looks more like a Young Republican. He played in nightclubs in Vienna and Budapest till a friend told him about America's current fascination with foreign musicians. He says he was tired of Europe anyway, so he bought a plane ticket and never looked back. But New York felt too much like Europe, "claustrophobic." Someone told him L. A. was different, so he purchased a train ticket.

As the train rolls down into the Hudson River Valley, Franz explains his quest in a soft, halting Germanic accent. "My family is musical—they trained me as classical guitarist from the time I was little boy. But once I first heard rock sound and knew that it came from electric guitars, I learned how to do it. Now—here I am."

Franz is enchanted with how easy it is to travel long distances in America without anxious border crossings. "The worst thing about Europe, let me tell you how bad."

Franz and his girlfriend were visiting Budapest last year. One day a man bumped into her on a busy city street and snatched her purse. Franz chased the man for several blocks and retrieved the discarded purse, expecting to find it empty of valuables. Surprisingly, his girlfriend's money and some jewelry were still there; they concluded that the chase had thwarted the robber's intent and soon forgot the incident.

But at the border stop on the train returning to Vienna, when the Hungarian authorities demanded passports, Franz discovered what the thief had been after. "It's common in eastern Europe—valid passports are valuable on black market. So stupid not to think of that." Without passports, Franz and his girlfriend were taken off the train and detained at gunpoint in the cold outside a desolate border guard-post until an inbound train could take them back to Budapest under arrest. There they had to wait a week till the Austrian consulate rescued them with new passports.

"We took night train to Vienna, clutching our passports . . . just wanted out and never come back." But at the border stop, they encountered the same customs guard who had stopped them before. Though their passports were in order, the guard vaguely remembered them and, associating them with trouble, put them off the train again, perhaps thinking that the passports were forged. For six hours they waited again under guard outside that miserable frontier hut. Telephone calls were made, and they were finally allowed to leave on the next train.

Franz has never been able to cross a European border without fear ever since, but in America the dread is transformed into a thrill every time he crosses a state line.

I will discover in the next six months that the melting pot still bubbles, especially on trains.

Accustomed to shorter traveling distances and unaccustomed to the preeminence of auto travel massively subsidized by government-built highways, foreigners in America take the train as a matter of course, just as they do at home, where railroads are still promoted, rather than neglected, by their governments.

At Albany, Franz and I detrain to stretch our legs and say farewell to our Irish friends, who are greeted lustily at trackside by their waiting compatriots. One of the group has brought a six-pack of Budweiser in a paper bag and pops one for each of us right on the platform. Ignoring the disapproving glances from the stationmaster on duty, I feel a sense of initiation into an American ritual normally outside the experience of natives. When the rowdy young Irishmen disappear into the night and Franz and I reboard the train, I hear one of them shout out a line from a U-2 song, " . . . into the arms of America."

Now the Boston section is clunked onto the New York section and I am finally able to settle into my sleeping compartment, which had originated in New York. This is one of the pleasurable moments for which there is no equivalent in other kinds of travel. For this ride I am in Amtrak's cheapest sleeping accommodation, a slumbercoach room. With incredible economy of space it contains a small but comfortable cushioned seat; a bed that folds down from the opposing walls in two halves that meet; pillows, sheets, and blankets; a flush toilet; a sink with running hot and cold water that folds down over the toilet; a mirror and shelf with washcloths, towels, and soap; adjustable lighting fixtures; heat and air-conditioning controls; a 120-volt electrical outlet; a tiny closet; and, most important, a large window on the passing world with a pull-down shade. For $34 additional to Chicago, not bad, not bad at all.

When we think of comfortable sleeping cars on trains, we think of George Pullman—the words "Pullman" and "sleeper" have become almost interchangeable. According to the myth, George Pullman suffered an excruciating ride on this route from New York to Chicago in 1858 which prompted him to a burst of inventiveness resulting in the Pullman Palace Car. The comforts of the Palace Car were so attractive that by the end of the Civil War every American railroad with overnight runs placed orders, creating a spontaneous monopoly for Pullman's company. Europeans flocked to America to copy these wonders of American ingenuity, and thus Pullman established luxury rail travel worldwide.

The true history of passenger sleeping railcars is a skewed variant. Indeed George Pullman was invited in 1958 to assist the Field brothers of Chicago in designing a sleeping car specifically for the Chicago & Alton Railroad, running to St. Louis. The comfort and functional design of the cars were abominable. Beds were formed simply by dropping the seatbacks of hard wooden coach seats, there were no partitions or compartments, lighting was by candle, heat was from woodstoves at each end of the car and the wheel trucks were taken directly from freight cars with heavy, stiff springs. But Pullman was an early practitioner of packaging and promotion. He created the illusion of luxury in these cars with such accoutrements as cherrywood paneling, heavy tapestries, and white linen.

By the end of the Civil war, Pullman was ready to revolutionize the railroading world with the Pioneer, the forerunner of his famous Palace Car, but it was too big for the rights-of-way of most railroads' tracks. Pullman saw his opportunity in Lincoln's assassination when he managed to convince Mrs. Lincoln that the Pioneer was the only fitting carriage for the body of the beloved President in its cross-country funeral procession. In deference to Mrs. Lincoln's grief, railroads along the route made the necessary enlargements to their rights-of-way. Thus in one stroke Pullman was able to recover from an engineering blunder while accomplishing one of the truly remarkable promotional stunts of that or any century. All along the route people gazed not only at the body of the slain President but also at Pullman's revolutionary railroad car. The orders began to roll in.

That first transcontinental *Pullman Hotel Express* of 1870 was another characteristic promotional coup. Pullman's genius for publicity is evident in the brilliant device of publishing editor Steele's newspaper on the train en route. Distributed at stations along the way and carried into posterity after the trip by the illustrious passengers on board, the paper guaranteed the association of the Pullman name with both luxury and long-distance travel. The elaborate masthead portrayed a brooding Indian on a rock ledge in the foreground watching a great train steam across the plains toward distant mountains. On each car in clearly legible letters appeared the words "Pullman Pacific Car Company."

Within a decade, Pullman was able to ruthlessly buy out, drive out, or swindle competitors till, with one notable exception, he had achieved a virtual monopoly of sleeping-car travel. To cement that monopoly he insisted on contracts with the railroads stipulating that Pullman cars would be manned only by Pullman personnel. Thus came about the one Pullman innovation which would make a concrete contribution to the comfort of travelers: the through car, which afforded continuous service, making it unnecessary for passengers to make connections as they traveled over long routes involving several railroads.

The one rail system Pullman would not conquer in the nineteenth century was the Vanderbilt system, including the Lake Shore & Michigan Southern, over whose route today's Amtrak *Lake Shore Limited* travels. Commodore Vanderbilt personally insisted on contracts with Pullman's only surviving rival, the Wagner Company. It wasn't that the Wagner cars were more comfortable—though they were—but that the great rail monopolist could not abide being the victim of another monopolist in his own business.

Testimony is ample that nineteenth-century travel in Pullman's Palace sleepers and diners provided something less than luxurious comfort. Concerning the dining service, Mark Twain wrote in 1866 of "flabby rolls, muddy coffee, questionable eggs, gutta-percha beef, and pies whose conception and execution are a dark and bloody mystery." Concerning the highly touted sleeping cars, Twain commented that their only advantage over European coaches was that they were at least intended as sleeping cars. Frequent complaints of other travelers, including Robert Louis Stevenson and Charles Dickens, included the low backs of the hard seats, excessive heat or cold, dim lighting, sleeping berths so crowded that one usually slept with someone's feet in one's face, lack of privacy and provision for undressing, and questionable cleanliness of blankets.

The evolution of modern sleeping cars with private compartments happened in Europe, and Pullman was only incidentally involved. Spurned in love, one Georges Nagelmackers, the man ultimately credited with luxury long-distance travel in Europe, came to America in 1866 to bury his hurt and investigate this marvelous American invention, the long-distance luxury train. He returned to Europe disappointed by Pullman's open berth design but convinced that the through car was the key. In the meantime, the American confidence man Colonel William d'Alton Mann, who had made his fortune selling bogus Pennsylvania oil wells, brought his concept of "Boudoir Cars," sleeping cars with partitions and separate compartments, to Europe after being locked out of the American market by Pullman. In 1868 he took up with Nagelmackers and formed the Compagnie Internationale, which established the first long-distance luxury railroad routes across Europe. By 1869, Pullman wanted a piece of this action, but Mann was able to repay Pullman for his kindness in America with a clever campaign warning Europeans of the licentiousness and debauchery promoted by the Pullman cars' open-concept berths. Ironically the privacy afforded by the European closed compartments made them very quickly a popular spot for trysts and even the place of business for rail ladies of the night. But the ruse worked, and with its European monopoly firmly established, the Compagnie Internationale was able to provide Europeans with truly luxurious long-distance travel from 1870 on.

Americans would not see this quality of accommodations until the next century. The train was the New York Central's *20th Century Limited*, forerunner of today's *Lake Shore Limited*. The cars, built in my family's hometown, Bloomington, Illinois, would be provided by the Pullman-Standard Company. The date was 1904, and a new generation of managers ran both concerns.

Sleep comes slowly on the first night of a train ride. The slumbercoach bed is not very wide and runs lengthwise in the car; my usual drifting-off position on my side doesn't work because of the rocking motion. I finally decide to adjust and sleep on my back, and apparently succeed, because after Syracuse and Rochester, I miss the stops at Buffalo and Erie and don't wake up till Cleveland. This is the last night I will have trouble falling asleep for the next nine thousand miles.

I awake to the clatter of George, our car attendant, making up beds in adjacent compartments. George, is an attractive and striking buxom, thirtyish black woman with a wide smile and a gold upper front tooth. "Ah hate these eastern trains, slave work here. Ah got two dozens bedrooms to deal with in one car. Ah like the western trains better. It's easier. But Ah'm quittin' it altogether after this run." She smiles too much to be a woman who takes her own complaints very seriously. Despite her oath, somehow I think I just might meet her again somewhere down the tracks.

I have breakfast, eggs over, sausage, fried potatoes, toast, tomato juice, and two refills of coffee, with Tom and Jane, and their new friend, Suzie Picharski. Suzie, a pretty curly-haired blonde of twenty, is running away to California too. The three met at the pay phones in the Albany station last night, where the two girls were calling their mothers. Suzie's mom cried and asked about what Suzie had had to eat on the train. "I don't eat, see" she says. "My mom drives me crazy about it. That's why I'm going to California to live with my sister, so I can do what I want."

Suzie loved high school, has pictures of herself on prom night, youthfully glamorous but a little heavier in a red dress. She passes them around the table, and tears appear in Jane's eyes while Tom clenches his fists. This is what they have missed by running away.

Suzie was a Polish dancer, has toured, danced in Macy's parade, and appeared on television with her high school dance group. But graduation was like a death. "Nothing ever happened after that. Every-thing was boring." She moved to New York with a friend and went to work as a teller at Citibank. She was too afraid of the city to go out much and spent most of her free time listening to the likes of Mötley Crüe and Ozzy Osbourne on her Walkman. "So I decided to get thin. It makes me feel good." Then last week she quit her job and called her sister in California.

My runaway companions remind me of an incident that happened at my old fishing cabin in the woods back in New Hampshire. One morning I found a broken window and a dead partridge (called grouse outside of New England) amid the glass on the floor. My knowledgeable fishing buddy explained that this is a common thing. At the age of one year, the equivalent of human adolescence, the young partridge is possessed of what is called "the crazy flight"—it leaves the nest in a sudden spasm of wild flight. If it survives the crazy flight, the bird finds itself in the territory where it will make its nest. If it doesn't. . . .

Back in my slumbercoach compartment watching the icy shores of Lake Erie drift by, I search for perspective. Tom and Jane riding west to escape dysfunctional families, Suzie pursuing her anorexia to the sunset—are these the personal tales behind the "crazy flight" romanticized as the urge to go west in our national mythology? The stories of the young foreigners I have already met more nearly fit the myth, yet we all began as foreigners at some time on this continent; and, in a sense, both my young friends and I are sojourning aliens today—they toward a future they can't conceive, I toward a past scarcely remembered.

At Toledo the train pauses for a refueling and servicing stop and I get off to take pictures. It is rainy, misty, murky. The Toledo station is emblematic of the recent history of American passenger rail travel. The tracks have been pulled up from several now abandoned platforms, but the crumbling platforms themselves have not yet been removed, testimony to a nation's continuing indecisiveness about the future of its heritage. Meanwhile the platform at which our

train has stopped buzzes and clatters with activity and bustle.

The full consist of the *Lake Shore Limited* is now pretty impressive after the junction at Albany. There are two F-40 engines, three mail cars (I'm told that rail mail sorted en route is still faster than air mail between big cities), the Boston sleeper, the two Boston coaches, a lounge car (bar car), a diner, three New York coaches, a New York slumbercoach (my car), two New York sleepers, and a trailing baggage car—two engines and fifteen cars, all full. When the New York Central discontinued this train's predecessor, the *20th Century Limited*, in 1967, the *Limited* was limping along with one failing engine and two ragged coaches of mostly empty seats.

Cornelius Vanderbilt—the Commodore—boasted that he never built a railroad in his life. Instead he bought existing railroads. He had already made his fortune as a young man with ferries and steamboats operating in the harbor on New York, but at the age of sixty, when most men would be content to enjoy the fruits of success, he risked his fortune and reputation on the new-fangled transportation technology. He began his march toward a railroad empire by buying two rickety roads, the New York & Harlem and the Hudson River, which, when combined, yielded a through route all the way to Albany.

Erastus Corning had established the precedent in 1853 when he welded a series of small upstate routes into the old Central to provide competition for the Erie Canal. Corning was never paid a penny for his management of the road but made a fortune anyway by making his ironmongery business its sole supplier. This was the era one historian has called the "age of bare knuckles." There were few rules governing private enterprise, and there was an enormous opportunity. The Erie Railroad, hailed as the "work of the age," already provided a rail link, via the southern tier of the state, to the Great Lakes, but it quickly became the financial football of men like Daniel Drew, Jay Gould, and Jim Fisk who plundered it regularly in a series of infamous corners and short-selling operations.

Its moribund condition left plenty of room for another well-run railroad to the Great Lakes when the Commodore's Harlem and Hudson lines built a bridge over the river to connect with the Central lines at Albany. Corning's Central continued for some time to transfer its freight and passengers to riverboats for the trip down to New York. Vanderbilt got a piece of the action only when the rivers froze and his riverside rails were the sole option for continuing passage to the city. But in the icy winter of 1867, Vanderbilt refused to send his trains across the bridge to make connections with the Central.

Passengers trudged through the snow across the bridge, and freight piled up. Legislators in Albany called upon Vanderbilt to know why his trains wouldn't make the connection. He produced an old forgotten law, instigated by the canal people, forbidding his trains from crossing the river. He shrugged and the legislators departed. The price of Central stock plummeted, and Vanderbilt began buying. Soon he had control. He united the Central lines to his own and, taking their name, improved the route with major infusions of capital. Thus was born the New York Central of modern times. With the additional acquisition of the Lake Shore & Michigan Southern and the Boston & Albany, the Vanderbilts had put together the line over which runs today's *Lake Shore Limited*.

The *Pullman Hotel Express* of 1870 was a harbinger of great things to come in passenger railroading. In addition to the baggage car carrying W. R. Steele's printing press and five ice closets, it included a smoking car with a wine-tasting room, a shaving salon, a card room with mahogany euchre tables, and an office for editor Steele. There followed two hotel cars, each containing a library, a Burdett organ, and a drawing room. Then there were two sleeping cars and finally the commissary and dining cars. All were finished with extravagant hangings, plush upholstery, and dark polished woodwork. But that train was a one-shot spectacular. It wasn't until the turn of the century that American passengers on scheduled runs would see anything like that kind of luxury.

Ironically it was Vanderbilt's great failure to purchase the competing Erie Railroad in the 1870s which led to the grand service the New York Central would provide on the *20th Century Limited* in the next century. Convinced of the necessity of monopoly, Vanderbilt tried again and again to purchase a controlling percentage of Erie Railroad stock and was thwarted each time by the Erie's simple expedient of printing more stock. When Vanderbilt enlisted the aid of injunctions from a friendly New York City judge, Drew, Gould, and Fisk fled across the river to New Jersey with such haste that they literally left a paper trail of documents which had been desperately stuffed into their pockets. Vanderbilt eventually accepted the defeat with stoicism, saying that he had enough money to buy all the stock and injunctions he needed, but he could never get enough money to buy the Erie's printing press.

Disorderly as it was, the episode affirmed limits to monopoly and firmly established that competition over routes serving the same terminal points was possible. It forever changed the assumptions in the railroad game. And down along the rivers, canals, and ridges of Pennsylvania, a far greater threat than the Erie was taking shape in what would become the Pennsylvania Railroad. Out of the clash of these two rail behemoths, the next century would see the classic textbook argument for the advantages to the consumer of American capitalist philosophy.

By 1900 there were twelve competing truck routes from the urban east to Chicago, but the dominant players were the Pennsylvania and the New York Central. The NYC had already made its first luxury run with the *Exposition Flyer* over the route for the Chicago Columbian Exposition in 1893. The consist included three Wagner sleeping cars, a library/smoker car, a luxury diner, a parlor car, and an observation car with an open platform. Various versions of the train made the run in twenty hours over the next nine years and received such good press that the railroad inaugurated the first *20th Century Limited* on June 15, 1902. The name was a stroke of genius, playing as it did on the hoopla hailing the new century as America's. By 1904 the Pullman-Standard Company had taken over the sleeping accommodations, and the intense competition with the Pennsylvania's rival *Broadway Limited* established the service of these two trains as the class of the world.

In 1914 the schedule of the two routes was down to eighteen hours. The *20th Century* at this time offered the first all-steel cars (some feared these would attract lightning), aboard which were a barber, a manicurist, a stenographer, valets, lady's maids, bathrooms with fresh and salt water, and a stock-market ticker. In 1926, for safety reasons, the two railroads negotiated a mutual twenty-hour schedule.

In 1938, Pullman finally dropped its open berth cars (the kind one sees in old movies in which only a curtain separates the sleeper from the corridor) in favor of the European-style compartments one finds on Amtrak today. In this year the schedule reached its all-time fastest, sixteen hours from Grand Central Station in New York to Union Station in Chicago

(the *Broadway Limited* matched it).

After World War II, the NYC bravely struggled, as did most American railroads, to promote a new era of rail travel. But the federal subsidy of highways and airports for the auto and aviation industries, along with the clear preference of the new American traveler for the freedom and speed those industries promised, was already creating an environment in which passenger service would become increasingly unprofitable. There is some question today whether American passenger travel ever really made money for the railroads. The New York Central, the Pennsylvania, and others had always fostered the illusion of profitable passenger service, but the real money was in freight, and passenger trains existed primarily to promote a corporate image and to generate freight business along the routes. Current evaluation of accounting methods of those times shows all sorts of expenses not included in the ledgers of passenger service. By today's accounting standards, it is quite possible that America's most lucrative passenger train never showed a profit.

In the late forties and early fifties, the New York Central introduced through cars with the Union Pacific to San Francisco—lightweight stainless-steel cars with modern conveniences—and a host of special programs and incentives to attract riders. But ridership continually declined until, in 1958, the *20th Century* stopped carrying sleeping cars and luxury accommodations. The publicists put a brave face on it by announcing that the great train had been brought within the reach of the common man, but the end was in sight. In 1967 the *20th Century Limited* was dropped from service.

As the train rattles westward over the flat farmland of northern Indiana, five watchers sip Cokes and munch potato chips in the lounge car. Tom, Jane, Suzie, Franz, and I have coalesced into a group of travel companions in which I am the senior member. By now I have told my story and my young friends are helping me to look for my roots as we approach Elkhart, where I lived as a small child.

The landscape is impossibly nondescript, so much so that Suzie begins to yawn, fidget, and chain-smoke her Tareytons. It is Franz who first mentions the windmills that rise in an infinite variety of postures. Here is one that is overgrown with ivy, a steel-and-vegetation sculpture of surprising beauty. There is another broken and falling over like a neglected metal scarecrow, looking as though the next breeze will bring it down. And finally a working windmill, all of its blades intact, whirls and pumps with well-oiled productivity.

The same variety of existential conditions appears in the farms. They range from the overgrown to the merely derelict to the white-fenced, manicured and scrubbed, prosperous and proud Stark Farm, its name and founding date, 1926, in bold black on a brilliantly white-washed barn. This is encouraging, since I'm looking for something from only as far back as the early fifties.

Soon we enter Elkhart, where thirty-five years ago on my way to kindergarten I would wait with my lunchbox for New York Central freights to cross Division Street. Somewhere near the tracks there is a duplex house where Lionel electric trains raced around a Christmas tree, and hoboes off the line could count on my mother's handout sandwiches at the back door. There are also memories of a dog and a treehouse my father built, of a terrible fire in the shacks across the river where "the bums" lived, and of one glorious Easter with visiting grandparents when the joy of being a small boy on a sunny Indiana spring morning was so intense that it hurt forever.

Today there are residential streets with duplex houses, but we roll through without my seeing anything but a quickly passing town that looks like any other. There the McDonald's arch triumphs, and there sprawls a parking lot and its mall. Only at the downtown crossing is there a hint of this town's past and uniqueness—in the brick train station and block building housing the original establishment of Florsheim Shoes. But the station has been converted to retail shopping, and Florsheim has become a national chain. The train pulls on past the downtown crossing to stop at a tarmac platform behind a cinder-block warehouse. Memory is too feeble, change is too formidable.

After Elkhart, the services chief announces that there will be no lunch served on this train. I find this unusual and irritating. Other Amtrak trains squeeze in one last meal before arrival at the end of the line, and since we have crossed a time zone, that means that my stomach will interpret our arrival time of 1:15 as 2:15. I eat a piece of the wretched microwave pizza you can buy in the lounge car and ride through Gary, Indiana, sullen and sulking while the youngsters play cards. This wouldn't have happened on the *20th Century Limited.*

But the *Lake Shore Limited* does arrive in Union Station on time, eighteen and a half hours out of New York, two and a half hours slower than the *20th Century* at its zenith, three hours faster than Amtrak ran it when it took over in the early seventies, two days faster than the *Pullman Hotel Express.* Editor Steele described an immense crowd of dignitaries and curious common folk who greeted the first transcontinental at the station. Speeches were made on the platform as passengers hung listening out of their open windows. Later the Chicago Board of Trade celebrated their Boston counterparts' successful passage of one-third of the continent with feasts and more speeches.

As the *Lake Shore Limited* backs into the station

today there are no dignitaries on hand to toast my passage, and I play travel guide for my young companions. To the right looms the huge Great Lakes Warehouse and ahead towers the post office, under which arriving and departing trains have passed in my memory since the beginning of time when I would wait for my grandfather's train at the end of the platform. Inside, the train sheds are just as dark as they have always been, and the train makes a safety stop and then a final stop short of the track-end bumper just as my grandfather explained it would eons ago. I show the kids the spot on the platform where I would stand waiting for his train to pull in from Bloomington, where even now another small boy wearing a St. Louis Cardinals cap waves at this train.

NIGHT TRAIN TO MOSCOW: WAGING PEACE

from *The House on Via Gombito: Writing by American Women Abroad*

Maureen Hurley

California writer, poet and photo-journalist Maureen Hurley has served as Director of Poetry Across Frontiers: Sonoma Heritage in Santa Rosa, a student poetry and art exchange program with the Ukranian town of Cherkassy. She has been the recipient of numerous awards, including seven California Arts Council grants.

"Though this land is not my own I will not forget it."
—Anna Akhmatova

We ride across the limitless snowbound Russian steppes by train in Car #17 to Moscow from Cherkassy. Once reserved for high-ranking Communist officials, the car with its russet wooden paneling reveals an earlier era. In fact, one still can't officially buy tickets for this well-appointed carriage at the train station. We get them through a friend. Connections mean everything in the USSR: in a country of perennial shortages, anything is available for a price. Out of the grimy window blanketed with coal soot, a monotonous landscape rhythmically repeats itself. My partner, Oleg Atbashian, says, "Siberia is like this; only it goes on forever."

We are leaving the Ukraine, where few villages have survived the many wars. Instead, industrial high-rises now punctuate the landscape, holding the low cloud ceiling aloft. Battered about for eighteen hours by train, we see that it could be any city—the curious sensation of *déjà vu*, and of arriving without ever having left. In frozen fields, haystacks hibernate like slumbering mastodons under a coat of snow. Poet Nazim Hikmet was right: No European hills or chateaux skirt the rivers here. There is nothing lovelier than birch trees in winter. Birch trees are as Russian as vodka. We eat small dark Ukrainian cherries steeped in liquor, and I hum "Moscow Nights," but not much is left in the way of onion domes to inspire me. Not much is left of the Oriental architecture of the Tartars, the Golden Hordes that once taxed the Slavs of the steppes into submission. In the morning, the *dezhurnia* brings us sweet amber tea in delicate lead crystal glasses confined in flowery brass holders.

I visited the USSR twice; during August 1989, and again the following December and January to set up a poetry and art exchange. I met with artists, writers, and publishers in Moscow, Leningrad, and Cherkassy, a Ukrainian town near Kiev. Armed with a crazy dream and a Macintosh computer, printer, and modem to revolutionize the cultural exchange with Cherkassy, the sister city of Santa Rosa, California, I met poets and artists everywhere: in cafés, video bars, and homes. Impromptu gatherings formed on street corners and trolleybus stops. We read poems, shared art, sang, made toasts, and talked of everything under the sun until late into the night. Sleep was often forsaken as we demystified the myths. Summer was sultry—lingering sunsets followed by incredibly long twilights, the white nights that lasted until dawn. Long walks along the Dnieper River, a wide expanse that moves without hurry through the drowned valley.

At home in California's wine country, people doubted my sanity when I made a return visit to the USSR in the dead of winter. Winter solstice. Then the dark that stretched past forever, a hungry tiger following us. Spectacular dawns and sunsets followed in rapid succession, and the long curtain of night beating against window panes announced its Arctic origins. To understand another culture, we must forsake fair-weather travel; we must see it even in winter. I came to the Soviet Union by accident, but I'm not an accidental tourist. As a writer, the world is my teacher, my inspiration. Stripping away acculturation, like so many layers of clothing, we discover we are alike in the flesh, after all.

"We Americans and Soviets are sentenced to understand one another," someone said. It was easy to begin. I was impressed with the openness and generosity of these people—most of whom had never met an American. I was part of a home-stay program, living with Soviet families in small crowded flats where I was treated like a long-lost relative—in a country where suspicion and distrust are inbred after generations of government terror, and repression is as common as the borsht we ate three times a day. It was not always easy. Misunderstandings arose—and required careful translation even from English to English. From this, I learned what "détente" really meant. Distrust sometimes went to funny extremes. At a birthday party, Oleg's grandmother thought I was a spy, but when—after politely parroting *chut-chut* too many times—I nearly slid under the table, she decided I was all right. *Chut-chut* is not a national toast as I first thought (since everyone was saying it)—it means "a little more!"

Glasnost, which literally means "open door," has done much to tear down the walls of misunderstanding on both sides of the American/Soviet power equation. Like many, I too was a product of the Period of Stagnation, raised in the ignorance and misinformation of our McCarthy era, and of the Stalin/Breshnev periods in the Soviet Union. Another reason I went to the USSR was to banish ghosts. When I was a child, my best friend's mother, a Russian translator for the United Nations, blacklisted during the Red purges, took a drink for solace, and died, branded by fire. Coming home from school, we were moths circling the blazing house. An accident, they said—blaming a crossed wire in the dryer. But our political climate killed her—surely as if they'd set the fire themselves. . . . Because of glasnost, I was able to move in relative freedom around the country and discover what Citizen Diplomacy, a natural grass-roots evolution based on personal contact, friendship, and sharing—is all about. When we shared the stories about our fears during the Cuban Missile Crisis, and the Bay of Pigs—the stories were identical, only our nationalities were different. The Russians have only one word, *mir*, for both world and peace.

FROM WALL TO WALL: FROM BEIJING TO BERLIN BY RAIL

Mary Morris (1947–)

Mary Morris's journeys to China, Mexico, Central America, Russia and Europe have provided most of the background for much of this global wanderer's writings. Her first book, Vanishing Animals and Other Stories, *appeared in 1979, followed four years later by the novel* Crossroads. *Other fiction includes* The Waiting Room *(1989),* A Mother's Love *(1993) and* Acts of God *(2000). Morris is best known for the travel book* Nothing to Declare: Memoirs of a Woman Traveling Alone *(1988).*

Train travel for me is the fictive mode. Trains are the stuff of stories, inside and out. From windows I have seen lovers embrace, workers pause from their travail. Women gaze longingly at the passing train; men stare with thwarted dreams in their eyes. Escapist children try to leap aboard. Narratives, like frames of film, pass by.

On the inside I have had encounters as well. I've met people who have become briefly, for the length of the ride, a lover or friend. A strange and sudden intimacy seems possible here. On the Puno-Cuzco Express through the Urubamba Valley of Peru I met a man I thought I would follow across the Andes. On the night train from Chungking a woman stayed up half the night telling me the story of her life. On an Italian train I met a woman who pleaded with me to go to Bulgaria with her, saying she knew it was where I needed to be. I've been invited off trains into homes, into beds, asked to walk into people's lives, all I am sure because people know a train traveler will never leave the train.

My life even as a little girl was intimately tied to trains, with those fast-moving machines that raced across the Midwestern plains. When I was five, my parents concocted a train journey to Idaho, a family vacation at Sun Valley. My father was not with us on that ride. He would be joining us later, flying in after a meeting, coming for a short spell, his vacation time always being trimmed like lean meat.

So it was my mother, brother, and myself in our tiny compartment, my mother a frazzled woman, alone with these children on a long train ride, lonely I think, but dedicated, as mothers were then, to us. She didn't get angry about the toothpaste flushed down the toilet, the small suitcase that kept falling on her head. She wore lipstick and a blue dress and high heels to dine in the dining car and secured our water glasses with glove-covered hands as the heartland sped by. My mother's agenda was London, Paris, Rome, maybe Hong Kong, but we were en route to Boise, Idaho.

So I escaped and sat, hour after hour, beneath a glass dome, staring at the light over the cornfields, I sat—a dreamy, somewhat forlorn child of five whose father had too much work to do, whose mother was left with the unwelcome task of ushering us to a place of horses and duck ponds—watching the stars coming on like city lights, until my mother retrieved me back into the warm womb of our cramped compartment. Here I kept my eyes open, peering into the night at the passing towns, at the dark expanse of prairie, through a turned-up corner of the window shade as the world as I knew it receded and we moved into the West.

In the morning before daybreak I made my way, still in my night clothes, back to the domed car, to await the rising sun. Slowly it came as the train sped, never changing its pace, and the light opened on the plain. There before me suddenly stood the white peaks of mountains. I had never seen a mountain before and these shimmered—their glacial caps sheathed in sunlight—against the endless blue sky and the flat, green Midwestern plain from which they rose. There on that Union Pacific Railroad, carrying these reluctant travelers to our indeterminate destination, the mountains came upon me as my first truly complete surprise—the way the remarkable events of life have come upon me since.

As the train hurtled to those mountains, even my mother, as she came wearily to find me and try to coax me back to our compartment, paused for a moment in awe.

In the high-ceilinged, dark-wood waiting room for the Trans-Siberian Express, Chinese Muslims, the women with veils over their heads, sat on sacks of bulgur and rice. European students studied their travel guides or slept on their duffel bags. Eastern European diplomats in dark navy suits and shirts with frayed collars milled close to the doors. The noises were those of train travel. Announcements in Chinese blared overhead through static speakers. Anxious travelers—bound for Ulan Bator, Moscow, Warsaw, Bucharest, Belgrade, Berlin, London, and some even for Mecca—checked their watches or bid their good-byes, though there was none of the frenzy I'd seen at the Chinese International Travel Services office.

I sat on my duffel and went through my papers as well. My ticket, Mongolian transit visa, Soviet visa. Everything seemed in order as I leaned into my duffel, once again suddenly overcome with fatigue as if I had sunk there never to rise again. But suddenly the doors to the waiting room were opened and a surge went through the travelers as we headed like an obedient flock for the door.

I moved slowly from the rear, dragging my duffel behind until I passed through the doors onto the platform. There it stood. An army-green train with perhaps a dozen or so cars, circa 1950, "Peking-Moskau" on its side, Chinese porters in red caps standing at each car, ready to show us to our cars. I stood amazed and thrilled.

I made my way to carriage number 3 where a very tall, very un-Chinese-looking porter, who would take care of our car for the entire ride to Moscow and who spoke enough English and French to make brief conversation possible, took my duffel out of my hand. He led me into the first compartment on that car. Dropping my duffel on the lower berth, he wished me a pleasant journey.

I stared at the lace curtains, the small lamp, the writing table with lace tablecloth, the chair, the small sofa that would convert into a bed. On the advice of a friend I had purchased a deluxe ticket, as opposed to first-class. First-class consisted of a hard bed and four people in the compartment. Deluxe was a soft bed and two people in the compartment. For six days, at a cost of two hundred dollars, I knew I had made the right choice.

I tossed my duffel overhead, pulling out just what I'd need for the day—the copy of *Anna Karenina* I'd planned to reread, my journal, some snacks, and a toothbrush. Then I inspected the compartment more closely. The sofa felt relatively comfortable and I thought that it would make an adequate bed. I opened the door to the semiprivate bath which consisted of a hose shower and a sink, so that at least I'd be able to bathe instead of taking what I'd come prepared for—Wash n' Dri sponge baths.

I sat down at the small table by the window. Travelers scurried outside. Porters helped them with their bags. My porter brought me a pot of tea and said that the samovar was always hot.

I breathed a sigh and settled in. I was opening my journal when Cecilia arrived. She sported a full pack and a loud Liverpool accent. "So here we are. We're roomies. Isn't this great!" She dumped her pack on the floor, hurled a few things onto the top bunk. She was large, a dishwater blonde with square features and a boisterous voice. In a matter of moments I learned that Cecilia was English, living in Singapore with her second husband and her two children, having marital problems, and also, she hinted, an affair. "Going to London," she said. "I needed a break."

I predicted rather accurately that Cecilia would not stop talking for the entire six days and that I'd learn more than I ever cared to know about her, her private life, her feelings for the royal family, her politics, and that if I wanted to think or rest I'd have to work my way around her, which did not seem very easy in an eight-by-six-foot room.

I got up to stretch and Cecilia took the seat at the

table by the window, facing the direction in which the train was traveling. There she planted herself for the rest of the trip where she'd sit with her tea, her rock 'n' roll tapes, and the snacks she'd eat all day long, never seeming to have a meal

I left the compartment and stared out the window. Soon there came a whistle, a brief announcement in Russian and Chinese. The wife of a Yugoslav diplomat who had the compartment next to ours stared out the window as well. When she heard the announcement she turned to me and said in English, "Now we are leaving." She gave me the only smile I would see on her face the entire trip. Suddenly the whistle came again, piercing and more insistent this time, and in a matter of moments I felt the tug of wheels, the power of engines as the journey began.

I found a jump seat at the window. I pulled it down and sat there for a long time. I watched as the residential streets of Beijing drifted away; the stream of bicycles receded, then disappeared. Rice paddies came into view. Farmers in broad-brimmed straw hats bent, legs in upside-down V's, planting in the sodden fields. Oxen pulled plows across the yellow-earth fields. I was oblivious to the other travelers, all with noses pressed to the glass, until someone shouted, "the Wall, the Wall." There it was, snaking across the mountains, crumbling here and there, careening down a ridge, only to rise again; the Great Wall of China wended its way like a mythological beast, fortified and useless against the ostensible fears. Then slowly it diminished until it was only a thin line, like a crack in the earth. And then it was gone. . . .

The dining car looked more like a Chinese laundry than a restaurant—noisy, frenzied, boiling hot. Warm Chinese beer was being handed out and I grabbed one from a passing tray as everyone else seemed to do. The car was packed and I saw no seats, but then Pierre, the French saxophone player I'd met at the Mongolian Embassy, waved from across the room, pointing to half a seat. "So," he said, putting an arm around my shoulder, "you made it." He was sitting at a boisterous table of European travelers—Swiss, French, German and Dutch. They were all speaking assorted European languages, though French seemed predominant. When I joined them they switched to English but I told them French or German was all right.

A small fan blew overhead, the kind a secretary might put on her desk, but the heat continued to rise. Everyone was sweating. Plates of delicious fried meats, sautéed vegetables, rice, were being passed. "Open the window," Pierre shouted in French. Someone who spoke broken Chinese shouted the same thing. The soaking waitress ignored our pleas. Someone opened a window and the cook went wild, screaming in Chinese, slamming it shut. "Dust," he yelled which someone translated, "dust." We drank our warm beer and ate hot food as we baked in the sun.

The heat did not let up and felt close to a hundred and twenty at times. None of the Chinese porters would permit windows to be open. "The desert," our porter explained to me. But finally in our car protests were mounting. At last he let us open the windows in our individual compartments if we kept the doors shut. Cecilia had gone to the dining room to sit, for I don't believe she actually ever dined, and left me alone at the open window, dust blowing in my face.

The landscape had altered. From the farmlands and rice paddies we moved into a mountainous, more arid terrain as we crossed the Northern Chinese province of Inner Mongolia. Though we had yet to reach he desert, a scrub grassland reached to the horizon with occasional sheep grazing. I sat as the day shifted to evening and the heat subsided.

At eight-forty that evening we reached the out-post of Erhlien, the border town between Inner and Outer Mongolia. It was the gateway to Russia, Mongolia being a Soviet protectorate. The station was old-fashioned, like something out of the American West—a small, wood-slat structure. Chinese border guards came onto the train. After checking our passports and visas, they told us we could leave the train.

I stood on the platform, breathing the cool evening air. It was unclear how long our stop was, but to my surprise and almost fear, suddenly they took the train away. I watched as it receded, disappearing behind us. The Chinese Muslim men smiled benignly, but the Europeans seemed dismayed. Then I recalled the words of a friend who'd taken this trip before. "At the borders," he'd told me, "they take the trains away." They have to change the wheels because the track has a different grade, which in part makes international hijacking impossible across Asia and Europe. Also they take the train away because each country has its own dining car and now for Mongolia the new car must be attached.

I was happy to leave the train and walk in the cool night air. It was a lovely night now and a full moon shone overhead. All the travelers went into the station house, but I walked the platform. Chinese Muslim men strolled, but their women were nowhere in sight. In fact the Chinese Muslim women would never leave the train. They would not be seen in public. Instead they remained in their compartments, facing Mecca, eating from the giant sacks of food they had brought and cooking on small portable stoves in their compartments. I always knew where East was and roughly the time of day because the Muslim women would be facing East at specific times.

I went into the station where a small postal service was open. I bought stamps and began to write post-cards from the border of Inner and Outer Mongolia, to many people seemingly the most remote place on earth, though in fact it was fairly accessible. I bought a bag of stewed apricots and a warm orange soda from a small stand. I sat in the station on a wooden bench, writing cards while border guards patrolled around me and a bolero of bullfighting music played incongruously on the overhead speakers.

On the platform an hour or so later, I ran into the Chinese Muslims I'd sat next to on the floor of the Chinese International Travel Services office. We greeted one another like long-lost friends. They laughed, happy to see me, and pointed to my pen which remained in my hand. One made a sweeping motion as if to wipe sweat off his brow, indicating how hot they had been. Then they pointed to the yellow moon over Mongolia, clasped their hands as if in blessing, and smiled.

At about midnight the train returned with new wheels and a Mongolian dining car and we crossed into the People's Republic of Mongolia. The temperature had dropped considerably and it was actually cool. I grabbed a sweater from my compartment. Then after perhaps half a mile the train stopped and Mongolian passport officials boarded. They had wide bronze faces, reminiscent of the indigenous peoples of America. Some theories of human migration say that these ancient Central Asian peoples crossed the Bering Strait and were the first inhabitants of the Western Hemisphere, the people from whom all the Native Americans descended.

But now their being part of the police state was clear. The train was thoroughly searched. Beneath bunks, overhead racks, suitcases were moved aside to search for contraband. Then, at 1 A.M., they left and we entered Mongolia.

I found I could not sleep so I wandered to the

darkened new dining car, which, with arching windows, scalloped seats, red curtains, looked more like a mosque than a dining car. Pierre was sitting with two Dutch girls. The Mongolian dining crew—a man and his wife—were already setting up for breakfast. They worked noiselessly in the background.

Pierre ordered a bottle of Mongolian vodka and poured drinks all around. The man, who wore a small, brightly colored skullcap, and the woman, with a scarf around her head, both with sharp Mongolian features, wide, flat faces, brought glasses out and joined us. They raised their glasses and we raised ours. Then we sat in the darkened car, watching the beginnings of a moonlit Gobi rush by, drinking Mongolian vodka into the night.

ABOARD THE CRESCENT

Chapter 1 from *Booked on the Morning Train: A Journey through America*

George F. Scheer III

Writer and Revolutionary War historian George F. Scheer III is best known for his first book, Rebels and Redcoats: The American Revolution Through the Eyes of Those Who Lived It, *co-authored with F. Rankin. He has also contributed to* American Heritage *magazine and* The New York Times Book Review.

In a Pullman berth, a man can truly be alone with himself. (The nearest approach to this condition is to be found in a hotel bedroom, but a hotel room can be mighty depressing sometimes, it stands so still.)

—E. B. White, "Progress and Change,"
December 1938
(Collected in *One Man's Meat*)

The bags—the big red pullman, the square brown bookbag, the squat gray camera bag—sat by the door, neatly packed. The thick bundle of tickets lay under the lamplight on the desk. I was due to catch the Amtrak Crescent at Greensboro, North Carolina, at 12:30 in the morning as it passed through on its way to New Orleans.

My plan was to ride as many of the overland routes as I could, keeping in mind the heritage of American train travel but not letting myself be tyrannized by it. The glimmering days and nights of rail travel, when the dining tables were clothed with linen, the sleeping rooms were paneled with exotic woods, and train crews included hairstylists, barbers, and wine stewards, are gone and will never return. We may take pleasure in recounting them, in reminding ourselves that progress is not always a straight line, but I see no point in pining for their return. No woeful lamentations for a gentility gone forever and founded in part, if we look around to the back door, on some social conventions we have done well to leave behind. No paeans to the golden days. I would take my journey on its own terms.

The last day had become an endless quickstep of cross-continent telephone calls, quick recalculations of the itinerary, and quickening misgivings as the pieces got harder and harder to fit together and the threads threatened to unravel.

On my last evening, I sat on the sofa and looked around. The house was still in dishabille from the exterminator's visit. The contents of kitchen drawers were piled in cardboard boxes on the living room floor. Clean clothes and dirty laundry were heaped together on the bed. Books and letters and papers from two works in progress were piled haphazardly on my desk, with more filed stack by stack on the study floor. Somewhere among them all must have been the previous month's unpaid electric bill: the power company was threatening to pull the plug. In my last several frantic days of preparation I had reduced my surroundings to such confusion that my only hope lay in escape, pure dishonorable retreat.

I was tired, grumpy, frustrated, and nervous. I longed to be on the road and leave my troubles behind. And still I was troubled by the prospect. Travel cuts us loose from our moorings. It's why we want to go, but at the last minute it seems so snug in the harbor. Travel takes practice. I was rusty.

Boarding passengers were already waiting on the platform in Greensboro when we pulled into the small parking lot ten minutes before train time. The station itself was one of a number of nondescript cracker boxes erected by Amtrak to replace city stations that have been razed or are no longer feasible to maintain. It was too late to check any of my bags. I carried them through the gap in the chain link fence straight to the platform, and just as I set them on the concrete the locomotive's headlight appeared down the tracks. When the Crescent rolled up to the platform, air brakes hissing, the ground shook, and I had to steel myself not to jump back. It is easy to forget what an awesome kinetic force rides with a railroad train. It's like a toppling building, something so heavy moving so fast. Remember how the locomotive of your childhood electric train was so heavy, so dense, such a surprising mass in your small hand

and how it made the floor rumble when it pounded around the track? A big train has the force of a river.

Boarding at Greensboro I experienced the sudden, giddy freedom of the traveler, who by the simple expedient of climbing aboard leaves at once his workaday cares behind. It seemed so simple now: farewell to friends, just two steps up, all the way to your left, stow your luggage, find your seat, and for six weeks, everything would follow from there.

I stored my suitcase and bookbag in the luggage rack at the head of the coach and walked softly through the aisle, past huddled passengers all trying to ignore the intrusion on their sleep. I found an empty seat, slid my camera bag in front of it, and sat down. This was the moment I had been looking forward to for months, the cusp where anticipation became experience. It went uncelebrated. I sat in the dark and longed for some human contact, even a conversation about the weather. The passengers on the Amtrak Crescent that night were not interested in my story. They wanted only to pass the night in peace.

Later I would realize that there is a continuity to train travel that distinguished it from, for instance, air travel and helps define the experience. Planes go from here directly to there. Fellow passengers share a common experience, a common schedule, common expectations. An overland train is something different. On it ride passengers who may have boarded at any one of dozens of points and may be headed to any of a dozen more. Stops come regularly, all through the day and night, and no one stop is an event. Travelers finishing their journey get off, travelers beginning their journey get aboard, and most just keep on. I got on at Greensboro. All around me my fellow travelers just kept on.

I waited apprehensively in the dark car for the conductor to come and collect my ticket. My arrangement with Amtrak was unorthodox and I was uncertain of its reception from the railroad conductors, who were then officials of the independent railroads, not Amtrak employees, and who are a law unto themselves on the trains. But the conductor accepted my thick book of tickets without comment, as most would do throughout the journey, and I was soon alone again.

The Amtrak car attendant followed closely behind, marking and posting seat checks, and he changed my seat to afford me two unoccupied seats side by side so I could stretch out a bit. I thanked him for the courtesy, and he asked me, "Is this your first time on a train?" The first in many years, I told him. He commented on my bulky camera bag, and we spoke for a few minutes about my plans and his work, the first of many impromptu conversations I would have with Amtrak people in the wee hours of the weeks to come.

As I looked around, the night coach seemed like steerage in an ocean-going vessel, with determined emigrants huddled amidst their belongings. Some held children, others cuddled together, limbs entwined. A few stretched out, legs scattered, breathing or snoring through a slack mouth. The darkness afforded us all an illusion of privacy.

By dumb luck I stumbled that first night on the secret of survival in coach by realizing that I was free to move about and seek my own company. I tucked my camera bag like a precious bindle into the aisle seat and made my way to the rear, out for a stroll. I passed the Amtrak attendants in their seats at the rear of the coach, stepped through the clamorous vestibule, walked with a wobbling gait, still unaccustomed to the swaying train (I decided many weeks later that one never grows accustomed to it, because even the train crews who spent their working lives aboard stumbled about like rank cabin boys), through several more coaches of slumbering passengers, and finally found life in the lounge car.

What I found was the dregs of a cocktail party. Most nights, on most long runs, the lounge car of a passenger train is the neighborhood tavern for a neighborhood that exists for one night only astraddle the rails. An evening drama in a lounge car progresses through the same scenes staged every night in the local around the corner: a few determined souls start the evening with the sun barely over the yardarm; the cocktail crowd stops by for a pick-me-up on the way to dinner; the brandy and cigar crowd relaxes after dinner (allowing for the fact that Amtrak prohibits the smoking of both pipes and cigars in the lounge cars, a rule that is occasionally broken but seldom abused); a little later celebrants looking for a night on the town congregate in noisy conclaves; and as the night wears down, the lounge thins out, leaving by the wee hours the usual assemblage of overindulgers, truly gregarious creatures, insomniacs, and those who have nowhere else to go.

It was after one in the morning, well past last call. Toward the end of the coach, a young man on leave from the navy sat alone at his table, a meaningless grin on his face and an evening's worth of bar litter—empty cellophane pretzel bags, a couple of overflowing metallic paper ashtrays with crimped edges, scattered poptops, and three or four empty beer cans—on the table around his elbows. Neatly arrayed along the edge of his table were three more unopened cans laid in at last call.

The conversation at the center of the coach was about railroads. A young Southern Railway trainman, deadheading home to Salisbury, was discussing the advantages of concrete ties with a beefy German, who, with elaborate ceremony, filled, tamped, and smoked a large Scandinavian freehand briar. I never learned the German's trade, but he had traveled extensively over the American rails, which suggested that his work afforded him time and opportunity, and he was obviously sensitive to mechanical matters. There were two other passengers in the lounge car: a quiet and apparently sober man sitting to my left and an overbearing drunk across the aisle, who desperately wanted someone to listen to tales of his days in military intelligence and to his analysis of American defense policy, an analysis that benefited from some mysterious insight he constantly hinted at but could never explain. Eventually he found in the young sailor an appreciative audience for his tales of whoring in old New Orleans. Together they hatched elaborate and boastful plans for a night on the town in that wicked city.

As we passed Spencer, North Carolina, the young trainman pointed out the former site of the old Spencer shops, the largest railroad repair shops ever built in the South. From the turn of the century onward, the steam behemoths that were the motive power for the Southern Railway were repaired, rebuilt, and kept in their distinctive green and gold trim here in a shop that included a roundhouse with more than thirty stalls. Spencer was named for the Southern Railway's president, Samuel Spencer, who died in the wreck of Southern No. 37 at Lawyers, Virginia, south of Lynchburg, in 1906. Three years prior, another Southern train, the Southern Fast Mail from Washington, D.C., to New Orleans, left the tracks on that same run and derailed straight into folklore:

Oh, they handed him his orders at Monroe, Virginia,
Saying, "Steve, you're away behind time.
This is not 38, but it's old 97
You must put 'er in Spencer on time."

The trainman left at Salisbury, headed home to a

new wife. He had told me that he had a boy from a previous marriage and wanted desperately to father a girl. Salisbury was just past 1:30 in the morning, and the German, the sailor, the traveling salesman, and the quiet man to my left were all traveling through to New Orleans, so they spoke their parting words, promising to meet for breakfast, although I doubted any would make the first call, and made their way to their respective nights' rest—the German and the salesman, traveling on his expense account and proud of it, to their sleepers in the rear of the train, the sailor forward to snore away the remaining night hours in a coach. The quiet, informally dressed man at my left, who might have been a high school football coach, or even a biology teacher, turned out to be an engineer from upstate New York working for a company that manufactures and installs oil drilling equipment. He commuted every month to Slidell, Louisiana, outside New Orleans, to be near the Gulf.

"Do you usually take the train?" I asked him.

"Never done it before. One of our representatives takes the train to conferences now and then and he persuaded me to try it. Said it had improved. And I'm tired of flying. If I hurry down there, I'll just be on a chopper for the Gulf in the morning, so I thought I'd take my time."

We were alone in the lounge car at ten past two when my car attendant, a young, redheaded woman working one of her first runs, came to fetch me. "Charlotte in ten minutes."

The once-a-day schedules of most Amtrak long-haul trains dictate awkward arrival times for many intermediate destinations. A train that runs only once a day cannot arrive everywhere on its route at five in the afternoon. Fortunately, I have a very good friend in Charlotte, one willing to meet my train at two-twenty in the morning.

I spent twenty-four hours in Charlotte while the Crescent rolled on to New Orleans without me. At 3:00 A. M., by the time Celia and I had gotten my bags out of her Karmann Ghia and into her apartment, the Crescent was leaving Gastonia, North Carolina, its next stop. At 4:00 A. M., while Celia and I were sitting in her tiny kitchen drinking a beer and talking, the Crescent was changing crews at Spartanburg, South Carolina, its next division point. As we slept, the Crescent traveled on, reaching Tuscaloosa, Alabama, about the time we arose at noon.

I spent the afternoon calling ahead to confirm arrangements, repacking my bags, reconsidering my provisions. After lugging my suitcase down just two station platforms, I was tempted to jettison everything except a pipe, a necktie, and a change of underwear. At about six-thirty in the evening, while Celia and I were still waiting for a table in a Mexican restaurant, the Crescent was arriving in New Orleans without me. But that afternoon, another train, another Crescent, had left New York's Pennsylvania Station at two-thirty, and when it arrived in Charlotte twelve hours later, at two-twenty on Thursday morning, I would be there to board it.

Celia ran four stoplights in downtown Charlotte, which was deserted at 2:00 A. M., to get me back to the station by train time. I knew that somewhere down the line I would miss a train, but this was not to be it.

"Look," she told me, "if you want to miss one next week, that's your business, but you're not doing it on my shift!"

We dashed through the station and up the steps just as the Crescent rolled up. On the platform, Celia handed me a going-away present, a blue toothbrush with the name "RICK" on the handle in white letters.

"Don't you think it's funny?" she said

I climbed aboard the sleeper car for my first encounter with a roomette.

The Amtrak attendant, a black man in his late fifties, gave me a ritual demonstration of the roomette's features. He showed me how to work the lights—there were four of them in my little warren, with one doubling as a night light, emitting a pale blue light that was at first eerie but soon became soothing.

On its long-distance routes east of the Mississippi, Amtrak employs what it calls its Heritage Fleet, refitted and completely re-equipped cars inherited from the private railroads. This car I was riding to New Orleans might once have seen service on the Santa Fe line, or the Union Pacific, or in the Chessie system.

In a space no larger than a closet, I found a seat, a toilet, a table or hassock, a coat closet, a sink with hot and cold water taps, a water fountain issuing potable water and stocked with a supply of paper cups, a shoe locker, four lights positioned variously about, a folding bed, a window, and a mirror large enough to reflect it all. The sink was particularly clever—an oval stainless steel bowl with no drain but instead an opening along and just below its back rim. When the sink folded upward into the wall, the water held in its bowl escaped through that opening down a pipeway that also drained the water fountain immediately above. The shoe locker higher up was a reminder that these cars were designed for an earlier and more formal day, and that train travel once offered grace notes of service found today only in luxury hotels. There were no rough edges or sloppy fittings, and the overall impression was of impenetrable construction. In its solidity the Heritage sleeper reminded me of my '55 Chevy. Dated though it was, my little cubbyhole seemed to be the product of a superior design tool: common sense. It fit a human being just about right. At least I thought so until the first time I needed to use the toilet in the middle of the night and discovered that, to raise the bed and get to the toilet beneath it, I had to poke my own caboose into the hall.

I slid the heavy steel door closed, dropped the latch, propped myself up in bed, unpacked my typewriter and papers, and spent the hours writing notes and letters, pausing for minutes, hours it seemed, to watch the hypnotic lights of the night. Frequently I would douse my own dim light to allow my eyes to penetrate farther into the shadowy world passing my window. Night in a railroad sleeper, particularly a single berth, is too glorious a glimpse of solitude to waste entirely in sleep; I relished it as we rocked on through the darkness, past the farm villages, small towns, and little cities of North Carolina—Juneau, Belmont, Lowell, Gastonia, Bessemer City, Kings Mountain, and Grover—and of South Carolina—Blacksburg, Gaffney, Thickety, Cowpens, Clifton, Converse, and Zion Hill.

Between Charlotte and Atlanta, the Crescent stops roughly once each hour. The stations seemed old and shopworn at night, with baggage carts that would have looked at home trailing behind a mule, simple wooden beds riding on spoked wheels with strap-iron rims. Sometime in the dark morning hours, somewhere in South Carolina, I stood in the open doorway of the vestibule savoring the night air, looking at a long row of these venerable carts lined up beneath the overhang of a station's shed roof, and wondering how a station could have changed so little in so many years.

On the way back to the lounge car, I passed through the empty dining car where a trainman sat quietly by himself reading his Bible. He seemed willing to put it aside for a moment and talk. I noticed he was somewhere in John. He suggested that I could find something to drink a the Greenville stop, coming up soon. "If you walk ahead about three cars, there will be a door open, and you can get off and find yourself a soft drink in the station. Don't worry, we don't leave Greenville until 5:00 A.M., and we're running plenty ahead right now. We'll probably get in there sometime around four-forty. They spend some time on the train at Greenville, checking it out, putting on water, changing engineers, looking under the cars for problems."

We drifted into a conversation about the way Amtrak had changed things. "I went to work for Southern in 1968, and it was a different company then, a different atmosphere," he said. "Nobody at the company cared about drinking. I would see men come to work so drunk they couldn't do their job at all. Somebody would put them on the train and then just look out for them until the day was over. The company people knew what was happening but they were interested in the bottom line, and as long as the jobs got done they didn't care who did them or how they got done. It's true, they showed some heart. A lot of the worst were nearing retirement and the company just carried them along until their time was up. But it's not like that anymore. The company changed completely in about five years, which might seem slow to you, but for a man who has been with the company a lifetime, his whole career, it seemed like overnight. And now the company doesn't care that you get the job done, as much as they care that you don't break any of the rules."

He voiced an opinion I would hear again from other trainmen on other roads. "You know, Amtrak is always trying to get control of the trains. They want us to work for them, just like the dining car waiters and the porters. But I don't think the Southern will ever let that happen. If we worked for Amtrak, they'd never be able to hold us to the same

standards that Southern can, even with the unions." Amtrak, naturally, has argued just the opposite and has since acquired control of the crews on many of the trains.

We made Greenville ahead of schedule a few minutes before five in the morning. My first night in a sleeping compartment was nearly over. So, while it was still dark, somewhere south of Greenville, I clambered again onto my bed, reached back and slid the door closed, dropped the latch, undressed, and slipped between the sheets. I lay half-upright, drifting between sleep and wakefulness, as we crossed from South Carolina into Georgia. A few minutes past seven I began to notice the sun, not yet over the horizon, beginning to color the morning sky. In a field, I could just make out the dark forms of cows lying scattered about, their forelegs tucked up tightly like snoozing house cats.

By quarter of eight, we were moving slowly through the outskirts of Atlanta, past lumberyards and building supply lots, past an abandoned railroad trestle now leading nowhere, covered with kudzu. We stopped, started, and then stopped again, and in a moment a Southern locomotive tandem passed with a freight behind, flatcars of building materials: Weldwood, Westar, plywood. Road crews were building a freeway overpass. The work day had begun. The sun already glared. It promised to be hot long before noon.

The grim energy of Atlanta in the early autumn heat and the new passengers crowding onto the train seemed oppressive after the lonely overnight run through the Carolinas. As lagniappe for travelers in sleeping cars, Amtrak offers morning coffee, tea, or juice, and often a local morning newspaper. I cracked my door just long enough to take the coffee and the paper, latched it shut again, drank a few sips, checked the headlines for catastrophes, pulled the shade down tight, and fell asleep before we left Atlanta.

When I lifted the shade, the late afternoon Mississippi sun flashed through the trees, stuttering through the gaps and hitting my window like a strobe. The dazzling light flickered across my retinas and ricocheted around in my eyeballs and made me queasy. I was on the right-hand side of the Crescent, the western shoulder of the consist.

I slowly came awake and after a while I began my housekeeping. I sifted through the notes I had taken the night before and set aside a letter to be mailed from New Orleans. I crawled to the foot of the bed and, kneeling there, brushed my teeth and splashed cold water on my face. I took my pants and shirt from their hook on the wall of the compartment between the window and the mirror at the foot of the bed, lay back down, and wriggled into them. Dressing from the supine position is a humbling experience, shared by railroad travelers and campers in mountain tents. I pulled myself back to my knees and rummaged blindly under the foot of the bed for my shoes. During the night, they had walked too far back beneath the bed to be reached from above, so I gave up and opened the door. I stepped out in the aisle in my stocking feet, my shirttail hanging loose and my belt unfastened. As I fell to my knees to grope for my shoes, I heard my porter say, "Well, cowboy, I see you're gonna get up today."

By the time I had collected myself and rearranged my compartment from night to day configuration, from bedroom to sitting room, the sun was getting low and red. A few minutes after I settled into my chair the trees fell away and we rolled slowly out over Lake Pontchartrain, 630 square miles of brackish water. The Crescent crosses this wide lake on a rickety causeway, built a century ago, that is five and three-quarters miles long, still one of the longest railroad bridges in the world. The trestle is so low and so narrow that nothing of it can be seen from the coaches. Look out and you see only water. The sun hung swollen in the thick atmosphere just over the lake. Its rays skipped off the light, even chop, ticking each crest.

The open water became a cove and then a marsh and then sandy soil, and I heard the announcement for New Orleans. The Crescent approaches the city through its northeastern suburbs, skirting the south shore of Lake Pontchartrain, crossing the Inner Harbor Navigation Canal, and then turning south to cut through City Park. When I saw the bright white masonry burial vaults of Metairie Cemetery, built above ground because the terrain is so low and wet, I knew we were in New Orleans. When I stepped down to the platform in Union Station, the first thing I noticed was the ballast between the rails: pearly white oyster shells.

My watch said almost seven-thirty. I thought we were more than an hour late. In towns all up the line—Choccolocco, Eastaboga, Cook Springs, Weems, Burstall, McCalla, Coaling, Cottondale, Moundville, Boligee, Cuba, Toomsuba, Enterprise, Pachuta, Moselle, Okahola, Talowah, and Pearl River—men and women were just coming home from their work, stowing away the tools of their trade, briefcase or pipe wrench, sitting down to dinner, and contemplating the end of their day. It was early evening and my day was just beginning. In New Orleans, chefs and bartenders and musicians and pickpockets were beginning theirs, too.

PRETORIA, JOHANNESBURG, SOWETO, A GOLD MINE, AND THE BLUE TRAIN TO CAPE TOWN: 1991

from *Pole to Pole with Michael Palin*

Michael Palin (1943–)

"Monty Python" acting alumnus Michael Palin has written and appeared in numerous movies and television programs, written children's books and, in the early 1980s, filmed a travel piece for BBC's "Great Railway Journeys of the World," which led to his 1989 re-creation of the travels of Phineas Fogg from Jules Verne's Around the World in Eighty Days, also for the BBC. In the early '90s, Palin traveled North to South, from Pole to Pole, by camel, river raft, train and balloon.

DAY 127. JOHANNESBURG TO CAPE TOWN

Discomfort in my back at night is still acute. Time will heal, people keep reassuring me, but I wouldn't mind a bit of help. A cheerful and obliging Johannesburg chemist recommends arnica, a homoeopathic remedy, and bonemeal tablets. They join the growing stash of pain-relieving drugs which have just about made up in weight for the bag lost in Lusaka.

Johannesburg station is deserted at 10.15 a.m. apart from a straggle of passengers and their porters booking in beside the sign "Bloutrein Hoflikheids Diens." The Blue Train porters must be the smartest in the world, in their blue blazers, grey trousers with knife-edge creases and leather shoes polished to a mirror-like sheen. Sadly, they wear rather sour expressions as if they all might have toothache, but as our man leads us into a lift he makes it pretty clear what he's surly about.

"Sorry about the smell," he turns to pull the gate across, "it's the coons. They piss all over the place."

A group of fellow-travellers is squashed onto a piece of carpet at a specially erected check-in area, in the middle of an otherwise long and empty platform. They look a little nervous and exposed, as if the ability to take the Blue Train marks you out as one of the world's most muggable prospects. Some are scanning the information board which gives details of unashamed luxuries that await us.

"Dress is smart casual for lunch and elegant for dinner."

Rack my brains to think of anything in my depleted wardrobe that could by any stretch of the imagination be described as elegant. Fail.

Two azure-blue diesel locomotives, bringing the 17 coaches of colour coordinated stock down from Pretoria, ease into the curve of the platform and quietly glide to a halt, whereupon stewards move smartly forward to layout matching carpets, monogrammed with the letter "B," before each door.

And so it goes on. My compartment has a wall of a window—big and double glazed—air-conditioning, carpet, individual radio and temperature controls, half a bottle of champagne, a newspaper and an electronically operated Venetian blind. Just before 11:30 a husky female voice breathes over the intercom, "The Blue Train is ready to depart," and barely noticeably, we begin to pull out of Johannesburg, due to cover the 900 miles to Cape Town in 22 hours. For the first time since Tromso we are moving west of our 30 degree meridian and may not meet it again until, God willing, I reach the South Pole.

A travel-worn maroon and white local from Soweto passes us, heading into the city. We gather speed through grubby stations like Braamfontein and Mayfair, whose platforms are crowded with blacks in headscarves and sweaters, accelerating into the smarter suburbs with names like Unified and Florida. It is the most comfortable train ride I've ever experienced, and combined with the aircon and the thick glazing and the wall to wall carpets it is like being in an hermetically sealed capsule, enabling the passenger to observe the outside world whilst remaining completely detached from it—an unconscious paradigm, perhaps, of the apartheid systems, officially abolished only five months ago.

There are 92 people in 17 coaches—as opposed to 4000 in 18 on the Nile Valley Express. No one is allowed to travel on the roof. On Zambian Railways the restaurant car was out of food altogether, on the Blue Train I count 13 pieces of cutlery in front of me at lunchtime. Terrine of king clip (a local fish) and Cape salmon are served as we move across the wide, flat expanse of the High Veldt. Grain and gold country. Far in the distance the mountains are temporarily obscured by a thunderstorm.

The Johannesburg Star carries more evidence of the rapid emergence of the country from the years of isolation. South Africa is to be allowed to take part in the Olympics for the first time in 30 years. There is an advert for the resumption of South African Airways services to New York and a report that Richard Branson hopes to bring Virgin Airlines into Johannesburg by 1993. Meanwhile uniformed attendants move discreetly along the carpeted corridors collecting clothes to be pressed. Muzak lightly dusts the tranquil atmosphere, occasionally interpreted by train announcements:

"You can look out for some rhinos now on the compartment side."

We search unsuccessfully for rhinos. All I can see is telegraph poles.

"Well, we don't seem to be in luck today." Fade up Strauss waltzes.

But they don't give up easily. Fade down the Strauss waltzes.

"Ladies and gentlemen, you can now look out for flamingoes on the corridor side."

Have a shower before dinner, and taking my all-purpose tie out to add that indefinable touch of elegance, saunter down to the bar. The windows are of such size, with minimum partitions giving maximum view, that one has this strange sensation of floating, unsupported, over the countryside. Fraser says he saw a car coming towards him on a road running alongside and instinctively moved to one side. Poor old sod.

The barman Matt is put to work by Basil to make the perfect martini, but after three attempts Basil drinks it anyway. Matt comes up with the surprising information that the noisiest tourists he dealt with are the Swiss.

"Swiss people are noisy?"

He relents a little: ". . . Well, not noisy, but they're happy drinkers."

A glorious sunset over the town of Kimberley which boasts of being the home of the World's Largest Man-Made Hole. At one time there were 30,000 frantic diamond prospectors digging in the hole at once. When it was closed in August 1914 it was three and a half thousand feet deep with a perimeter of a mile.

Meet one or two of my fellow-travellers. A couple from Yorkshire whose daughter manages a vineyard on the Cape, a Swiss tour-guide (Swiss and Germans are the most numerous tourists), a lady from the Irish Tourist Board who thinks that they have similar problems to South Africa in attracting visitors—beautiful countries but political problems—and an exotic couple, she Colombian, he German, who are working in Gabon. We get back to the hoary old subject of malaria. Their view is that the pills are as bad for you as the disease, quite seriously affecting digestion and eyesight.

Fortunately my digestion is, for once, settled, as I move through to the restaurant and the mountain of cut-glass that awaits me.

DAY 128. JOHANNESBURG TO CAPE TOWN

5.30: Woken with piping-hot tea in a white china pot. For the first time since Victoria Falls I was able to sleep without a pain-killer, and for the first time in Africa I was able to sleep well on a train. I now regret that I gave such enthusiatic instructions to be woken at sunrise.

We are travelling across the Karoo, a wide landscape of bare mountains and scrubby plain, deriving its name from the Hottentot word meaning "thirstland." Stimulated by this information I make my way down to the restaurant car, past train staff already polishing the door handles.

We are close now to the end of Africa. Beyond a succession of tightly folded mountain ranges lies Cape Town, the richest corner of a rich province. God's Own Country. Sit and watch the sun warming the mountains and allow myself a nostalgic drift back to a sunrise in August as we drew in from the Mediterranean and saw the lights of Africa for the first time. It's now late November and high summer has turned to early spring. I don't exactly know what lies ahead but I have a sudden surge of optimism that everything is going to turn out right. We have been tried and tested by Africa in every possible way and, bruised and battered maybe, we have survived. My children call these moments of mine "Dad's happy attacks," and, as we glide out of an 11-mile tunnel into a dramatic, sweeping bowl of land filled with vineyards. I know that this one may last some time.

The magnificent landscapes of Africa build to a tremendous climax. Towering haze-blue mountain ranges—the Matroosberg, the Swarzbergen and the Hex—part like stage curtains to reveal the final epic image of Table Mountain and the wide Atlantic. It is a breathtaking display of natural beauty and one which raises all our tired spirits.

WHEN A MONKEY SPEAKS

from *When a Monkey Speaks and Other Stories from Australia*

Damian Sharp

Damian Sharp's debut work, When A Monkey Speaks *(1994), is a collection of eleven short stories set in his native Australia. His interest in Asian philosophy surfaces in later works, such as* Simple Feng Shui *(1999),* Simple Chinese Astrology *(2000) and* Simple Numerology *(2001).*

It was now the middle of the afternoon and she sat by the window with the louvered shutter up, looking out at the high sand dunes alongside the tracks. The dunes shone brightly and were as deep and as high as a canyon, shutting out the view of the desert plain and the immensity of blue sky.

"You don't have to be that way," she said. "There are other things you could do that would make me happy." She watched the shadow of the train sliding across the wind-rippled, yellow surface of the dunes.

"Like what?" he said feebly.

"It doesn't take much. A bit of imagination. A new approach. You're smart enough. The same thing all the time gets boring. All you have to do is please me and then things'll be fine. We can have a good time, even out here."

They were alone in the compartment and the blinds on the door and the corridor windows were drawn. The man sat facing the woman. His pants were still undone and his shirt was out and he was perspiring uncomfortably in the heat.

"Why does it go so slow?" she asked, turning her face from the window and looking at him.

"It's he heat. It buckles the rails during the day. You notice how we roar along at night, to make up for time?"

She didn't reply but turned back to the window and he looked at her with hot eyes, his face red and hot and wet and his lips dry.

"You know," he said musingly. "I've thought about you a lot lately. You're a very curious person. I don't think I understand you."

Alongside the tracks now, half buried in the sand, were three derailed freight cars lying on their sides in a haphazard line. She looked down at them and the shadow of the train as they moved slowly by.

"Malcolm, please stop trying to be interesting."

She sighed and leaned back and ran her fingers through her hair.

"No. I mean it. I think you're fascinating. Difficult but fascinating."

The sand dunes started to level out and now she could see the plain and the sky and the bright shimmer of the heat on the flat horizon. They were in a second-class passenger carriage on the end of a long freight train, directly in from of the caboose, traveling from Adelaide to Alice Springs across the Simpson Desert, in the dry center of Australia.

"Why don't you give your mind a rest and look at the desert," she said impatiently.

"I've already seen the desert."

She stood up and opened the blinds on the door and the interior windows. Through the glass, across the corridor and through the outside windows, she could see the great, flat, glaring white expanse of a salt lake.

"That must be Lake Eyre," she said, sitting down.

"Yes, I believe it is," he said flatly and his bored tone immediately irritated her.

"It was your idea to get on this wretched train instead of the regular express," she said shrilly. "So why don't you be creative and take something in instead of drooling over me. Climb up on the roof. Leap between the carriages like in a Western, the way you were going to. Remember? You said that was the one thing you've always wanted to do. Well, now's your chance, and we're only doing ten miles an hour."

He stood up and did his pants.

"You know, Vivian, you're an inspiration. That's exactly what I'm going to do."

He stepped out into the corridor and slammed the sliding door shut behind him. He would climb onto the roof and get himself burned black and then, probably, he'd be able to sleep. He hadn't slept properly in three days, not since they got on the train, and it was all because of her. She was difficult to be with at times, lonely; as though nothing much mattered to her except herself. And although he knew she'd be miserable for a time if he left her, she could accept being alone better than he could. She didn't seem to need affection or be reliant on him the way he thought he would like her to be. A lot of men had come and gone in her life, and when she talked about them it was always as though that was what she had expected. It was all she had ever really wanted. It was different with him, of course. But he too could go like the others and she let him know it wouldn't mean the end of the world. She had always been self-sufficient, and that had nothing to do with the fact that she was born rich and American, although she admitted it made her different—being rich. She could be cruel, he thought, capable of a subtle and cold terrorism if she didn't get her way. He was in love with her and he didn't quite know how to handle her. Yes, he thought, opening the carriage door and looking out at the glaring salt flats. She could be cruel and hard. She called it honesty. He saw it as evidence that she didn't really need anybody because her life had always been well provided for and that she had suffered for it. Yes, suffered. In a private, lonely way.

She was not what most people considered beautiful. She was striking. Very tall and long legged, with a powerful, sexual body and a handsome face with clearly defined, patrician features. She had dark, thickly handsome eyebrows and long, slanted, bewitching green eyes. The eyes were beautiful. They had a mysterious look that spoke to him of some ancient race in her blood. Like the eyes of Medea, he thought. Jason had looked into those eyes and drowned. She was striking and handsome in the street or in a restaurant with her dark, leonine mane,

but in bed she was beautiful. Most men could sense that; and those who couldn't, he quickly concluded, were simply not very intelligent. All men knew she was difficult, though. A real handful. So did the women, especially the older ones. Since he had been with her he had been told on several occasions by women much older and wiser than himself that she was "very interesting" and "a special kind of challenge." She was unique but no devastating beauty in the traditional sense, although she was certainly beautiful out here in the desert.

He climbed out between the cars and a hot wind blew against him and immediately he felt the sun burning his skin. As he started to climb the ladder on the caboose the train came to a lurching, skidding and screeching stop and he heard men shouting further down the tracks.

Inside the compartment Vivian sat by the window just out of the sun. She had been looking across the low dunes to the plain where dust devils whirled and danced, at a mob of red kangaroos, when the train started to skid on the tracks and then there was the crashing boom of couplings hitting and she was thrown forward as the train jolted and then stopped. For a moment she thought they had been derailed and she remembered Malcolm on the roof and sat perfectly still, listless in the heat, and waited solemnly to see what had happened. She thought about getting up and going out to look, but she was tired and irritable because of their failure to pass the time in lovemaking and because of the endless, heat-soaked desolation that surrounded her, and she did not feel like moving nor care about anything.

She heard men's voices shouting and laughing from the other compartments. They were a strange lot, these outback men, she thought. Wild and crude and reckless, uneasy in the company of women and apparently drunk all time. She had managed to shun their immediate assumption of intimate friendship toward them as a couple, and the men now left them alone and maintained a polite distance, although she still sensed them stalking, looking for the smallest opening to engage Malcolm and draw him into their back-slapping circle. Well, she thought, right now they can have him. Let them get him rotten drunk. It'd probably be good for him. Right now I'm sick of him. He's one of them, really, even if he doesn't know it himself.

The conductor came angrily out of the caboose, and as he walked by the compartment she heard him mutter: "Bloody fuckin' ants."

She stood up and went to the door and called out to him.

"Excuse me."

He stopped and turned around. He was a heavy man about five feet, ten inches tall and dressed in a battered wide-brimmed hat and a blue singlet and baggy shorts and dilapidated, knee-high Texas-style cowboy boots. His shoulders and arms were covered in black hair and he was deeply sunburned and had a round, fat, beard-stubbled face. He looked at her with expressionless, dull blue eyes.

"What's that you said, about ants?" she inquired.

"Yes, miss." He tipped his hat awkwardly. "Pardon my French, but the fuc—" He caught himself, twisting and rolling the syllables, struggling to disguise the obscene slip of the tongue. "—frolickin' ants."

"Frolicking?" Her voice sounded both amused and quizzical.

"The ants get on the tracks, miss. Millions of 'em, followin' the straight an' narrow. Then a train comes along, mushes 'em up, and skids to kingdom come. Where are you from? You're an American, ain't ya?"

"That's right," she said, giving him a big, white-toothed American smile. He looked at her, obviously puzzled as to why she was on this particular train.

"Well, out 'ere, miss, ants derail trains." He turned and continued down the corridor shaking his head. She went back and sat by the window and looked out at the desert and saw that the kangaroos were gone. The train started to move again, only in reverse, going back into the high dunes.

AMTRAK DIARIST: TRAIN PEOPLE

Michael M. Lewis (1961–)

Michael M. Lewis is a former Wall Street bonds salesman for Salomon Brothers who has written books and articles on popular culture as well as the financial world. He is perhaps best known for his book on life as a bond trader in the 1980s, Liar's Poker: Rising Through the Wreckage on Wall Street *(1990).*

The preferred topic of conversation on trains is airplane crashes. The second favorite is near misses. Third is all the things a train can hit on the track without the passengers feeling a thing, a category that apparently includes all vehicles up to the size of an 18-wheeler. Running a distant fourth among things one might discuss with strangers in the bar car are the sights to be seen outside.

I know this because I have just spent 26 hours in the bar car of the Amtrak Crescent, riding from New Orleans to Washington. Train people fall into two broad categories. There are those with wanderlust, time on their hands, and a high threshold for discomfort. And those who regard boarding an airplane as an act of insanity. Train people, it should be said, are different from plane people. They simply ignore the various weird statistics that show flying to be safer than walking down the stairs, spitting, or watching the sun rise. They are not scientific but intuitive. "I just think that pilots do magic, and if you get up in the air, and he forgets his magic, kaboom," said one of the three doctors of philosophy in the bar car. He was traveling to Washington to sign copies of his latest book, and he wouldn't dream of flying.

My conductor told me that the number of airplane neurotics increases with the surge in publicity about plane crashes. The nice thing about trains, he accurately noted, is that "when the engine quits, you don't fall." The other nice thing about trains is that taxpayers subsidize your ticket. The bill that Amtrak presented to Congress this year came to $581 million. I would like to say now how appreciative I feel toward taxpaying Americans. But really, you shouldn't have.

Maybe because they are so thankful to be paid to stay on the ground, train people have an anachronistic tendency to talk to people they don't know. Or perhaps they recognize a soulmate in a fellow passenger who has said no to planes. Anyway, train people are very touchy feely. And once they dispense with the Continental Crash in Denver, the congestion at National Airport, and the dozens of poor souls the Crescent has hit (train disasters, it is assumed, happen to those on the *outside*), they prove to be able and willing tour guides.

I traveled with a British photographer who had never been south of the Mason-Dixon line. As I am from the South I know that Southern towns, no matter how tiny, possess at least one beauty parlor and one Baptist church, invariably called the First Baptist Church (might there be a Second Baptist Church?). My British companion, however, found this riveting. And I have to admit, even I was impressed when, in an Alabama hamlet, we passed a hybrid called B & J's First Baptist Church *AND* Beauty Parlor. Yet another surprise was the number of mobile homes parked beside the tracks. I asked my conductor, who has been riding over the same rails for 28 years, why, if you can park your home anywhere, you would put it beside the railroad tracks. "Life is full of mysteries," he said, right as rain.

One of life's mysteries is how, in the six-by-four-foot space that was my berth, a 1950s genius in spatial relations managed to fit a bed, a sink, a lounge chair, two closets, a luggage rack, a toilet, three coat hangers, and a trash can. Granted, there wasn't much room left for a mixer, but I would suggest to those who gnash their teeth and pull their hair thinking about overpopulation in the 21st century that old railroad men may have the answer. The cars were built over 40 years ago, and are considered quaintly adequate by their users. Twenty years ago, however, a partition ran down the center of the car, separating black passengers from white. As a result, the cars have bathrooms in the back and the front, with the ones in the front being conspicuously larger. Now, of course, they aren't black and white, but men's and ladies'. Guess whose is bigger.

Like most city boys, around country folk I have the bad habit of encouraging homespun wisdom. One of my private fantasies is to chew tobacco on the front porch of a house in a town with a name like Hicksaw Ridge. Seated in rocking chairs, me and the other citizens of Hicksaw Ridge take turns spinning yarns. One of us might even hold a finger up toward the clear blue sky and say, "Gonna rain." This said, black clouds immediately appear on the horizon.

On the Crescent, I came the closest I ever have to living my fantasy. OK, so no one had ever heard of Hicksaw Ridge. But nearly everyone in the bar car was from some small Southern town. There was a moral to every story, and a story about every place we passed. Bet you never heard of Tallapoosa. It sits on the border of Alabama and Georgia, beside the tracks of the Crescent. Back at the turn of the century, recalled one of the conductors, it was called Possum

Snout. But folks there just didn't like the sound of Possum Snout, and changed the name. In itself, this was mighty suspicious—change your name and maybe you got something to hide. Sure as shootin', just 80 years later the mayor of Tallapossa gets caught with 11 other Tallapoosans siphoning as from the public utility's pipeline. There's even been a book about it, called *The Dirty Dozen*.

As dusk fell, the Crescent was about 40 miles shy of Atlanta. We rode through a town called Donaldsville. The best thing about Donaldsville, said my conductor, is its unusual Baptist church. Since, with the exception of B & J's, every Baptist church I had seen looked like every other Baptist church, I squinted to catch sight of a Baptist anomaly. As I expected, it was the same unimaginative square building, with the same white wooden sign in front. But since my conductor hadn't yet steered me wrong, I squinted harder. And sure enough, on the sign were the words: Second Baptist Church of God. Goes to show you, miracles will never cease.

DOWN TO THE PACIFIC SHORE

from *Sierra*

William Poole (1945–)

A San Francisco–based writer, William Poole has spent years writing for publications such as VIA *and* Sierra. *In his travels, he has covered most of the Pacific Northwest, followed California's Mission Trail and hiked through the Fern Canyon.*

reamt the train had slipped onto the smoothest track of the trip. So smooth was this track that the *Zephyr* had ceased all rocking, all clickety-clack, even the hum of the sleeper's climate-control system had stopped. After two days of train noise and motion, the stillness was profound, although I could feel my body flying forward, forward, at 80 miles an hour. But how did they ever make it so smooth?

Gradually I came awake. Outside the window was a darkened train yard, and in the corridor was a kitchen worker headed for the dining car to prepare breakfast.

"Where are we?" I whispered.

"Elko." His voice blended resignation with disgust.

An hour late and counting, the *California Zephyr* sat dead on the tracks in eastern Nevada, its umbilical to the engine severed and undergoing repair. Cold leaked through the metal skin of the sleeper. An hour and ten minutes late . . . an hour and twenty minutes late . . . the train jolted to life and pulled out past the carnival glow of Elko's casinos. Waiting for breakfast outside the dining car, some passengers computed how tardy they would be at Sacramento. But I secretly thanked the locomotive gremlins for an extra hour of daylight in a favorite part of the world.

We picked up the skimpy Humboldt River then. Mark Twain once wrote of this stream that a man could leap and releap its thin flow until thirst consumed him—and could then proceed to drink it dry. Another moody morning, the sagebrush brown, bedraggled, with muddy puddles beside the track; and with even the abrupt mountain ranges—sometimes two or three visible at once in as many directions—blanched by snow and smothered in cloud. "Go back to sleep" was the message most of the *Zephyr*'s passengers discovered in this brooding transit. For much of the morning the observation car held only a man with a book, me, and a pair of lovers, for whom even this privacy seemed not private enough.

We dawdled along on rock-and-roll track, following the route of 19th-century wagons, while trucks and busses on Interstate 80 passed us by. Through Winnemucca (named for a Paiute chief, the route guide said) and into Lovelock, exactly an hour and forty minutes late. Near here the Humboldt disappears, exhausted from the simple effort of being a river in such country, and the *Zephyr* inclined southwest for a last bolt across scabrous volcanic rock and all-but-unvegetated saline flats to the California mountains.

"Very little of note save dust and brightness of the glittering sand, now and then a grave," wrote pioneer John Clark in his diary, crossing this desert in 1852. Even today the *Zephyr*'s passengers seemed to heave a collective sigh when we picked up the Sierra Nevada—born Truckee River and followed its oasis canyon into Reno. As if on cue, the clouds thinned, and with another mountain range ahead, the observation car filled with camera-toting tourists. For several miles the train courted the river, first from one bank, then the other, chunky hawks decorating the fall-bronzed cottonwoods along its banks and ducks dotting its placid surface.

At Reno we picked up a party of gamblers headed back over the mountains to California, and an interpreter from the California State Railway Museum in Sacramento. We were now ascending Truckee Canyon, the interpreter announced over the train's public address system, and it was near here that in 1846 the Donner party of California-bound emigrants—20 wagons, 87 suffering men, women, and children—were trapped and ultimately reduced to cannibalism by another early

November snowstorm.

For there was snow again for this mountain passage—not as much as doomed the Donner Party, but enough to fly up off the wheels of the engine during the long horseshoe ascent of Coldstream Valley, as Donner Lake appeared below us in a wintry bowl. As in Colorado, here also were snow-encumbered firs and pines and half a horizon of assertive peaks.

We broke out of the summit tunnel into sparkling sun. Down the Pacific Slope now, almost home, feeling our way above the American River Canyon, a 2,000-foot-deep absence of mountain on our left. Chinese laborers blasted this right-of-way and laid these tracks, the man from the railroad museum said. He pointed out the old hydraulic-mining scars along the route, still festering after more than a century. The snow was softening now, sloughing from the trees, the sun pushing back the season where aspens glowed like candles beside the tracks.

We crept downhill through the heart of California's Gold Country, through Dutch Flat to Gold Run, where we found ourselves once more idling on a siding. Five minutes . . . ten . . . before the conductor made his announcement. We were stopped for an important train to pass. Soon we heard the whistle, and the massive silver nose slipped into view, striped blue and white and red. Here was our sister train, today's eastbound *Zephyr*, and I wondered who might be aboard, off to see the country from its rocking vantage.

Ahead on our own route lay the Sacramento Valley, its rice paddies burnished in the setting sun, and further yet (the *Zephyr* two hours late by now), a littoral of lights around San-Francisco Bay. And while I would have been sorry to miss these glories, part of me would just as soon have made a great leap at Gold Run, have traded one *Zephyr* for another and my exhausted stack of tickets for a fresh one. Let's see, from Denver I could catch the *Pioneer*, and the *Empire Builder* from Seattle . . . and from Chicago. . . .

Well, who could tell?

THE "VIRGIN DE GUADALUPE" EXPRESS TO BARCELONA AND BEYOND

from *The Pillars of Hercules: A Grand Tour of the Mediterranean*

Paul Theroux (1941–)

Valencia Railway Station was picked out with ceramics of figures and fruit, and prettily painted, with flags stirring and a gold ball and eagle. It had the whimsy and hospitality of the front gate of a fairground. Entering it gave a pleasant feeling of frivolity if not recklessness to any onward train journey. The bullring next to the station was huge and well-made, elaborate brickwork, arches and colonnades, not old, but handsome and a bit sinister, like the temple of a violent religion, a place of sacrifice, which was what it was. There were no bullfights that week in the Valencia bullring, but there were plenty on television. Televised bullfights I found to be one of the irritations of eating in cheap restaurants—the way the diners stopped eating when the bull was about to be stabbed, the close attention they gave—to the stabbing—a silence in the whole place—and then the action replay, the whole length of the sword running into the bull's neck, the bull dropping and vomiting blood in slow motion. It's not really a Catholic country, the Spaniards told me, but this express train to Barcelona was dedicated to the Virgin Mary. I asked the conductor why this was so. "It's just a name," he said.

The Virgin sped out of Valencia and along the Mediterranean shoreline of gray sand and blue sea, a plain of gardens and trees and square houses of brown stone, the hills rising to mountains in the background, a classic Spanish landscape of dry overgrazed hills, some of it hardly built upon. But most of it, especially around the coastal town of Tarragona and beyond, is overdeveloped, full of houses. Yet even the most unsightly place was relieved by vineyards or lemon trees, orchards, palm trees. It did not have the nasty urban desolation of industrialized Europe. There were mainly Spaniards on the train. A few foreigners were heading to Barcelona, others to Port-Bou, the last stop in Spain before the train entered France. There

were clusters of Japanese, and Frenchbusinessmen, and Moroccans. And Kurt, who was heading back to Germany. He was very fat and bearded, in a leather vest, with a tattoo on his wrist, and very drunk at two in the afternoon, in the buffet car.

"This tattoo—I made it myself! I got drunk and took a needle and just went plunk-plunk-plunk for three hours."

The tattoo seemed to show a hot dog in a man's hand, but Kurt helped me to see that it depicted a bulky submarine being crushed by an enormous hairy fist. Above it were the words Germany-Navy and below it, Killer Submarine Crew.

"Why are those words in English?"

We were speaking German. Kurt did not speak English.

"They just are."

"Were you in the navy?"

"For twenty years, based in Wilhelmshaven, but I also traveled."

It seemed an unlikely question because he was not much older than I was but I asked, "Did you destroy any submarines?"

"No, but I would have if I had to. I knew how."

"Why did you leave the navy?"

"Family problems. My son is a diabetic. He needs my help. And my wife is in the hospital."

"Serious?"

"Yes. She jabs herself—with a needle, you know. She is not a fixer, not really. She is sick."

"What brought you to Valencia?"

"Football. Karlsruhe was playing Valencia."

"Who won?"

He growled and made a face. "Valencia," he said, and uttering the word seemed to make him thoughtful. He was probably thinking of the defeat, the details of the game. He drank for a while longer, and while he was lost in his thoughts I started to slip away.

"Wait," he said. "See this tattoo?" He rolled up his sleeve. "This one was much easier to do. I did this one myself, too."

Eventually I went back to my seat. As this was an express, the Virgin had a TV in each car. The video that trip was a soft-porn film of the Blue Lagoon variety—castaways, jungle, friendly parrot, and plenty of excuses for the man and woman to get their clothes off.

Headphones were sold, though hardly anyone bought them. Most of the passengers looked out the train window at the pretty coves and the rocky shoreline, the steep cliffs, the pines and the small port villages. We had passed Sagunto and Castelión, and the Desierto de las Palmas, a high ridge with an eighteenth-century monastery to the west. Past miles of fruit trees and tenements by the sea, and after Tortosa on the River Ebro we were traveling ten feet from the sea, known in this corner of the Mediterranean as the Balearic Sea.

In spite of its fragrant herbaceous name, Tarragona was a grim place. That seemed to be the rule on this part of the Mediterranean shore. The town had been the subject of poems by Martial. The wines had been praised by Pliny. "The emperor himself wintered here in 26 B.C. after his Cantabrian campaign." Now it was mainly an oil-cracking plant and a strip of littered shore. The sour stink of sulfuric acid is an unmistakable indication that you have entered an industrial suburb. Sitges, farther along, once a fashionable resort, was now known mainly for its strip of homosexual beach.

OUT OF PRETORIA, BY LUXURY TRAIN

from *The New York Times*

Donald G. McNeil, Jr.

McNeil is a Paris reporter for The New York Times *who was formerly based in South Africa. He has published columns on biotech-food protests in Europe, the environment, AIDS, ape massacres in Africa, copper mines in Zambia, India's generic drug companies and conflicts in Romania and Hungary among many other topics.*

We've all known him. The little boy whose devotion to the details of his 1:87 scale model steam train is so obsessive that he paints the microscopic lenses of its tiny lamps just the right shade of amber.

Now imagine that little boy at about 2:1 scale, and 51 years old.

Now imagine that his train is a full-grown one, too, though it's a good deal older than he is, a rolling museum of the glory days of the chemin de fer. And imagine that you can buy a ticket on it, and sleep inside its rumbling coaches of polished mahogany, or watch the starlit savanna roll by from the observation car while dignified waiters hand you flutes of Champagne, your children play board games with new friends at your feet, and grass fires started by cinders from the locomotive leap into the African night.

That's what it's like to ride Rovos Rail.

The train starts in Cape Town, one of the world's loveliest cities, traverses the length of South Africa, following the tracks that Cecil Rhodes once dreamed would stretch the British Empire from the Cape to Cairo, makes a left at Pretoria (capital of the Boers, one of the major stumbling blocks to Rhodes's dream), slips into Botswana and Zimbabwe and ends at Victoria Falls. On the last mile of the four-day trip, as you pull literally into the front yard of one of the great old hotels of the British Empire, you can just see the mist rising from the falls like steam from a cauldron.

It's all true. It ain't cheap, but it's true.

Rovos Rail is not the only luxury train prowling South Africa's rails. The recently refurbished Government-owned Blue Train, which also runs from Cape Town to Pretoria to Victoria Falls, is certainly the most famous. But none so completely reflect the personality of its owner as Rovos, the full-size toy of Rohan Vos, a former auto parts magnate from the town of Witbank whose hobby, restoring old railway carriages, turned into a career after he was snubbed by South African Railways. According to one of his train managers, Paul O'Connell, he asked the railroad how much it would charge him to use its tracks to take his family on vacation on a small train he had restored. "They named some extortionate sum," Mr. O'Connell said. "He said it was ridiculous. They said, 'So sell tickets.' So he did. That was eight years ago—and he's been losing money ever since."

If Mr. Vos is indeed losing money, it is perhaps because of his spare-no-expense attention to details, his appetite for more trains—he now has two, the Edwardian Pride of Africa and the Classic Pride of Africa—and the expensive delays caused by Government bureaucracies. He has put together his long green-and-gold trains— ours, the Classic, had 21 cars—by buying them from scrap yards, little railway museums, private collectors and other sources. Most were built between 1919 and 1970, but he even has an 1893 locomotive. They are refurbished at his sheds in Pretoria, rebuilt in a way that blends traditional woods and fixtures with modern conveniences like hidden minibars and roomy bathrooms.

He tries to see each train off himself, flying to Cape Town to usher guests down the red carpet laid on the station platform, then flying to Pretoria three days later to wave good-bye on the second leg of the trip.

When he rides, Mr. Vos gets even more hands-on. Other passengers have seen the tall, lean man with the clipped British accent trotting beside the train in a rainstorm to throw gravel under slipping wheels. He has even shucked his dinner jacket to shovel coal. "I've lent a hand every so often when the chaps get exhausted," he told me.

The two Rovos Rail trains run several routes, with the trip from Cape Town to Pretoria to Victoria Falls the most popular. There are also two 24-hour trips: one from Pretoria to the Mozambique border, with a stop for a safari in Kruger Park; another from Cape Town along the mountainous southern coast to Knysna. Since 1993, there have been five grand 25-day round trips to Dar es Salaam in Tanzania. Next year there will be an experimental jaunt through the Namibian desert to Swakopmund. Most passengers ride one way, or even one leg of a trip, and fly back.

For my family—my wife, Suzanne Daley, and our daughters Avery, 11, and Galen, 7—the trip began in Pretoria, where we gathered at 9 A. M. one Monday in early August in a creaky but charming 1892 hotel, the Victoria, right across from the elegant old Pretoria Station designed by Sir Herbert Baker, architect of many of South Africa's best civic buildings.

Even the 11-room hotel, which also houses the company headquarters, is a train buff's delight. While porters strap nametags onto your luggage, you can wander halls illuminated by stained-glass windows and peek into rooms with pressed-tin ceilings, claw-footed bathtubs and brass beds. The walls are full of photographs of steam trains and framed financial instruments that laid the rails. My favorites were an 1887 share certificate for the Keokuk & Des Moines Railway Company and a 5 percent gold bond for the Lung-Tsing U-hai Railway with the coupons printed in English, French and Chinese.

Passengers—a maximum of 72—gather in the dining room for a short speech by Mr. Vos, which combines a welcome, a history of the train and the rules of the rails: Don't pull the emergency brake for fun. Do shut your windows when not in your carriage, since some thieves can run as fast as the train. Don't throw cigarettes out the windows. Do dress for dinner—black tie optional—which will be announced by a gentle gong.

And keep a sense of humor about delays. There are two customs posts and seven engine changes on the Pretoria-Victoria Falls leg, and sometimes the locomotive hasn't arrived yet. "It's not easy running a Swiss-watch train service through Africa," Mr. Vos said.

Even the walk to the station was fun. We were encouraged to snap one another's photographs on the two steam engines that would do the first haul—Tiffany, a dainty 1893 engine imported when Johannesburg was a city of only 50,000 people, and Bianca, a 1938 model. (They are named after two of Mr. Vos's children.) Both had every copper pipe and brass strap shined and their black paint picked out in red and gold trim. The Blue Train's diesels may be more dependable and do not need to stop to take on tons of coal and swimming pool-sized loads of water, but it's impossible to beat the romance of the clouds of steam chuff-chuffing through the landscape.

Rovos Rail claims to have the world's biggest compartments; there were only three in our car, and two in the fanciest one.

Ours measured about 18 feet by 6 feet—large enough so that the double beds don't fold away. Each carpeted room is paneled in beautiful West African sapele mahogany and has a writing table, minibar, air-conditioner, etched-glass reading lamps, electric outlets and real closets. In the closets were bathrobes and, in case one wanted to lean out the window, a pair of plastic goggles, as a protection against cinders. Each also has, by railway standards, a huge bathroom, with a real glass-and-mahogany shower. The bigger compartments have tubs. And each compartment had an ancient telephone for calling the hostess, though ours didn't work.

That was the only thing I missed on the train—

any sense of connection to the outside world. There is one cellular telephone for emergencies, but otherwise the lack of television, phones and the like is deliberate, in keeping with the spirit of old-time travel. I did get my short-wave radio to work by leaning out the window. But I think more sensible, less news-addicted passengers enjoyed the 48 hours of isolation.

In any case, to call the hostess, all one had to do was leave the door ajar. Ours, Karien Coetzer, could not have been nicer. When our daughters returned from dinner the first night, they found their bed turned down, Galen's dolls tucked in and cups of hot chocolate on the table. She had also picked up their room, a feat in itself.

"We were spoiled because that nice lady was doing our carriage," Galen said.

But first, on departure, Mr. Coetzer had explained our rooms to us—how to work the air-conditioner's remote control, where the fresh milk was kept if we made ourselves tea at midnight.

Remembering the one train ride of my youth, I gave my daughters the only warning I could remember: "Don't flush the toilet when we're in a station."

"Oh, it's all right," Mr. Coetzer said instantly. "Go ahead. They fine us, but we pay. We want our guests to be comfortable."

That was my introduction to the slightly cavalier attitude that being a passenger in a rolling cocoon of wealth and finery traversing Africa's poverty inevitably makes one a party to.

We did not have a moment like this, but a colleague who was on the first Dar es Salaam run remembers a table full of travelers enjoying dessert with Champagne while a crowd of children in rags gathered outside the window and stared.

"Someone pulled the shade," he said.

In fact, tossing bread rolls out the window in a Marie Antoinette gesture might have been just as rude. Once you're aboard, it's hard to know how to react—liberal guilt is pretty meaningless, given the stark contrasts, since it's so evident that you are rich and everyone outside is poor. Life in South Africa is one long study in that difference, of course, but most whites never roll through black shantytowns as this train does. On our trip, the people we passed generally smiled and waved and, when the train was stopped at a border post, walked up to the observation car's deck to say hello. Most riders—90 percent of whom were European, American or Australian—responded in friendly fashion.

The attitude I found really startling was toward the brush fires the engines started. Coal-fired engines spew out hot ashes, and the train started two big blazes in the first hour. The bartender in the observation car took it in stride. "People burn the veld here," he said. "It germinates seeds." I know that to be true—two years in South Africa has made me used to driving past fields and hillsides burning without a firefighter in sight. Trees are scarce, most residential areas are protected by walls or firebreaks, and the fires usually burn out at the nearest road. But still, it's odd to hear the arsonist shrugging it off.

In fact, Mr. O'Connell said, the company isn't really that casual. "We used to have a truck following us, putting out fires," he said. "And we can't use steam down in the Cape anymore, since we were sued after we burned down some vineyards." Mr. Vos is converting a steam engine to burn diesel fuel so there will still be the steam but without the sparks.

Other than people and fires, the scenery from the train is vast and romantic, but a bit monotonous, on the central African plateau—consisting of dry farmland and dry savanna with thorn trees twisted into ghostly shapes. The mountains around Cape Town are stunning, and the Matopo Hills and balancing rocks of Zimbabwe are pretty, but there are long stretches of flatland in between.

Once you are settled in, there isn't too much to do except read, talk, eat and drink, so meals take on great importance. There were two dining cars, enough for all the passengers, so there was no rushing through a first sitting or waiting hungrily for a second. The "Letaba" was particularly beautiful, a 1924 car with seven pairs of carved-roof arches and graceful aluminum fans. Unlike other cars Mr. Vos rescued from scrap yards, it was part of a museum and then used for V.I.P. dinners by a brandy distillery.

Even the mismatched cutlery on the white linen was intriguing—each piece bore the initials of a railway line. "That butter dish is older than I am," the wine steward, Bruce Parkinson, said appreciatively, translating its initials as the Afrikaans ones for South African Railways Catering.

Each meal was a set menu, five courses with a choice of two entrees, and if one didn't like the grilled duck breast in an orange liqueur sauce, one would probably like the portobello mushroom in a tomato coulis or the rainbow trout with hollandaise. There were two sparkling wines, two whites and two reds, ports and brandies, all South African—surprisingly good, middle-priced wines.

Galen wasn't having any of it. She likes grilled cheese sandwiches and ungarnished pasta—even a sprinkle of parsley ruins it. The kitchen graciously accommodated her. There were six children on board (all beautifully behaved—whether well brought up or simply intimidated, I couldn't tell), and the staff even offered to serve them before the 8 P.M. dinner.

There were two club cars, each with comfortable couches and a convivial barman. A few guests overdid it with the free drinks, but in a dignified way—and frankly, you stagger so much trying to walk the length of a moving train that it's hard to tell.

And thus to sleep. A word about sleeping on trains: Some people love it. Some don't. It can be wonderful but unpredictable. It's a bit like being lulled in a cradle tended by a teen-age boy—it may sway gently for hours, then suddenly lurch violently or stop.

The first night, I slept beautifully until 2 A. M., then woke up; we were marooned on a siding somewhere in Botswana. An hour later, as we pulled shudderingly out, I was awakened again by having my head smacked against the wall a few times. So I slid down the window shutter and watched the moon over the desert.

The second night, I slept better. When I awoke and checked a map, I found that we were deep in the hills next to Hwange Game Park and had covered hundreds more miles than I thought. The crew did say the Zimbabwean rails were smoother than the Botswanan ones, which haven't been relaid in 100 years.

There were several delays. We were never individually questioned at customs, and the Botswanan crossing was fairly quick, but the Zimbabwean agents decided to count every bottle of wine for tax purposes and held us up for four hours, which meant our three-hour tour of Bulawayo had to be canceled.

Nonetheless, we made it to our last stop 10 minutes early, gliding into the front yard of the Victoria Falls Hotel.

"That was great," was Avery's verdict. "It was like a hotel, only better, because the scenery kept changing."

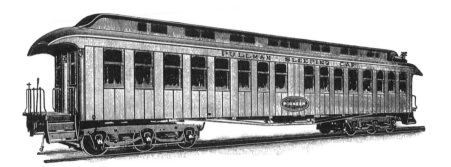

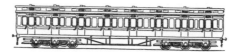

TAKE THE F

from *The New Yorker*

Ian Frazier (1951–)

Comic, affectionate essays on rural America form the core of Ian Frazier's work. Twenty-five of his stories, previously published in The New Yorker, *were collected in Frazier's first book,* Dating Your Mom *(1986). A year later, he published a second collection of short stories,* Nobody Better, Better Than Nobody. *His additional titles include* Great Plains *(1989),* Family *(1994) and* On the Rez *(2000).*

Brooklyn, New York, has the undefined, hard-to-remember shape of a stain. I never know what to tell people when they ask me where in it I live. It sits at the western tip of Long Island at a diagonal that does not conform neatly to the points of the compass. People in Brooklyn do not describe where they live in terms of north or west or south. They refer instead to their neighborhoods, and to the nearest subway lines. I live on the edge of Park Slope, a neighborhood by the crest of a low ridge that runs through the borough. Prospect Park is across the street. Airplanes in the landing pattern for La Guardia Airport sometimes fly right over my building; every few minutes, on certain sunny days, perfectly detailed airplane shadows slide down my building and up the building opposite in a blink. You can see my building from the plane—it's on the left-hand side of Prospect Park, the longer patch of green you cross after the expanse of Green-Wood Cemetery.

We moved to a co-op apartment in a four-story building a week before our daughter was born. She is now six. I grew up in the country and would not have expected ever to live in Brooklyn. My daughter is a city kid, with less sympathy for certain other parts of the country. When we visited Montana, she was disappointed by the scarcity of pizza places. I overheard her explaining—she was three or four then—to a Montana kid about Brooklyn. She said, "In Brooklyn, there is a lot of broken glass, so you have to wear shoes. And, there is good pizza." She is stern in her judgment of pizza. At the very low end of the pizza-ranking scale is some pizza she once had in New Hampshire, a category now called New Hampshire pizza. In the middle is some OK pizza she once had at the Bronx Zoo, which she calls zoo pizza. At the very top is the pizza at the pizza place where the big kids go, about two blocks from our house.

Our subway is the F train. It runs under our building and shakes the floor. The F is generally a reliable train, but one spring as I walked in the park I saw emergency vehicles gathered by a concrete-sheathed hole in the lawn. Firemen lifted a metal lid from the hole and descended into it. After a while, they reappeared, followed by a few people, then dozens of people, then a whole lot of people—passengers from a disabled F train, climbing one at a time out an exit shaft. On the F, I sometimes see large women in straw hats reading a newspaper called the *Caribbean Sunrise*, and Orthodox Jews bent over Talmudic texts in which the footnotes have footnotes, and groups of teenagers wearing identical red bandannas with identical red plastic baby pacifiers in the corners of their mouths, and female couples in porkpie hats, and young men with the silhouettes of the Manhattan skyline razored into their short side hair from one temple around to the other, and Russian-speaking men with thick wrists and big wristwatches, and a hefty, tall woman with long, straight blond hair who hums and closes her eyes and absently practices cello fingerings on the metal subway pole. As I watched the F-train passengers emerge among the grass and trees of Prospect Park, the faces were as varied as usual, but the expressions of indignant surprise were all about the same.

Just past my stop, Seventh Avenue, Manhattan-bound F trains rise from underground to cross the Gowanus Canal. The train sounds different—lighter, quieter—in the open air. From the elevated tracks, you can see the roofs of many houses stretching back up the hill to Park Slope, and a bumper crop of rooftop graffiti, and neon signs for Eagle Clothes and Kentile Floors, and flat expanses of factory roofs where seagulls stand on one leg around puddles in the sagging spots. There are fuel-storage tanks surrounded by earthen barriers, and slag piles, and conveyor belts leading down to the oil-slicked waters of the canal. On certain days, the sludge at the bottom of the canal causes it to bubble. Two men fleeing the police jumped in the canal a while ago; one made it across, the other quickly died. When the subway doors open at the Smith-Ninth Street stop, you can see the bay, and sometimes smell the ocean breeze. This stretch of elevated is the highest point of the New York subway system. To the south you can see the Verrazano-Narrows Bridge, to the north the World Trade towers. For just a few moments, the Statue of Liberty appears between passing buildings. Pieces of a neighborhood—laundry on clotheslines, a standup swimming pool, a plaster saint, a satellite dish, a rectangle of lawn—slide by like quickly dealt cards. Then the train descends again; growing over the wall just before the tunnel is a wisteria bush, which blooms pale blue every May.

I have spent days, weeks on the F train. The trip from Seventh Avenue to midtown Manhattan is long enough so that every ride can produce its own mini-society of riders, its own forty-minute Ship of Fools. Once a woman an arm's length from me on a crowded train pulled a knife on a man who threatened her. I remember the argument and the principals, but mostly I remember the knife—its flat, curved wood-grain handle inlaid with brass fittings at each end, its long, tapered blade. Once a man sang the words of the Lord's Prayer to a mournful, syncopated tune, and he fitted the mood of the morning so exactly that when he asked for money at the end the riders reached for their wallets and purses as if he'd pulled a gun. Once a big white kid with some friends was teasing a small old Hispanic lady, and when he got off the train I looked at him through the window and he slugged it hard next to my face. Once a thin woman and a fat woman sitting side by side had a long and loud conversation about someone they intended to slap silly: "Her butt be in the *hospital*." "Bring out the ar-*tillery!*" The terminus of the F in Brooklyn is at Coney Island, not far from the beach. At an off hour, I boarded the train and found two or three passengers and, walking around on the floor, a crab. The passengers were looking at the crab. Its legs clicked on the floor like varnished fingernails. It moved in this direction, then that, trying to get comfortable. It backed itself under a seat, against the wall. Then it scooted out just after some new passengers had sat down there, and they really screamed. Passengers at the next stop saw it and laughed. When a boy lifted his foot as if to stomp it, everybody cried, "Noooh!" By the time we reached Jay Street-Borough Hall, there were maybe a dozen of us in the car, all absorbed in watching the crab. The car doors opened and a heavyset woman with good posture entered. She looked at the crab; then, sternly, at all of us. She let a moment pass. The she demanded, "*Whose is that?*" A few stops later, a short man with a mustache took a manila envelope, bent down, scooped the crab into in, closed it, and put in his pocket. . . .

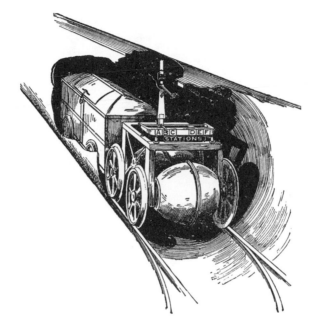

EXCERPT OF THE MAN WITH FIRE

from *Yesterday's Train: A Rail Odyssey through Mexican History*

Terry Pindell (1946–)

At the train station in Mexico City, there is a fuss out on the platform as we are waiting to depart for Querétaro. People crowd at the windows on the left side of the train to see what is going on. "*Rateros,*" someone says—a rat, a thief has been caught. Outside I can see a fair-skinned Mexican grasping a younger, darker, shirtless fellow by the hair. He has been caught stealing food from the train, someone says. The police have been called. Meanwhile the vigilante yanks the hair of the miscreant as if intent on pulling it all out by the roots. The thief is younger and physically much bigger than his assailant, but still he passively cries that he didn't take anything and begs to be let go. When two policemen arrive, people on the train quickly lose interest. "What will happen to the *ratero*?" I ask.

"They will take him to jail and beat him and then let him go in a few days," shrugs one of the passengers. "And then he will try to steal again when he gets hungry."

The train ride to Querétaro is full of images of Mexican life bursting from the sun-warmed earth. We pass men gathering brick from ruins of abandoned homes, pointed maguey and rounded nopal, and trackside laughter and horseplay. We also see Mexico's poverty—the beggar child, the crippled woman crawling on her cracked and bleeding knees—and the power of emotion that springs from it in the yearning faces young and old that crowd around the train at station stops. But on this ride we begin to see a paradox. All along the route the corn grows taller even than in the American Midwest. Orchards are heavy with oranges, mangos, bananas, and pears. There is good land enough here for prosperous-looking cattle ranches. In the pueblos, market stalls are piled with fruit and vegetables and meat. Even the smallest homesteads have goats and chickens in the corral and neat gardens of beans,

corn, squash, and nopal cactus out back. Except in some of the regions of the arid north and the mountains, Mexico is everywhere a land of abundance. And yet, everyone below a certain rung on the socio-economic ladder suffers from some degree of malnutrition. The government is probably correct in claiming that over the years that rung has moved lower and lower, but the fact remains that vast numbers of the Mexican people are hungry in a land of plenty. And the harsher fact is that full bellies and Spanish blood go hand in hand. After spending months in Mexico, when one pictures hunger, one sees gaunt ribs under dark skin. When hungry people are bonded together by their skin color as well as their deprivation, violent solidarity is a powder keg just waiting for a spark of leadership.

It's a rainy evening in Querétaro on the Plaza de la Corregidora. Querétaro is a pleasant city of leafy trees, gardens, and well-preserved colonial architecture. Like most Mexican cities it presents a visage of prosperity that belies the social crisis endemic to so much of the countryside. We have settled in for the evening at El Regio, one of the canopied sidewalk cafes that ring the square, where a magician moves from table to table doing his tricks. But there's not much action here on this rainy evening, so he ends up sitting down and giving us a private show. He is José Martínez Somarriba, aka "Artístico Gran Giuseppe," and his energy soon attracts the girlfriend of one of the owners of the cafe, Angélica Hernández Solís, who also joins us.

José lives in the pueblo of Apasio el Grande, near the railroad tracks. He leaves home around 1:00 P. M. and works here till nine in the evening, then relaxes for a while and gets back home near midnight. He was originally attracted to the city because of the bright lights and the hope of a better life, and he worked as a waiter until a magician began teaching him tricks. Then he saw his dream and sprang for it. He believes he is fortunate to have come from a humble pueblo and found this life in the city. And while his compatriots are out scratching the fields in the morning, he gets to sleep in late.

Angélica's family is also from a rural pueblo. They liked to cook, so their dream was to open a restaurant here in the city. Like José, Angélica and her family have found what they sought. They are both dark complected and of humble origins. But they demonstrate the possibility of an upward mobility that runs counter to an otherwise fixed caste structure.

Angélica says that the city people of Querétaro are regarded as "closed-minded" by the folk of the countryside. When we press her to explain what she means, she says that she doesn't use the term in a moral sense. It's not that they are closed-minded to new ideas or to modern lifestyles. If anything, what she means is just the opposite—they are not accepting of the simple and traditional ways of the countryside. They regard country people as bumpkins. She won't go so far as to say that it's a matter of race; she and José are themselves examples of the fact that it is teasingly possible for those who are adaptable and ambitious, if darker skinned, to migrate upward by moving to the city. It's a matter of the second-best opportunity for the good life. If you can't be born with fair skin, at least you can move to the city.

Angélica suggests that we visit the Temple of the Crosses, the site of a miracle that draws the true believers. There we will see the soul of the simple, traditional country people who make pilgrimages here to bear witness to something too spiritual for the sophisticates of Querétaro. At the temple there are trees growing in the soil where an Indian was martyred that have ever since blossomed with cross-

es instead of flowers. Today the crosses are harvested, encased in plastic, and sold as key chains.

Lourdes and I try to imagine what kind of natural phenomenon could be interpreted as such a miracle. Perhaps the flowers have only four petals, thus looking like a cross. Perhaps there is some subtle pattern in the bark or the flowers themselves that true believers see as crosses. We make our own pilgrimage to the temple the following day when the rain has stopped. In the nave of the chapel hangs a black Christ with long Indian-style hair. We see earnest peasants shuffle in, poverty showing in their worn clothing and their calloused feet. They wet their hands in the holy water, sit down, and swoon into a spiritual trance. Their features relax, their shoulders lower, their eyes glaze. Concerns about work, hunger, domestic trouble, or safety seem washed away during these quiet moments, and I think of Marx. "The opiate of the masses" may be right. But these people come here seeking peace and they find it. Despite everything else, it is the miracle of the church.

The miracle we came here to see is a little harder to get to. The convent where the trees are located is closed just now, and I suspect machinations to cloak the truth of the supposed "miracle." But as we wander the cloisters, Lourdes approaches a novitiate who takes us to see the trees. They grow only in one interior courtyard, unceremoniously sharing the space with a couple of old pickup trucks. Behind a makeshift barrier of chicken wire, stand the trees, similar in shape and foliage to small locusts, a type of tree we have frequently seen elsewhere in Mexico. At first glance we see no crosses and I think, well, this is something that is going to take some imagination.

But then Lourdes finds them, so large and obvious I missed them at first because I was looking for something subtle—all along the branches, three-pronged thorns in the perfect shape and proportion of crosses with pointed tips. Some are as big as two inches in length. The novitiate explains that the convent has attempted to transplant.

"Life is good," she says. "You will take a piece of me with you, and I will take a piece of you with me." Lourdes sighs, "We materialistic Americans. The piece of us is just money." But later it occurs to us that maybe it wasn't. The piece of us was also the train ride home—mobility. And as I think of this and admire the patterns in my new tablecloth, I'm

FROM *IN A SUNBURNED COUNTRY*

Bill Bryson (1951–)

Bill Bryson's written work falls into two categories: best-selling travelogues and linguistic explorations. His travel writings include The Lost Continent: Travels in Small-Town America *(1989), which was a Book-of-the-Month Club alternate selection,* Neither Here nor There: Travels in Europe *(1991) and* Notes from a Small Island: An Affectionate Portrait of Britain *(1995). His linguistic writings include* The Facts on File Dictionary of Troublesome Words *(1984) and* The Mother Tongue: English and How It Got That Way *(1990).*

Chapter 2

I believe I first realized I was going to like the Australian outback when I read that the Simpson Desert, an area bigger than some European countries, was named in 1932 for a manufacturer of washing machines. (Specifically, Alfred Simpson, who funded an aerial survey.) It wasn't so much the pleasingly unheroic nature of the name as the knowledge that an expanse of Australia more than 100,000 miles square didn't even have a name until less than seventy years ago. I have near relatives who have had names longer than that.

But then that's the thing about the outback—it's so vast and forbidding that much of it is still scarcely charted. Even Uluru, as we must learn to call Ayers Rock, was unseen by anyone but its Aboriginal caretakers until only a little over a century ago. It's not even possible to say quite where the outback is. To Australians anything vaguely rural is "the bush." At some indeterminate point "the bush" becomes "the outback." Push on for another two thousand miles or so and eventually you come to bush again, and then a city, and then the sea. And that's Australia.

And so, in the company of the photographer Trevor Ray Hart, an amiable young man in shorts and a faded T-shirt, I took a cab to Sydney's Central Station, an imposing heap of bricks on Elizabeth Street, and there we found our way through its dim and venerable concourse to our train.

Stretching for a third of a mile along the curving platform, the Indian Pacific was everything the brochure illustrations had promised—silvery sleek, shiny as a new nickel, humming with that sense of impending adventure that comes with the start of a long journey on a powerful machine. Carriage G, one of seventeen on the train, was in the charge of a cheerful steward named Terry, who thoughtfully provided a measure of local color by accompanying every remark with an upbeat Aussie turn of phrase.

Need a glass of water?

"No worries, mate. I'll get right on 'er."

Just received word that your mother has died?

"Not a drama. She'll be apples."

He showed us to our berths, a pair of singles on opposite sides of a narrow paneled corridor. The cabins were astoundingly tiny—so tiny that you could bend over and actually get stuck.

"This is it?" I said in mild consternation. "In its entirety?"

"No worries," Terry beamed. "She's a bit snug, but you'll find she's got everything you need."

And he was right. Everything you could possibly require in a living space was there. It was just very compact, not much larger than a standard wardrobe. But it was a marvel of ergonomics. It included a comfy built-in seat, a hide-away basin and toilet, a miniature cupboard, an overhead shelf just large enough for one very small suitcase, two reading lights, a pair of clean towels, and a little amenity bag. In the wall was a narrow drop-down bed, which didn't so much drop down as fallout like a hastily stowed corpse as I, and I expect many other giddily experimental passengers, discovered after looking ruminatively at the door and thinking, "I wonder what's behind there?" Still, it did make for an interesting surprise, and freeing my various facial protuberances from its coiled springs helped to pass the half hour before departure.

And then at last the train thrummed to life and we slid regally out of Sydney Central. We were on our way. Done in one fell swoop, the journey to Perth takes nearly three days. Our instructions, however, were to disembark at the old mining town of Broken Hill to sample the outback and see what might bite us. So for Trevor and me the rail journey would be in two parts: an overnight run to Broken Hill and then a two-day haul across the Nullarbor. The train trundled out through the endless western suburbs of Sydney—through Flemington, Auburn, Parramatta, Doonside, and the adorably named Rooty Hill—then picked up a little speed as we entered the Blue Mountains, where the houses thinned out and we were treated to long end-of-afternoon views across steep-sided vales and hazy forests of gum trees, whose quiet respirations give the hills their eponymous tinge.

I went off to explore the train. Our domain, the first-class section, consisted of five sleeping cars, a dining car in a plush and velvety style that might be called *fin de siècle* brothelkeeper, and a lounge car in a rather more modern mode. This was provisioned with soft chairs, a small promising-looking bar, and low but relentless piped music from a twenty-volume compilation called, at a guess, "Songs You Hoped You'd Never Hear Again." A mournful duet from *The Phantom of the Opera* was playing as I passed through.

Beyond first class was the slightly cheaper holiday class, which was much the same as ours except that their dining area was a buffet car with bare plastic tables. (These people apparently needed wiping down after meals.) The passage beyond the holiday class was barred by a windowless door, which was locked.

"What's back there?" I asked the buffet car girl.

"Coach class," she said with a shudder.

"Is this door always locked?"

She nodded gravely. "Always."

Coach class would become my obsession. But first it was time for dinner. The PA system announced the first sitting. Ethel Merman was belting out "There's No Business Like Show Business" as I passed back through the first-class lounge. Say what you will, the woman had lungs.

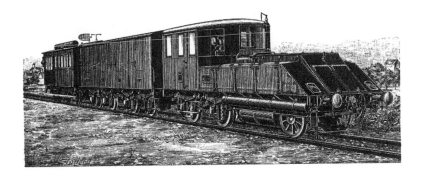

GRAVY TRAIN: A PRIVATE RAILWAY CAR

from *Fresh-Air Fiend: Travel Writings 1985–2000*

Paul Theroux (1941–)

I was sitting in the sunshine in the last car of a train heading west, feeling utterly baffled, and thinking, *I have never been here before*. It was not just the place (early morning in the middle of Colorado); it was also my state of mind (blissful). I was grateful for my good fortune. To think that riding a train, something I had done for pleasure all my traveling life, had been improved upon. In the past, what had mattered most in any long train journey through an interesting landscape was the motion, the privacy, the solitude, the grandeur. Food and comfort, I had discovered, are seldom available on the best trips: there is something about the most beautiful places having the most awful trains. But this was something else.

My chair was on the rear observation platform of a private railway car called "Los Angeles," formerly part of the Southern Pacific Railway. My feet were braced against a brass rail, and the morning sunshine was full on my face. I had woken in Fort Morgan, and after a stroll in Denver had reboarded to have breakfast with family and friends in the private dining room of this car: orange juice, home-baked blueberry coffee cake and muffins, scrambled eggs and fresh juice and coffee. Then the morning paper in the private lounge, and finally settling myself in the open air on this little brass porch as we started our climb through the foothills of the Rockies. An hour out of Denver it was epic grandeur, moving past frozen creeks, pines, and rubbly hills, destination San Francisco. I was very happy.

From this position on a train, eye contact is possible, and as we passed through Pinecliffe, in Gilpin County, a woman stopped at the level crossing, stuck her head out of her car, and waved at me, making my day.

"Anything I can get you?" This was George, the steward, holding the rear door open. "Coffee? Cookies? More juice? Hot chocolate?"

There were four armchairs and a big sofa in the parlor just inside, and off the corridor, four bedrooms, two with double beds, and hot showers. Farther along, the dining room and the gourmet kitchen, and beyond that a big long Amtrak train, the *California Zephyr*, pulling us on its usual route from Chicago to San Francisco, via Denver and Salt Lake City.

As for the rest, I was ignorant. Happiness has no questions; bliss is not a state of inquiry. Whatever squirrelly anxieties I possessed had vanished a long way back, probably soon after we boarded in Chicago, or else at Galesburg. Bliss had definitely taken hold as we crossed the Mississippi, because I remember standing right here on the rear platform and gawking at it, the chunks of ice gleaming in the lights of Burlington, Iowa, on the distant riverbank, the clattering of the bridge, the sense that I was in the night air, hearing and seeing the water, and smelling it too, this damp winter night, the marshy muddiness of the great river.

We had left Chicago the previous afternoon in fog so thick that airline passengers had turned O'Hare into a gigantic dormitory, and departing flights were so thoroughly canceled that there was a slumber party at each gate. The fog was news, so I was excited just slipping out of it. I glanced from time to time at the Amtrak route guide, which gave helpful information. We passed Princeton, Illinois ("Pig Capital of the World"), and Galesburg (associated with Carl Sandburg, and the Lincoln-Douglas debates, and "Popcorn was invented in Galesburg by Olmstead Ferris"), then through Monmouth (birthplace of Wyatt Earp). But all I saw were dark houses, dim lights, and the vast midwestern sky, and here and there a small nameless town, not noticed by the guide, and a filling station on a side road, or a bowling alley, or the local diner filled with eaters.

It is easy to understand the envy of the traveler for the settled people he or she sees, snug in their houses, at home. But I could not have been snugger here in the private railway car. Thinking of the days that stretched ahead, all of them on rails, I was put in mind of Russia, of long journeys through forests and prairies, past little wooden houses half buried in the snow, with smoking chimneys. It was like that, the size of the landscape, the snow, the darkness, and the starry night over Iowa.

After hot showers, we assembled for predinner drinks in the parlor and toasted our trip and talked about the train.

"This was the car that Robert Kennedy used for his campaign in 1968. He made his visit to Los Angeles on it." Christopher Kyte said.

Christopher was the owner of the "Los Angeles," having bought it some eight years ago and restored it at great expense to its former glory. It had been built and fitted out at the height of the boom in the 1920s, and finished just in time for the crash in 1929.

That Robert Kennedy had used it, and made whistle-stop speeches from the rear observation platform, was a solemn thought, but it had been used by many other people—actresses, tycoons, foreign royalty. Sam Rayburn and Lyndon Johnson had made hundreds of trips on it, between Texas and Washington, D. C. It had seen drunks and lovers and millionaires. It was not a mere conveyance, any more than a ship was—people had spent a part of their lives on it.

"Los Angeles" was for weeks at a time Christopher Kyte's own home, one of the mobile aspects of his California-based company. A humorous, self-mocking fellow, whose innocence and innate good will made his humor all the more appealing, Christopher reminded me of Bertie Wooster. He was especially Woosterish when he was in his double-breasted dark suit, recalling a scandalous episode, with George the steward at his elbow, helping with a name or a date. George was Jeeves to his fingertips—efficient, helpful, silent, good at everything, eighteen years on the Southern Pacific. "I've looked after Tom Clancy," he told me. He was as kindly as Christopher, and it was a wonder, given their dispositions, that the company made any money at all. But it has more than prospered.

Nostalgia is not the point, nor is it the glamour of an antique railway car. The idea is comfort, privacy, forward motion. It is a grand hotel suite on wheels, with gourmet food and fine beds, and a view of the Great Plains, and any stopover you like.

"I'd like to spend a day skiing," I had told Christopher a few weeks before we left on the trip. I knew we would be traveling through Colorado, Utah, and snowy parts of California. "What if we stopped for a night somewhere in Utah?"

We decided on Provo, about sixteen miles from the narrow, snowy canyon in the Wasatch Range where Sundance is located. That would be our second night.

"We'll drop you in Provo," Christopher said. "A car will meet you at the station. Stay at Sundance that night and ski the next day. Then meet us at the station in Salt Lake City, and plan to have dinner on board. The chef will have something special."

Meanwhile, the Iowa plains were passing and we filed into the dining room for our first night's dinner, six of us around the table, feasting on pot roast, braised southern style. The conversation was enlivened by a mealtime quiz of guessing celebrities' real names (significant answers: Reg Dwight, Gordon Sumner, Malcolm Little, Bill Blythe, Newton McPherson).

That night the *Zephyr* pulled "Los Angeles" through Nebraska, from Omaha ("Boys Town . . . is west of town") to Benkelman, near the Colorado border ("one hour earlier if going west"). But I was still asleep in Colorado. I roused myself around Fort Morgan, in the high plains, and a little later watched people gathering for the National Western Stock Show in Denver, just next to the tracks—cattle, cowboys, stock pens—the year's big event. I got off to buy a newspaper in Denver, and soon after, in the clear bright day, I was sitting on the rear observation platform in the sunshine for the long climb through the foothills of the Rockies, amid the pines and aspens.

Snow and cold drove me inside around lunchtime, and soon we came to the small town of Winter Park, not far from Fraser (which "proudly calls itself 'the ice-box of America'"). That afternoon we had a long snowy ride under the steep pinnacles of shale in Glenwood Canyon, to Glenwood Springs, and where the rock was uncovered it was the color of honey in the fading daylight. Skiers got off the train to make their way to Aspen and Vail. We followed the course of Spanish Creek, which flowed toward the Colorado River.

"Who has been your oddest passenger?" I asked Christopher over dinner as we clattered down the canyon.

"Most of our people are wonderful," he said. But he was smiling, remembering.

There was once a man, traveling with five strangers, who showed up in the dining room one morning stark naked, just as someone was saying "Pass the sausages, please." The naked man was five foot four; he weighed three hundred pounds. This was not a welcome sight at the breakfast table.

"You have no clothes on," Christopher said to him.

"I always eat breakfast like this," the naked man said, and began to sip his coffee while the rest of the diners averted their eyes.

Ever the diplomat, Christopher suggested that the man would be more comfortable having his breakfast served on a tray in the privacy of his room.

Oh, yes—Christopher was still smiling gently—and there was the transvestite who was a rather sedate man during the day, and at night put on a wig and a dress and mascara, and drank far too much Drambuie, and turned cartwheels on the rear platform with such energy that Amtrak threatened to uncouple "Los Angeles" and leave it on a siding in Omaha.

And the man who bedded down with his stuffed giraffe and teddy bear. And the man who celebrated his divorce by boarding in Reno and setting off on a ten-day trip in the car with a little harem, five young women who took turns visiting him in his room. And the large, ill-assorted family who used a cross-country trip as the occasion for a noisy three-day binge.

"The minute they boarded I knew there'd be a problem." Christopher said. "They were the sort of people who use the word 'party' as a verb. Very bad sign."

We were by now on dessert, and also near the top of the Wasatch Range—Soldier Summit, almost seventy-five hundred feet high, snow everywhere. From here we traveled in loops and through tunnels to Provo, where a van was waiting. It was about midnight.

"Have a good time skiing," Christopher said.

"Dinner will be served at eight tomorrow," George said. "We'll be waiting for you."

The mist at the station gave way to sleet outside town, and before we had reached Sundance it was snow, drifting down the canyon. There had been so much snow already that we could see the slopes, the lifts, and the stands of white-clad pine gleaming in the lights of the resort.

All night the snow fell, and it was still falling the next morning. Fortified by the late dinner, we had some juice and set off for the wooded cross-country trails. We rented skis, poles, and boots; we had all the rest of our gear. After the eating and drinking of the train, this was perfect—kicking and gliding across the meadows and woods of Sundance. A break for lunch, and then a whole afternoon of skiing. The snow still fell, and the air was mild, hardly freezing. Except for a flock of crows and one invisible woodpecker, the woods were silent.

At dark we handed back our ski gear and were taken to the Salt Lake City train station, about an hour away. There, solitary, detached, at a platform in the middle of the train yard, its lights blazing, was the "Los Angeles."

A movable feast, I was thinking, as a woman in a white smock greeted us.

This was the chef, Regina Charboneau, just in from San Francisco, where she owned a restaurant and a blues bar. The southern cuisine was Regina's inspiration, but it was southern cooking with a difference, traditional ingredients served with a flourish —the sweet potatoes and crab cakes and buttermilk biscuits we had been eating. Tonight we were being served pheasant and okra gumbo, salmon with potato crust over creamed hominy grits, and warm chocolate bread pudding. The pheasant and okra gumbo, hearty and flavorful, was meant to restore us after our day of skiing. The gumbo, the bread pudding, and the biscuits were full of her own innovations.

"My sous-chef said, 'What about lentils with the salmon?'" Regina said. "I told him, 'Everyone does that. Let's rethink the lentils.'"

The grits they tried had come from Regina's childhood. She had gotten to San Francisco by way of Natchez (where she was one of nine children, her father a chef and restaurateur), Missoula, (where she gained a sense of reality), the settlement of Chignik Lake, Alaska (where at the age of twenty-three she was camp cook), Paris (the Cordon Bleu school), and Anchorage (several successful restaurants). Her stories could not top Christopher's naked passenger, cartwheeling transvestite, and cross-country harem, but they were very good, and included a plane crash in Alaska, strange times at the work camp, and at least one marriage proposal by a young Aleut male: "Marry me," the man said. "You damn good cook. You paint the shanty any color you like. I not beat you very much."

Later, in my room, full of food and warmth and a pleasant fatigue, I began to understand the meaning of the expression "gravy train"—not the sinister implication of voluptuous self-indulgence, but a friendly journey where everything is rosy.

Sometime during the night, the westbound *Zephyr* snatched us from Salt Lake City station and whisked us across the Great Salt Lake Desert at ninety-five miles an hour. We were still in high desert in the morning, a landscape like Tibet, arid stony ground with the peaks and ridges of snowy mountains showing in the distance on almost every side.

"Those are the Ruby Mountains," Christopher said, indicating a great white wall to the east. A bit later, about eighteen miles out of Reno, "And that's Mustang Ranch."

It was pinkish and sprawling, three or four one-story buildings by the side of the tracks. Not very glamorous, the Mustang had the look of a boys' camp, which in a way it was. Reno itself, part circus, part residential, seemed a blight on the landscape, "kitsch in sync," in the words of one wag. Those people who boarded the *Zephyr* here did not look like winners; in fact, no one looked like a winner here at all.

Some friends of mine and their child had been driven from their home in Colfax, farther down the line in California, to join us here. They got on board, and all along the route of the Donner Party we ate and drank. One of them brought me a copy of *Ordeal by Hunger*, the story of the Donner tragedy, by George Stewart, and there I sat as we clunked past Truckee—deep in snow—and Donner Peak and Donner Lake, where the awful events of death and cannibalism unfolded. I sat all afternoon reading and wolfing down coffee cake.

It was downhill after that, in every sense, through the foggy forests of ponderosa to Colfax and farewells; to Sacramento in the dusk; and the moonrise at Martinez, where Howard Hughes's *Glomar Explorer* was riding at anchor.

"Joe DiMaggio was born here," Christopher said. "And so was the martini. Maybe."

Then we were rolling through the Bay Area's back yard.

"May I suggest we put the lights out?" Christopher said with his usual grace. "The last time we came through here some young people threw rocks at our windows. I'd pay each of them two hundred dollars not to! But this way no one will see us."

The darkness inside "Los Angeles" revealed everything outside—the lights of the bay, the distant bridge we had just crossed, the muddy little docks in the foreground, Oakland just by the tracks, the skyline of San Francisco, Emeryville up ahead, where we glided to a stop.

I hated separating myself from the snug comfort of "Los Angeles." Taking nothing for granted, I travel hopefully; but I am not surprised when things go wrong. I am very grateful when things turn out well. If bliss can be described as an exalted state of not wishing to be anywhere else, then this had been bliss.

PERMISSIONS ACKNOWLEDGMENTS

Ambrose, Stephen E.: Reprinted with the permission of Simon & Schuster, Inc., from NOTHING LIKE IT IN THE WORLD: The Men Who Built the Transcontinental Railroad, 1863–1869. Copyright © 2000 by Ambrose-Tubbs, Inc.

Auden, W. H.: "Gare du Midi," copyright 1940 & renewed 1968 by W. H. Auden, from W. H. AUDEN: COLLECTED POEMS by W. H. Auden. Used by permission of Random House, Inc. and Faber and Faber Ltd.

Baker, Russell: Reprinted by permission of *The New York Times* News Services Division Rights & Permissions Department. Copyright © *The New York Times*.

Barcelo, François: Translation by Matt Cohen of *The Man Who Stopped Trains* from INTIMATE STRANGERS, reprinted with permission of Patricia Aldana and the estate of Matt Cohen, through Anne McDermid & Associates and Strickland Ltd

Beauvoir, Simone de: Excerpt from AMERICA DAY BY DAY, translated/edited by Carol Cosman. Copyright © 1954 Editions Gallimard. Copyright © 1998 Regents of the University of California. Reprinted with permission of University of California Press.

Behrend, George: Excerpt from NO TRAIN TONIGHT reprinted with permission of HarperCollins Ltd.

Berry, Scyld: Excerpt from TRAIN TO JULIA CREEK: A JOURNEY TO THE HEART OF AUSTRALIA, reprinted with permission of Hodder and Stoughton Publishers, a member of the Hodder Headline Limited Group.

Bryson, Bill: From IN A SUNBURNED COUNTRY by Bill Bryson. Copyright © 2000 by Bill Bryson. Used by permission of Broadway Books, a division of Random House, Inc. Also reprinted by permission of Doubleday Canada, a division of Random House of Canada Limited.

Burton, Marda: *Whistlin' Through Dixie* reprinted with permission of *The Saturday Evening Post*. Copyright © 1990 by BFL&MS, Inc.

Dos Passos, John: "Bedbug Express" from ORIENT EXPRESS, reprinted by permission of Lucy Dos Passos Coggin, Owner & Assignee of Copyright.

Fitzgerald, F. Scott: Reprinted with permission of Scribner, a Division of Simon & Schuster, Inc., from THE GREAT GATSBY (Authorized Text) by F. Scott Fitzgerald. Copyright © 1925 by Charles Scribner's Sons. Copyright renewed 1953 by Frances Scott Fitzgerald Lanahan. Copyright © 1991, 1992 by Eleanor Lanahan, Matthew J. Bruccoli and Samuel J. Lanahan as Trustees under Agreement Dated July 3, 1975, Created by Frances Scott Fitzgerald Smith. Reprinted by permission of Harald Ober Associates Incorporated.

Fitzgerald, F. Scott: Reprinted with permission of Scribner, a Division of Simon & Schuster, Inc., from TENDER IS THE NIGHT by F. Scott Fitzgerald. Copyright © 1933, 1934 by Charles Scribner's Sons. Copyright renewed © 1961, 1962 by Frances Scott Fitzgerald Lanahan. Reprinted by permission of Harold Ober Associates Incorporated.

Fleming, Peter: "A Crash on the Trans-Siberian Railway" from ONE'S COMPANY by Peter Fleming, reprinted with permission of John Johnson (Authors' Agent) Limited.

Frazier, Ian: "Take the F." Copyright © 1996 by Ian Frazier reprinted with the permission of The Wylie Agency

Govenar, Alan B. and Brakefield, Jay F.: From Alan B. Govenar and Jay F. Brakefield, DEEP ELLUM AND CENTRAL TRACK: WHERE THE BLACK AND WHITE WORLDS OF DALLAS CONVERGED (Denton: University of North Texas Press, 1998). Copyright © 1998 by Alan B. Govenar and Jay F. Brakefield. Reprinted by permission.

Hamilton, Virginia Van Der Veer: "Wartime Washington" excerpt from LOOKING FOR CLARK GABLE AND OTHER 20TH CENTURY PURSUITS, reprinted by permission of The University of Alabama Press copyright 1996. Originally published as *Of Time and the Train* in *The New York Times* 1987.

Hood, Clifton: Reprinted with permission of Simon & Schuster from 722 MILES: THE BUILDING OF THE SUBWAYS AND HOW THEY TRANSFORMED NEW YORK by Clifton Hood. Copyright © 1993 by Clifton Hood.

Hughes, Langston: *Homesick Blues* and *Pennsylvania Station* from THE COLLECTED POEMS OF LANGSTON HUGHES by Langston Hughes. Copyright © 1994 by The Estate of Langston Hughes. Used by permission of Alfred A. Knopf, a division of Random House, Inc.

Hurley, Maureen: *Night Train to Moscow: Waging Peace* from THE HOUSE ON VIA GAMBITO: WRITINGS BY AMERICAN WOMEN ABROAD, edited by Madelon Sprengnether and C.W. Truesdale. Copyright © 1997 by Maureen Hurley. Reprinted by permission of the author.

Kisor, Henry: From ZEPHYR: TRACKING A DREAM ACROSS AMERICA by Henry Kisor. Copyright © 1994 by Henry Kisor. Used by permission of Time Books, a division of Random House, Inc.

Lewis, Michael: *Amtrak Diarist: Riding the Amtrak Crescent* from THE NEW REPUBLIC, 1988, reprinted by permission of the author.

Lloyd, Roger: Excerpt from WATCHING THE TRAINS GO BY reprinted with permission of HarperCollins Ltd.

Mansfield, Katherine: "The Little Governess" and "Father and the Girls" from THE SHORT STORIES OF KATHERINE MANSFIELD by Katherine Mansfield, Copyright © 1923 by Alfred A. Knopf, a division of Random House, Inc. and renewed 1951 by John Middleton Murry. Used by permission of Alfred A. Knopf, a division of Random House, Inc.

Maund, Alfred: Chapter One from THE BIG BOXCAR reprinted by permission of the author. Copyright © 1957 by Alfred Maund.

McCarthy, Mary: Excerpt from "The Cicerone" in CAST A COLD EYE. Copyright © 1948 and renewed 1976 by Mary McCarty, reprinted by permission of Harcourt, Inc.

MacLeish, Archibald: "Burying Ground by the Ties" from COLLECTED PO EMS 1917–1982 by Archibald MacLeish. Copyright © 1985 by The Estate of Archibald MacLeish. Reprinted by permission of Houghton Mifflin Company.

McNeil, Donald G., Jr.: Reprinted by permission of *The New York Times* News Services Division Rights & Permissions Department. Copyright © *The New York Times*.

Millay, Edna St. Vincent: "From a Train Window" by Edna St. Vincent Millay. From COLLECTED POEMS, HarperCollins. Copyright © 1934, 1962 by Edna St. Vincent Millay and Norma Millay Ellis. All rights reserved. Reprinted by permission of Elizabeth Barnett, literary executor.

Morris, Mary: From WALL TO WALL: FROM BEIJING TO BERLIN BY RAIL by Mary Morris. Copyright © 1991 by Mary Morris. Used by permission of Doubleday, a division of Random House, Inc.

Morton, H.V.: Excerpt from IN SEARCH OF SOUTH AFRICA by H.V. Morton, 1948. Copyright the estate of H.V. Morton, used by permission of Methuen Publishing Limited.

Naipaul, V. S.: "In The Middle of the Journey" from THE OVERCROWDED BARRACOON by V. S. Naipaul, used by permission of Gillon Aitken Associates Ltd. Copyright © 1972, by V.S. Naipaul.

INDEX